PRAISE FOR
"SIMON GREY AND THE MARCH OF A
HUNDRED GHOSTS"

"This exciting adventure filled with humor, great characters, and lively writing will drive young readers under the covers with flashlights to read late into the night. This is a winner!"
– San Francisco Book Review

" A terrific adventure, filled with strange and amazing creatures, and steeped in Japanese culture. The story is intense and compelling, the characters are fascinating and jump off the page, and the writing is superb. This will delight middle-graders, both boys and girls."
– Manhattan Book Review

"A ton of action, never a bland chapter, with some iconic laugh-out-loud dialogue. Watch out, Rick Riordan!"
– The Book Insider

"Unique and exciting, layered and rich in details that bring this world to life by weaving history, samurai, Asian mythology, and magic into an addictive adventure!"
– Readers' Favorite

"A creative mix of historical fiction and mythology. Very educational, but fun and light at the same time. Imaginative, funny, mystifying, and empowering!"
– Pages for Thoughts

" A beautiful historical story, culturally rich, laced with unlimited adventure. An absolute entertainer!"
– The Reading Bud

CHARLES KOWALSKI

SIMON GREY
AND THE CURSE OF THE DRAGON GOD

THE SECOND SIMON GREY ADVENTURE

EXCALIBUR
BOOKS

For Kento and Kay

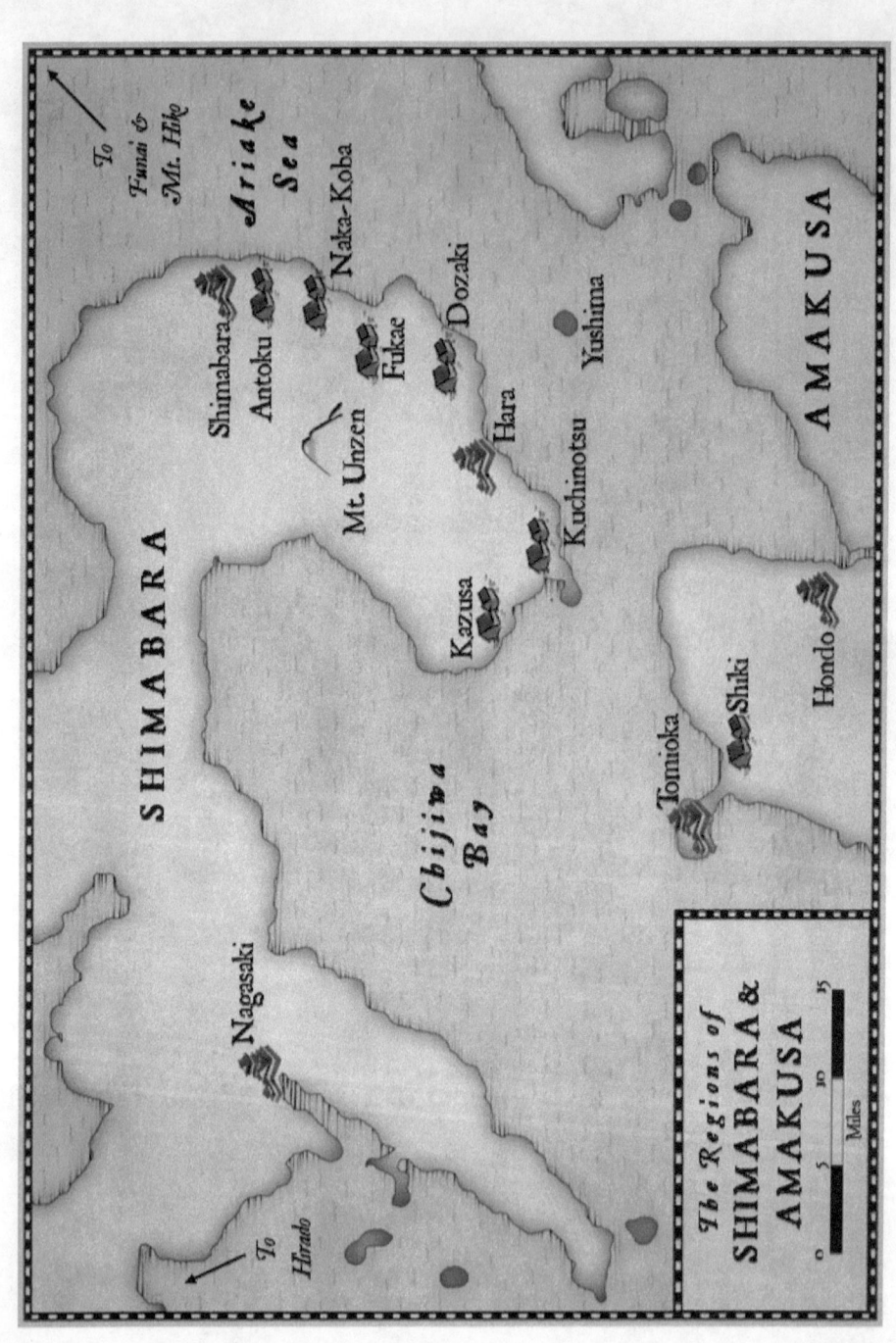

The Regions of
**SHIMABARA &
AMAKUSA**

Miles
0   5   10   15

SHIMABARA

Chijiwa Bay

Ariake Sea

AMAKUSA

To Funai & Mt. Hiko

To Hirado

Nagasaki

Shimabara
Antoku
Naka-Koba
Mt. Unzen
Fukae
Dozaki
Yushima
Hara
Kazusa
Kuchinotsu
Tomioka
Shiki
Hondo

DRAMATIS PERSONAE.

The REBELS:

AMAKUSA SHIRO, supreme commander
ASHIZUKA CHUEMON, chief strategist
CHIJIWA GOROEMON, commander
MORI SOIKEN, commander
YAMADA EMOSAKU, captain of Simon Grey's division
KOMAGINE TOMOFUSA, master gunner
ARIMA GENSATSU, doctor
ASHIZUKA SANAI, son of Ashizuka Chuemon
YOZAEMON OF KUCHINOTSU, a farmer
TOTOEMON, a fisherman, and his wife ONAMI*
OBOTAN, an actress from the Kabuki theater in Edo*
JINZAEMON (a.k.a. JAMES), a young volunteer*
SIMON GREY and OYUKI WINTER*

The SHOGUNATE:

MATSUKURA KATSUIE, lord of Shimabara Province
TAKEDA SOHO, enforcer and tax collector for Matsukura*
ITAKURA SHIGEMASA, commander of the first wave
MATSUDAIRA NOBUTSUNA (a.k.a. IZU THE WISE),
    commander of the second wave
ARIMA NAOZUMI, lieutenant to Izu the Wise
MIYAMOTO MUSASHI, most famous duelist in Japan
DOMON YASUNARI, military magician*

Others:

ARIMA HARUNOBU (a.k.a. DON PROTASIO), lord of Hara Castle
NICOLAES COUCKEBACKER, chief of the Dutch trading post
Samurai, soldiers, farmers, ghosts, and yokai

*Characters marked with an asterisk are entirely fictional.
Others are based on actual historical figures.
In Japanese name order, the surname comes first.*

Chapter 1:
The Palace of the
Dragon God

第一章・竜宮城

Our first night at sea came and went without any sign of ghosts.

This was not something I could take for granted. Two years earlier, in 1620 by the calendar I was most used to, I had signed up as a cabin boy aboard a ship bound for Japan, hoping that a long sea voyage would provide some relief from the ghosts that always haunted me on land. But as it turned out, our ship had once been the scene of a bloody mutiny, and every night, the ghosts of the old crew had felt obliged to stage a re-enactment of the battle...right by my pillow.

The *Hereford*, however, appeared to be ghost-free, and as far as I was concerned, that was all the voyage needed to make it perfect. We were sailing along one of the most beautiful coastlines I had ever seen, a shore both lush and rugged, with green forests on top of rocky cliffs, and sprinkled with innumerable little islands. But the most beautiful sight was aboard the ship with me: Oyuki, daughter of John Winter, an English sailor who stayed in Japan and became a samurai. Having heard rumors that the Shogun of Japan, Tokugawa Hidetada, was planning to drive all foreigners and half-bloods out

1

of the country, Oyuki's father had thought it prudent to head back to England. I was eagerly looking forward to going home, and even more eagerly to sharing the long voyage with Oyuki.

John Winter had generously offered to pay my passage, but I was an experienced ship's boy and didn't mind working my way, especially under the jolly captain who had first brought me to Japan. All his crew called him Captain Shakespeare, because he liked to relieve the boredom of long voyages by putting on Shakespeare plays. I was waiting for an opportune moment to suggest that this voyage offered the perfect chance to stage a production of *Romeo and Juliet*.

But the moment never came.

* * *

It was our second day out from Hirado, home to the one English trading post in Japan – whose days, if the rumors were true, were numbered. I was swabbing the deck, half-listening as Captain Shakespeare and John Winter speculated on how long it would be before our Dutch rivals would have to close up shop and head home as well, when Oyuki suddenly pointed off our port side and cried with excitement: "Look!"

We followed her point just in time to see, at the mouth of a cove that sheltered a little fishing village, a dolphin as it leapt into the air, impossibly high, then dived down again in a graceful arc. As soon as it struck the surface, a second one leapt up, even higher, and turned a somersault before splashing down on its back. Then the first one jumped again, higher still, and performed both a somersault and a half-turn before diving again. It was almost as if they sensed they had an appreciative audience, and were competing to outdo each other in feats of gymnastics.

As we watched in admiration, a small fishing boat disrupted our view. There were four men aboard: two rowing, one holding one end of a long net anchored to the land, and one carrying two metal rods. This last one, as the boat described an arc around the mouth of the cove, began to beat one rod against the other, creating a cacophonous noise that jarred our eardrums, even across the distance that separated their boat from the *Hereford*.

The boat continued to head for the far shore, dragging the net behind it to corral the dolphins into the cove. Oyuki turned to us, the delight in her face suddenly changed to apprehension. "What are they doing?" she asked anxiously, although her tone of voice made it clear that she had already guessed the answer.

"They're hunters," John Winter replied indifferently.

Oyuki gasped in horror. "They're going to kill those magnificent creatures?"

"Where you see magnificent creatures," her father said, "they see their daily food."

Oyuki looked from her father to Captain Shakespeare with a pleading expression. "And we're just going to sail on by and do nothing?"

Her father shrugged and spread his hands. "What would you have us do? If we tried to tell them to stop hunting dolphins, they would pay us no more mind than we would if they came to England and told us to stop eating beef or mutton."

"Your father's right, my dear," said Captain Shakespeare. "This is their land. What right have we to tell them what to do? What fish or beasts they may or may not eat?"

Oyuki made no reply, but flounced off and leaned against the wall of the captain's cabin, her hands behind her back and a sullen pout on her face. I hesitated a moment, then went over to her, although I had a hard time thinking of anything to say that might give her any consolation.

But I had no chance to say anything. Oyuki's feigned sulk lasted only as long as it took for her to untie her sash. Then, in one moment, she slipped off her outer kimono and leapt up onto the rail. And before anyone could stop her, she made a graceful swan dive into the sea.

"Man overboard!" shouted the lookout. "I mean, girl overboard! I mean..."

"Argh! Plague upon that girl and her hot head!" Captain Shakespeare exclaimed, then turned apologetically to her father. "Begging your pardon, Master Winter, sir."

"No need to apologize," John Winter muttered, his baleful eyes following Oyuki as she swam toward the fishermen's boats. "I know my daughter."

Captain Shakespeare turned towards the forecastle. "Gunner! Port cannon! Powder, but no shot."

The gunner hastened to carry out his order. He placed a packet of powder and a cloth wad into the muzzle of the cannon, seized the rammer, and used it to shove them down the barrel. But instead of putting in a cannonball after them, he gestured to his mates to heave the tackles and run the gun out to its port. "Ready, sir!"

"Prepare to fire upon my order. Fire!"

The gunner struck a match, fitted it into a long linstock, and held it to the touch hole. Everyone on deck covered their ears as the cannon fired, straining against the breech rope and delivering a noise like a thunderclap, a flash of fire, and a cloud of smoke. We knew it was unloaded, but the hunters didn't, and if all went well, the flash and bang would serve to scare them away.

The hunters stopped and looked up in alarm, and for a moment, it looked as though the cannon had done its job. But a moment later, their attention was back on the dolphins and Oyuki.

"Another volley, lads," Captain Shakespeare commanded. "Make ready! Fire!"

We covered our ears again as another shot from the cannon shook the boards. I looked toward the hunters, hoping the second shot would help them get the message. But they seemed to be wise to our strategy, and after one glance in our direction, they continued on their course.

Oyuki, by this time, was almost at their boat. One of them saw her coming, and raised his harpoon as though threatening to spear her with it.

Without pausing to ask leave from John Winter or Captain Shakespeare, or even really to think, I vaulted up onto the rail and plunged into the water.

When I came back up to the surface, I could hear the captain's distant voice shouting from the deck: "Simon! Belay! What are you doing? Blast you!" But I was already on my way out to where Oyuki was preparing to confront the hunters.

As I approached the boat, another shot thundered from the *Hereford*'s cannon. This time, a white fountain burst forth from the sea near the boat, as a ball struck the water just off its bow. I prayed fervently that the gunner knew what he was doing. It was very hard, I knew, to fire cannons at sea with any degree of accuracy, and if he miscalculated, he could easily hit the hunters, me, or worst of all, Oyuki.

But this shot finally seemed to get the message across. With baleful glares in our direction, the hunters turned their boat around and rowed back to shore.

The dolphins swam over to us, circling around us, nuzzling us playfully with their long noses. They chattered…and to my great surprise, I found that I could understand them.

Oyuki and I both perceive the world in a slightly different way from most people. We can see, hear, and otherwise sense the spirit world. When I first arrived in Japan, I made the acquaintance of the supernatural beings known collectively as *yokai*, and discovered that, even though I hadn't yet learned a word of Japanese, I could communicate with them in a way that transcended language. I had, however, never been able to understand animals before. But now, the dolphins were trying to communicate with us, and I could understand them too.

Thank you, they said. *Thank you both.*

"Not at all," Oyuki said. She had heard them as clearly as I had. "I couldn't bear to see them hurt you."

Come with us, they said.

Oyuki and I looked at each other.

Come with us, the dolphins repeated. *We want to show you something special. Something humans almost never see.*

We hesitated. "Where are you going to take us?" I asked. "We can't breathe underwater."

With us, you can.

Oyuki cast an anxious glance back toward the *Hereford*. "They're waiting for us."

It won't take long.

"We should at least tell the captain," I said.

Of course.

The dolphins turned around, offering us their backs. After another moment's hesitation, Oyuki and I sat astride them, locking our fingers around their back fins for lack of any other place to hold on. With a speed that nearly made us lose our grip, they took off across the water towards the *Hereford*, and once they were alongside, took a flying leap that brought them nearly level with the deck. We barely had time to shout, "Wait just a minute!" to the astonished John Winter and Captain Shakespeare, before the dolphins fell back down to the sea.

6

I took a quick breath, just before my dolphin went under and swam at a speed that would do credit to the swiftest of ships. The rush through the water was so exhilarating that I forgot about holding my breath. By the time I noticed, I realized that I had been breathing as naturally as if I were a fish or amphibian, just as the dolphins had promised.

The dolphins swam deeper, weaving among mounds of deep-green coral. It was like traveling through a valley that wound its labyrinthine way through steep, forested mountains, except for the rainbow-colored fish that constantly flitted across our path. Then, as we rounded a bend, we suddenly saw that the dolphins had not been exaggerating: they had led us to an amazing sight that surely no human being had ever seen before.

It was an undersea palace. It was bigger than the Shogun's castle in Edo, which was the largest castle I had ever seen on land. The walls were made of coral in a myriad of vibrant colors, the towers topped with minarets that looked like giant cone shells. The palace grounds consisted of dozens of interconnected buildings, including one that I took to be a temple, judging from the solemn procession of monkfish. The courtyard was a meticulously manicured garden of kelp, with fountains that sent streams of bubbles up through the water. The entire complex was lit up, as at a festival, by long strings of lanternfish.

We approached a gate that looked like a giant scallop shell, which swung down to let us through. The dolphins took us through a long, arched tunnel of coral, where swordfish stood guard like sentries, saluting as we passed.

After a while, the dolphins turned sharply upward, toward a hole in the roof of the tunnel, and we broke through the surface into a space full of the air we were used to breathing. After a moment's hesitation, we dismounted from the dolphins, climbed out of the pool, and examined our surroundings.

We were at one end of a long, elliptical gallery. The floor on which we stood seemed to be made of solid sand, studded with shells of every shape and color, and the walls, which came together to form a vault like a cathedral's in place of a ceiling, were as transparent as glass, giving us a spectacular view over the rooftops of the palace.

At the far end of the gallery was another pool like the one we had just come out of. As soon as we noticed it, we heard a low, mysterious sound that I guessed was the blowing of conch shell horns. The water in the far pool churned, and up from the depths rose a coral throne whose back, like the palace gate, was a giant scallop shell. And on this throne sat the most beautiful woman I had ever seen.

Like the Lady of the Lake from the legend of King Arthur, she somehow managed to look perfectly elegant and composed even after she had just emerged from the water. Her clothes were iridescent, constantly changing color like the sea itself. Under a gossamer garment, white but shimmering with all the colors of the rainbow, she wore a kimono of some unearthly material that sparkled with shifting shades of blue. Looking at it was like watching the sunbeams dancing on a tropical sea. A loop of the translucent white material behind her head looked like a halo or aureole, as you might see in an icon of a saint.

She stood up and spread her arms wide. "Welcome to Ryugujo, the Palace of the Dragon God," she said. "My name is Otohime."

Unsure of how to address her, Oyuki and I made somewhat awkward bows and introduced ourselves.

"My messengers inform me," Otohime said, stepping down from her throne, "that you saved their lives."

I glanced at Oyuki, who looked down with a slight blush. "I couldn't have done otherwise."

Otohime beamed. "It gladdens my heart to meet someone who still remembers that any living thing on land, in the air, or in the sea, can be one of the Eight Million Gods. If you honor them, they will honor you."

"They've certainly done that," I said, with an admiring look around. "This is a pleasure I don't imagine many…surface-dwellers ever have."

"The pleasure is mine," Otohime replied. "As you say, I don't get many visitors from up above. Although we did have one just a week or two ago, a delightful lad by the name of Urashima Taro. I don't suppose you know him?"

"Urashima Taro?" Oyuki echoed, with a distant look as though trying to remember where she had heard the name before. "It sounds familiar, but I can't say I've ever met him."

"Oh, well," Otohime said, with a note of disappointment in her voice. "I just wondered how he was doing. But anyway, you must allow me to offer you some refreshments."

She clapped her hands, and immediately a low table appeared out of nowhere, spread with a greater variety of seafood than I had ever known existed. There were three cushions side by side on the floor next to it. Otohime knelt on the middle one, and gestured to us to be seated on either side of her. Oyuki, who had grown up in Japan, slid gracefully to her knees just as Otohime had. I, who was still getting used to the Japanese manner, sat cross-legged.

As we served ourselves, we saw through the transparent dome that an underwater pageant was beginning outside. To the accompaniment of guitarfish, drumfish, and sea bass, a troupe of mermaids and tritons performed spectacular dances and feats of acrobatics (or aquabatics), spinning and turning somersaults in perfect time to the music.

"Synchronized swimming," I marveled. "Do you suppose we humans could ever do that?"

Oyuki shook her head. "Not in a hundred years."

After the dances came a circus performance, with sea lion tamers followed by a school of clownfish that had us doubled over with laughter. Next, Otohime tried to coax a recitation out of a Shy Hamlet, but that reminded me that Captain Shakespeare and the *Hereford* were waiting for us. The dolphins had promised that it wouldn't take long, but it already felt as though we had been in this magical undersea kingdom for hours. I could imagine John Winter going mad with worry for his daughter, and Captain Shakespeare – in eloquent blank verse, of course – cursing at the delay.

"Otohime-*sama*," I said, giving her the honorific used for royalty and nobility, "thank you very, very much for your hospitality. This has truly been an experience we'll never forget. But our captain, and Oyuki's father, are waiting for us. We've been under water a long time, and they're probably afraid we've drowned."

"Of course," Otohime said, sounding sad but still gracious. "My messengers will carry you back up to the surface. Where would you like them to take you?"

"To our ship. The same place they found us."

"As you wish. And before you go, I'd like to give you a little present."

From the folds of her kimono, she took out a small bag on a cord, woven from the same iridescent, gossamer material as the ring of cloth behind her head. Inside was a box, tied with a red cord, and made of some mysterious substance. Its surface constantly shimmered as though reflecting the sunlight dancing on the surface of the sea.

"This is a *tamatebako*," she said. "Keep it always with you. It will be a talisman to protect you. But promise me one thing: Never, upon any account, are you to open it."

Oyuki and I exchanged a glance. What kind of present was it, I had to wonder, if it could never be opened? From the puzzled look on Oyuki's face, she was thinking the same thing.

"What's in it?" I asked.

"Promise me," Otohime repeated more insistently. "You will never open it, for any reason on earth."

"All right," I said. "I promise."

Her face relaxed back into her usual gracious smile. She looked toward the pool at the end of the hall, where we had first arrived. When next she opened her mouth, the sound that came out sounded more like dolphin chatter than human speech, but as with the dolphins, I could understand her meaning: *We're ready.*

A moment later, the two dolphins who had brought us swam up to the surface of the pool. We lowered ourselves into the water, sat astride them, and grasped their dorsal fins.

"Thank you, Otohime!" we said together.

"Thank you for coming," she replied. "It was a delight to meet you. And if, by any chance, you should happen to see Urashima Taro, give him greetings from Otohime, and tell him she misses him and thinks of him often."

We waved one last farewell as the dolphins dived. They swam back through the corridors of Ryugujo and the valleys between coral mountains, before taking us back up to the surface, letting us off, and immediately diving back down into the depths.

As soon as we were back in the open air, the first thing I noticed was how cold it was. The weather had been pleasant when we left, sunny and still warm even though it was the end of September. Now, the sky was grey, and a chill wind swept across the water, blowing an icy spray into our faces.

The second was that the *Hereford* was nowhere in sight.

* * *

We treaded water, our eyes sweeping the horizon in vain for any sign of a sail.

"What could have happened?" I asked. "Why didn't they wait for us? We weren't gone that long." But even as I said it, I realized "that long" was a relative term. Time had passed quickly for us in the Palace of the Dragon God, but from the point of view of someone waiting up above, we were gone much longer than anyone could be expected to survive underwater. As much as I hated to believe it of John Winter and Captain Shakespeare, it would have been understandable if they had given us up for lost.

Oyuki scanned the horizon again. "Where could they have gone?"

"They wouldn't just have sailed on and left us," I said, to reassure myself as much as her. "If they thought we might have gotten lost at sea, maybe they went back to Hirado to wait for news."

Oyuki's gaze returned to the cove where we had seen the dolphin hunters, and the fishing village barely visible at the end of it. "Or maybe they docked in that village?"

My eyes followed hers. "That cove doesn't look deep enough for a tall ship," I said. "But maybe someone there saw something. It's as good a place to start as any."

The longer we talked, the more keenly I felt the chill of the air and water. Any way to get us moving, and hopefully someplace warm and dry, would be welcome.

We swam towards the village. As we rounded the promontory and headed into the cove, we saw a small boat manned by a lone fisherman.

"Hello!" Oyuki called to him. "Can you help us?"

The fisherman looked in our direction. As soon as he saw us, his eyes widened in surprise. I was used to that by now – outside of the ports frequented by foreign traders, it was how most Japanese reacted when they saw me – but I had never seen anyone do what he did next: take an anxious look around as though afraid someone might catch him in some forbidden act.

Once he had assured himself that no one was watching, he extended a hand and helped us aboard. As he did, I saw that the skin on his arms, chest, and neck was red and scarred, as if he had suffered terrible burns.

"Get down! Down!" he ordered before we could even say a word of thanks. As Oyuki and I hunkered down below the gunwale, he took another furtive look around before returning his attention to us. "Where on earth did you come from?" he demanded, in a voice barely more than a whisper.

"From the ship that was here a couple of hours ago," Oyuki answered, gesturing in the general direction where we had last seen the *Hereford*. "I don't suppose you know what happened to it?"

The fisherman looked at us as though we had gone mad. "Ship?" he repeated. "I've been out here all day, and I've seen no Dutch ships."

"She was British," I said.

He shrugged as if it were all the same to him. "I've seen no foreign ships of any kind. What happened? Did you fall overboard?"

"You could say that," Oyuki said. "Two, maybe three hours ago."

The fisherman took another wary look around. "Well, you two little fish have snared me in quite a sticky net. I can't very well throw you back, but if I'm caught with you, all of us will be on the chopping block."

Oyuki gave him an uncomprehending look. "What do you mean?"

The fisherman gaped. "How could you not know? Any foreigner or half-blood caught on the mainland, or anyone caught harboring them…" He moved his hand across his neck in an unmistakable gesture.

Oyuki turned to me, looking as shocked as I felt. We had heard the rumors, of course, but it was hard to believe the law could have been put into force so quickly.

"Since when?" she finally asked.

"Since the Shogun issued the Maritime Seclusion Edicts. Three years ago, at least. Where have you been?"

Oyuki shook her head. "That can't be right. We knew Tokugawa Hidetada was mulling the idea of driving foreigners out of Japan, but if he had issued an order like that, we would have known about it."

The fisherman gave us another incredulous look. "Hidetada? This order was issued by the present Shogun."

We waited, hoping to hear a name, but none was forthcoming. Oyuki prompted him, "Who is…?"

"You don't know?" The fisherman's eyes bulged, then narrowed as he spoke in a lowered voice as though afraid that the mention of the name might summon an evil spirit. "Tokugawa Iemitsu."

This was too much for me to follow, and a glance at Oyuki told me that she was feeling just as lost. "I'm sorry," she said to the fisherman. "As you've gathered, we seem to have fallen a little behind on the news. When did he become Shogun?"

The look on the fisherman's face was rapidly shifting from disbelief to anger. "What kind of game are you trying to play with me? Before you were born, by the look of you. Fourteen years ago."

14

Oyuki's bewilderment and alarm were clearly mounting at the same rate as mine. "Please, bear with me," she said to the fisherman. "I hope you don't think I'm mad for asking, but…when Iemitsu became Shogun, what year was it?"

The fisherman gave us one final stare before looking up in thought. "I believe it was the ninth year of the reign of His Majesty the Emperor Genna."

Oyuki's face froze. I could practically see the calculations going on in her mind, leading to a conclusion that she couldn't believe any more than I could.

"When we left," she finally said to me in English, "it was the eighth year of Emperor Genna's reign."

She and I were silent for a moment, as we did the same arithmetic and arrived at the same incredible, but inescapable, result.

"If what he says is true," Oyuki said through pale lips, "it would mean that, by the Western calendar, it's now 1637."

I lay there, stunned, as the import of her words sank in. I could barely manage to speak above a whisper.

"We were underwater for fifteen years."

Chapter 2:
Takeda

第二章・武田

My thoughts flew back to England. Even before our visit to the kingdom of the Dragon God, I had been starting to worry about my parents, thinking they must be beginning to wonder when I would be coming home again. They knew I was on a long sea voyage, but would certainly have expected me back within five years, at the very most. Now that fifteen had passed, they would surely have assumed the worst. With all my heart, I wished I could fly over land and sea to my home in London, leap into the arms of my now grey-haired mother and father, and shout over the cries of the children that my brothers undoubtedly had by now, "I'm here! I'm alive!"

I could barely hear the fisherman's voice when he spoke again, breaking into my thoughts before I had even begun to come to grips with this revelation. "Now," he said, "we need to figure out what to do with you. The only places where foreigners are allowed anymore are Hirado and Dejima."

"Dejima?" Oyuki repeated.

"An island they built in Nagasaki harbor. All foreign ships have to dock there."

"Can you take us there?" she asked.

As if by way of answer, the fisherman picked up a bucket and bailed out some of the water that had begun to seep in through a tiny crack in the hull. "Even if this little boat could take you that far, every ship entering or

16

leaving is closely inspected. And when I say ship, I mean the big trading ships. Can you imagine what they would do if a little fishing boat like mine rowed up to the sea-gate with two foreign children on board?"

"Could we get there by land?"

The fisherman scoffed. "And do what? Walk across the bridge and knock on the gate? You don't understand, do you? Just by setting foot on Japanese soil, you'd be breaking the law. If you think they'll be merciful to you because you're children, you don't know the Shogun."

Oyuki and I exchanged glances, at a loss for what to do. We were marooned in a country where our very existence was a capital crime.

Finally, the fisherman gave a sigh as though resigning himself to the inevitable. "Stay down," he said, and took up the oars.

We hunkered down, as close to the bottom as we could, while the fisherman rowed. The water seeping in through the leaky hull would have soaked our clothes if they weren't already soaked, and every so often, the fisherman had to stop and bail with his bucket. Finally, he shipped his oars, jumped over the gunwale into the shallows, and pulled the boat ashore.

"Stay here," he said in a whisper, "until I come back for you. Don't make a sound."

His footsteps receded. We waited, huddled in the bottom of the boat, until we heard his footsteps approaching again. Finally, he reappeared, leaning over the gunwale and holding out two pieces of cloth.

"Cover your heads," he said. "Wait for my sign, then come with me."

We hurriedly tied the improvised kerchiefs around our heads, as the fisherman looked around. Once he was satisfied that the coast was clear, he motioned to us, and we quickly climbed out of the boat and followed him. The chill wind blew right through my sodden clothes, making me shiver. I had little time to notice anything else but that we had landed behind a house, with rows of mackerel hanging on bamboo poles to dry. Before I could take in any more, he led us around to the front of the house, ushered us inside, and slid the wooden door shut behind us.

We stood in the packed-earth entryway that doubled as a kitchen. On the raised straw-mat floor, next to the open hearth in the center of the house, a woman knelt, watching us. When she saw us, she recoiled for a moment, but quickly put a brave face on it and motioned to us to step on up. We had nothing on our feet – we had both kicked off our sandals before diving off the deck of the *Hereford* – so the fisherman handed us a rag to wipe the dirt from our soles.

"Now," the fisherman said in a low voice once we were seated around the fire. "I think introductions are in order. I'm Totoemon, and this is my wife, Onami."

The woman bowed as her husband said her name, and Oyuki returned the bow. "I'm Oyuki," she said. "This is Simon."

"Where did you come from?" asked Onami.

"Simon's from England," Oyuki replied. "I was born here." For the moment, she declined to mention that her father was English.

"I mean, how did you get here?"

"We told your husband," Oyuki said, "but..."

"But your story made no sense," Totoemon interrupted. "If there's anything you've been keeping secret, you need to tell us."

Oyuki glanced at me. "If we told you," she said to Totoemon, "you would think we were mad."

"I'm already more than halfway convinced of that. If you want to change my mind, you might as well tell me the whole story."

Oyuki hesitated. "Very well," she said at last. She told him how we were on our way out of Hirado aboard the *Hereford*, saw the dolphins threatened by hunters, followed them to Otohime's undersea realm, and resurfaced to find that fifteen years had passed.

As Onami listened, her eyes widened steadily, less in disbelief than in astonishment. When Oyuki finished, she was silent for a moment, then nodded slowly. "Like Urashima Taro?" she said at last.

"Urashima Taro?" I echoed, recognizing the name Otohime had mentioned. "Isn't that…"

"Yes!" Oyuki exclaimed, slapping her knee with sudden recollection. "Now I remember where I heard the name before. A friend of my father's once joined a diplomatic mission to Europe and the Americas. He was away for seven years, and when he came back, there was a new Shogun and everything had changed. He said he felt like Urashima Taro."

I turned back to Onami. "Maybe he can help us," I said. "Is there someplace we can find this Urashi… Urashima…?"

"Find him?" Totoemon gave a disbelieving laugh. "I heard his story from my grandfather, who heard it from his, who heard it from his, and it was an ancient legend even then. If Urashima Taro ever really lived, it must have been hundreds of years ago."

I looked at Oyuki in puzzlement. "Otohime said he had been there just last…"

My voice trailed off, as the situation became clear. We had spent, at most, three hours in the Palace of the Dragon God, to find that fifteen years had passed on the surface. At that rate, a week would easily be the equivalent of several centuries.

"Then is there no one who can help us?" Oyuki pleaded.

Totoemon gave his wife a significant look. "I can think of one."

Onami replied with an emphatic shake of her head. "No. I know what you're going to say, and we've been through this before. If anyone saw you talking to him, and word got to Takeda..."

"Do you know anyone else who could be trusted not to betray us?" Totoemon asked.

Onami thought about this, and apparently had no ready answer.

"Do it quickly," she finally said. "And don't let anyone see you."

Without another word, Totoemon got up and stepped down into his sandals. He slid the door open, looked both ways, and slipped out, sliding the door closed behind him.

"Who has he gone to see?" I asked.

"Better you not know," Onami said. "If by any chance they find you, you won't be able to tell them."

"They?" Oyuki asked. "Who do you mean by 'they'?"

"Takeda and his men."

"Who's Takeda?" I asked.

Onami gestured to me to keep my voice down, while looking around anxiously, as if she expected this Takeda to be waiting just outside the window. "The chief enforcer for Lord Matsukura," she said, her voice little more than a whisper.

"Lord Matsukura?" I echoed, in a low voice to match hers.

"The *daimyo*. The lord of the province of Shimabara. To pay for that monstrosity of a castle, he's been taxing the heart and soul out of the people. Every time we turn around, they've come up with some new excuse to squeeze even more out of us." She gestured to the window. "If we have a window in our house, we pay a window tax. If we have a *kamado*..." she gestured to the clay oven in the kitchen, "...we pay a tax on that. He taxes us from the moment we're born until the moment we die. And even after that, our heirs have to pay a death tax. If we can't pay our taxes, the punishments..." She lowered her voice. "Like my husband. He came up just a little bit short, but that was all the reason they needed to make him dance the *mino* dance."

She said it in an ominous undertone, but Oyuki only looked at her in puzzlement. "Mino?" She pointed to a sheet of plaited straw, hanging on the wall by the door. "Is that what you mean? A straw raincoat?"

Onami nodded.

"They punished your husband by…making him dance in it?"

Onami lowered her voice further. "They bound him hand and foot, put the mino on him, doused it with oil, and set it on fire."

Oyuki and I both gasped. That explained the burn marks that covered Totoemon's body.

"How horrible!" Oyuki exclaimed.

"There are worse fates," Onami said. "He's scarred for life, but at least he's still alive. Others were not so fortunate. Some were tortured to death. Some, especially those who were suspected of working for Bateren, were taken to Unzen and never seen again."

"Bateren?" Oyuki echoed.

"You don't know?" Onami asked incredulously. "You must know. This tall," she said, holding a hand high above her head. "With black wings like a bat, a head like a *kappa,* and a nose like a *tengu.*"

I knew about bats, of course. And I knew about kappa, the river-dwelling yokai with dishes of water on top of their heads – in fact, one of them had guided Oyuki and me on our journey from Edo to Hirado. But I hadn't heard of tengu, nor could I form a clear picture of the composite creature Onami was talking about. Oyuki, I had always thought, knew every yokai in Japan, many of them personally. But the name "Bateren" didn't seem to have any more meaning for her than for me.

Before we could find out any more about Bateren, or where Unzen was and why Onami's voice sounded so ominous when she said the name, we heard footsteps approaching outside. My first thought was to wonder how Totoemon could have made it back so soon, but then I heard voices, and it was clear that there was more than one person on the path. When I looked back at Onami, she had panic in her eyes, and was gesturing frantically at us to keep silent and escape through the back window.

However much Totoemon and Onami had to pay in window tax, they – or, more accurately, we – got their money's worth out of it that day. Oyuki climbed up and out effortlessly. As for me, I got stuck partway. Onami pushed me from behind, none too gently, and when I landed on the ground with a thud, she slid the window shut behind me. Oyuki was in the process of turning Totoemon's boat over. I gave her a hand, and once we had it bottom up, we hid underneath.

We huddled there, conscious of how our breathing echoed in the hull of the boat, until we heard footfalls coming our way. At first, I thought it was Onami coming to tell us the danger was past, but then we heard her voice, pleading so fervently that she was practically screaming: "Takeda-*sama!* Have mercy! We can barely feed ourselves as it is! And now you tell us that our taxes from next year will be *doubled?*"

"I'm afraid I haven't made myself quite clear," said another voice. "I didn't say next year. The tax increase is retroactive. Effective immediately, you owe Lord Matsukura the amount you underpaid for the past *seven* years."

A silence fell, so heavy that even the footfalls ceased, as though this news had stopped Onami cold in her tracks. "There's no way…"

"You must have *something* of value," the other voice said. "Lord Matsukura is quite fond of salt mackerel. Those will be an excellent…" The voice suddenly stopped. "Onami, I thought you said your husband was out fishing?"

22

No reply came from Onami. The evidence of her lie was right in front of them, and we were under it.

The voice barked an order. Then, with a sense of impending doom, we saw the boat above us move. Two pairs of hands turned it over, leaving us blinking in the sunlight.

A man stood next to Onami. He wore a black jacket and a helmet arched in front like a turtle shell, and two swords hung at his side. He looked at us as if he had just overturned a log and found a venomous snake. Two others, similarly dressed but without the helmet, had just moved the boat to reveal us.

"Well, well, well," said the man with the helmet. By his voice, this was the one Onami had called Takeda. He gestured to his guards. One pulled me to my feet, twisted my arms behind me, and held them in a painful grip. The other did the same for Oyuki.

Takeda turned to go, and the guards marched us behind him.

"Takeda-sama!" came Onami's pleading voice, but Takeda raised an impatient hand to cut her off.

"After I've interrogated them," he said, "I will determine what your punishment should be for harboring them."

Takeda continued on his way. Twisting our arms further, and making us grimace with renewed pain, the guards led us after him.

Chapter 3:
The Tengu

They marched us to a stockade surrounded by a wooden wall, and through a heavy wooden gate into a courtyard. The guard holding Oyuki took her one way, and the other led me to a building with a roof supported by wooden bars, making a kind of cage open to the elements. Through the bars, I could see that the cage was full of men, along with some boys my age or younger, packed so tightly that there was barely room for all of them to stand.

The guard watching the gate slid it aside, and the one holding me pushed me in. When the gate slid shut behind me and I had a closer look at the other occupants of the cage, I could see that some had been there for a very long time. Their hair, beards, and nails had grown to alarming lengths, and judging from the smell, they hadn't been able to change their clothes or wash since they first passed through the gate.

As I looked at them, they looked at me, with expressions all along the spectrum from curiosity to suspicion. One of them sidled over to me, leaned in close, and in a voice too low for the guard to overhear, muttered something that sounded like, "*Abé.*"

I glanced around. The prisoners nearest me were watching me intently, clearly waiting to see how I would respond, but I had no idea what the word meant or what kind of reply was expected of me.

I shook my head. "I'm sorry, I don't understand."

24

The one who had spoken to me looked away with a disappointed expression, followed soon by the others. I was left on my own, to wonder how long I would have to stay here.

The sun reached its zenith and began its descent. My stomach started to growl. My last meal, after all, had been in Ryugujo, and that had been…well, by the reckoning of the ordinary world, over a decade ago.

I had no idea how many hours passed, but eventually, two guards came and slid open the door of the stockade. The other prisoners recoiled slightly when they did.

One of them pointed at me. "Give us that boy," he said.

The other prisoners huddled even closer together to make room for me as I shouldered my way to the gate. The guards took me and escorted me into an open, dusty courtyard. At one end was a pavilion where Takeda sat, next to another official of some kind, flanked by two more guards. The guards escorting me stopped in front of them, and gave my shoulders a rough shove. I fell to my knees.

"Now then," said Takeda. "Suppose you tell me who you are and where you came from?"

The official sitting next to him said something that I guessed was supposed to be a translation of his words. However, he apparently spoke no English, and what came out of his mouth sounded like mixed fragments of Dutch and Portuguese. By this time, I knew enough Japanese to understand most of what Takeda was saying, so among us, we managed to communicate, although less than perfectly.

"My name is Simon Grey, sir," I said. "I'm from England. I'm sorry if I've broken any of your laws. All I want is to go home. Please, if you can send us on our way to Nagasaki, we'll gladly take the next ship back to Europe."

"How did you get here?"

"We were on a trading ship heading home from Hirado, sir. We fell overboard and lost sight of our vessel."

"What ship? Of what country?"

"The *Hereford*, sir. British."

Takeda gave me a stern look. "You will find it very unwise to play games with me, boy. The last British ship left Hirado before you were even born. I can only see one reason for your being in Japan. You're working for Bateren."

There was that name again. "Bateren, sir?"

Takeda glared at me impatiently as the interpreter struggled to explain. "You must know. A servant of the demon Yaso. It bewitches people into thinking that if they eat human flesh and drink blood, and their bodies are buried whole without burning, Yaso will raise them from their graves and make them into an army to overthrow the Shogun and conquer the world."

This terrifying description still brought me no closer to identifying what he was talking about. "Sir, I've never heard of such a yokai."

Takeda stared. "Yokai? They're men. From your country."

Men? From my country? I stood there for a few moments in utter bewilderment. Then, in a flash, realization dawned.

I should probably point out that Japanese doesn't have a simple way of distinguishing singular from plural like the "s" in English. After studying Latin and being forced to memorize endless charts for all the possible combinations of number, gender, and case – *equus, equi, equo, equum,* "a horse, of a horse, to or with a horse," and all that – I found Japanese grammar mercifully easy. But it also made things confusing when *uma* could mean "that horse" or "those horses" or "some horse or horses somewhere" or "horsiness in general." I

26

had assumed that *Bateren* was the name of a single creature, but it could equally well be a plural.

Knowing that, and knowing how Japanese tended to push, pull, twist, and chop words from other languages to make them fit its strict pronunciation rules, it wouldn't be too great a leap from *bateren* to *padre*.

He was talking about Catholic priests. I recalled Onami's description, and I could see how their shaven heads might remind Japanese people of kappa.

As for the other horrors Takeda had just listed, as much as I hated to admit it, I could see where his nightmare images had come from. *Eat my flesh and drink my blood, and I will raise you up on the last day.* When you heard those words every Sunday, knowing that "flesh and blood" just meant ordinary bread and wine, you didn't usually think twice about them. But if a hostile outsider wanted to portray Christians as cannibals plotting a zombie apocalypse, our own scriptures would testify eloquently against us.

I shook my head. "No, sir. I don't know any… bateren."

"But you are Kirishitan?"

"I'm sorry, sir?"

"You believe in a god called Deus, who had a son called Yaso by a woman called Maruya."

Things continued to fall into place. *Kirishitan* meant "Christian." *Deus* was the word for "God" in both Latin and Portuguese. I could also see how they got from "Jesus" to "Yaso," and from "Mary" or "Maria" to "Maruya."

"Well?" Takeda prompted. "Are you, or are you not?"

It was a good question. In England, I had gone to church every Sunday because that was what you did when your father was a vicar, but I had never really thought about what I believed. Because of my gift, I had always known with certainty what others speculated about: the spirit realm was real. The more I saw of it on my travels, the more vast and diverse it seemed, and the harder it was to believe it could all be united under the rule of one monarch any more than the mortal world. But if it was, I devoutly hoped the supreme ruler was the merciful and loving God I had been taught to believe in.

"I was raised in the Church of England, sir," I finally said. "We have nothing to do with the bateren."

"Then I ask again: What are you doing here?" Takeda demanded. "What is an English boy doing in Japan, when all the English traders packed up and went home long ago?"

I sighed internally. "If I told you the truth, you'd think I was mad."

"It would be better for you to be regarded as a madman than a spy."

He had a definite point. I took a deep breath and rolled the dice.

"Very well," I said. "You know the story of Urashima Taro, right, sir?"

"What has that to do with the matter at hand?"

"What would you say if I told you it was true?"

Takeda laughed. "You're right. I would say you were mad."

For a moment, I thought of showing him the tamatebako as proof. The guards hadn't searched me when they put me in the stockade, so I still had it with me. But Otohime had given me strict orders never to open it, and I was afraid that if Takeda saw it, he would take it from me and open it himself. I had no idea what was inside, but I had heard the story of Pandora's box, and the message had stayed with me: If a supernatural being gave you a magical box and told you to keep it closed, that was exactly what you did.

Instead, I haltingly told him of our visit to the Palace of the Dragon God. I wondered how much I should say about Totoemon and Onami, not wishing to get them into any worse trouble on our account than they were already in. But before I even got that far, Takeda and his officers were laughing so hard they could barely hear me. Takeda raised a hand to stop me.

"Say no more," he said. "You certainly tell an entertaining story, but I can see we aren't going to hear the truth from you today. Perhaps you really are mad. In which case, the simplest solution would be to send you to Dejima and let your own people decide what to do with you."

My heart gave a leap, and I bowed deeply. "Thank you, sir."

"You swear you aren't working for the bateren?" he continued.

I gave my head an emphatic shake. "No, sir. I mean, yes, sir. I swear it, sir."

"Then you shouldn't have any trouble giving us a little demonstration to prove it."

He gestured to the interpreter, who took what looked like a flat piece of wood from under his chair, rose, stepped forward, and laid it at my feet. When I took a closer look, I saw that the wood was a frame around a stone carved in relief. The picture was of the Crucifixion. It was a work of art, carved in meticulous detail, except that the figure on the cross had no face.

"Well?" Takeda demanded. "What are you waiting for?"

I looked from the stone carving to Takeda. "What do you want me to do, sir?"

Takeda looked at me as if it should have been obvious. "Step on it."

"What?"

"Put your foot on its face."

So that was why the figure was faceless. Its features had been worn away by the feet of countless other prisoners put to the same test.

"Go on," Takeda said. "Step on it. Prove that this Yaso means no more to you than the dirt under your feet."

I looked back at the carving. The faceless figure hanging on the cross made no judgment. It was as if he were leaving the next move entirely to me.

It's a piece of wood and a block of stone, I told myself. *That's all it is. All I have to do is give it a little tap with my toe, and we'll be on our way home.*

I closed my eyes, took a deep breath, and raised my foot.

In that instant, a vision flashed through the darkness behind my eyelids. For the briefest of moments, I was no longer in seventeenth-century Japan but in first-century Jerusalem, in the crowd watching Jesus carry his cross the last mile. What would I have done? Helped him to his feet when he stumbled under its weight? Tried to hide among the crowd, hoping no one would notice me? Or jeered and spat along with the others, not because I had anything against him, but because the soldiers were watching me and I was afraid of what they might do to me if I held back? The answer to that question, I suddenly knew with certainty, lay on the ground in front of me. Whatever I did to this stone carving now was the same thing I would have done to the flesh-and-blood man then.

A verse rushed into my mind: *Whosoever shall deny me before men, him will I also deny before my Father which is in heaven.*

Before I knew it, my foot was back on the ground.

"You can't," came Takeda's voice. It was a statement, not a question.

I opened my eyes to see him glowering at me.

"I could kill you," he snarled. "I could have you burned at the stake. But that would be just what you want, wouldn't it? You would sing as the flames rose up around you, and die with the name of Yaso on your lips.

30

In the eyes of your people, you would be a martyr, and I would be a demon for sending an innocent little boy to his death. That's exactly your plan, isn't it?"

Actually, nothing was further from my plan. If there was anyone capable of singing songs of praise while being burned alive, I knew with certainty that it wasn't me. But if Takeda was trying to talk himself out of killing me, it seemed most prudent to keep silent and let him.

"Well," he went on, "I am not going to give you that satisfaction! But before I'm done with you..." he gestured to the carving on the ground, "you'll be begging me for another chance to step on the *fumi-e*."

He motioned to the guards. They seized hold of my arms, bound my wrists together with rough cord, and then lashed my arms to my waist. Once my bonds were tied so tightly that the blood could scarcely move through my veins, they took me to the gate, which opened at a word from them. My only choices were to walk or let my feet drag on the ground, as the guards, holding my arms in their iron grip, marched me out of the stockade, down the road, and onto a path that led through a forest and up to a swiftly flowing river.

The procession stopped at the riverbank. In the middle of the current, I saw a bamboo cage big enough to hold a grown man, at the end of a plank also made from bamboo stalks. The guards marched me along the plank, and when I reached the end, gave me a rough push over the edge.

I plunged into the frigid water. As I pushed my head back above the surface, gasping and spluttering, they swung a lattice hatch closed, fastened it with a stake, and left me up to my neck in the current of icy water.

On a scorching summer day, I might have found it refreshing – for a minute or two. As it was, going from the cold autumn air to the colder water, I was chilled to the bone within seconds.

"We'll be back," said one of the guards, "to see if you've changed your mind." And with that, they went their way.

Within a few minutes, I was shivering uncontrollably. When I exhaled, my breath chilled my lips. I didn't dare to move, because my mind had fixed on the idea that what little heat remained in my body was warming the water around me a fraction of a degree, and if I moved, the current would be even colder.

I looked up at the hatch. It was a simple arrangement, almost primitive. If I could free my hands, I could reach between the bamboo stalks, pull out the stake, open the hatch, and climb out with scarcely any exertion. But with the ropes binding me – tightly at first, and even more tightly now that they were waterlogged – I was completely helpless.

The minutes turned to hours, and the sun began to set. I realized that, of course, there would be no way of getting any sleep tonight. Even if I could manage to fall asleep with the frigid water flowing around me – which, in my state of exhaustion, I thought might actually be possible – there was no place or position where I could rest. If I did anything but stand, my head would sink below the surface and I would drown.

As night began to fall, I heard a sudden flapping of enormous wings over my head, and I wondered grimly whether a vulture had seen me and flown down in anticipation of a soon-to-be-frozen treat. But when I looked up, I saw a giant bird unlike any other I had ever seen, coming down to perch on a branch. At least I supposed I had to call it a bird, since it had wings, feathers, and a long, pointed beak. But it was also my size. It had a human body with human hands, even though its legs ended in bird's talons that were now gripping the branch. It wore human clothes: a red jacket with round, fluffy tassels on the lapels, and something that looked like a round, black box tied to its forehead. It had a sword tucked into its sash.

I started when I saw it. When it noticed my reaction, it blinked, and turned its head sideways to focus one of its wide-set eyes on me. "Well, well!" it squawked. "One of those, eh? You can see me."

I nodded. I wanted to ask, *What are you?* But the question felt rather rude, and I couldn't think of a more polite way of phrasing it. Instead, I cut to the chase: "Can you help me?"

"Help you do what?" it asked, in what sounded like genuine puzzlement.

"Help me out of here."

The bird-man cocked its head. "You mean you're not in there on purpose?"

"No!" I exclaimed, wondering whether it was joking or whether it really thought we humans liked to lock ourselves into bamboo cages in rivers just for fun.

"How long have you been in there?"

"I'm not sure. But I know it's been hours."

"Weakling!" it said, with a squawk that sounded like a derisive laugh. "The *yamabushi* meditate under freezing waterfalls for days on end."

I had no idea what a yamabushi was, but I made up my mind then and there that I never wanted to be one.

"Can you help me?" I repeated. "Please?"

The creature looked at me through its beady eyes. "What will you give me?"

"What?"

"It's a simple question. Come on, it's not every day that a bird gets to enjoy the sight of a human in a cage. If I let you out, what do you have that would make it more worth my while than that?"

I couldn't think of anything to offer. We had nothing of any value.

I hesitated so long that the creature made a suggestion of its own. "Can you sing?"

"What?"

"You humans expect caged birds to sing, don't you? If you want me to help you, first you should have a little taste of how it feels."

Even at the best of times, I was no one's idea of a great singer. And at that moment, my teeth were chattering so hard that I could barely speak, let alone sing. But the birdlike creature was perched there expecting a performance, and I had no chance of being let out unless I gave it one.

From my numb lips came a stammering rendition of *Greensleeves*. "A-l-las, m-my l-love, you d-do m-me wr-wrong, to c-c-cast m-me out so d-d-disc-c-court-t-teous-s-sly..."

The creature grimaced and pressed its hands to its ears. "Stop! Ugh! Is that the best you can do? I tell you, if I were the one keeping you in that cage, and you gave me a performance like that, I would take away your feeder."

I let out a breath that felt as if it would turn to ice crystals on contact with the air. "Fine, then," I said. "Go your way. I'm sure you couldn't help me anyway."

Perhaps it was my imagination, but I thought the creature's eye narrowed. "What? What makes you say that?"

"Look how scrawny you are," I went on. "I bet you're not strong enough to lift me."

The creature glared at me. "Foolish boy!" it squawked. "You must just have gotten off the boat from whatever barbarous country you came from, if you don't know there's nothing a tengu can't do!"

So this was a tengu. I was a little puzzled by Onami's comparison of its nose to those of priests, but Japanese people did often tend to comment on the length of European noses, and maybe they thought a bird's beak was an apt comparison.

34

"I've never met any tengu before," I said, "but I have trouble believing that you, who are barely bigger than me, could lift a waterlogged boy out of this cage."

"Are you joking? I could do it before breakfast!" And without another word, the tengu swooped down, perched on the edge of the bamboo plank, drew out the stake, and opened the cage. It took hold of my arms under the armpits and pulled. As it did, my feet kicked frantically under the water, until they finally came within reach of a cross-piece that I could use as a step. With one last heave, it pulled me out and helped me to my feet. I stood dripping and shivering on the plank as the tengu untied the cords that bound me.

"Now do you believe me?" it demanded.

"Amazing!" I said, as I rubbed my wrists to get the blood flowing again. "It's true! I never knew what a tengu was until today, but from now on, I'll be praising your legendary strength to anyone who'll listen! Oh, and by the way, I don't suppose you happened to see a girl about my age anywhere nearby?"

The tengu looked at me in some annoyance, as though it had just realized it had been tricked. "Yes," it said. "In a cage like yours, a little way upstream. But you'll have to get her out yourself."

The tengu launched itself into the air and flapped away. By what little light remained in the darkening sky, I made my careful way along the path as it followed a bend in the river. As soon as I was around it, I came to another landing. And there, in a cage like mine, was Oyuki. Child of snow that she was, I was sure she had greater resistance to the cold than I did, but she was still shivering.

"Simon!" she said as she looked up and saw me. "How did you get out?"

"I had some help," I said. "I'll tell you in a moment."

I opened the cage and tried to pull Oyuki out as the tengu had done with me. I soon discovered that it was nowhere near as easy as the tengu had made it look, but between some determined pulling on my part and some carefully timed jumps on hers, soon we both stood on the plank, unbound.

We scrambled along the dark path, heading back downstream. But before we had gone far, we saw the flicker of torchlight ahead, and heard voices.

We looked around frantically for a place to hide, but there was none. To one side of us was the river, and to the other, a sheer wall of rock.

Takeda's guards rounded the bend and saw us. Before we could run or put up any resistance, they had seized us by the arms, which they twisted painfully behind us. One of them ran ahead while the others marched us back down the path and into the stockade.

Takeda was standing in the courtyard. His face, looking even more sinister in the flickering shadows cast by the torches, showed a mixture of anger and astonishment.

"How did you get out?" he demanded.

Oyuki and I exchanged a helpless glance. From her silence, I guessed that she had no more idea what to say than I did.

"So it's true, what they say," Takeda said slowly. "I didn't believe it at first, but now I've seen it with my own eyes. You Kirishitan really do practice witchcraft."

He turned to the guards. "Lock them up," he said, "and keep a close eye on them tonight so they can't conjure another escape. In the morning, we'll take them to Unzen."

Chapter 4:
Unzen

第四章・雲仙

The stockade was so tightly packed that we had to sleep in shifts, some lying down while the others pressed themselves against the bars to make room for them. I stood through the night. The combination of cold and fear kept me from even thinking about trying to sleep.

In the morning, the guards came for me. We met with the other contingent bringing Oyuki from the women's side, and Takeda led the way up a steep mountain path winding among tall pines and cedars. The forest was so cool and quiet that it was hard to believe any horrors awaited us at the end of the journey. But still, remembering the way Onami had said "Unzen" filled me with trepidation.

As we approached the top of the mountain, I saw a plume of white vapor rising above the treetops. But instead of the smell of smoke I expected, the air carried the odor of rotten eggs.

Then we emerged from the forest. And suddenly, it was as if we, like Dante, had wandered out of the woods and into the mouth of hell.

The trees ended abruptly on a crest overlooking a grey depression. I could see no growing things in it at all, nothing but bare rocks in all shades from the greyish-white of unrefined sea salt to obsidian black. From the gaps between the rocks crept tendrils of sulfurous steam, leaving behind sickly greenish-yellow

37

crusts. Puddles of thick grey sludge bubbled and steamed like witches' cauldrons. The way the mud leapt from the pools, hissing like a snake, it was all too easy to see it as a living, breathing, malevolent creature, ready to seize any unwary soul who ventured too near and drag him into the boiling slime.

The place looked alarming enough even to my eyes. But to Oyuki, it must have looked like a literal hell. She was one of the bravest people I had ever met, but there was one thing that I knew terrified her. Her mother was a *yuki-onna*, a snow spirit in the shape of a woman. When Oyuki was still very small, her mother had met her untimely end in a hot spring. Ever since then, Oyuki had been mortally afraid of hot water. Knowingly or not, Takeda had chosen the worst torture imaginable for her.

Takeda stopped and turned to face us. As if reading our thoughts, he pronounced with a cruel grin: "Welcome to hell!"

The guards marched us along the path, deeper into the nightmare zone, as Takeda gleefully played the role of infernal tour guide. "These hell-pools were named by the monks who used to meditate here long ago, to keep them mindful of the horrors that awaited them in the next world if they disobeyed the laws of Buddha. Now, Lord Matsukura has put them to a more…shall we say, down-to-earth use, to keep his people mindful of the horrors that await them in *this* world if they disobey the laws of the Shogun." He pointed at a pool by the side of the path. "*Suzume-jikogu*, the Hell of Sparrows. If you listen closely, you'll notice that the noise that the steam makes when it pipes through the vents sounds like the warbling of little birds. Poetic, those monks, weren't they?"

He led us farther along, until we rounded a bend and saw what must have been the source of the great steam cloud I had seen from a distance. The grey rocks sloped up to form a crater from which sulfurous vapor spewed skyward. We couldn't see what lay beyond the rocky barrier, but we could hear it. Where the other hell-pools hissed, this one gave out a continuous deep-throated roar, as though a dragon had its lair under the mountain, from which it might break forth at any moment.

Beside the crater stood three wooden crosses.

Takeda stopped and indicated the crater with a grand gesture. "*Daikyokan-jikoku*," he announced dramatically. "The Hell of the Great Scream. And having heard the sound that men make when they're thrown into it, I can personally tell you that the monks who named it were more right than they knew."

He gestured to his men, who marched us over to the crosses. They untied the ropes binding our wrists just long enough to pin our arms to the wooden beams and tie them there, Oyuki on the left, me on the right, leaving the one in the middle vacant. I wondered whether the symbolism was intentional: There was no one there who could reassure us, "Today, you will be with me in paradise."

Takeda walked over to one of the pools, from which the steam billowed so thickly it sometimes hid him from view. When the wind blew it into my face, I felt waves of dizziness and nausea. A moment later, Takeda emerged from the cloud with a bucket in one hand and a ladle in the other.

"Nothing better than a nice soak in a hot spring, I always say," he said conversationally. "But not here. No, definitely not here. If you took a dip in one of these pools, you would be boiled alive in a matter of minutes. But I don't think we'll have to go that far." He dipped the ladle into the bucket and lifted it, pouring down a cascade of steaming water. "Not just yet, at any rate."

He walked over to us, passed by me, and stopped in front of Oyuki. She twisted and strained against the ropes that bound her, and I knew it was taking all her self-restraint not to scream.

"Stop!" I shouted.

Takeda turned to look at me.

"You win," I said. "I'll step on that fumi-e thing, if you let her go."

Takeda grinned. "I knew you'd eventually see reason." He turned and gave a nod to one of the guards, who had apparently been carrying the fumi-e just for this occasion. He placed it on the ground in front of me.

I looked down at the faceless figure on the cross. *Forgive me,* I prayed in the silence of my heart. *But this is to save a life. And not just any life, but Oyuki's.*

I closed my eyes and raised a foot.

Out of the clear and cloudless sky, I heard a sharp crack of thunder.

I hurriedly put my foot back on the ground and opened my eyes.

Takeda swayed, then fell and lay motionless on the grey earth. What I had first taken for a thunderclap, I now realized, was the report of a musket.

I looked up. On the wooded ridge above the crater stood three men in full samurai armor, with muskets at the ready and swords at their sides. The one who had fired his musket set it aside, but the other two still held theirs, aimed at Takeda's guards. As I watched, the one in the lead drew his sword, lifted it high, and shouted something that sounded like, "Santiago!"

Takeda's guards looked in alarm from their fallen leader to his attackers. They had clearly thought their day's work would simply be to escort condemned prisoners to their doom, not to fight a battle. They were dressed in simple uniforms and armed only with swords, no match for fully armored warriors carrying firearms. They scattered and fled.

The three warriors made their hasty way down the steep slope. The one who had given the call to arms stood in front of me, as the others started to loosen our bonds. When I had a closer look at their faces, I saw a similarity among them. They were all old enough to be my father, or perhaps even grandfather, and their faces all bore a look that I had seen in some sea captains I had served under, particularly one who had fought against the Spanish Armada in Sir Francis Drake's fleet before turning his hand to merchant vessels. It was the look of men who had been in battle, who had given orders and seen other men die following them.

"Simon Grey, I presume?" said the one in front of me. His voice sounded gruff, accustomed to shouting orders across the battlefield, but kind as well. "And you must be Oyuki?"

We both nodded, as the last of the cords that bound us fell away and we stood rubbing our chafed wrists.

"Ashizuka's the name," he said. "Ashizuka Chuemon. This is Yamada Emosaku, and this is Chijiwa Gorozaemon."

"We heard about you from Totoemon." Yamada said. "And when his wife told us you had been taken by Takeda's men, we thought we might find you here."

"Totoemon!" Oyuki exclaimed. "Is he all right? And Onami?"

"They're both fine," Ashizuka assured us. "You'll see them soon. But let's move quickly, before Takeda's men come back with reinforcements."

We headed down the mountain, by a different path than the one we had taken. I cast an occasional anxious glance around me, still afraid of seeing Takeda's guards. But even if we did meet them, I felt much less afraid of them with three warriors accompanying us.

After about an hour's march, we reached the foot of the mountain, and a while later, we came to the seashore. A small, one-masted ship was anchored off the coast, a rowboat lying across its bow. I could see no crew aboard.

"Abé!" Ashizuka called to the ship.

"Maruya!" an unseen voice replied.

A fourth, who had lain hidden behind the gunwale, suddenly appeared. Judging from his long grey hair and beard, he was at least as old as the others, but instead of armor, he wore a brocade jacket and a band of purple paper that kept his hair bound in a ponytail. He pushed the rowboat into the water, and once it was afloat, climbed in and rowed it to shore.

"Simon Grey? And Oyuki Winter?" he asked as he helped us aboard. "Mori Soiken. Delighted to make your acquaintance." As he took the oars, he asked the other warriors, "Any difficulties?"

"For us, or for them?" Yamada asked, eliciting a chuckle from the others.

Ashizuka added more seriously, "Takeda is dead."

Mori nodded as though this was news he had been expecting. "The first shot in this battle has been fired. There's no turning back now."

Once we had reached the ship, all the warriors worked together to bring the boat aboard, weigh the anchor, and set the sails. I helped as best I could. As soon as we were underway, Mori settled down in the stern and unfurled a sky-blue parasol.

I looked around at our company, wondering how to phrase my next question. "Are you… samurai?" I asked hesitantly, addressing no one in particular. From what I understood, samurai were like knights in the service of a lord. But the only lord I knew of in these parts was Matsukura, and these men were clearly no friends of his.

"Depends on who you ask," Mori replied, eliciting some chuckles from his companions.

"What lord do you serve?" Oyuki asked.

"The lord of heaven and earth," Chijiwa replied pompously. "Deus, and none other."

The others exchanged a look of wry tolerance: *There he goes again.*

"We're what you might call *ronin*," Mori explained.

Oyuki quickly filled me in: "Samurai whose masters have died or fallen out of favor with the Shogun."

"Exactly," said Mori, "although one does tend to go along with the other. The point is, at our current station in life, our allegiance is to the people of Shimabara and Amakusa, and to seeing justice done for them."

"The password and countersign you exchanged," I said. "What do they mean?"

Chijiwa gave me the *You don't know? You must know!* look I was getting very accustomed to by now. "The words spoken by the *arikanjo* to Maruya."

I looked at him in puzzlement for another moment, and then it became clear. *Ave Maria*, the Latin prayer based on the words the archangel – hence *arikanjo* – had supposedly said to Mary at the Annunciation. The words had changed over time to suit Japanese pronunciation, but I could see where they came from.

"And 'Santiago'?" I asked.

"The battle cry of the Kirishitan in Spain," Chijiwa said, "when they took their land back from the infidels. Wasn't it?"

"I suppose," I said.

Oyuki looked out to sea. "Where are we going?" she asked.

"To Yushima," Yamada replied.

"Yushima?" Oyuki echoed in alarm. "As in 'Island of Hot Water'?"

"Yes." He hastened to reassure her: "But it's nothing like the place you just came from."

"As I'm sure you know from Totoemon," Ashizuka said, "the common people of Shimabara have been suffering for years under Lord Matsukura. They work like slaves and never get to enjoy any of the fruit of their labors. It all goes to Matsukura and his samurai. Higher and higher taxes every year, even in the middle of a famine. And for those who can't pay, more and more terrible punishments."

I thought of the scars on Totoemon's body from the "*mino* dance," and shuddered.

"Well, they've finally decided enough is enough," Ashizuka went on. "It's time to take a stand."

"The time is right," Chijiwa added, "now that the Chosen One has appeared."

"The Chosen One?" I echoed.

Chijiwa leaned forward and fixed me in his penetrating gaze as he continued, "Mamakos the Great foretold it in the *Mirror of the Future*, exactly twenty-five years ago:

When five times five years have passed,
Japan will see a remarkable youth,
All-knowing without study.
Behold his sign in the sky:
In East and West the clouds will burn.
Dead trees shall put forth flowers,
And white flags shall flutter on the sea.
Fires shall engulf fields, mountains, grass, and trees
To usher in the return of the Anointed One.

There was a moment of solemn silence, as heads nodded all around the ship, and all eyes seemed to be on me.

I looked uncomfortably from one to the other, and finally said, "Uh...I think you have me confused with someone else."

Chijiwa gaped at me, then gave a disbelieving laugh.

"Did you think we were talking about *you?*"

Everyone on the ship, including Oyuki, burst into uproarious laughter. My face burned.

"Who were you talking about, then?" I asked, an eternity later when they finally calmed down.

"Amakusa Shiro," Chijiwa said reverently, as his head turned to gaze back out to sea. "By the age of four, he already knew how to read, without anyone having taught him. Without question, he is the one foretold in the prophecy, the youth sent from Heaven to guide us."

I was still flushed with embarrassment. Ashizuka, gallantly changing the subject, asked us: "So how did you come to be here? Totoemon told us you had an adventure like that of Urashima Taro."

Oyuki told him the story. I could follow most of what she said, and when she got to the part about Otohime's parting gift, she motioned to me. I pulled the bag from its cord around my neck, loosened the drawstring, and opened the bag just enough to give the ronin a glimpse.

"A *tamatebako!*" Mori exclaimed.

"You know it?" I asked.

"I've never seen one, but all the stories about Urashima Taro says he received one from Otohime. This must be it."

"What was in it?"

"According to the legend," Mori explained, "it contained all the time he spent at the bottom of the sea. Otohime gave him strict orders not to open it, but when he got back to the surface and found the world changed, he couldn't see anything else to do. And all that time caught up with him. Depending on which version of the story you hear, either it was several decades and he suddenly became an old man, or it was several centuries and he turned into a pile of dust."

I hastily put the bag back under my shirt.

The ship reached a tiny island, small enough that you could stand on the hill in the middle and see the sea in all directions. There were already several other boats docked all the way around the shore, and a crowd had gathered on the hill. From a distance, I guessed there were around five or six dozen.

When we disembarked and made our way towards the crowd on the hill, I heard a voice shout: "Simon! Oyuki!"

Onami ran to us and clasped our hands, with Totoemon following close behind her. "You're all right!" She turned to Ashizuka and bowed deeply. "Thank you, sir."

"Thank *you*," he replied. "Without you, we would never have found them."

Ashizuka took his leave of us and stepped up to the highest point of the hill. "Abé!" he shouted over the general hubbub.

"Maruya!" came some scattered replies. The voices died down as the crowd turned to face him.

"We all know why you're here," Ashizuka began. "You're here because you've had enough. Enough of toiling endlessly in your fields, only to see all your rice go to fatten the greedy bellies of Matsukura and his samurai while you scrounged for roots and ferns. Those of you who are Kirishitan have had enough of practicing your faith in secret, always having to pray with one eye open and one ear alert for the approaching footsteps of Takeda and his men. And all of you have had enough of living with the constant fear that, if you couldn't keep up with Matsukura's never-ending demands, you would meet a fate like that of Yozaemon of Kuchinotsu. I'll let him tell his story in his own words."

Ashizuka stood aside as an old farmer, with a weatherbeaten face and sad, sunken eyes, stood up to speak.

"I came up thirty bags of rice short of my annual tribute," he said. "I pleaded with Takeda to give me just a little more time to come up with the rest. But my pleas fell on deaf ears. He arrested my daughter-in-law, who was with child, and put her in a water jail."

The entire audience gasped. I shivered, remembering my own experience with that particular torture device, and I could see Oyuki having a similar reaction.

"After six days," Yozaemon went on morosely, "she died. With my only grandchild still inside her."

The crowd was silent. Every face on the island looked as sad as Yozaemon's.

"It would have been better if they had killed me," Yozaemon went on. "Then, at least, my heirs would have lived on after me. Now, I'll have to live out my days in the knowledge that when I finally die, my family line will end with me."

A grave silence hung over the assembly as Yozaemon rejoined the crowd, and Ashizuka stood up to continue his oration.

"As for me," he said, "I proudly served under Arima Harunobu, who had more honor and decency in the tip of his little finger than Matsukura has in the whole of his fat body. It boils my blood, as I'm sure it would boil his if he were alive, to see his domain fall into their greedy hands. I would be able to go to my grave with a satisfied heart if I could wage one last campaign."

He paused for a dramatic moment.

"To take it back. To storm Shimabara Castle and topple Matsukura from his seat."

The audience, which until now had been listening in rapt silence, now broke out in a flurry of murmurs, some excited, some incredulous.

Ashizuka let them continue for a while before shouting over them: "The time is right. Matsukura and his retinue are away in Edo, leaving the castle in the care of a castellan with a small garrison. Now is the time when it is at its most vulnerable. And our numbers may be small now, but they will grow. Who wouldn't want to join us? Who wouldn't seize the chance to live free from fear? To see the crops from their own fields go to feed their own families instead of Matsukura's soldiers? Is that not worth fighting for? Some may not live to see it, but knowing that all mortal men eventually die, who wouldn't choose to die fighting for a noble cause?"

"Do we really stand a chance against them?" said a voice, sounding half hopeful, half doubtful. When I looked for the source, I saw that it came from Totoemon.

Ashizuka gestured to the other ronin. "Many of us have been wielding swords ever since the Battle of Sekigahara, more than thirty years ago. Among us, we have nearly two centuries of military experience. We can teach you everything you need to know about strategy and the martial arts. Today, your strong hands plough furrows in the earth. Tomorrow, they will plough furrows in the flesh of Matsukura's minions."

"And the lords of the surrounding provinces?" said another voice. "Won't they all rally to Matsukura's defense?"

"Not one of them," Ashizuka replied, "can put a whisker outside his own domain without orders from the Shogun. There might be an army amassed just across the border, but for all the help it will be to Matsukura, it might as well be in Edo. And we have something on our side that Matsukura and his minions can never hope for."

He nodded to a young man, who stood up as Ashizuka stepped aside. His dress was a mixture of Japanese and Western, with a red vest over a white kimono, a ruffled collar, and a cross hanging around his neck. His long hair was bound back in a pony-tail, like Mori's. This, I thought, must be Amakusa Shiro.

There was only one word to describe him: *beautiful*. It wasn't just his long hair, smooth skin, and refined and delicate features, but he seemed to have a halo about him, as though he had stepped out of a stained-glass window. I doubted he was much older than me, but his eyes spoke of a wisdom beyond his years. It was as if the angels had given him a glimpse of heaven with orders to keep it a secret.

I took a brief glance at Oyuki. She didn't notice, because her wide-eyed gaze was fixed on Shiro.

I felt an unpleasant stirring just under my heart, as if I had swallowed a snake that was now trying to bite its way out of my stomach.

"We have the blessing of Deus," Shiro said. He had a pure, clear, high voice, as reassuring as his expression. "We fight on the side of the Almighty, who promises us that every valley will be exalted, and every mountain and hill laid low. He will show the strength of his arm and scatter the proud in their conceit. He will cast down the mighty from their thrones and lift up the lowly. He will fill the hungry with good things and send the rich away empty. He has already sent us a sign of his favor: an emissary from a distant land, to show us that we are not alone in our struggle, that the thoughts and prayers of his faithful followers all around the world go with us every step of the way."

To my surprise and alarm, he gestured toward me. The crowd between him and me parted like the Red Sea, and seventy pairs of eyes turned to look at me.

I froze. Listening to Ashizuka's speech had made my heart pump faster – from excitement, or fear, or both, I couldn't be sure. Like any English boy, I had been raised on tales of Robin Hood, and without question, Matsukura was at least as bad as the Sheriff of Nottingham. Part of me thrilled at the prospect of joining a merry band of outlaws plotting to rob the rich and feed the poor. At the same time, our main goal was to reunite Oyuki with her father if we could, and get back to England alive. Storming a castle full of heavily armed samurai didn't seem like the best way to accomplish that.

"What do you say?" Shiro pressed. "Will you join our cause?"

"Uh…" was my eloquent reply.

"I'm sorry," Oyuki broke in, giving voice to the thought that occupied half my mind. "Truly, we wish you the best in your struggle. But my father, and

49

Simon's parents back in England, haven't heard from us in years. They must be afraid we're dead. All we want to do is find our way back to them. We need to get to Nagasaki."

"And you shall," said Chijiwa. "Once Nagasaki is ours."

We gaped.

"Nagasaki," Chijiwa went on, "is a fortress to the seaward side, but soft and defenseless to the landward. Once we've taken Shimabara, we can expand our domain westward until it encompasses Nagasaki as well. And when the port of Nagasaki is in our hands, we will reopen what Tokugawa Iemitsu closed. Ships, goods, ideas – and weapons – will once again be able to travel freely between Japan and the outside world. The Shogun can do what he likes with the rest of Japan, but *our* domain, if no other, will be free!"

It was certainly an ambitious goal – and, a large part of me said, a worthy one. But it also sounded like one that would take years to accomplish, even in the unlikely event that the Shogun failed to rally his forces and put a stop to it.

"It's an honor to be invited to help the cause of justice," I said. "But, as Oyuki said, our most urgent task right now is to find Oyuki's father and get back to our country."

"Of course, I understand," Shiro replied. "This isn't your land, and it isn't your battle. We have no right to ask you to risk your lives for our sake. If you don't feel that our cause is worth fighting for, we can simply put you ashore and send you on your way with the blessing of Deus."

His words were gracious enough, but the implication behind them was clear. If Oyuki and I were caught wandering through Matsukura's domain – or anywhere in Tokugawa Iemitsu's Japan – it would take a great deal more than a blessing to save us. We were fugitives in a hostile country, and these rebels were the only ones who could offer us any protection.

Before either of us could reply, Chijiwa stood up and raised a hand to the sky. "Look!"

All eyes, including ours, followed his point. The sun was just sinking into the sea, looking like a ball of fire dancing on the water. Above, as far as the eye could see from horizon to horizon, the clouds glowed bright red in the fading sunlight.

"The sign!" Chijiwa exclaimed. "From the Mirror of the Future! Clouds will burn in East and West!"

There was a moment of awed silence. Then, Shiro raised his hands, turned his face toward the sky, and started to sing in a pure, high tenor voice. The words of the song sounded like, "*Daodate domino ohne zente.*" I had no idea what they meant, which I first thought was because of my limited Japanese, but when I glanced at Oyuki, she seemed to be struggling just as hard to catch them. But the song was clearly familiar to the audience, because as soon as Shiro began, about half the crowd joined in: "*Rodate iyoni, ishi poporiya.*"

When the song was over, some of the crowd took out cooking pots, while others set about building fires. Soon, the smell of steaming rice filled the air, and my long-empty stomach rumbled like thunder. When the rice was ready, and the cooks shaped it into salted balls and passed them around, people's faces lit up as if they had just been served the choicest cut of meat. They took the rice balls reverently in their hands and ate them slowly, savoring every bite with rapturous expressions on their faces, licking every last clinging grain off their fingers.

I looked around in puzzlement. "Aren't they rice farmers?" I asked Totoemon. "Why are they acting as if it's such a treat?"

"Do you still not understand?" he replied. "Do you have any idea how long it's been since they've been able to taste their own harvest? Up until now, every grain of rice from their fields went to Matsukura."

I had wondered whether the few cooking pots would yield enough for such a large crowd, but when the meal was over, everyone looked as satisfied as I felt. It wasn't quite as impressive a feat as feeding five thousand people with five loaves and two fish, but it did make me wonder whether Shiro really did have some power that bordered on the miraculous.

And so, without knowing exactly how it happened, Oyuki and I found ourselves joining the ranks of the Shimabara rebel alliance.

Chapter 5:
The First Battle

第五章・初戦

From Yushima, we sailed back to the Shimabara Peninsula. The little sailboat we had come in, as it turned out, was the flagship of the fleet; most of the other vessels were no larger or more seaworthy than Totoemon's fishing boat. Each one flew a white flag bearing the sign of the cross. I wondered whether this was an intentional way of fulfilling another verse from the prophecy: *White flags shall flutter on the sea.*

Our first port of call was the village of Kuchinotsu, the hometown of Yozaemon who had told us his tragic story. When Shiro stood in the village square to speak, everyone gathered to hear him. At first, he said not a word, but stretched a hand skyward. As if on cue, a sparrow came to perch on his finger. When it flew away again, it left an egg in the palm of his hand. He held the egg up to show everyone, and then cracked it open. Inside was a small strip of paper, which he proceeded to unroll as the audience cheered and gasped in awe.

I saw him perform that trick time and again, in one village after another. To this day, I have no idea how he did it. Could he really perform miracles? Or was he just exceptionally skilled at sleight of hand?

"Consider the sparrows," he read from the paper. "They neither sow nor reap nor gather into barns. And yet, all their needs are provided for. Are you not worth more than many sparrows?"

From the expressions on the faces of those watching, you could see that they welcomed Shiro's words the way parched earth welcomes rain. Judging from the way I had seen Takeda treat the common people of Shimabara, I wondered whether any of them had ever been told they were worth more than a sparrow.

"Come to me," he exhorted his listeners, "all you who are weary with toil and labor, and you shall find rest! Come to me, all you who hunger and thirst, and you shall be satisfied! Come to me, all you who groan under the weight of injustice, and I will break the chains of slavery and shatter the yoke of oppression! Come and follow me, for the world is about to turn!"

Growing up in the church, I had to listen to my father's preaching every Sunday. As dearly as I loved my father, the closest I had ever come to a religious experience while listening to one of his sermons was the occasional prayer along the lines of "Please, God, let him finish quickly" or "Thank God he's done." By contrast, Shiro was on fire, and everyone who listened to him caught a spark from his flame. They were ready to follow him through hell if he told them that was the way to heaven.

Ashizuka's words proved prophetic. As we marched from village to village, we often left ghost towns in our wake, as everyone in the village packed up and followed us. I later learned that most of the village headmen in the area had been present at the council on Yushima, and it usually took only a single word from them to set the entire village in motion. Shiro hardly needed to speak at all in those places, but still, when he talked about rest for the weary, justice for the oppressed, and divine retribution for the wicked – meaning Matsukura – everyone's face lit up with unaccustomed hope. The force that started with seventy soon grew to seven hundred, and I wouldn't be surprised if it eventually topped seven thousand.

Everyone was in high spirits, and they often sang as they went. One of the common songs was the one we had heard on Yushima: *Daodate domino ohne zente, rodate iyoni ishi poporiya.*

"What language is that?" I asked Oyuki. "Is it some local dialect?"

She shook her head. "I was hoping you could tell me."

These peasant farmers, I thought, must have felt a hundred times more alive marching behind Shiro than toiling in their fields for Matsukura's sake. As for me, with hundreds of rebel allies around me and dozens of former samurai protecting us all, I also walked with a spring in my step. For the first time since resurfacing from our ill-fated visit to Ryugujo, I felt safe.

At one point, as I was walking along beside Oyuki, Shiro fell in step next to us. I wondered why he was interested in talking to me. Or perhaps, as the serpent in my stomach whispered, maybe he just wanted to talk to Oyuki and I was in the way.

"You've read the Bible, Simon?" he asked.

"Some," I replied. I heard it read aloud every Sunday morning, of course, and I had once tried to read through the whole of King James' new translation, but had run aground somewhere between Leviticus and Chronicles.

"How have I been doing?" he asked anxiously.

It came as something of a shock to realize that the Chosen One was asking *me* to evaluate his theology.

"Very well," I replied, and I meant it. "Where did you learn? Did you go to Catholic school?"

Shiro shook his head. "I wish I could have. The last *collegio* in Japan closed before I was born."

"So you just read it on your own, then?"

"A little, but only a few bits of it were ever translated into Japanese. I did manage to get a copy of the Gospels and read it once, before it was taken away and burned."

"That's all? How can you quote it so accurately?"

He shrugged. "I just say the words I was given to say."

"Given by whom?"

"Just given."

Before I could press him further, he went on, "I can't help envying you a little. You come from a country where everyone can read all of it freely."

"I suppose everyone *could*," I said, "but not everyone *does*. Maybe I know more than most because I grew up in the church. My father is a vicar."

He looked at me in puzzlement. "Your...father?"

I remembered that the only clergy he was likely ever to have met would have been the notorious *bateren* – Catholic priests, who were forbidden to marry. "Yes," I said. "In my country, ministers of the church are allowed to marry and have children."

"Really?" he asked, with great surprise and what sounded to me like an excessive degree of interest. Was it my imagination, or did his gaze flicker ever so briefly in Oyuki's direction?

I cursed myself. It could well have been that Shiro had felt a calling to the priesthood, and therefore resigned himself to a life without marriage or family. And I might unwittingly have planted the seed of a thought in his mind that it was possible to have the one without giving up the other. Had I accidentally made the Church of England its first convert in Japan?

After passing through a village called Dozaki, we crossed a bridge over a wide, swiftly flowing river incongruously named the Mizunashigawa or "River of No Water," and stopped for the evening in another village called Fukae. As in others we had visited, the headman had already pledged his loyalty to Shiro, and everyone else enthusiastically followed his lead. The villagers kindly billeted us in their homes, cramming as many people into each house as it could possibly hold, but our arrival had increased the population of the village several times over, and there wasn't enough roof to go over all our heads. Families with children were given priority, followed by single women and girls, which meant that most of the men and boys were left outside to find whatever improvised shelter we could. At least it wasn't raining.

Once we had gotten settled into our lodgings, we reported to the village square for our tasks. Ashizuka instructed us: the men would train for battle, while the women, and any children big enough to help, would prepare the food. I automatically went in the direction of the men, but Ashizuka stopped me.

"Women and children that way," he said, pointing towards the cooking area.

His words brought me up short. "I can fight," I said. "I want to." For the moment, at least, I honestly believed both of those.

"I'm sure you can," Ashizuka replied. "And I appreciate your willingness. But you have a family in your country waiting for you to come back to them, and it's more than my conscience will bear to send a boy so young into harm's way."

I pointed to a young man I saw doing preparatory exercises near us. "That boy there," I said. "He can't be much older than me."

Ashizuka looked where I was pointing. "That boy," he said, "is sixteen. And he is my son." He raised his voice and called, "Sanai!"

The young man immediately ran to join his father. "You haven't been properly introduced," Ashizuka said. "This is Simon Grey."

Sanai gave me a brief, disdainful glance, then turned away and spoke to his father. "I don't speak the southern barbarians' language."

"Fortunately for you," I said in Japanese, "my language skills are not as limited as yours." I tried to say it in a lofty tone, hoping all the while that I hadn't made any laughable mistakes.

"*Chichi-ue*, he should not be here," Sanai said, still addressing his father and giving no sign that he had heard me. "If there's even one foreigner among us, Matsukura will tell the Shogun and the other lords that the bateren are the puppet masters of our movement. They'll be much more willing to believe that than the truth, that we rose up against Matsukura purely because he deserved it. And then they'll have a perfect excuse to crack down on every Kirishitan in Japan."

"We must be grateful for all the help we can get," Ashizuka told his son sternly. "Everyone in this movement, no matter where they're from or how old they are, has a useful job they can perform." He turned to me. "And yours is over there."

I sullenly went to join the cooks. At least, I thought, I would have the compensation of being close to Oyuki. But as it turned out, she had been assigned to a fire far removed from mine, so all I could do was take an occasional glance in her direction as Onami instructed me in how to cook rice and shape it into the salted balls called *onigiri*.

Once the sun set, I helped distribute the rice balls to the men I wished I had been training with. Shiro went through the line last, making sure that everyone else was served before him. When Oyuki handed him an onigiri, he favored her with a dazzling smile. "Thank you, my dear," he said.

As he went off to have his dinner, Oyuki's head turned to follow him out of sight. The snake under my heart stirred, and sank its fangs into me as it once again tried to bite its way out. My gaze still on Oyuki, I scraped the bottom of the pot for one last portion of rice and slapped it into an onigiri, so vehemently that a few grains fell from my hand and landed on the ground.

Onami saw me, and to hear the howl she gave, anyone would have thought I had dropped an entire treasure chest into the sea. She immediately fell to her hands and knees, picked up every last grain, and frantically brushed the dirt from them while calling loudly for water. When Oyuki handed her some, she splashed it over the rice she held in her hand, trying to wash away as much dirt as she could.

"Perhaps you never knew starvation in your country," she scolded as she pushed the fugitive grains onto the onigiri I was making, "but these people know it like their own families. One grain of rice is more precious than the most valuable of gold coins. You know why? Because you can't eat gold!"

I flushed with shame. It was probably an exaggeration to say that everyone in the camp had witnessed this tongue-lashing, but that was how it felt, and one thing certain was that Oyuki had been standing right by her and heard every word. I took my rice ball and retreated to a far corner of the camp, away from the others, to eat it alone.

When dinner was over and we prepared for bed, I railed silently at the injustice of the situation. Apparently, I wasn't considered a man when it came time to train for battle, but when it came time to sleep, I was...which meant I got to join a thousand-voice choir of snorers.

I was exhausted enough that I somehow managed to fall asleep, but I woke up again when the birds started singing their pre-dawn chorus. Unable to go back to sleep, I got up, walked to a secluded spot at the edge of the campsite, and sat down to stew in my own seething thoughts.

After I had been there for an unknown number of minutes, various thoughts swirling in my mind, I was suddenly jerked back to the present moment by the beating of enormous wings over my head. I looked up in alarm to see a huge, dark shape alight on a nearby bough. When it held still long enough to make out its silhouette, I realized it was the same bird-like creature that had visited me in the water jail, the one called a tengu.

"A young lady, is it?" the tengu squawked.

I stared at him. "What?"

"When a young human male sits brooding like that, it usually has something to do with a young human female. Am I wrong?"

I didn't feel inclined to share the thoughts of my heart with this rather rude creature. I looked down and said nothing.

"An ancient worthy once said," the creature went on, "When there is dust in the eye, all things in heaven and earth are shut out. But when the mind and heart are without a care, your whole life is at ease."

"Easy for you to say," I muttered. I wondered briefly whether creatures in the yokai realm experienced love, embarrassment, or jealousy the way we did.

"Freeing the heart and mind from distraction," it squawked, "is essential if you are to master the way of the warrior."

"I'm not a warrior," I said, picking up a rock and flinging it angrily at the nearest tree. Of course, I missed. "At least, according to them I'm not. I'm just a child, only fit to help the women and girls cook the food and serve it to the real men."

"Hmm." The tengu cocked its head. "So they won't even let you help defend the camp against the army that's coming your way?"

My head snapped up to stare at him. "What?"

"They just left that big castle," the tengu said, gesturing in what I took to be the direction of Shimabara. "They should be here by noon."

I leapt to my feet. "How many?"

"About two or three hundred."

As the tengu flapped off, I ran back to the village as fast as I could, and found the village headman's house where the senior officers were quartered. I slid open the door without knocking, having seen that this was how it was done in Japan: the patch of earth inside the front door was apparently regarded as an extension of the road. "Sir!" I called. "Enemy on the way!"

Ashizuka appeared in an instant. "Where?" he demanded. "How many?"

"On the road from Shimabara. Two or three hundred."

"How do you know?"

I paused. "A…little bird told me?"

Ashizuka gave me a look of bewilderment, but before he could inquire further, Mori, Chijiwa, and the village headman appeared. Ashizuka told them what I had told him.

"We knew the day would soon come when we would have to meet the enemy in battle," said Chijiwa. "Let's take defensible positions and wait for them."

"Just a moment," said Mori. "I have another idea. Where's the main temple in this village?"

"Not far," said the headman. "I can show you the way."

"And the priest?"

"He's been taken captive."

"Excellent," Mori said. "We'll tell the good people of Fukae just to go about their lives as if nothing out of the ordinary were happening. But let the best food they have be brought to the temple. And especially sake, as much as they can provide."

Chijiwa gaped at Mori as if he had gone mad. "What on earth are you on about?"

"Tell our forces to withdraw to Dozaki and wait there until we give the order to march," Mori went on without answering him. "When the enemy first appears, they are to charge…but when the first answering volley is fired, they are to scatter, reconvene in Dozaki, and wait there until the next day dawns. Understand?"

"If you say so," Ashizuka said. His voice sounded as though he couldn't entirely disagree with Chijiwa's assessment of Mori's sanity, but also that this was not the first time he had heard such a mysterious plan from Mori.

Under Ashizuka's guidance, all of us, except the villagers of Fukae and a few officers who had stayed behind, withdrew to Dozaki, which was eerily empty after all the villagers had left their homes to follow Shiro. When a messenger finally came running from Fukae, we set off: those with muskets in the lead, followed by able-bodied men with farm tools that could be used as weapons. I, of course, was relegated to the back ranks.

When we were nearly back to Fukae, Ashizuka stopped us and ordered the musketeers to take cover in the pines surrounding the road. The rest of us stood our ground as the enemy forces finally came around the bend.

The contrast between their side and ours could not have been more stark. Those in the lead rode fine horses and wore suits of armor. Unlike the armor I had seen in England, made simply of chains and plates, theirs seemed made to attract admiration as much as to repel arrows, with studs, braids, and other ornaments bedecking the armor, and a crescent-moon device rising from the helmet like a pair of horns. Some of the warriors had long bamboo poles strapped to their backs, with a vertical banner hanging from a crosspiece: on a white field, a black circle surrounded by eight smaller circles. This, I was to learn later, was a *kamon*, the identifying symbol of a noble house, like a coat of arms for British nobility. In this case, it was the Nine Sunrises, symbol of House Matsukura.

"Rebels!" came the voice of the mounted warrior in the lead. "Lord Matsukura has no wish to see the blood of his people shed. We come only with a warning. If you return at once to your homes and your fields, your lives will be spared. If you persist in this rebellion, you will be utterly destroyed."

"You can take this message back to Lord Matsukura," Ashizuka replied, and drew his sword. "Santiago!"

His cry was taken up by hundreds of voices, as our forces surged forth in a charge.

The musketeers, from their places of concealment, opened fire. Some of the enemy soldiers fell. As soon as the first volley had been fired, our infantry, with their farm tools, charged the soldiers.

The enemy commander shouted an order: *"Nerae!"*

With one motion, as if with one mind, the musketeers assumed a firing stance, the back row standing, the front kneeling.

At the command of *"Hanate!"* those in the front rank discharged their muskets, then immediately pulled back to reload as the next rank formed up and took aim.

But before the second rank could fire, our forces scattered as ordered, with expressions of terror that I wasn't sure were entirely feigned.

Oyuki and I ran into the pine forest. The pines, under the constant pressure of the wind from the sea, grew at an angle to the ground, and their branches hung low. Their branches reached out treacherously to claw the faces of unwary travelers, and their trunks to bash their heads. From the voices we heard behind us, our pursuers were encountering the same difficulties, but still they pressed the chase.

The occasional backward glances I risked showed no sign of Matsukura's troops, but still we ran, until we came to a riverbank. This, I recalled, was the Mizunashigawa, the so-called River of No Water. I was in too great a panic to appreciate the irony.

We waded into the shallows and began to cross. I wondered apprehensively how deep it was going to get.

Oyuki suddenly let out a shriek.

I was about to say something sharp to her for giving away our location to the soldiers, when I nearly screamed myself instead. Under the water, a cold hand, with sharp claws, took an iron grip on my ankle.

Chapter 6:
Shimabara

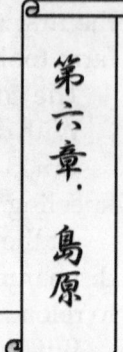

第六章、島原

My glance in Oyuki's direction might well have saved my life. Thinking quickly, she had seized a low-hanging branch of one of the pine trees that leaned over the river. I hurriedly followed her example. The unseen hand tugged fiercely at my ankle, but the more it pulled, the tighter I gripped the branch, even though it felt as though the conflicting forces would tear me in half.

A greenish head emerged from the water.

For a moment, I thought it was a kappa, which would have been a relief. Even though kappa have been known to plague humans with mischief that was not always completely harmless, one of them had been a good friend of ours. But this head was not like theirs. It was elongated like a mink's or otter's. Its piercing eyes and sharp teeth reminded me of a tiger, but instead of fur, it was covered in shiny green scales.

The rest of the creature's body followed its head out of the water. It was smaller than me, but I still wouldn't have wanted to get into a wrestling match with it. It was covered in scales like the head, with webbed hands ending in the sharp claws I had felt on my ankles. Additional claws that looked like a tiger's – complete with a ring of orange fur – protruded incongruously from its kneecaps. I could almost imagine a couple of particularly capricious Japanese gods, after consuming a cask or two of the sake they were rumored to enjoy as

64

much as their devotees here below, saying to one another: "Hey, let's create an aquatic version of the tiger. We'll give it scales, and webbed hands and feet so it can swim more efficiently. What's that you say? That leaves nowhere to put a tiger's claws? O ye of little faith..."

Two others rose up around it. The first one curled its hand into a fist and thrust it skyward. "Bengals!" it shouted, and the other two took up the cry.

"*Suiko,*" Oyuki said. The trepidation in her voice answered my unspoken question about how dangerous they were. "Water tigers."

The first one looked at her. "Oh, so you're one of those?" it said. "You can see and hear us? Well then, when we drag you under, let this be your last thought: It was the Bengals that did it!"

The other two cackled raucously. One of them waded my way, claws extended.

My first instinct was to get back to the bank as fast as I could and run. These creatures were made for swimming, and I doubted they could outrun us on land. But that would take us back in the direction of Matsukura's troops.

My second was to let go of the branch and prepare to defend myself. But I was none too confident in my chances against these creatures, especially since I couldn't be sure I was seeing all of them. For all I knew, there might be more lurking under the surface, waiting to grab me again and drag me under if I gave them the opportunity.

I pulled myself up by the branch, and with both feet, dealt a kick to the belly of the one coming towards me. It lost its balance and fell back, but its hard scales had protected it from the blow. I had delayed it temporarily, nothing more.

Oyuki, I saw, had pulled her way back to the bank hand over hand and started to climb the tree. The suiko under her jumped frantically to try to catch her, but she was already beyond its reach. Once again, I followed her lead. I pulled myself up as far as I could, and after one or two failed attempts, managed to curl my legs around the branch.

The suiko glared at us in frustration and anger. Apparently, they couldn't climb trees, so we were safe from them for the moment. But if Matsukura's men pursued us this far, we would be easy targets for them.

"What are you playing at, boys?" the suiko in the lead demanded of his followers. "Do you want to lose the chance to bring fresh humans down to the Big Boss Below? Do you want him to rank the Siberians ahead of us?"

"The Big Boss Below?" I echoed, almost involuntarily.

The suiko in the lead gave me a startled look. Understandably, it looked unused to having its prey join in its conversations.

"Who are you talking about?" Oyuki asked.

"What's it to you?" the one in the lead snarled. But at the same time, one of the others had already said, "The Big Boss at the bottom of the sea."

"Do you by any chance mean the Dragon God?" Oyuki said. "The one who lives in an undersea palace with the lovely Otohime?"

The leader looked momentarily surprised, but its expression quickly reverted to its usual menacing sneer. "So you've heard the story of Urashima Taro, I see. So what? Everyone in Japan knows that one."

"We've done more than hear it," I said. "We've been there. We've met Otohime."

"That's right," Oyuki chimed in. "We're under the protection of the…the one you call the Big Boss Below. He'll be most displeased with you if you harm us."

The leader scoffed. "Why should I believe you?"

"Have you seen one of these before?" I reached under my shirt, pulled out the bag I wore around my neck, took out the tamatebako, and held it high. In the twilight, it glowed with a preternatural light, as if, even though the sun was setting here above, the noonday sunlight

66

was always dancing on the sea from which this had come.

The jaws of all three suiko dropped.

"Forgive us," said the leader, humbly folding its hands and bowing its head. "We had no idea."

"Will you allow us to cross the river without further trouble?" Oyuki asked.

"Yes," said the leader. "By all means. We'll help you across."

Oyuki and I exchanged glances. The reaction of these creatures to the sight of the tamatebako had seemed genuine, but her expression told me she didn't trust them any more than I did.

As we hesitated, we heard a shout behind us and a thrashing in the pines. A quick glance behind was enough to confirm that Matsukura's men had caught up with us.

I turned back to the suiko. "As for those men," I said, gesturing their way, "they've never met the Big Boss Below. I'm sure he'll consider them fair game."

The suiko looked at one another, nodded with malicious grins, and submerged back under the river.

I looked at Oyuki. "Here goes," I said.

I leapt from the branch, as far from the bank as I could, into the river. Oyuki did the same.

As we waded to the far side, I waited apprehensively for the crack of a musket, but I heard none. Either our pursuers weren't carrying firearms, or else they were so intent on the chase that they hadn't stopped to reload. What I heard instead was splashes as they waded into the river after us, followed by the same cries of alarm I had heard from Oyuki, and cries of terror abruptly cut off as their heads went under water.

We made our hurried way through the forest. It was the hour when there was still some light in the sky, but the shadows of the trees made the forest a treacherous place. It would be easy to stumble, or get lost, or wander into the clutches of some yokai even worse than the suiko.

But before long, we emerged back onto the road we had taken to Fukae, and followed it south until we saw the thatched roofs of Dozaki, welcoming us with the promise of a fire to dry ourselves, a good meal, and a roof over our heads.

The next morning, we rose before dawn and headed back to Fukae. When we arrived at the temple, we found a crowd of jubilant villagers waiting for us. Among them, to my great surprise, stood a shaven-headed Buddhist priest, in a purple robe with a long string of prayer beads around his neck.

To my even greater surprise, the priest smiled and bowed as we approached. "Welcome back," he said.

I hadn't recognized him with his hair and beard shaved, but his voice gave him away. It was Mori.

He gleefully told us the story, which spread like wildfire among the rebels, gaining richer detail with each retelling. When Matsukura's soldiers rode into Fukae, Mori, disguised as the temple priest, had run up to meet them. "Thank all the gods and Buddhas you're here!" he said. "Those madmen have been going from village to village, slaughtering everyone who refused to join their cause. Some villages have gone along with them, either out of fear or because they really are believers in this vile Yaso. But I assure you, everyone in Fukae is a loyal subject of the Shogun and Lord Matsukura. Please, mighty samurai, defend us! Oh, and when you've routed the rebels, do please come back to the temple for a victory party."

Encouraged by the speech and the invitation, Matsukura's forces had sallied forth to meet us. When we ran away as ordered, they gave token pursuit before returning to the temple for what they thought was their well-earned victory party. They gorged themselves on the food and sake the villagers had generously provided, boasting all the while about how the job had been more easily done than they had thought. And once the soldiers had drunk themselves into oblivion, Mori had signaled the villagers to come in and relieve them of all their armor and weapons, which they then proceeded to distribute among the rebels: forty suits of armor, forty bows, fifty spears, and seventy muskets with powder and shot, as well as various other supplies that our side could put to good use.

"And the soldiers?" asked Shiro.

Mori gestured back toward the temple. "When they wake up, they'll find that the doors and windows have all been nailed shut."

Everyone who heard him laughed. Even the ordinarily dour Chijiwa couldn't suppress a satisfied smirk.

"Excellent," Chijiwa said. "Let's burn it."

Mori's smile evaporated. "I hardly think that's necessary," he said. "By the time they wake up and find a way to break out of the temple, we'll be long gone, with all of their weapons in our hands. It will almost be worse for them when they go back to Shimabara and have to tell their superiors what happened. That is, if they have the courage to go back at all."

"If we let them live, they won't rest until they've had their revenge," Chijiwa said. "And any temple to a pagan god left standing is an affront to Deus. Burn it. It will help our side, it will hurt the enemy, and it will please Deus."

"Be that as it may," Shiro cut in, "it will *not* please *me*. There will be no death or destruction that can possibly be avoided. Let it be as Soiken says."

Chijiwa, with a disbelieving look at Shiro, opened his mouth to speak again, but Ashizuka cut him off. "You have your orders."

Chijiwa gave him a baleful look, but said no more.

* * *

We continued our march toward Shimabara. Somewhere along the line, we had acquired a banner to march behind: a large square of cloth, painted meticulously in bold colors with the image of a host hovering over a chalice, flanked by two angels kneeling in supplication.

The mood among the rebels had changed noticeably. We had just faced a well-armed, disciplined force numbering in the hundreds, and by a combination of determination and guile – and, Shiro might have added, the blessing of Deus – we had survived. But now the real battle was about to begin, and those of us who hadn't already known what that entailed, did now.

As we went, new members continued to swell our ranks, bringing with them food, weapons, and news. Some rebels knew where Matsukura kept a stash of weapons as part of a half-formed plan to invade Corea someday, and they had raided it, adding to our arsenal. Others had stormed the stockade where Oyuki and I had been held captive, and freed the prisoners, most of whom thanked us by joining our cause.

When we arrived at Shimabara, there was no mistaking it. The castle keep, a tiered pagoda five stories high, towered over the town, awe-inspiring even with the bamboo scaffolds that still surrounded it. The last castle I had seen anywhere near that size was Edo Castle, seat of the Shogun himself. The grounds that Shimabara Castle stood on were smaller, of course, but the keep was no less imposing. I could see why Lord Matsukura had drawn such condemnation, from both his people in Shimabara and his master in Edo, for building something so much grander than his actual rank warranted.

My heart dropped into my bowels with the weight of a cannonball. The crowd around me surged inexorably forward, and there was nothing I could do but go along with it as it swept me towards a collision with this hulking, immovable symbol of the highest authority in the land. I felt as though I were part of a great wave about to break against a cliff. And in such cases, the word "break" always applied to the wave, never the cliff.

The wave gathered momentum as we approached the castle wall. As I looked up at the bulk of the fortress, the barrels of muskets emerged from the holes in the walls. Then I heard the sharp crack as they fired. Our side replied with a cry of "Santiago!" and quickened our pace.

The castellan had stationed a hundred or two of his defenders outside the castle walls. He must have thought they would make short work of a handful of rebellious peasants, but he had grievously underestimated our numbers, our skill, and our determination. After just one volley from their muskets, the rebels surged forward and surrounded them, barely giving them time to draw their swords.

Amid the chaos, a thought came to my mind: *This is war. This is what I read about in books.* But reading about it was no preparation for the real thing. I wasn't watching a performance of *Henry V*, and I needed no narrator to apologize for not being able to cram whole armies into the theater. I didn't have to look at one man on stage and imagine a thousand, or hear the word "horse" and mentally provide the sound effects of pounding hooves and terrified neighs. The sounds were real, like the crack of muskets, the bone-shaking boom of cannons, the battle cries, the screams of the fallen.

The siege continued until nightfall. Of the defenders, those who survived had retreated within the castle gates. Despite our side's best efforts to pursue them inside, they had managed to close the gates and shut us out. At night, the more seasoned warriors among us took it in shifts to keep watch over the castle gates to stop any of the defenders trying to attempt a sally, while the rest of us took up lodgings in the town. Apparently, the castellan had gathered the citizenry of Shimabara inside the castle walls, so the only ones left outside were those sympathetic to our cause. Shimabara was now divided: Matsukura's men controlled the castle, while our side controlled the rest of the town.

In the houses where friendly citizens hosted us – and in the abandoned ones we commandeered – families and neighbors tended to stay together, with the result that the town became a miniature map of the entire region of Shimabara and Amakusa. As for those of us without families – without families *here*, I hastened to correct my thought – some of the larger houses were made into barracks, with men and women billeted separately. Once again, I found myself sleeping in a confined space with a vast choir of virtuoso snorers.

The pallet next to mine was occupied by a boy about my age. As soon as we settled down for the night, he turned to me. "Excuse me," he said eagerly. "Are you really from Oranda?"

He had just called me a Dutchman. It was an honest mistake, so I decided against challenging him to a duel. Instead, I corrected him gently: "I'm from England."

He gave me a blank look. "Pardon me?"

"England," I repeated. "I'm English."

His face lit up with comprehension. "*Igirisu!*" he exclaimed. "Yes, I've heard of that. What part of Oranda is it in?"

The Dutch must be delighted, I thought ruefully, to have established themselves here so well that in the mind of at least one Japanese person, their country comprised the whole of Europe.

"It's not part of Oranda," I said. "It's a whole different…" Here I broke down. The same word – *kuni* – was used both to distinguish one nation from another and one part of Japan from another. I knew of no way to clarify the matter.

I gave up and turned the tables. "How about you?" I asked. "Are you from Shimabara originally?"

He shook his head. "I'm from Funai, across the Ariake Sea. I came here as an apprentice to my uncle.

He's a carpenter, and he came here to work on the castle. When the rebels arrived, he followed the order to take shelter inside the walls. But as for me..." He paused. "I knew how Matsukura treated the common people. I knew it wasn't right. So when I saw the people taking a stand against him...well, I ran away and joined in."

My annoyance with him diminished somewhat. "I'm Simon," I said. "Simon Grey."

"Jinzaemon," he said. "So what brought you to Japan, Simon?"

"An English merchantman," I replied, honestly if evasively.

"And how long have you been here?"

"Uh..." I was saved from having to come up with an answer to this deceptively simple question by a gruff voice somewhere in the darkness.

"Will you boys quiet down?" it said. "There are people trying to sleep."

* * *

It soon became apparent that, even with all the collective military experience that our side boasted, no one had quite planned for what we would do after we arrived at the castle and found the gates shut against us. To get into the castle grounds, we would have to scale a high outer wall, and we had no siege ladders or anything that might help us accomplish that objective. And from what I heard, even if we got over the outer wall, we would still have to cross an inner moat before reaching the castle keep.

As for the defenders' side, after yesterday's initial assault, musket shots from the ramparts grew less frequent. Our leaders told us that when Matsukura had left for Edo, he had taken a large retinue with him, leaving only the castellan and a token garrison to defend the castle. Their supplies of powder and shot, apparently, were also limited, and they were rationing them carefully. This was good news for our side, but it seemed to betoken a stalemate rather than a victory.

We surrounded the castle, and what began as an assault turned into something more like a demonstration. And there were only so many times you could brandish a pitchfork and chant the Japanese equivalent of "Hey, hey, ho, ho, Matsukura's got to go!" before it began to grow tiresome. I tried to beguile the time by writing my own bits of doggerel, like:

Matsukura went to Edo
On orders of the Shogun's.
He came home and found
His castle surround-
-Ed, and his men with no guns!

But astonishingly, none of my compositions was ever adopted by the rebels as a battle chant.

On the third day, Yamada found me in the crowd. "Simon," he said, "Shiro wants to see you."

I followed him to the house where Shiro and the senior officers were staying. When we arrived, I found Oyuki already there, along with Shiro, Ashizuka, and Mori, all gathered around a table poring over a map. Chijiwa was conspicuous for his absence.

"There you are," Shiro said, nodding to me as I entered. "Here's the situation: The siege of Shimabara Castle is at an impasse. The enemy can't get out, and we can't get in. But time is on their side. All they have to do is wait until reinforcements come and pin us against the castle walls, so we'll be under attack from both sides. If we want to secure a stronghold for ourselves, we need to send a larger force against a smaller castle."

Chijiwa arrived, his face streaked with soot like a chimney sweep's. Shiro gave him a sharp look. "Where have you been?"

"Executing the judgment of Deus on the infidels." Under the mask of ash and smoke, I thought I saw an expression of vindictive satisfaction.

Shiro gave him a questioning look, but said nothing more to him, turning his attention back to the map instead. "This will do," he said, pointing at a spot across the water from Kuchinotsu. "Tomioka Castle."

I looked apprehensively at the place where he was pointing. Tomioka Castle seemed to be built in a very defensible location: on a peninsula connected to the mainland only by a narrow strip of land. Even if we had the advantage of numbers – which, by this time, we might well have – it would count for nothing if the enemy could simply pick us off as we tried to march across the causeway.

"We can attack the castle on two fronts," Ashizuka said, as if reading my thoughts. "March on it overland, while at the same time, bombarding it with cannon fire from the sea."

That last part mystified me. "Do we *have* any cannons?" I asked. "Or ships big enough to carry them?" Neither of those had been in evidence when we sailed to Shimabara.

"That's where you come in," Shiro replied. "I would like you two to be part of a special envoy to see if you can get any help from your people."

"My people?" I echoed.

Before I could remind him that all the English had been driven out of Japan fifteen years ago, Shiro went on: "Mori is going to Hirado to talk to the head of the Dutch trading post, someone by the name of Nicolaes Couckebacker. We'd like you to go with him. With the blessing of Deus, maybe this Couckebacker can be persuaded to give us some help, or at least to spread the word of our resistance movement abroad."

Shiro, it seemed, was making the same mistake as Jinzaemon, lumping all Europeans together. But before I could explain to him that the English and Dutch had been fierce rivals for time out of mind, Oyuki spoke up. "Go to Hirado?" she asked excitedly. "And could we stop in Nagasaki on the way? At this new port...this Dejima?"

"That's the plan," Shiro said. "If you can get support from Couckebacker in Hirado, we hope he might send orders with you for the Dutch ships anchored in Nagasaki. It's worth a try."

Oyuki practically jumped with delight. My heart did the same. If we could stop in Nagasaki, maybe someone there could tell us what had happened to Oyuki's father and Captain Shakespeare.

We joined Mori aboard the little sailboat, which seemed adequate for the voyage as long as we stayed close to shore. As we put out from Shimabara, I saw columns of smoke rising from the town. When I looked more closely, I saw that they were rising from the sites of Buddhist temples and Shinto shrines.

So that was what Chijiwa had meant by "executing the judgment of Deus on the infidels."

I recalled Oyuki's and my first adventure in Japan, in what I had come to think of as another lifetime, before our fateful visit to Ryugujo. We wouldn't have made it without the help of the priests at the temple of Ikegami Honmonji in Edo and the Seimei Shrine in Kyo no Miyako. Would Chijiwa have condemned them as "infidels" too, simply for following the way of their ancestors instead of a new way imported from a distant country barely a century ago?

I had often wondered: What happened to people who never had the chance to hear the Gospel, simply because they had lived either too long ago or too far away? As far as anyone had ever been able to tell me, the best they could hope for was a place among the Virtuous Pagans – the pleasantest part of hell, but still in hell. This hardly seemed a fair treatment for those whose only "sin" consisted of being born in the wrong place and time. And it seemed even less fair that those born in remote continents had to wait *fifteen centuries* before the people entrusted with the Gospel learned to build ocean-going ships. God clearly knew the shipbuilder's craft well enough to give Noah detailed plans for an ark, so why couldn't he have thrown in a few words about how to square-rig a galleon? When Jesus told his disciples to preach the Good News to the ends of the earth, how much would it have cost him to add, "And for that, you'll need this instrument called a compass"? I had been assured that everything happens in God's good time, but still, I couldn't help wondering: What took him so long?

It took two days to reach Hirado, but the voyage went quickly as Mori regaled us with tales of his adventures. It seemed that, long ago, his master, the daimyo of Kumamoto, had lent his naval power to an ill-fated attempt to conquer Corea. Mori had been in command of a supply ship, which ran into a storm and capsized. He had been rescued by a Dutch trading vessel and taken to Holland, where he spent four years, with a year or two in China on the way back. His tales might have been tall, but they were entertaining.

At one point, we sailed past the mouth of an inlet, where several other vessels were coming and going. I crouched anxiously below the gunwale while Oyuki asked Mori, "Is that the way to...?"

"Nagasaki," he confirmed.

"Didn't you say we were going to stop there?"

"On the way back," Mori answered gently. "If all goes well, Couckebacker will accompany us himself, or at least send us with a message for the chief of Dejima."

With a last longing look toward Nagasaki, Oyuki acquiesced.

Finally, we arrived in Hirado. We put ashore by the Dutch trading post, a large, white building with gabled roofs that looked decidedly out of place in a Japanese town. Bamboo scaffolding still surrounded the nearly completed building, and a crew of Japanese roofers and painters were hard at work. But the building itself was closed, and we saw no sign of any Dutch traders anywhere.

Mori asked for directions to Couckebacker's house, and one of the workers answered his questions with no more than a cursory glance at Oyuki or me. Since this was one of the two places in Japan where the Dutch were allowed to conduct business, I thought, perhaps the sight of foreign or mixed-race children was not so unusual.

Mori attempted to follow the directions we had been given, but Oyuki confidently took the lead and guided us to an inlet of the sea, across a stone bridge, and to a house that also looked as though it had been picked up in a distant country and carried to Japan.

"Have you been here before?" Mori asked, clearly impressed with her sense of direction.

"Often," Oyuki replied, in a melancholy voice. "This house used to be mine."

Chapter 7:
The Battle of Hondo

第七章. 本渡城戰

Mori slid aside the door and took a tentative step into the foyer. From inside, we heard sounds of frantic activity, as though Couckebacker already had numerous guests and the kitchen staff were bustling to get everything ready.

"*Gomen kudasai?*" Mori called. "Hello?"

A dark-skinned footman in a tunic, leggings, and turban – from Jakarta, I guessed, or one of Holland's colonies in the East Indies – appeared and regarded us silently.

Mori spoke to him in Dutch. "Please inform Heer Couckebacker that an emissary from the Lord of Kumamoto begs his pardon for the sudden intrusion, but desires an urgent audience."

"Please, come in," the footman said with a bow.

As we took off our shoes and stepped up into the house, I once more admired Mori's cleverness. Nothing he had said could really be called a lie. He had, at one point, served the Lord of Kumamoto; he simply neglected to mention that his former master had been dead for decades.

The footman ushered us into the same parlor where Oyuki and I had sat with John Winter, scarcely two weeks ago for us, but fifteen years ago for the rest of the world. It was the same mixture of Japanese and Western styles: sliding lattice doors covered with translucent rice paper, a folding screen painted in Japanese style, and straw tatami mats on the floor, but covered with carpets from India upon which stood chairs and tables that would have looked more at home in Amsterdam.

This mixture of strangeness and familiarity was an unsettling sensation even for me, who had only been here briefly as a visitor. As for Oyuki, who had called this house her own, I could only imagine the sense of unreality she must be feeling, even though her face was perfectly composed.

We all stood as the footman announced Couckebacker's arrival and a door slid open to let him in. He had a pleasant face with a neatly trimmed beard and moustache, and was dressed in a doublet and leggings, with a white ruff around the neck that reminded me of Shiro.

"Heer Couckebacker," Mori said once we were seated again, "please forgive our intrusion at such a busy time, but we've come with an urgent appeal."

The footman set before each of us a blue and white porcelain cup-and-saucer set decorated with scenes of life in Holland, and filled it from a matching pot with a steaming, dark-brown liquid. The aroma was sharper than tea, an earthy fragrance that made the eyes and nostrils widen. It smelled enticing enough, but when I took an experimental sip, it tasted as though someone had boiled mud and run it through a filter. I gamely swallowed, but the bitter, acidic taste lingered in my mouth. It was all I could do to suppress a grimace.

"This is *kaffee*," Couckebacker explained. "It comes from a type of bean grown on the island of Java. It's all the rage back in Holland these days, but I suppose it *is* an acquired taste. Perhaps a little sugar?"

I made no protest as the footman stirred a spoonful of sugar into my cup, but I doubted it would make this brew much more palatable. There was no accounting for Dutch tastes, but I couldn't imagine this concoction ever catching on anywhere else.

As I pretended to sip my kaffee, Mori told our story. His Dutch, rusty though it may have been, was much better than mine. I struggled to follow what he said, and when he occasionally got stuck for a word and glanced at me in the hope I could prompt him, I could only shrug helplessly.

Throughout Mori's narration, Couckebacker listened attentively in between sips of his kaffee. When Mori finished with an impassioned plea for help, Couckebacker was silent for a moment, and then asked, "So what exactly is it that you would like me to do?"

"Send ships and cannons," Mori said. "Help spread the word of the rebellion, so other countries will come to our aid."

Couckebacker set down his cup. "Mori-*sama*," he said with a sigh, "you have my sympathies. Truly, you do. But I'm a trader, not a fighter. As you know, this is one of only two Dutch trading posts remaining in Japan. And as the Shogun never tires of reminding us, we're only here by his good graces. To take part in an uprising against him would be more than my life is worth."

"And to turn away from fellow Christians in their time of need?" I spoke of my own accord, before Mori could say anything, and I was as surprised as anyone else to hear the bold words coming out of my mouth. "That's more than your soul is worth."

Couckebacker gave me a long, hard look. "What are you hoping to accomplish?" he said at last.

"To overthrow Matsukura, of course! To bring freedom to the oppressed."

"How, exactly? How do you imagine the story of your rebellion will end?"

Mori, Oyuki, and I looked at one another in awkward silence. Clearly, none of us had a ready answer for this question.

"Suppose you *had* succeeded in taking over Shimabara Castle," Couckebacker went on. "What do you think would have happened then? I'll tell you: All the local lords would have rallied to Matsukura's support. You'd have been under a siege like no other in history."

I recalled what Ashizuka had said at the meeting on Yushima. "None of the local lords can send soldiers outside their domain without permission from the Shogun," I said.

"But what good does that do you, other than to buy you a little time?" Couckebacker rejoined. "Do you really think Tokugawa Iemitsu will just sit back in Edo Castle and allowed a band of...meaning no disrespect...peasants to stage an uprising against one of his lords? He'll throw everything he has at you. He won't allow any of his vassals to rest until your rebellion is completely crushed."

"That's exactly why we need support from other countries," Oyuki chimed in.

"And which countries did you have in mind? Holland's position in Japan, I've already told you, is too precarious to get involved. And the English are long gone."

"The Portuguese would help," I said. "Or should. It's because of their missionaries that the people of Shimabara are in these straits."

Couckebacker gave a one-shouldered shrug. "If you think that will convince them, the nearest Portuguese territory is Macao, off the coast of China. You're welcome to send an emissary there and plead your case. But even if Portugal, Holland, England, and every other country in Europe rallied to your cause, what then? Under the best possible conditions, it would take a good four years for any messengers to sail from here to Europe and come back with help. What do you think your chances are of holding off the Shogun's armies that long?"

"The Dutch have a whole fleet in Batavia," I said. "Just a few days' sail from here. Haven't you?"

"And if you think you could persuade the Governor-General to send them to your aid, you're welcome to go try. Myself, I wouldn't wager much on your chances."

"The writing is on the wall, Heer Couckebacker." The boldness of my words continued to astonish even me, but the time for cautious diplomacy was past. "First the Spanish, then the Portuguese, then the English. How long do you think it will be before your turn comes? When they finally send you packing, you could at least go home knowing you struck a blow on the side of justice."

"Fine words, Simon Grey," Couckebacker replied. "But unlike the Spanish and Portuguese, we have no interest in evangelizing, only in trading. And no offense meant, but unlike you English, we actually have a market here for our merchandise. So I foresee we'll be here for quite a while yet. Unless we decide to throw away everything we've worked so hard to build, by doing something extraordinarily foolish like siding against the Shogun in a domestic uprising that's of no concern to us."

I glanced at Mori, who had a defeated look. Clearly, he had no more idea what to say than I did.

"I'm terribly sorry to send you back empty-handed," Couckebacker said. "But I hope, at least not empty-bellied. Since you've come all this way, perhaps you'd care to join us for Christmas dinner?"

I looked at Oyuki, and saw the same shock of realization on her face that I felt. By the Japanese lunar calendar, today was the entirely unremarkable tenth day of the eleventh month. It had completely escaped us that, by the Gregorian calendar, it was the twenty-fifth of December.

"Heer Couckebacker," said Oyuki, "we're so sorry to have disturbed you on Christmas Day. We wouldn't want to impose."

"Oh, it would be no imposition. The cooks have really outdone themselves. They've prepared more than we can possibly finish. Three more guests will scarcely matter."

We looked at Mori, who nodded acquiescence. "We will humbly accept the privilege of being allowed to take you at your gracious word," he said in highly formal Japanese.

Oyuki suddenly turned to Couckebacker and asked the question that must have been burning in her mouth from the moment we crossed the threshold. "Mijnheer, may I ask you something? You must know my father, John Winter. The former owner of this house."

Couckebacker blinked. "Of course," he said. "Everyone knows him."

"Have you heard anything about what happened to him since the English were driven out of Japan?" she asked anxiously.

Couckebacker inclined his head ambivalently from side to side. "Well, there are several rumors. One can never be sure which to believe, but…"

"Tell me all of them," she interrupted breathlessly.

"Supposedly, he left Japan aboard the last British ship. Something like the *Cow* or *Bull*, I think it was…"

"The *Hereford*?"

"Yes, that might have been it. But some people have reported seeing him in Japan since. One saw him here, another there…"

"Where is 'here'?" Oyuki interrupted anxiously. "Where is 'there'?"

"Literally, all over. I've heard of sightings as far away as the domain of Mutsu, way up at the northern end of Japan. But if you ask ten people, you get ten different stories. Some say he died, but no one seems to know where he's buried. Some say he went back to England, but no one can say exactly when or how. His fate is one of history's unsolved mysteries."

The door to the adjoining room opened, and the footman, standing behind it, silently bowed.

Couckebacker rose to his feet. "Ah, dinner's ready," he said. "If you'll follow me?"

He escorted us into the dining room. Except for the tatami mat underfoot, we could have been in the house of a wealthy merchant in Amsterdam. Around the table sat Dutch men dressed like Couckebacker. A few had Japanese wives by their side, mostly in kimono, but some in Dutch dresses. Mori looked out of place, like a visitor from a distant land, even though he was one of the few on his native soil.

The long table was covered with a pristine white tablecloth and laden with such a lavish dinner as I had rarely seen even in England. Each of the plates on the table already bore a little loaf of bread and several slices of roast beef, and bowls stood ready to be filled with soup from the covered tureens. Up and down the table, the light from the abundant candles flickered over a menagerie of earth, sky, and sea: roast chicken, grilled fish, whole roasted quails with their heads peeping over the rim of their porcelain nest, a ham hock studded with cloves, and in the very center, a boar's head with an apple in its mouth.

I could say my mouth watered. But that might give the impression of a slight leak between inexpertly tarred boards, when the actual sensation was more like the entire hull shattering on the breakers. At sea, my diet had consisted entirely of rock-hard biscuits and meat doused with salt in a futile attempt to keep it from rotting, and in Japan, plain rice supplemented occasionally by pickled vegetables or a bite of fish. It took all my self-restraint to keep from rushing at the table and tearing into the food before it turned out to be a dream or mirage. Even as the aroma pierced my nostrils, a sense of guilt pierced my heart as I thought of the rebels back in Shimabara, who would be muddling along on their usual meager rations while we sat down to such an extravagant feast.

Oyuki clapped a hand over her mouth, turned on her heel, and ran, back through the sitting room and out the front door. After a moment's hesitation, I ran after her, as Mori, Couckebacker, and all the guests looked on in bewilderment.

I emerged from the house into the chill December night, looked up and down the street, and saw Oyuki on the bridge we had crossed on our way from the harbor. She was leaning over the rail, sobbing, her tears dropping into the inlet to blend with the salty sea. She had faced enchantment, imprisonment, the threat of the worst torture she could imagine, and the guns and blades of battle, all without shedding a single tear. But the last straw, apparently, was to be in her own house and see her own table laden for Christmas dinner, just like every other Christmas of her life...except that everyone sitting around it was a stranger.

I ran onto the bridge, stood beside her in silence for a minute or so, then laid a tentative hand on her shoulder. She didn't resist my touch. I wondered whether she even felt it.

"This is all my fault," she said, when she could take enough of a breath between sobs to speak. "If only I had listened to my father. If I hadn't tried to save those dolphins..."

"Then I would have," I said.

She looked at me through wide, tearful eyes. "Really?"

I hesitated. "Actually, I don't know whether I would have. I would have wanted to, but I don't know whether I could actually have done it. All I know is that you have the kind of courage I wish I had. And because of that, I know that we *will* get through this. We *will* find your father. And we *will* find a way home."

She looked back out to sea. "I feel so small," she said. "So helpless. So alone."

"Small, maybe," I said. "But 'helpless' has never been a word I would use for you." My heart continued speaking before my mind even knew what was coming: "And as long as I'm alive, you'll never be alone."

Oyuki turned to me and laid her head on my shoulder. I hesitated, then put my arms all the way around her. After a moment, I felt hers around me. The heat from my heart radiated throughout my limbs and banished the cold in an instant.

Something told me there would never be a more opportune time to say what was burning in my heart. I summoned my courage and prayed for a Christmas miracle.

"Oyuki," I whispered into her ear, "I love you."

As quickly as if I had turned into a burning ember, she let me go, pulled away from my embrace, and backed up to the far side of the bridge, with a look of wide-eyed horror.

"You should never say that," she said, "on a bridge after sunset."

"What?" I replied in bafflement. "Why?"

From somewhere under the bridge came a scream that made me jump a mile. It was like the scream I had once heard from the cook when she caught the cat eating the fish meant for everyone's dinner, but a hundred times louder.

Oyuki closed her eyes and heaved a sigh. "That's why."

Out of the water rose an apparition, like a woman as tall as the keep of Shimabara Castle, scowling in fury, ghostly white except for the streaks of red on her face. She wore a white gossamer kimono, and on her head, an iron crown surmounted by candles. Clamped between her teeth was a torch, lit at both ends. How it, and the candles on her head, managed to stay lit underwater was a mystery.

She thrust an accusing finger at me. "You lie!" she screamed. She had no difficulty making her words unmistakably clear, even around a mouthful of blazing wood. "You are false, like all men! Confess it!"

"Do as she says," Oyuki instructed me.

"But I wasn't lying," I protested. "I..."

"Just do it," Oyuki said more urgently.

I sighed. "Fine," I said, and turned to the apparition. "You're right. I didn't mean it."

The woman in white nodded in grim satisfaction, and with a last venomous glare at me, sank back into the water.

I turned back to Oyuki, my heart still pumping from the shock. "Who, in the name of all that walks in the night, was that?"

She let out a long breath. "Hashi-hime," she said. "The Bridge Princess of Uji."

My knowledge of Japanese geography was still sketchy. "Uji? Is that close to us?"

"Nowhere near, but it doesn't matter. She can appear under any bridge anywhere in Japan."

"What does she have against bridges?"

"It's not bridges, it's men. She was betrayed by her husband, so she put on the ritual garments you just saw and went to bathe in the Uji River every night for three weeks, in the dead of winter, to turn herself into a spirit so she could take revenge."

"On her husband?"

"On anyone she hates. And she hates happy lovers most of all."

As I stood there uncomfortably, trying to think of what to say to smooth over this most awkward of moments, Oyuki's eyes widened and she pointed over my shoulder, toward the sea. "Look!"

I turned and looked where she was pointing. Just coming into view was a ship, as big as the *Hereford*, with two masts and square sails. It was packed to the gunwales with armed men, and from its prow flew a white flag with a crest that looked like waves with three sails above and three rudders below.

A moment later, another ship flying the same standard hove into view, and then another, and another.

We stood there, watching and counting the ships with mounting apprehension, until it became clear that an entire fleet was rounding the peninsula and heading south.

"I don't suppose I get any prizes for guessing where they're going?" I said.

"Come on," Oyuki said over her shoulder, already running for Couckebacker's house. "We have to tell Mori."

We ran back to Couckebacker's house, and breathlessly told Mori what we had seen. When we described the crest on the flags, his eyes widened.

"Terasawa Katataka," he said. "The lord of Karatsu has joined the battle. We have to warn the others." He stood up from the table. "Heer Couckebacker, we thank you most humbly for your hospitality, and we deeply regret the rudeness we must commit, but there is no time to lose."

Couckebacker nodded. "Of course."

Mori turned to go. With a last, longing look at the banquet I hadn't tasted, I followed him. Oyuki went with me, then paused and turned back to Couckebacker. "Mijnheer, can we ask you one last favor?"

"Certainly."

"Oyuki Winter and Simon Grey are among the Shimabara rebels. Please, spread the word as far and wide as you can. Maybe someday it will reach my father, and he'll know we're still alive."

* * *

Our little vessel sailed back down the coast toward Shimabara, with Mori casting anxious glances astern all the while as though expecting Terasawa's fleet to catch up with us at any moment. Conversation between Oyuki and me was strained, consisting mostly of practical exchanges about the proper trim of the sails. There was so much I wanted to say to her, but aboard this little boat with Mori, it was impossible to catch her alone. I had the horrible feeling she found that a relief.

The following day, we came the inlet that led to Nagasaki. Mori, however, kept our southeast heading.

Oyuki gazed at the inlet in increasing alarm as it became evident that Mori had no intention of changing course, then turned on him accusingly. "You promised!"

Mori spread his hands. "I'm sorry," he said. "But speed is of the essence. We have no message for anyone on Dejima, and an urgent message for our leaders in Shimabara. If we don't get back in time to warn them before Terasawa's fleet arrives, this whole trip will have been for nothing."

Oyuki made no reply. But from the way she gazed at the inlet as we passed it, I was more than a little worried that she might jump overboard and try to swim for it.

As the boat rounded Kuchinotsu and prepared to head north toward Shimabara, our course crossed with another boat going the other way. Mori tried to make an inconspicuous change to our heading, to give it a wider berth. But as it came within earshot, we heard a shout from the other craft: "Abé!"

"Maruya!" Mori shouted the countersign and steered us closer to the other vessel. Once we were within conversing distance, the pilot of the other boat said something across the gunwales to Mori, who then turned to tell us the news as the two vessels changed course and set off together in a southerly direction.

"It seems the castellan of Tomioka, a samurai by the name of Miyake Tobei," he explained, "has gotten wind of our coming and sent his troops out to meet us. Our forces are engaged with his at the town of Hondo, on Lower Amakusa."

We sailed down the coast. As we approached a narrow strait, presumably between Upper and Lower Amakusa, the sounds of battle grew louder: musket fire, war cries, and the eerie sound of the conch-shell horns that our side used as a call to arms. As we drew nearer, the sharp smell of gunpowder smoke hung in the air, and we saw the sea of waving white banners from our side, and across the river, an elaborate eight-spoked wheel, which I took for the standard of Miyake.

Mori beached our craft among the others, and we joined the throng. From observing, and listening to the snippets of information that came down the line, we could piece together an idea of the situation. Miyake's forces had poured down from their outpost, a small castle on top of a hill, to meet ours at the bridge over the point where the Machiyamaguchi River – a mouthful of a name meaning "mountain river whose mouth is in the town" – met the sea. Our forces were pressing on them from the south, and more of ours were landing even now at Mogine Beach to the north, but Miyake's forces still held the bridge and the castle.

"Stay behind," Mori ordered us, as he shouldered his way forward to meet the other leaders. We could only watch from a distance as our musketeers and Miyake's exchanged fire across the river, and his banner, slowly but inexorably, pushed ours back across the bridge.

Suddenly, I had a flash of inspiration. "Oyuki," I said, "I have an idea. Are you willing to go with me to the bridge?"

"All right," she said dubiously.

We joined hands and wove through the crowd of fighters until we reached the foot of the bridge. Miyake's forces had almost fought their way across, and ours were desperately trying to hold the line.

I found a spot on the bridge, just behind the front rank of our warriors, and stepped onto the wooden planks.

"Oyuki," I said, loudly enough to be heard above the clash of arms, "I love you."

She gaped at me in disbelief and alarm, as though sure I had gone completely mad. "What? Simon! This is hardly the…"

A deafening shriek came from under the bridge. The noise of battle suddenly stopped, as all the warriors on both sides looked frantically around them for the source of the nightmare sound.

A moment later, the gigantic figure of Hashi-hime rose up out of the sea to tower over the bridge. The soldiers, who evidently could see her, cowered behind the walls.

"You lie!" she shrieked, thrusting her finger at me as before. "You are false, like all men! Confess it!"

"No!" I shouted back.

"You lie!" she screamed even louder. "You are false, like all men! Confess it!"

"No! I'm telling the truth!"

"You lie!" Her voice reached such a pitch that some of the soldiers dropped their weapons and pressed their hands to their ears. "You are false, like all men! Confess it!"

I lifted up my head and shouted as loud as I could: "I will not! I'm telling the truth!"

Hashi-hime let out a howl of rage. A sudden gale-force wind blew in from behind her, whipping the sea into a frenzy.

"Fall back!" came the order from Ashizuka.

"Let's go!" I said to Oyuki, taking her hand. We ran off the bridge, along with the frantically retreating forces on both sides, just as a huge wave rolled in and crashed over the bridge. When the waters subsided, the bridge was gone.

Miyake's troops on the far side were now pinned between our troops and the river, their backs exposed to our musketeers firing from across the water. An armored, mounted figure – presumably Miyake himself – tried to leap across the gap where the bridge had been, but fell short, and horse and rider both plunged into the river.

Oyuki turned to me and clapped her hands. "Simon, you're a genius! What a brilliant strategy!"

Do you think it was just a strategy? I wanted to ask. But before I could, the conch shells started blowing again. My first thought was that it was a warning of enemy reinforcements arriving. But this time, the conchs were joined a moment later by drums and flutes, and the music sounded more like a celebration than a call to arms.

The rebels hastened back towards the beach where our craft had landed. We followed the crowd in time to see a boat coming in with five people aboard. Two rowed, and two more held lanterns that illuminated the figure of the fifth: Shiro.

He wore an embroidered robe over a plain kimono and breeches, with a crown of ramie grass on his head that I supposed was meant to resemble the Crown of Thorns. In his hand, he carried a wand with white paper strips hanging from it. His costume seemed purposely designed so that any rebels who looked at him would see what they wanted to see: either the vestments of a Christian priest, or the plain clothes of a Japanese peasant and the wand that looked as though it had come from a Shinto shrine.

The lantern-bearers disembarked, and the oarsmen gave Shiro a hand as he stepped delicately over the gunwale, as though taking care not to get sand on his clothes. The crowd parted as Shiro and his retinue, preceded and followed by lantern-bearers, made their way in a solemn procession towards the center of Hondo.

It reminded me of the triumphal entry into Jerusalem, and I was clearly not the only one who had that image in mind. The crowds on either side of him were shouting: "Banzai! Blessed is the one who comes in the name of Deus! Banzai!"

To see all the commotion, anyone would have thought *he* had won the Battle of Hondo. Or, at the very least, been anywhere near it.

Chapter 8:
The Castle of Heaven

第八章．天の城

With Tobei gone, we could have taken over his castle quite easily. But as it turned out, while we had been fighting in Hondo, Shiro had been busily recruiting new followers in his home territory of Amakusa, meaning that our forces now numbered more than ten thousand. Hondo Castle – a small fortress made to house a small garrison – was apparently nowhere near adequate. Shiro and the other commanders handed down the order to press on for the destination I had heard them name before our mission to Hirado: Tomioka.

I could feel a renewed sense of purpose in the air as we resumed our march. Any doubts the rebels may have been feeling after the stalemate at Shimabara had apparently been swept away by our victory at Hondo.

I was hoping that, while we were on the march, I could get a word in with Oyuki. But she was always buried deep in a protective crowd of women and girls. Getting past the defenses of a castle felt like an easy task compared with getting anywhere close to her.

We marched all day, with the wind from the sea whipping a cold rain into our faces. The weather didn't seem to dampen the spirits of the rebels any, however, as they continued to sing the mysterious song: *Daodate domino ohne zente, rodate iyoni ishi poporiya.*

"What are they saying?" I asked Jinzaemon, who tended to gravitate to my side as we marched.

94

He gave me a surprised look. "You can't understand? Isn't it a language from your country?"

"It's certainly not English."

"It's an *orasho*. Something their parents or grandparents would have learned from the bateren."

It finally became clear. *Oratio* was the Latin word for "prayer." They were singing a psalm that would have begun *Laudate Domino omnes gentes*, "Praise the Lord, all peoples." Over the years, the words had changed, but you could still see the original Latin behind them if you knew what to look for.

"Well, it helps take the mind off this wretched weather," I said. "At least it's not snowing."

"Oh, you have winter in your country too?" he asked. "You have seasons?"

Now it was my turn to look surprised. "Are you joking?"

"I just thought, since your country was so far south of here..."

I shot him a look of annoyance. "England is farther north than the northernmost part of Japan," I explained. "You don't know what winter is until you've spent it in London."

The more time I spent with Jinzaemon, and the more of his eager questions I answered, the clearer an image I formed of my world as he envisioned it. According to him, I came from a vast country called Nanban, roughly meaning "South Barbary" (so named since, after all, all our ships approached Japan from the south). Like Japan, it was divided into smaller domains, with names like Oranda, Porutogaru, and my home province of Igirisu. These were ruled by local lords who were always skirmishing with one another, often over trivial matters like the best way to pray, but all of whom owed at least nominal allegiance to the Divine Emperor in the glorious capital city of Roma. Jinzaemon sympathized with my supposed struggles in getting used to Japanese customs that must have seemed outlandish to me, such as observing no fewer than four distinct seasons, eating fish and rice, and (the unkindest cut of all) bathing – a custom which the Japanese, judging from the smell of sailors just off the boat after a two-year voyage, had concluded must be unknown in Europe. But he also envied me for growing up in a country where we could feast on roast beef and cake every day, and all the girls were beautiful blue-eyed blondes.

It was easy for me to laugh at his misapprehensions. But I reminded myself that when I had first set sail for Japan, I knew far less about his country than he knew about mine.

From a distance, Tomioka Castle looked as if it were on an island. Only when we drew closer did the narrow strip of land connecting it to the mainland become visible. The way the hills curved around the castle, I heard from some of the rebels, had given it the nickname of *Garyujo*, the Castle of the Sleeping Dragon. I felt a sudden surge of apprehension about what would happen when the dragon woke up.

The defenders had prepared for our arrival. The houses on the isthmus between the mainland and the castle had been hastily demolished, to leave a clear field with nowhere for us to hide. And because of our failed mission to Couckebacker, we didn't have the seaborne reinforcements we had hoped for – but the defenders of Tomioka did. The Battle of Hondo had apparently given Terasawa's fleet enough time to reach its destination, and we could see several of the troop barges and cargo ships docked behind the castle.

"Well," Ashizuka told us, "they were kind enough to leave us all this lumber. Let's put it to use."

We rummaged around the razed houses, grabbing doors, planks from walls, anything that could be used to make a shield. When we finally came within range of the castle, we held them over our heads to protect us from arrows and musket balls.

From the ramparts, a cannon fired.

I held my breath. If a cannonball fell into our ranks, our improvised shields would be no more protection than paper screens.

But I heard no sound of impact. Instead, I heard another sound from the castle: an odd clank of metal, and several shouts of consternation.

I almost laughed out loud. "They've blown their breech!" I exclaimed.

"What?" said Jinzaemon.

"Whoever sold them that cannon must never have told them they needed a rope to secure the breech end. That shot blew it right out. The cannon is useless now."

It must have been the only cannon they had. We heard the crack of muskets, but no more cannonballs came our way.

Word spread swiftly among the rebel forces, and in no time at all, the destruction of the Tomioka cannon became a sure sign that Deus favored our side. Encouraged, we surged forward at a swifter pace.

I heard a shout from somewhere behind me. When I looked, I saw that one of our soldiers had dropped his shield. An arrow was embedded in it, and to the arrow was fastened a packet of gunpowder. It had ignited and set fire to the wood.

Another fire arrow struck one of our shields. And then another, and another.

Our improvised wooden shields were suddenly worse than useless. And when we lowered them, the rain of fire became a storm, as muskets thundered and balls pelted down on our unprotected heads.

We beat a hasty retreat back across the causeway, and reconvened at the village of Shiki. The village boasted a sprawling shrine to Hachiman, the Shinto god of war, overlooking the sea. Rather than allow Chijiwa to put it to the torch, Shiro had commandeered it as his temporary headquarters. If Hachiman really existed, I wasn't sure which of these was likely to upset him more.

A dejected, anxious mood hung over our forces as we waited for word about the next step. Was Shiro going to rally us for another assault on Tomioka? But the next day, news spread through the camp, including a darkly whispered word: *Hara.*

Jinzaemon conveyed the message to me. "They're talking about a different destination. Hara Castle."

"Another castle?" I asked with a grimace. "What makes them think this attack is going to go any better than the ones at Shimabara or Tomioka?"

"There's no one to defend it," he replied. "It belonged to the former lord of Shimabara, before the Shogun gave the domain to Matsukura's father. According to the Shogun's law, no domain can have more than one castle. So when construction started on Shimabara Castle, Hara was abandoned."

"So we'd just be moving into an empty castle?"

"That seems to be the size of it."

"Why do people sound so apprehensive about that?"

Jinzaemon lowered his voice. "They believe it's haunted."

* * *

With the new recruits Shiro had gathered, along with those who had joined on the march from Hondo to Tomioka, the rebel force now numbered more than thirty thousand. We crowded aboard our patchwork flotilla, filling every boat to capacity, and made what our enemy must have thought was an ignominious retreat across the water, back to the Shimabara Peninsula. Soon, we came within sight of a promontory, crowned with the sad remains of what must once have been an imposing castle. The exterior wall was crumbling, and the three-storied pagoda-like castle keep – the *tenshu,* I later heard it was called – was falling into ruin.

We landed on a beach at the foot of a cliff, and used the steep, narrow pathways to climb up to what was to be our new home. It may not have looked very welcoming to us, but as a preliminary inspection of the castle grounds showed, it would look even less so to our enemies. The cliff where it stood was high enough to make it a difficult shot for ships' cannons. The sea surrounded it on three sides, and from the fourth, the only reliable approach was a narrow isthmus at the north end of the promontory. South of that was a tidal flat that, as we saw over the course of our first day there, was ankle-deep in mud at low tide and completely underwater at high tide.

It was a good, secure location, but I could see why the elder Matsukura had abandoned it in favor of his new construction. Shimabara Castle, with its high keep and commanding view of the harbor, could defend the entire town, while Hara Castle couldn't defend much besides itself. However, for our purposes, that was all it had to do.

Once all our people and goods were safely atop the castle mound, Shiro mustered us into the courtyard in front of the tenshu.

"This is the castle of heaven," he said, spreading his hands and turning around to encompass all the castle grounds.

The Japanese word for "castle" – *shiro* – sounded almost identical to his own name. And if even I noticed the subtle wordplay, of course everyone else would. By bestowing that nickname on the castle, was he, at the same time, indirectly proclaiming himself the messenger of heaven?

"If we live," Shiro continued, "we live in prosperity as masters of this castle. If we die, we go straight to paradise. Either way, generations yet to come will thank us for standing up for the poor and downtrodden. Blessed be Deus, our strong rock, the castle that keeps us safe, our fortress, and our refuge. And now, to work!"

Of that, there was plenty. The keep was cleaned, and huts were built inside the outer wall, again creating a miniature map of Shimabara and Amakusa. Bamboo stalks were harvested from the nearby forests and bound into bundles called *take-taba* – which, when lashed to a slanting wooden frame, could supposedly absorb the impact of a cannonball.

The boats in our flotilla were dismantled, leaving only a couple for fishing excursions, and the wood used either to build houses or to shore up the outer wall. Mori, displaying once again his talent for clever ruses, had the idea of covering the wooden planks with clay or white paper, and darkening the tops with pine-charcoal ink. From a distance, it looked like a real Japanese castle wall, whitewashed and topped with black tiles. I was impressed, but I was also reminded of the Spanish explorer in the New World who scuttled his own ships as soon as his men came ashore for a campaign of conquest, to cut off all possibility of retreat.

It was victory or death. And Couckebacker's question still echoed in my mind: What would victory for our side look like?

As the sun was setting and most people were in their improvised huts with their families, I chanced to see Oyuki, crouching and examining something in the ground. At first, I thought she was pulling weeds. All the courtyards were covered with them, except for the one called the "Tsume-no-maru," which had a patch about two yards across that was inexplicably bare. But when I took a closer look, I saw that she was holding a fragment of porcelain.

I approached her, trying to keep my knees from knocking. She looked up and saw me.

"Oh, hello, Simon."

I knelt beside her. "What have you found there?"

She showed me the fragment in her hand. "Do you suppose it's Dutch?"

"Maybe," I said, examining it. "But I've seen Chinese dishes in a similar style. It's hard to tell them apart."

"Look at this."

She had unearthed another piece of the bowl, this one containing the bottom. It looked like a floral pattern with four leaves of equal length.

"What about it?" I asked.

She traced the design with her finger. "It's the sign of the cross."

Now that she pointed it out, it was clear.

"Do you suppose it's a coincidence?" I asked.

"I doubt it," she said. "These days, it doesn't seem like anyone would risk having anything around that could raise even the slightest suspicion, unless they really were a true believer."

There was a moment of silence. I argued with myself about whether I should ask the question that had been preoccupying me. If I didn't now, I wondered when or if I would have another chance.

"Are you?" I asked.

"Am I what?"

"A true believer."

She gave me a puzzled look. "In?"

"In Shiro. That he really is who people say he is."

"Meaning?" She avoided my gaze by keeping hers on the fragment of pottery that she continued to turn over in her hand.

"A prophet. The Chosen One. A savior sent from heaven."

She was silent for a moment. When she spoke again, her voice made the evening air feel a degree or two chillier. "What I believe," she said, "is that you know far more about prophecies, saviors and that sort of thing than I."

"All I know is," I said, "from Shimabara to Hirado to Tomioka, and now here, nothing has gone according to plan. For a man who can supposedly talk directly to heaven, Shiro seems to be getting quite a lot of 'no' answers." I lowered my voice, even though there was no one around to hear. "Does he really know what he's doing?"

Oyuki finally looked at me. "If you aren't satisfied that he does," she said, "what do you propose doing about it? Do you see any other options?"

I was silent long enough that she answered her own question. "Unless you know how to conjure a ship and sail it to Nagasaki, I'd say this is the only place where we at least have a fighting chance."

"*Intruders!*"

A sudden cry out of nowhere made me jump. When I landed, heart pounding, I looked all around for the source of the voice.

What happened next made me think I was dreaming. The piece of porcelain in Oyuki's hand began to tremble – not because her hand was shaking, but of its own accord. Startled, she dropped it. All around it, other pieces were emerging from the ground, as though pushed from below by an unseen hand. As soon as they came to the surface, they took off and flew together. I ducked as they whizzed past my head, and looked up just in time to see them come together to make a figure that looked like a samurai made entirely of crockery. His helmet was a large bowl with a piece missing, his breastplate was an actual plate, and his arms and legs were articulated stacks of rice bowls. His fingers, made of tiny sake cups, curled around the handle of a large knife. Its blade was rusty, but I still wouldn't have wanted to be the one to test whether it still held an edge.

He glared at me from the dark depths of the sake flasks he used for eyes, and brandished the knife. "*Shiro-uneri!*" he called.

I had no idea what that meant, but I found out soon enough. Two pieces of cloth unearthed themselves in the same way as the pottery pieces that formed the warrior. I supposed they had once been white, but now they were so stained with mud and mildew that I had to take their original color on faith. The black-mottled, threadbare cloths twisted and folded themselves into something that looked like dragons, with claws outstretched towards us.

I had sometimes heard the cook at home chiding the scullery-maid for failing to hang out a dishrag properly: "If you leave it there too long, it'll come to life!" I had thought this was just a colorful expression, but now I saw it was the literal truth.

The two dishrags flew through the air with the speed of real dragons. One wrapped itself around my wrists, binding my arms behind me, and the other did the same to Oyuki.

"March!" the porcelain warrior ordered.

He stomped off on the large wooden rice ladles he used for feet, and the cloths binding my arms pushed me after him. Helpless to resist, Oyuki and I followed him to the castle keep. We climbed the external stairway, past the two floors where Shiro and the senior officers were quartered, until we came to the chamber at the top. Since part of the roof was missing, no one on our side had found a use for it. But apparently, someone else had: a ghost.

The phantom was clearly Japanese, with his hair done in the *chon-mage* style of a samurai. But his clothes looked European: a doublet with a high ruff on the collar like Shiro's. Around his neck hung an intricate filigree cross that might have been gold in its owner's mortal life.

"Sir!" the porcelain warrior said. "I captured these intruders and made a command decision to bring them to you for questioning, sir."

As soon as the ghost saw us, a delighted smile spread across his translucent face. *"Voce fala portugues?"* he asked. *"¿Habla español? Parlez-vous français? Cognoscisne linguam Latinam?"*

To be addressed in so many languages at once, by a ghost I hadn't expected to know any of them, brought on a moment of dizziness. "I'm English," I said. "My name is Simon Grey."

"I'm Oyuki Winter," said Oyuki. "Either English or Japanese is fine with me."

"It's a delight to meet you."

The ghost extended his hand. Oyuki, after a moment's hesitation, raised hers. The ghost took it – or rather, held his spectral hand under her solid one – and bent over as if to kiss it. But as he bowed his head, it fell off his shoulders, landed on the floor, bounced once, and rolled.

Oyuki screamed and stepped back, her hands flying to her face.

"Oh, dear me!" said the ghost's head from somewhere near his feet, as the rest of his body crouched and frantically groped along the floor, trying to find it by touch. "I'm terribly sorry! Please forgive me. I didn't mean to frighten you. Are you all right?"

"I'm...I'm fine," Oyuki said once she had caught her breath. "Just...a little startled."

The ghost finally found his head and placed it carefully back on his neck. "I do beg your pardon. It's so seldom I have company, and I must apologize for appearing before you so...discountenanced." He adjusted his head. "My name is Don Protasio."

"Don...Protasio?" I repeated.

"Yes. Well, my birth name is Arima Harunobu, but I thought you might find my baptismal name easier."

The Japanese name sounded vaguely familiar. "You're the lord of this castle?" I asked.

"I was. I suppose you could say I still am – what's left of it, at any rate." He looked over our shoulders at the crockery warrior. "Well done, General Seto. I'll take it from here."

General Seto clattered to attention and saluted. "Sir, thank you, sir!"

As he clanked back down the stairs, Don Protasio turned his attention back to us. "If I may be so bold as to inquire, what brings you here?"

We hesitated a moment, wondering where to start, and then began to tell the story of the rebellion. As soon as we mentioned the name of Matsukura, Don Protasio made a sound of disgust, threw his hands into the air, and cast his gaze toward heaven – a gesture that caused his head to tip precariously backward. He caught it just in time to keep it from falling off again. "Matsukura!" he exclaimed contemptuously once his head was back on straight. "Stayed here just long enough to make a ghastly mess, before deciding the castle that had been in my family for a century wasn't big enough for him, and tearing it down." He looked at us anxiously. "He came to no good end, I'll be bound?"

"You could say that," Oyuki agreed. We continued with the story of how the elder Matsukura's son Katsuie had taken his father's excesses to an even greater degree, thereby laying the kindling for the Shimabara Rebellion and providing the spark to ignite it. The more we told Don Protasio about the rebellion, the more pronounced his satisfied smirk grew.

"So your leader is this Amakusa Shiro?" he asked when we had finished.

"Well, you could call him our spiritual leader," I said. "Our main military strategist is Ashizuka Chuemon."

The ghostly glow around Don Protasio brightened. "Ashizuka!" he exclaimed in delight.

"You know him?"

"He was one of my best samurai."

That was where I had heard the name before. Ashizuka had mentioned his former lord at the meeting on Yushima.

"This explains everything!" Don Protasio continued. "When they came to take my head, I thought I would go straight to heaven as a martyr. You can imagine how surprised I was to find myself still here. To stand there, looking at your own head separated from your body, is not an experience I would recommend to anyone, let me tell you."

I wondered what he had done to warrant a sentence of decapitation. But I had spent enough time around ghosts to know how annoyed they get when mortals ask them, "How did you die?" Some of them find the question quite intrusive, and all of them find it quite unimaginative. Don Protasio, I trusted, would share the story when and if he chose.

"But everything happens according to divine plan," he continued. "Now I know the work I have to finish in this world: to make sure your rebellion succeeds." His face took on a wistful look. "I should very much like to see Ashizuka again," he said. "And to meet your Amakusa Shiro."

"I can introduce you," Oyuki said, a bit too quickly and a bit too eagerly.

* * *

The following day, when I looked over the ramparts, I saw columns of smoke rising from the horizon into an otherwise clear and cloudless sky. That could mean only one thing: the Shogun's forces were on their way, putting the abandoned villages to the torch as they went.

When we had made the castle as ready as we could, we were given our posts. Oyuki and I were both numbered among the defenders of the main keep, under Yamada's command. Oyuki, who had spent some years practicing the Japanese bow, was in the corps of archers. As for me, my experience aboard ship led them to place me among the gunners. Jinzaemon was in the same corps.

The master gunner was a gruff man by the name of Komagine Tomofusa. Either he was hard of hearing – not surprisingly for someone who had spent so many years with a musket by his ear – or he thought everyone else was. When he assigned the gunners to their posts, his voice could be heard all the way across the courtyard.

"And you boys," he said to Jinzaemon and me almost as an afterthought, "will run to the magazine and resupply the gunners when their powder runs low."

My shoulders slumped. So I was to be a "powder monkey." Aboard a ship, it was a job traditionally given to the youngest boys, since our small size allowed us to navigate the narrow spaces between decks quickly. An essential job, we were always told – but one whose chances of getting blown to bits were at least as great as the gunners themselves, without the corresponding hope of earning any glory.

The next morning, the sun rose as usual over the Ariake Sea. The sparrows greeted the sunrise with their usual chirping chorus, and the wind from the sea blew as always. Nature did as nature always does, completely oblivious to the bloody mess we humans were about to make in our little corner of it.

Early in the morning, they started to appear. The black-armored leader mounted on his warhorse. His standard-bearers, carrying flags with a device that looked like a spinning triple blade. Armored samurai, also riding proudly, with two swords hanging at their sides. Helmeted infantry carrying muskets slung over their shoulders, or spears more than twice as long as their bearers were tall. And behind them, another force with a different banner. Then another, and another – I counted at least nine in all. Matsukura's flag was among them, somewhere toward the rear.

It would have been a very impressive parade to watch from the sidelines, but it was an entirely different feeling to watch it from its destination. This procession of warriors, gathered from all the domains surrounding Shimabara, had assembled for just one purpose: to kill us.

And they looked as if they were eminently capable of doing so. There were over thirty thousand of us in Hara

Castle, but from the look of it, the enemy outnumbered us by four or five to one. To say nothing of the armor, weapons, and firearms that were so clearly superior to ours.

As we watched from the ramparts, every face around me reflecting the fear that I felt, the conch shells blew to summon us to the courtyard in front of our hastily constructed church. Shiro stood in front of the door, his arms upraised, and his high, clear voice carried over the anxious whispers.

"Brothers and sisters," he said to the assembly, "when Deus is with us, who can be against us? With Deus as our stronghold, whom shall we fear? When the wicked advance against us, it is they who will stumble and fall. It is they who will discover that no king is saved by his great army, and no warrior is saved by his great strength. Though an army may besiege us, we will have no fear. Though war may break out against us, our faith will never falter. We are equipped with the full armor of Deus: the belt of truth, the breastplate of righteousness, the shield of faith, the helmet of salvation, and the sword of the Spirit."

Cheers greeted his speech. I joined in, but I couldn't help taking a look around at my comrades in arms, all dressed in simple peasant garb except for the officers. The full armor of Deus was all very well, but I wished we were a little better equipped with the full armor of metal.

As we returned to watch from the ramparts, the procession came to a halt. One of the soldiers at the commander's side drew a bow and loosed an arrow, which sailed over the palisade and landed in the courtyard near where Shiro was standing. A scroll was tied around the shaft. This, I was to learn, was called a *yabumi*, an arrow-letter.

Shiro gestured to Yamada, who was standing nearest the letter when it landed. He picked up the arrow, untied and unfurled the scroll, and read aloud.

"In the name of His Majesty the Emperor, the exalted Shogun Tokugawa Iemitsu, and all the daimyo here assembled. For your rebellion against the lord appointed to rule over you by the Shogun, for the murder of his agents and the destruction of his property, and for your refusal to renounce your belief in the forbidden Kirishitan sect, the lives of all the criminals and rioters in Hara Castle are forfeit. However, the Shogun has no wish for the blood of his subjects to be shed to no purpose. Surrender, return to your fields, renounce all allegiance to foreign gods, and your crimes will be forgiven and your lives spared. If you refuse, know that you face a force against which you cannot hope to prevail. No stone of Hara Castle will be left standing, and no man, woman, or child therein will be left alive. The commander of the Shogun's forces, Itakura Shigemasa, awaits your reply."

Shiro listened to the recitation with a slight smirk on his face. When it was concluded, he called, "Emosaku!"

Yamada stepped forward and bowed. "Sir."

"It would be rude to keep them waiting."

While Yamada prepared paper, brush, and ink, Shiro sat with his eyes closed and his face upturned, as though praying for the right words. When Yamada was ready, Shiro opened his eyes and began to dictate his response.

"In the name of Deus, the one true Emperor of heaven above and all the earth below. We are indeed honored that such a mighty force of noble lords and samurai as are here assembled regards a simple band of – ahem – 'criminals and rioters' like us as worthy adversaries."

A chuckle went around the rebels as Yamada took Shiro's words down.

"Against such a force," Shiro continued, "as you so rightly say, we have no more hope of prevailing than a child has of measuring out the ocean with a seashell. We are, therefore, prepared to accept your gracious offer."

Yamada's brush stopped. "Sir?" His puzzlement was reflected on the faces of all those who were listening.

Shiro gestured for him to keep writing. When he reached the end of the paragraph, Shiro continued, "Under the following conditions: Matsukura Katsuie shall be relieved of all his lands and titles. Whoever is chosen to succeed him as Daimyo of Shimabara shall levy an annual tribute no greater than the farmers of the region can reasonably be expected to pay and still provide for their own families, certainly not to exceed half the amount levied by his predecessor. And everyone shall be free to practice their own faith according to their own conscience."

Yamada dutifully set down Shiro's demands. But even I, a stranger to the country, knew by now that there was no way they would be granted.

"We have every confidence," Shiro concluded, "that the Shogun, being a man of reason, will agree to these terms. If he does not, then may the one true Emperor fairly judge each one of us. May he welcome his faithful fallen into paradise, and as for those who have persecuted them, may he deal with them as their deeds deserve. With utmost respect, Amakusa Shiro."

When the ink was dry, Yamada rolled the message around the same arrow that had carried the enemy's message to us and handed it to the nearest archer, who happened to be Oyuki. I thought I saw a slight tremor in her hand, but when she drew her bow back and let the arrow fly, it sailed straight and true towards Itakura.

"We'd best take our positions," said Shiro. "And Deus be with us."

Amid scattered responses of "Amen," everyone hastened to take their places. I stood ready behind the gunners, who were lined up along the wooden palisades with the weapons whose names had been drummed into my head at top volume by Komagine. The matchlock muskets were called *tanegashima*, after the island where the Japanese had encountered their first missionaries from Spain – and with them, their first firearms. The light, shoulder-mounted cannons were

110

called *ozutsu*. And the ground-based cannons, including the mighty six-pounders, had the poetic name of *ishihiya*, "stone fire arrows."

Peering through one of the gun ports, I could see Itakura reading Shiro's reply to his arrow-letter. He was too far away for me to see his reaction, but I saw him turn his horse around and say something to his troops. Then he turned back to face the castle, drew his sword, and gave a battle cry that I could hear all the way from here: "*Ei, ei!*"

"*Ohh!*" came the reply from his troops, as they charged.

"*Santiago!*" came the answering cry from our side.

And so it began.

*　*　*

Arrows flew from both sides, and the musketeers took aim through the gun ports. Each port had three musketeers firing in rotation, because as soon as a musket was fired, the laborious work of reloading began: Measure powder into the muzzle. Put a wad of cloth in after it, rest the ball on top, and tamp it in with an auger and mallet. Put in another wad and push the whole assembly down the barrel with a long ramrod. Carefully tap another measure of powder into the pan, and even more carefully, fit the smoldering matchcord into the hammer arm. Put the stock up against your cheek, take aim, and pull the trigger.

An experienced musketeer, working under ideal conditions, still took nearly a minute to complete the process, and the ramparts of a castle under enemy fire were far from ideal conditions. And there was always the danger that the weapon would fail to fire, or the matchcord would touch the powder too soon and cause it to blow up in the gunner's face. Small wonder that, even with the armor-piercing power of the musket available, so many Japanese still seemed to prefer bows and arrows.

I caught only an occasional glimpse of the action unfolding down below. I spent most of the day running back and forth between the ramparts and the magazine every time someone yelled, "Powder!"

Some of the enemy leaned long bamboo ladders against the castle walls. But those were easy enough for our side to push over with equally long poles. Some attempted to scale the *ishigaki*, the sloping stone walls at the castle foundation. But the women on our side were ready for them. They had their fires burning and their pots full of water, oil, and sand, which they heated to the smoking point and dumped over the heads of anyone attempting to climb the wall. In addition to these, we made strategic use of another type of ammunition that was cheap, abundant, and highly effective even without heating: the contents of chamber pots.

By sunset, apparently the Shogun's forces had had enough. They withdrew to their camp, carrying the bodies of their fallen with them. From those who had been in a position to count, we heard numbers ranging from one hundred up to three hundred or more.

As for our side, not one.

"Did I not speak the truth?" Shiro asked rhetorically once the cheers had subsided enough to hear him speak. "Deus is on our side!"

For that moment, at least, it was easy to believe him.

* * *

After the failure of their first full-on assault, the Shogun's forces appeared to change their strategy to a waiting game. All the stories of battles I had read had failed to prepare me for all the tedium and uncertainty that took almost as great a toll on the mind as the battle itself did on the body. I woke up every morning expecting another attack. Throughout the day, occasionally the thunder of a cannon would send us all scrambling to the nearest take-taba, but the first volley would be the last. At night, I would go to bed thinking, *It didn't happen today. Maybe it will happen tomorrow.*

Of course, even without actual fighting, there was plenty to keep us occupied: training with swords and bows, cleaning firearms, foraging for food in the sea, cooking and serving our strictly rationed provisions. Life in Hara Castle was shaping up to look much like life in the rebels' home villages, with the small difference that any moment of any day, a cannonball might come crashing through your roof.

To relieve the monotony, Jinzaemon taught me to play *shogi.* I wasn't too bad at chess, but the Japanese version was much more complex. Some pieces were familiar, like the King, Knight, and the one they called the Angle-Mover since they couldn't very well call it a Bishop. Others were new to me, like the Gold General, Silver General, and Flying Dragon. The hardest thing to get used to was how captured pieces, instead of simply disappearing off the board, could be turned to fight for the other side. Many was the time I thought I had Jinzaemon surrounded, only to see one of the pieces I had lost to him suddenly appearing out of nowhere.

"Captured pieces ought to stay captured," I muttered after losing my third game in a row.

Jinzaemon gave me a triumphant grin. "The greatest strategy is to get your opponent to do your fighting for you."

I sighed. "Up for a rematch?"

"Tomorrow," he said. "Right now, I should probably go help prepare for the New Year's celebration."

"New Year's?" I repeated in puzzlement. It had been Christmas Day when we visited Couckebacker, and nearly two months had passed since then. By my reckoning, it was mid-February.

"Yes. You don't celebrate the New Year in your country?"

"Of course we do. Between Christmas and Twelfth Night."

As soon as I said it, I realized that I had been thinking in terms of the Gregorian calendar instead of the Japanese lunar calendar, where Christmas fell early in the eleventh month. That would mean it was now late in the twelfth month, almost the end of the year.

"It's going to be a grand celebration," he said. "Lots of food and sake, music and dancing."

"Dancing?" I repeated. Immediately, I started formulating strategies for how I would approach Oyuki and ask her for a dance before Shiro could.

* * *

In a castle under siege, with provisions rationed, I expected that New Year's would be a rather subdued affair. I couldn't have been more wrong. Embers burned in cressets, illuminating the courtyard as the sun set behind Mount Unzen. Over charcoal fires, fish sizzled on spits, and *mochi* – rice pounded into cakes and grilled – filled the air with the sharp smell of scorched soy sauce. Music rose into the evening sky, played on flutes, drums, and a three-stringed lute-like instrument called the *shamisen*. Everyone had come to Hara Castle carrying only the bare essentials, but when they put these essentials together, it was remarkable to see what a celebration they could produce.

Shiro, who usually sequestered himself in the tenshu these days and rarely appeared among the people, was out and about, greeting everyone and continually pouring sake, though I never saw him drink any himself. "Blessed be Deus," he said, "who spreads a table for us in the presence of all our enemies and fills our cup to overflowing."

It was a defiant celebration, a finger in the eye of the Shogun and his forces. The music and laughter, as the wind from the Ariake Sea wafted them westward over the enemy camp, carried a clear message: *You can surround us, isolate us, and rain cannonballs down on us, but you can't break our spirits.*

At the same time, it was impossible to ignore the feeling that the rebels were pouring heart and soul into this New Year's celebration because of the strong likelihood that it would be their last. The bright lights cast an inescapable shadow: *Eat, drink, and be merry, for tomorrow we die.*

Jinzaemon certainly took the first of those to heart. Every time I saw him, his plate was freshly replenished. I had to wonder where he put it all. The only other person I had ever met who could eat so much and still stay so thin was not even a person in the usual sense, but a yokai: Futakuchi-san, the woman with a second mouth in the back of her head that ate everything in sight and said everything that came into her mind. I wondered how she was doing. It was a comfort to remember, as I struggled to adjust to life after our visit to Ryugujo, that Japan and all the people in it could change, but our yokai friends would be here forever.

Then I saw Oyuki.

She was dressed in a kimono I had never seen before, patterned in the light and dark pink of the plum blossoms that were coming into full bloom around the castle grounds. A spray of the same flowers adorned her hair.

And she was standing alone.

Now or never. I summoned my courage and walked up to her.

"That kimono looks beautiful on you," I said.

"Thanks," she said. "It's borrowed, of course."

"It looks like it was made for you."

This was a transparent lie. It was clearly made for a grown woman, and while a few strategic tucks under the sash kept the hem from trailing on the ground, the voluminous sleeves swallowed her hands. But still, to my eyes, her beauty outshone any princess in Kyo no

Miyako. And she acknowledged my compliment with a modest smile.

I took my courage in both hands. "May I have this dance?" I asked.

She gave me a puzzled look. "If you want to dance, I don't suppose anyone would stop you."

I had imagined several possible replies, but this was not one of them.

When I looked back at the courtyard where people were gathering for the dance, I realized my error. I had envisioned something like an English country dance, in rows of couples, but it proved instead to be a big circle dance, all together. Oyuki graciously allowed me to stand near her, but that proved to be a gift with a sting in the tail. As the flutes, drums, and cymbals played a lively rhythm – *Ka-konka-danka-konka-danka* – the revelers danced to steps that everyone seemed to know but me, clapped to a rhythm that everyone seemed to know but me, and sang the refrain to a tune that everyone seemed to know but me. I stumbled my way through the dance, and bowed out when the music came to a merciful end.

Finally, the conch shells blew to usher the Year of the Ox out and the Year of the Tiger in. When we retired to our barracks, Jinzaemon had one last piece of cultural advice for me. "It's traditional to get up in time to watch the first sunrise of the new year," he said. "Hopefully, after having a fortunate dream. It's especially lucky if you see Mount Fuji, a hawk, or a *nasu*."

I blinked in confusion. I had seen Mount Fuji, and could easily see how its majestic symmetry could be a symbol of good fortune. I could also understand how the high-soaring hawk might be seen as auspicious. But the last one made me wonder if I had misunderstood his Japanese. The only meaning I knew for the word *nasu* was the purple, egg-shaped vegetable known in England as a mad-apple.

"Did you say *nasu*?" I asked.

"Yes. It sounds like the word for 'achieve.' If you dream of one, it's a sign that you'll achieve your goals."

I closed my eyes. It took me a while to fall asleep, since every time I started to drift off, a sudden fit of coughing from Jinzaemon would wake me again. But I concentrated on the image I would most love to see in a dream destined to come true: myself on the deck of a stout merchantman, with Oyuki by my side, holding her hand and gazing together at the sunset as we sped towards England. Just before I finally slipped away into dreamland, I hastily added one more detail: the cargo hold was packed to the gunwales with mad-apples.

In my actual dream, I was indeed aboard a tall ship. But the sailors were running around the deck, screaming in terror at the apparition off the stern: a walking skeleton, so huge that the sea only came up to its hip bones, while its skull was on a level with the crow's nest.

It wasn't exactly what I would have called auspicious. As I drifted out of the dream and into a semi-conscious state, I pondered what it could mean. Did the skeleton represent Death? Would I be trying to outrace it aboard a ship? And what was to become of Oyuki?

Before I could reach any conclusions, I was brought fully awake by a blast on the conch shells.

It was still dark, but all the men around me sprang from their pallets. They dressed as quickly as they could, considering how many of them were still under the lingering influence of last night's sake.

"To arms! To arms!" cried a voice from outside. "We're under attack!"

* * *

All of us were indeed up to greet the first sunrise of the new year, but not in the traditional way. As I ran to take my place among the musketeers, the rising sun illuminated scenes of confusion on both sides. As some of the enemy warriors charged the castle on the northern side, others emerged blinking from their tents, securing the last pieces of their armor as they went. Itakura was saddled up and barking orders to his troops, but even he was adjusting his armor. To my untrained eye, it looked as if one division of the Shogun's army had gotten impatient and begun the attack without waiting for orders, and the rest were scrambling to catch up.

"Ready!" came Komagine's order.

The first musketeer at my port finished loading his weapon and took his position.

"Aim!"

But before Komagine could say "Fire!" I saw a flash, and heard an explosion followed by a cry of pain. The musketeer's matchcord had touched the powder too soon. He dropped his musket as his hands flew to his eyes.

The second musketeer had his weapon already loaded and ready to fire, while the third was still halfway through the delicate process of loading his. After a moment's hesitation, the second handed his to me, and took his companion's arm to guide him to the infirmary. I was left there holding his musket.

"Ready!"

Seeing the other gunners up and down the line readying their weapons at the ports, I did the same, resting the barrel on the wooden palisade and putting the stock against my cheek as I saw the others do.

"Aim!" came the order from Komagine. But I had no idea what I should be aiming at. I chose the most conspicuous target: the black-armored Itakura on his warhorse.

"Fire!"

I pulled the trigger.

The blade sliced the smoldering end of the matchcord into the pan. When it touched the powder, the explosion set my ears ringing. The stock kicked against my cheek with a force that I thought would knock my teeth out, and I suddenly understood why all the gunners kept wads of cloth in their mouths. Sparks burst from the pan, and mindful of what had happened to the first musketeer, I turned my face away and shut my eyes.

When I opened them a moment later and looked down at the battlefield, I saw Itakura's horse prancing frantically, with no rider in the saddle. Itakura himself lay on the field, with his men rushing to gather around him. After a few moments, they took hold of his limp and motionless form, and dragged it back towards the camp.

It took me a moment to comprehend what had just happened. Itakura Shigemasa, the enemy commander, was dead. And my shot had killed him.

Chapter 9:
The Haimushi

第九章. 肺虫

I had often wondered: Did the people who made history know they were making history while they were making it? Was there a moment when they said, "Future generations are going to read about this in books, so I should record the date and time and make sure they spell my name right"? Or did the significance of the moment only become clear on later reflection?

Right now, I was inclined to believe the former. I knew I had not just witnessed a turning point in history, but caused it. From now on, whenever the history of the Shimabara Rebellion was told, it would include the line: "And then, Simon Grey, a boy..." no, "a young man from England, present there for some mysterious reason believed by some to have involved a journey like Urashima Taro's to the undersea realm of the Dragon God, fired the shot that felled Itakura Shigemasa, supreme commander of the Shogun's forces."

I supposed that made me a hero. So why didn't I feel like one?

Through my daze, I gradually became aware of a voice coming from farther along the ramparts: "I did it! I did it!"

I looked in that direction and saw Sanai. Smoke curled from the barrel of the ozutsu resting on his shoulder.

"I did it!" he repeated, grinning with triumph and pumping a jubilant fist. "I got Itakura! I got him!"

My first impulse was to set the record straight. But when I thought about the force with which Itakura had been blown off his horse, I realized Sanai could very well be right. I was no expert on firearms, but it was hard to see how a musket, at that range, could do much more than make a dent in his armor. It was much more likely to have been a ball from an ozutsu.

And, I realized, half of me – actually, a great deal more than half – *wanted* him to be right. Part of me was disappointed that my name wouldn't appear in the history books after all, but to the larger part, the possibility that I did *not* have the blood of another human being on my hands came as an enormous relief.

"No!" came a voice from behind me. "It was Simon!"

Sanai's head and mine both turned to look at the source of the voice. Jinzaemon stood behind me, looking defiantly at Sanai.

"What did you say?" Sanai demanded. His tone made it clear that any answer other than "Nothing" would be asking for trouble.

"It was Simon!" Jinzaemon repeated. "I saw it!"

Sanai set down his ozutsu and took a few menacing steps toward Jinzaemon. "Are you saying," he asked slowly, "that a southern barbarian boy, who never held a musket in his pathetic little life until someone put one into his hands by accident, hit the mark that the son of a samurai missed?"

Jinzaemon was clearly shaking in his straw sandals. But he stood straight, stuck out his chin, and looked Sanai in the eye. "Yes," he said. "That's exactly what I'm saying."

Sanai took a few more steps forward. I quickly stepped between them, facing Jinzaemon.

"It's all right," I said. "If it means that much to Sanai, we'll let that be the story."

Sanai grabbed me roughly by the shoulders and spun me around. "I said, it was me!" he shouted in my face.

I shook off his grip. "And I said, have it your way. If you won't feel you're a real man unless you get the credit for that shot, then go ahead and take it. I'm fine without it."

I turned and started walking away.

Two strong hands shoved me from behind, and I fell face down in the mud.

I rolled over to see Sanai standing over me, a smug look on his face. He took a step back and made a subtle gesture as though daring me to try him.

I struggled to my feet and charged at him.

The next thing I knew, I was face down in the mud again, this time with a terrible pain in my ankle.

"What's going on here?" came Komagine's booming voice from somewhere above me. "What did you do?"

"I didn't do anything!" Sanai replied. As I rolled over, sat up, and opened my mouth to protest, Sanai went on: "I just told Simon the truth. It was my shot that felled Itakura, not his. A moment later, he was charging at me. All I did was step aside."

I had thought Komagine's voice had no dynamic but *fortissimo*. I was wrong. He had mastered a whole range beyond that, as he promptly proceeded to demonstrate to me. I couldn't catch everything he said, since about half of it consisted of Japanese words I had never heard before, but the general gist came through with painful clarity.

"Simon, you (?) idiot! What the (?) are you playing at? The (?) guns we handle here are as big a (?) danger to our side as to the (?) enemy unless you're (?) careful, and if you (?) around near them, you're (?) likely to blow somebody's (?) head right the (?) off! Do you hear me (?) loud and (?) clear?"

"Hey!" I protested. "*He* was the one who..."

Komagine cut me off, his voice rising another level. Belatedly, I realized I had broken the first and greatest commandment: Thou shalt not speak in thy own defense whilst thy superiors are berating thee.

"Did I ask for your (?) excuses? The only (?) word I want to hear from your (?) mouth is '*Hai!*' Do you (?) well understand me?"

"*Hai,*" I said sullenly. There didn't seem to be anything else I could say that wouldn't make the situation worse.

Komagine gestured to Jinzaemon. "Take him to the infirmary."

I winced as Jinzaemon helped me up, and leaned on his shoulder, doing my best to keep my weight off my injured ankle. As we turned and started to head for the infirmary, I caught a glimpse of Sanai, giving me a triumphant look. I wished I could fire off a parting shot with Shakespearean eloquence like, "Beetle-headed flap-eared knave!" But unlike Komagine, my Japanese vocabulary was woefully limited when it came to curse words. I couldn't manage much beyond "Fool! You are noisy!"

Komagine's voice crescendoed into an even louder dynamic as he delivered his final salvo. "Come back when you're ready to stop (?)ing around like a little (?) boy and join the real men!"

Still leaning on Jinzaemon, I hobbled to the infirmary, painfully conscious of all the eyes on me. Somewhere among them, I was sure, were Oyuki's.

* * *

The camp doctor, Arima Gensatsu, was still occupied with the musketeer whose powder had ignited too soon, which gave me a few minutes to take in my surroundings: cabinets with minuscule drawers, shelves full of jars containing various herbs and strangely shaped roots, and charts on the walls showing the human body covered in labeled points connected by lines, like towns and roads on a map.

When Gensatsu finally finished with the musketeer, he turned his attention to my ankle. "Sprained, but luckily not broken," he said after a cursory examination. "Rest for a while and keep your weight off it."

James helped me to my feet, and I leaned on him as we hobbled together to the barracks. Once we were there, he gently eased me onto my pallet.

"Thank you," I said. "And thanks for standing up for me, back there. It takes a braver man than me to go toe to toe with Sanai."

Jinzaemon made a sound of contempt. "He thinks he can just walk over everyone," he muttered darkly. "Someone needs to show him otherwise."

"But in this case, as much as I hate to admit it, he might have been right."

Jinzaemon shrugged. "Well, that's still no reason for him to go around always thinking he is." He paused a moment. "Simon?" he asked shyly. "There's something I've been wanting to ask you."

"Go on," I said, preparing for another inquiry into the outlandish customs of my "southern barbarian" homeland.

"Could you give me an Igirisu name?"

"I'm sorry?"

"My grandfather had a baptismal name. He stopped using it after the Kirishitan ban, of course, but I admired him for having a name that could be understood anywhere in the world, and I always wanted one of my own. What do you say?"

Now that he mentioned it, I had heard a number of samurai, present and absent, referred to by their baptismal names: Don Protasio, Miguel, Augustin. If, among all these Catholic names, Jinzaemon wanted a good solid English name, then as far as I was concerned, he had earned a royal one.

"How about James?" I asked.

"*Jeimuzu?*"

"James. The king of England. At least the last one I knew." In fact, I had no idea whether the throne at Whitehall was still occupied by the same ruler as when

I left. For all I knew, he might have died and passed the crown on to the Prince of Wales. But for some reason, the name "Charles" just didn't sound too auspicious.

"James," he repeated. "I like it!"

"Very well," I said. "Henceforth, you shall be known as James."

His smile broadened. "Well, I had better get back to my post before Komagine fires another volley at me."

"Good hunting, James."

He hastened back to his post, leaving me alone with my thoughts.

So this was the glory of battle. I recalled the king's soul-stirring speech from *Henry V,* and wondered what he would have said in the present situation. "The lunar New Year's Day shall ne'er go by, from this day to the ending of the world, but we in it shall be remembered: we few, we happy few, we band of brothers. And gentlemen in England now a-bed will think themselves accursed they were not here, and hold their manhoods cheap whilst any speaks that fought at Hara upon New Year's Day."

What a load of rubbish. If any gentleman in England was cursing his fate because he had to sleep in a warm, soft bed in his own house, instead of chasing after honor and glory on a distant battlefield in a distant country and running the risk of leaving his bones on the far side of the globe, I would trade places with him in a heartbeat.

And half the people on the battlefield with me didn't even seem to think I belonged there. Komagine's parting shot rang in my ears: "Come back when you're ready to join the real men!" The more the words echoed in my mind, the more unfair they sounded. Sanai was just a few years older than me, but that was old enough to handle artillery. Shiro was even younger than him, but *that* was old enough to be both a military leader, with seasoned veterans three times his age calling him "sir," and a spiritual leader with tens of thousands practically worshipping him. As for me? It would seem that I was just one step to the wrong side of the line that separated the men from the boys.

There was no justice in this world. I was, after all, born a good fifteen years before Shiro. If all had their rights, I would be twice his age.

Without quite understanding how it got there, I noticed the tamatebako in my hands.

If I were to open it, all the years that had passed while Oyuki and I were in the palace of the Dragon God would catch up with us. I would be almost thirty, a fully grown man, and no one would question my fitness for any job in the castle. As for Oyuki, she would be a grown woman, much too old for Shiro, but just right for me.

The glimmers of light shifted and shimmered across the azure surface of the box, like the rays of the summer sun dancing on a cool, calm sea, inviting me to dive in.

Promise me, Otohime's voice echoed in my mind. *You will never open it, for any reason on earth.*

I continued turning the box over in my hand, bewitched by the endlessly swirling patterns.

The cloth over the doorway rustled.

I hurriedly hid the tamatebako and turned my head towards the doorway, feigning an expression of drowsy boredom as if the newcomer had caught me right in the act of doing absolutely nothing.

It was Yamada. I quickly prepared to stand to attention, wincing as I moved my ankle, but Yamada raised a hand to stop me. "Don't strain yourself."

He came to my pallet and knelt beside it, sitting on his heels in the way that I had never yet managed to do without my knees screaming in protest.

"I heard what happened today," he said. "Of course, it's impossible to know whose shot was the decisive one. Itakura, prancing around on his horse like that, was making himself such an attractive target that all the gunners must have taken aim at him together. Maybe it was your shot, maybe Sanai's, maybe someone else's, or most likely, a combination. In any case, though, it was brave of you to step up."

"Thank you, sir."

His tone shifted. "It seems you're not going to be doing much running around for a while. But once you can walk without pain again, I have another job in mind for you. Do you know *kabuki?*"

I didn't. But I knew that *ka* was one way of reading the symbol for "fire," and *buki* meant "weapon."

"Is that a type of gun, sir?" I asked. "Or cannon?"

He looked surprised, then chuckled. "Neither," he said. "It's a type of dance theater."

Again, I wasn't sure I had understood correctly. "Pardon, sir? Did you say 'dance theater'?"

"Yes. It seems one of the ladies, Obotan, spent some time with a kabuki troupe in Edo. Then the Shogun decreed that kabuki could only be performed by men, so she had to give up her career and come back to Shimabara. But she'd be glad to put her skills to use in a place where no one cares what the Shogun says. She's put together a few players, and she could use some new material. When I heard that, I remembered that you had been on the stage yourself, is that correct?"

"You could say that, sir." I had, in fact, been on the boards in more senses than one, having played numerous parts during an eighteen-month voyage under Captain Shakespeare. I was hardly a candidate for the Globe Theatre, but I could hold my own.

"Would you be able to help her?" Yamada asked.

I gave him a skeptical look. "Go from being a warrior to an entertainer, sir?"

"Here's the situation," he said. "When Itakura fell, it was a major blow struck for our side. But it seems a new general is already on his way from Edo. Hand-picked by the Shogun himself. Matsudaira Nobutsuna is his name. Also known as *Izu no Kami,* 'the Protector of Izu,' or *Chie no Izu,* 'Izu the Wise.'"

I seized on the shorter name. "Izu," I repeated.

"He has a reputation for being much more patient and cautious. After the losses their side suffered under Itakura, Izu isn't likely to risk another direct assault. Instead, we'll be facing a war of attrition. It will be a test to see which side can hold out longer. In such a situation, entertainers are no less valuable than archers or musketeers. Without them, our people would be in as much danger of dying from boredom as from cannon fire."

"I can understand that, sir," I said. "But shouldn't the warriors focus on war, and leave the arts to the artists?"

"Simon, have you ever heard the phrase *bun-bu-ryo-do?*"

I shook my head.

"It means," he said, "that a true warrior is an artist – and that includes the fine arts just as much as the martial arts. Would you call me any less of a warrior because I paint?"

"You paint?" I was so surprised that it took a moment before I remembered to add, "Sir?"

If Yamada noticed my lapse, he let it go. "You know Shiro's battle flag? That was my work."

"Yours, sir?"

"Sign-painter by trade, artist at heart. When all this madness is over, that's how I mean to spend the rest of my days: painting my masterwork. This is all by way of saying, not only is there no shame, there's honor for a warrior in mastering the fine arts. So what do you say? Is this something you could help with?"

Part of me leapt at the chance to be away from the worst of the fighting. But another part of me imagined how mercilessly Sanai would mock me if I were singing and dancing with the women while he was on the front lines with what Komagine would call the real men. Even being a powder monkey would be better than that.

"Thank you for thinking of me, sir," I said. "But if it's all the same, I'd rather be back among the warriors."

Yamada paused for a moment. "Simon," he said, "you have a mother and father waiting for you at home, don't you?"

"Yes, sir," I replied, devoutly hoping it was still true.

"So do I," he said. "If you listen to men like Ashizuka, or Mori, or especially Chijiwa, they'll fill your head with ideas about how the greatest thing a man can do with his life is to sacrifice it in battle for his lord. And of course, that's the way to get into the history books. You'll never see your name written there if you spend your days by your aging parents' bedside, feeding them when they can no longer feed themselves, washing them when they can no longer wash themselves. But is that any less an example of giving your life for a noble cause?"

I shook my head. "No, sir."

"My hope for you is the same as for myself and all the other men under my command," Yamada continued. "That you'll be able to live out your days in your own country, among those you love. So when you're given an opportunity to get out of the line of fire, I'd say you'd be wise to take it."

I was silent for a moment, digesting this. "Thank you," I finally said. "But is there any other job that might be more suitable for me?"

"If you insist, I could probably find one for you," Yamada said, with an exaggerated sigh of disappointment and the hint of a smile. "Well, I've already asked Oyuki if she would be willing to join in as well, and she said she was. I'll just go and tell her you weren't interested, shall I?"

I sat bolt upright.

"Wait," I said. "On second thought..."

* * *

Time proved Yamada's prediction accurate. Every day, when we looked over the ramparts, we saw more men and more banners on the landward side, and more sails on the seaward side, but there were no more charges like the one on New Year's Day. The Shogun's forces lobbed cannonballs over the ramparts at irregular intervals, sending us scrambling to take shelter behind the nearest take-taba, but as time went on, we began to regard even those as more a nuisance than a danger. The new commander, Izu, did indeed seem to be biding his time, building up his side while wearing ours down.

The first performance I saw by the kabuki troupe was about a legendary princess named Takiyasha-hime, daughter of the tenth-century warrior Taira no Masakado. Her father had led a rebellion on behalf of the downtrodden common people against the rich and decadent imperial court. When he lost, his daughter, vowing revenge, performed a midnight ritual at Kifune Shrine for twenty-one nights until the god of the shrine appeared and taught her the magical arts. She raised an army of yokai and almost succeeded where her father had failed, but Oyataro Mitsukuni, a warrior trained in the magical arts of *onmyodo*, finally defeated her.

"I was rather hoping she'd win," Oyuki commented, and I agreed with her. I supposed the original author had meant for the audience to cheer for Mitsukuni – whose very name, "Light of the Nation," seemed just a bit too on the nose – but I imagined that most of the audience in Hara Castle would be more sympathetic to her cause than his.

There was no need to ask which member of the troupe was Obotan. Among the farmers who made up the bulk of the rebel forces, men and women both tended to wear simple garments in plain earth tones, and her reddish-pink, peony-patterned kimono stood out like the first flower of spring amid the mud and slush of winter. She was further distinguished by her elaborate hair accessories, which looked like nothing so much as golden chopsticks, and a foot-long lacquered pipe in her mouth. The aromatic smoke curling out of the thimble-sized bowl made me cough as I approached her.

"You must be Simon," she said in a voice turned dusky from smoking, as one hand held her pipe and the other pinched my cheek, her long nails leaving painful indentations. "Ooh, that face is something like it. If you went to Edo, you'd have no trouble getting into the theater as a *wakashu*." Seeing my blank look, she clarified: "A boy who plays women's roles. But then again, the Shogun's goons might say the same about you that they said about me: You're too pretty to be on the stage. The merchants and samurai might start fighting over who gets a command performance."

My gaze returned to her pipe. When I left England, tobacco smoking had just become fashionable – much to the dismay of King James, who vigorously condemned "the black stinking fumes most nearly resembling the horrible Stygian smoke of the pit that is bottomless." It astonished me that the fashion could have spread to Japan so quickly, even allowing for the fifteen-year interval I had spent at the bottom of the sea.

Obotan noticed my gaze. "Do you smoke, boy?" she asked.

I shook my head.

"Good. Don't ever start. The pipe kills. Or so they keep telling me. But I figure if I live long enough to be in any danger from it, I'll already be ahead of the game." She leaned back and took another puff. "So, I hear you know some stories from Oranda? Let's hear one."

I decided against trying to correct her. "How about *Romeo and Juliet?*"

Oyuki looked at me as though she wasn't sure whether I was joking.

"What's that about?" Obotan asked.

"Two lovers from rival families who end up killing themselves."

Obotan nodded approvingly. "Love suicides. Always a crowd-pleaser. Does one of them come back as a ghost?"

"Well, no," I said.

"If it's vengeful ghosts you want," Oyuki chimed in, expertly pivoting away from my suggestion, "I was thinking of *Hamlet*. The ghost of the old king gets his son to take revenge on the brother who killed him and stole his throne."

Obotan nodded again. "Palace intrigue, revenge, *and* ghosts. That's something like it."

"And I know the perfect person to play the king," Oyuki went on. "If he doesn't mind being type-cast."

* * *

"I?" asked Don Protasio in astonishment. "On the stage?"

"The ghost of Hamlet's father is a key character," Oyuki explained. "And this might be the first time it was ever played by a *real* ghost."

Don Protasio looked rather flustered, but intrigued. "I...well, now, I've always been quite fond of the theater. I've sometimes fancied that, if I had been born into a different station in life, I might have made rather a name for myself as an actor."

"Would you care to read for it, then?"

"Certainly. I'll give it a go."

"You're the ghost of the old king," I told him. "Your brother told everyone you died from a snakebite, but the truth is, he poisoned you so he could take over the kingdom and marry your wife. In this scene, you're appearing to your son, to tell him the truth and get him to avenge your death. Got it?"

"I believe so." But Don Protasio's voice sounded less confident than it had a moment ago.

"Here's your line: 'If thou didst ever thy dear father love, revenge his foul and most unnatural murder.'"

Don Protasio hesitated a moment, but then gamely struck a dramatic pose. "If thou didst ever thy dear father love," he intoned in a deep, spectral baritone that couldn't have been more perfect for the part. "Revenge his foul and..." He faltered.

"Most unnatural murder," I prompted.

He started over. "If thou didst ever thy dear father love..." His voice trailed off again. He looked up at the ceiling, his eyes blinking, and I thought I saw drops of ichor on his cheek.

I had seen many ghosts in my life, but this might have been the first time I had seen one cry.

"Revenge his foul and...most unnatural..." He sat down suddenly. He leaned forward as if to rest his head on his hands, but it toppled off his neck, and before he could catch it, bounced off his knees and landed on the floor.

"Bother! Not again!" said his voice from the floor, as the rest of his body knelt and began to feel for his head. With a little guidance from us, he found it and put it back in place. "I'm terribly sorry," he said when he had pulled himself together. "But I'm not sure I can do this."

"What's the matter?" Oyuki asked.

"It...it hits a bit too close to home."

"What happened?" I asked.

Don Protasio was silent for a moment, blinking back more transparent tears.

"I had a son of my own," he said. "We christened him Miguel. When he was...well, about your age, he showed such promise as a warrior that I sent him to Edo, hoping that he could develop his skills further and attract the notice of someone who might help him on his career. And he did, more than I could have imagined: no lesser man than the Shogun, Tokugawa Ieyasu himself. He married a lovely girl named Martha, the niece of Augustin Konishi – the same daimyo, by the way, who once counted many of your leaders among his retainers. Mori, Yamada, Shiro's father, they all served him."

Don Protasio exhaled a luminous cloud of spectral vapor. "But then Ieyasu started the persecutions that continued under his son and grandson. Miguel, who had grown so close to Ieyasu and hoped for an even higher rank in his court, turned away from the faith I had taught him. When his wife refused to do likewise, he had her banished and married Ieyasu's granddaughter instead. And then…" He closed his eyes. "When a rumor reached Ieyasu's ears that I was plotting to kill the governor of Nagasaki over a land dispute, Miguel said nothing in my defense. That was how I lost my head."

"That's horrible," I said. Rather than Hamlet's father, I thought, his story was better suited to King Lear: "How sharper than a serpent's tooth it is to have a thankless child."

So the role of the ghost ended up being played, as usual, by an ordinary mortal in a white sheet. Oyuki played the equivalent of Ophelia, and myself of Hamlet. James had ultimately joined our troupe too, playing the equivalent of Laertes. The story had been shortened and adapted for our Japanese audience to such an extent that if Shakespeare were watching from heaven, even if he could understand the language, he might not have recognized his own work. But judging from the reaction of our audience, it was a success. The cheers and applause were so loud they must have carried into the besiegers' camp, hopefully causing some consternation. Oyuki and I took several curtain calls, each time stepping carefully around James, who was still lying on the ground after his dramatic "death" in the climactic duel with me.

A delighted Obotan threw an arm around each of us, squeezed us tightly, and exclaimed: "That was something like it!" This, I was beginning to feel, was the highest accolade in her repertoire.

Once she let us go, the next in line to congratulate us was no lesser person than Amakusa Shiro. "Simon!" he gushed. "That was brilliant! I hope we can get you back to London as soon as possible, otherwise England will lose a fine actor."

I bowed. "Thank you, sir."

"And Oyuki," he said, turning his attention to the leading lady. "Magnificent. Truly magnificent."

She blushed, smiled a brighter smile than I could ever remember her smiling for me, and curtsied. "Thank you."

"I'm not very well versed in the customs of other countries," he went on, "but I heard something like this was traditional?"

He handed her a bouquet.

It was made of the ordinary wildflowers that grew in the courtyards of Hara Castle. Weeds, I would have called them. But to see Oyuki's expression, you would think they were perfect roses, or the rare tulips that mad Dutchmen buy at auction for thousands of guilders.

"Shiro," she breathed. "I...I don't know what to say."

She didn't have to say anything. Her face said more than enough.

From the direction of the besiegers' camp came a sound like a distant peal of thunder.

Everyone knew what that meant, and sprang into action before anyone even raised the cry of "Cannonball!" Those who were near a take-taba, or other form of shelter, hurriedly took cover. But some were standing too far from the nearest one to reach it in time. Oyuki, Shiro, and I were among them.

Oyuki hurled herself at Shiro, knocking him to the ground and scattering the flowers she had just received from his hand. A second later, a spray of dust rose up from the place where he had been standing, as the cannonball embedded itself in the earth.

Shiro, lying on his back, looked over at the spot, then up at Oyuki – who, even though the danger was past, was still on top of him, her arms pinning his to the ground.

"Oyuki," he said, and it drove me mad to hear the tenderness in his voice as he said her name. "You saved my life. Thank you."

She smiled. "We can't have you going back to heaven just yet," she said. "This world needs you."

She stayed there, gazing into his eyes, for far longer than necessary. Then, with what looked to me like great reluctance, she stood up and held out her hands to him. He took them in his, and she helped him up.

Even after Shiro's feet were securely under him, their hands remained joined.

Only then, it seemed, did they become conscious of the people around them. Oyuki took a glance around. For the briefest of moments, her eyes met mine. Then she hurriedly looked down, and with an embarrassed look, let go of his hands.

I had seen enough. I turned on my heel and headed for the barracks. My heart sank into my stomach, where the serpent viciously tore into it.

From the moment I first met Oyuki, I had felt – well, it sounds awfully poetic and sentimental to say "we were made for each other," but that was how I felt. We had both grown up with one foot in the ordinary world and one in the spirit world – and, in her case and now increasingly in mine, one in England and one in Japan. And since then, we had been through more together than most people can even imagine, on adventures that took us from an evil sorcerer's dungeon in Edo Castle to the Dragon God's undersea kingdom. She had saved my life several times, and I think it's fair to say I returned the favor. I felt closer to her than I ever had to any other human being. But as soon as I tried to tell her my true feelings, a wall came up between us.

Then, along came Amakusa Shiro. And Oyuki, just like every other woman in Hara Castle, gazed starry-eyed at him as if he were an angel come down to earth. But unlike most of them, she was young enough – and, Deus knew, attractive enough – that if anyone could entice him to step out of his stained-glass window, lay aside his wings, and prove he was really a man of flesh and blood, she would be the one.

Before I knew what was happening, the bag containing the tamatebako was out from under my shirt. The box was out and in my hands. And the knot of the cord was untied.

"Simon?" came a small, hesitant voice from the entrance.

It was Oyuki's.

I hastily tried to stuff the box back into its bag, but she saw me and let out a shocked gasp.

"Simon!" she exclaimed. "What are you doing?"

"I...uh..." I couldn't think of a single thing to say.

"Didn't Otohime tell us never to open that, for any reason on earth? What, in the name of all that walks in the night, are you thinking?"

I couldn't very well tell her the truth. I hung my head and kept silent.

She turned and stormed out. I quickly rose and rushed out of the tent to follow her, although I had no idea what I was going to say when I caught up to her.

"Simon!" came a voice that made me jump. With that volume, it couldn't be anyone but Komagine.

I turned and saw him dragging a limp form towards the infirmary. "I could use a hand."

I took the patient's other arm, and only then did I see the pale face. It was James.

Between us, we half-carried him to the infirmary. With every step, I cursed myself. I had been so preoccupied with dark imaginings about Oyuki and Shiro that I had failed to notice that James had continued to lie in place even after the cannonball struck. Our audience might have thought at first that it was all part of the play, but I should have realized something was terribly wrong.

As Gensatsu prepared to examine him, James fell into a fit of coughing. In the midst of it, something small and reddish flew out of his mouth – and, rather than falling to the ground, flew upward in a spiral. Had James swallowed some kind of insect? And had it miraculously survived?

"Doctor!" I called. "Look at that!"

Gensatsu looked where I was pointing. "Look at what?"

"That! That bug that just flew out of his mouth!"

I did my best to track its movement with my finger as it flew erratically around the infirmary. Gensatsu tried to follow, but it was clear he couldn't see what I was pointing at.

"Can you see something I can't?" He rushed to his table and brought an empty glass jar. "Catch it! Don't let it get away!"

As Gensatsu frantically ran around, making sure all the doors and windows were shut, I chased after the fugitive bug with the jar in hand. As though sensing danger, it flew upwards until it finally reached the ceiling and clung to it.

"I can't reach it," I said.

Gensatsu quickly swept some books and scrolls off his table and pulled it over in my direction. I stood on it and extended the jar toward the bug. I tried to trap it against the ceiling, but it anticipated me and took off before I could reach it. I leaned over, slipped the jar over it, and quickly popped the lid into place, just before I lost my balance and fell from the table. I landed on my backside with a jolt that knocked the wind out of me, but the jar and its contents were intact.

"Are you all right?" asked James.

"Did you get it?" asked Gensatsu.

I gave James a grateful look, and Gensatsu an annoyed one. "Yes, and yes."

Gensatsu peered intently at the jar. "What does it look like?" he asked.

The bug was circling frantically around in the jar. "It's small," I said. "I can't see too well."

Gensatsu brought me a magnifying glass. "Does this help?"

I had never tried to look at a ghost or yokai through a lens, but I supposed it wasn't much different from looking through a window. I tried, and sure enough, I got a bigger view of the creature.

"It's about as big as the tip of my little finger," I said. "Its body is white. Segmented, like the larva of some insect, with...it looks like four...no, five pairs of legs. I see four wings, red, with some yellow and black around the edges. Its head is red, with..." I took a closer look to be sure I was seeing correctly, "a three-pronged mouth, like a fork. And...it seems to have a tongue at the wrong end. At its tail."

Gensatsu picked up a book and frantically flipped through the pages. "Does it look like this?"

He turned around to show me a page. In the middle of the text was an illustration that matched the bug exactly.

"Yes," I said. "That's it."

Gensatsu nodded. "A *haimushi*," he said as he read the description. "It lives in the lungs, but occasionally goes down into the stomach to feed. That explains both the cough and the inability to get any nourishment from food."

James craned his neck to look at the illustration. "Are you saying *that* was inside me?" he asked, his face contorted with disgust. "Ugh! Kill it!"

"No!" Gensatsu exclaimed. "No, no, no! When a *haimushi* leaves the body, it takes a piece of the soul with it. If it can't find its way back, the host dies. The only treatment is to let it back in and see to it that it meets its end while it's still inside you, so the part of your soul it carries can be absorbed back into your body." He hung a kettle on the hook over the fire. "The way to do that is with the Chinese herb called *byakujutsu*." He selected one of his jars and took out a dried slice of brownish root.

James craned his neck for a better view of the jar. "I can't see anything," he said. "Are you having us on, Simon?"

"Not at all," I said. "If I can see it but you can't, it must be a yokai."

"And it's well known that yokai are the cause of many diseases," Gensatsu said. "But how are *you* able to see them?"

I shrugged. "Some people seem to be born with the gift of seeing the spirit world," I said. "I'm one. Oyuki is another."

James sat up, eyeing me with interest. "Have you seen others?"

"Other yokai and ghosts?" I gave a mirthless laugh. "More than I ever wanted to. I've been seeing them all my life. That's why I went to sea in the first place, because the ghosts that always haunted me on land were getting to be too much. Most recently, it was something that looked like a cross between a man and a bird."

Gensatsu gave me a long look. "Was it wearing clothes? Like a tasseled coat?"

I looked at him in surprise. "That's right. How did you know?"

"A tengu!" he exclaimed.

"Have you seen one too?" I asked in astonishment.

"No," Gensatsu said, "but of course I've heard of them."

"So have I," James interjected. "My hometown isn't far from Mount Hiko. According to legend, the great warrior Kobayakawa Takakage was trained by the tengu there."

"Wait just a moment," Gensatsu told me. He poured the water from the kettle, steaming by now, over the root, then picked up the jar containing the haimushi. "Sorry about this," he said to James, holding the jar in front of his face.

James clamped his mouth shut.

140

"You'll have to open your mouth," Gensatsu said, "unless you would prefer it looked for another way in."

James screwed his eyes shut and opened his mouth as Gensatsu opened the jar. The haimushi flew back in.

"Drink this," Gensatsu said, carrying the hot beverage to James. "You'll taste both bitterness and sweetness, and you'll feel a warm sensation." When he had finished, Gensatsu turned back to me. "Now, you need to come with me."

Gensatsu led me out of the infirmary and toward the tenshu. We walked up the stairs to the floor below the place where we had met Don Protasio, and slid the door partly open with a tentative *"Gomen kudasai?"* When Shiro's voice replied, Gensatsu slid the door open the rest of the way, and led me into the room that had become the command post. On the wall behind Shiro hung the battle flag drawn by Yamada. Ashizuka, Mori, and Chijiwa, who had been conferring with Shiro, looked at us as we entered.

"Excuse me for interrupting, sirs," Gensatsu said, "but I've learned something about Simon you might not know. He just helped me treat a patient, by identifying a yokai no one else could see. And he says he's seen a tengu!"

All of them stared at me. Mori and Ashizuka with rapt interest, Chijiwa with alarm, Shiro impassively.

"Is this true?" Shiro asked.

"I've always had the gift of seeing the spirit world," I said. "And yes, I have seen a tengu. That's how I was able to warn you about the approaching army in Fukae."

"Why didn't you tell us sooner?" Mori asked.

"Well…" Almost involuntarily, I took a surreptitious glance in Chijiwa's direction. Mori noticed, and nodded as if that were all the explanation he needed.

"Imagine if we had a yamabushi on our side," Gensatsu went on excitedly. "Someone trained in the martial arts by the tengu themselves, just like Minamoto no Yoshitsune!"

The name was unfamiliar to me. But I had heard the word *yamabushi* before, from the tengu while I had been shivering in the river, and the reluctance I had felt then to have anything to do with them returned full force. From the expression on Mori's face, however, he was as enthusiastic about the prospect as Gensatsu.

"Even if we only had one yamabushi among us," Mori said, "he could train our entire army in the secret arts of the tengu. You know what they say about yamabushi? They can make their bodies resistant to blades and fire. They can transform themselves into beasts. They can turn invisible. Imagine how the advantage would shift if we had such powers available to us."

"Those powers would be of the devil," Chijiwa said dogmatically. "Tengu are demons. To seek aid from them would be to open the door to infernal forces."

Shiro also looked doubtful. "We've come this far by the power of Deus alone," he said. "If we enlist the help of creatures from some other part of the spirit realm, we risk forfeiting his aid."

For once, I found myself agreeing with him. There was nothing I fancied less than undertaking a difficult and dangerous journey to a distant mountain and putting myself at the mercy of the tengu. Especially if it left Oyuki here with Shiro.

"I would say, sir," said Mori, "that Deus has handed us this opportunity. We would be foolish not to take advantage of it."

"How say you, Simon?" Shiro asked.

I cast about for an excuse. "How could I possibly get to Mount Hiko?" I asked. "I don't know the way. And if I were caught, it would be the end of me."

"Jinzaemon said it wasn't far from his hometown," Gensatsu said unhelpfully. "He could take Simon there once he recovers."

Chijiwa scoffed. "So we would lose two instead of one."

"Only temporarily," Mori said. "And what we got back would be a warrior of superhuman ability."

"Then it's decided," Ashizuka said.

"Not quite," said Shiro. "The person most directly affected has yet to give his consent. Simon, will you undertake this mission?"

All eyes were on me. I tried desperately to think of a plausible reason to decline, other than "I don't want to."

I tried to expand the hole Shiro and Chijiwa had opened, hoping to give myself enough room to wriggle my way out. "As you said, sir," I began, "it's doubtful whether it would really be the will of Deus. And..."

"Look at it this way," Mori interrupted. "If you take the shorter voyage to Mt. Hiko now, it greatly increases your chances of surviving to take the longer voyage back to England in the future."

He had hit me in my most vulnerable place. It was the last thing I wanted to do, but I couldn't deny the truth of his words.

"All right," I heard myself saying. "I'll do it."

Chapter 10:
The Road to
Mount Hiko

第十章・英彦山への道

Gensatsu's treatment for James' *haimushi* worked better than I would have liked. Within three days, he was back to normal, ready and eager to escort me to Mount Hiko.

During that time, I kept hoping I could see Oyuki and try to mend things with her, even though I was still far from certain what I would say. With thirty thousand people crammed into a hundred acres, you wouldn't think it possible to avoid someone for long. That, however, was exactly the feat she somehow managed to perform. Had she learned to turn invisible, or had she discovered a network of secret passageways that bypassed the routes people usually used, or did she have spies to inform her whenever I came near? However she did it, she made herself as scarce as...well, these days, as a meal that left you feeling full.

Finally, the day appointed for my departure arrived. In a last desperate bid to say even one word to Oyuki before I left, I summoned my courage and walked into the lionesses' den, otherwise known as the barracks for unaccompanied women and girls.

It was built slightly differently from ours, with an anteroom through which everyone would have to pass to get into the sleeping area. This room was occupied by

Obotan, in her self-appointed role as guardian of the younger ladies. With a pang in my heart, I saw that she was wearing the kimono I had first seen on Oyuki on New Year's Eve, which Obotan must have lent her. A wooden chest of drawers, presumably holding more kimonos, stood in a corner, surmounted by a bewildering array of make-up brushes and containers. How she had managed to transport all this to Hara Castle, where most of the rebels arrived with only what they could carry on their backs, is a mystery that baffles me to this day.

She was engrossed in reading a sheaf of printed pages sewn together, with illustrations in vivid colors. But when I caught her attention with an involuntary cough caused by the smoke from her ever-present pipe, she looked up and hurriedly closed the book, as though trying to shield my innocent eyes from whatever might lie within.

"Simon," she said, "what are you doing here? No men allowed. Or boys. Just because you might qualify for a women's role doesn't mean you get to come into their dressing room."

"I need to see Oyuki."

"She's not here." The way she said *here* made me suspect it meant *willing to see the likes of you.*

"Please," I said. "I'm about to leave on a mission that I might not come back from. I need to talk to her."

"I said she's not here."

"Where is she, then?"

"I'm not her keeper," Obotan replied, even though she was doing maddeningly well at that very job. "If you want, I can give her a message."

There was nothing else for it. "Tell her I'm sorry," I said. "And give her this. It's safer with her than with me."

I took the bag containing the tamate-bako off my neck, and handed it to her. She took it from me with a cursory glance.

"I'll make sure she gets it," she said dismissively, and turned her attention back to her book.

* * *

That night, under a moonless sky, James and I left the castle by the Oe Beach gate and boarded one of the few boats that hadn't been wrecked and used as timber. We rowed out at first, as quietly as we could, scarcely daring to breathe for fear of attracting attention from one of the enemy vessels that patrolled the waters around the castle. The farther we rowed, the sharper the pain I felt in my heart, as though it were impaled on a fishhook with Oyuki holding the other end of the line. My grief lay onward and my joy behind.

Either the enemy were asleep or they didn't see us in the dark, because we made it away from the castle without being intercepted. Once the sails of the Shogun's boats were behind us, we began to breathe easier.

"I have to say, I envy you a little," James said when we judged it safe to speak.

"Envy me?" Right then, I felt like one of the least enviable people on earth. "Why, in heaven's name?"

"Oh, only because you can get away from the fighting and the crowds and the short rations for a while. *And* you get to learn from real live tengu. Is it true that you've seen them?"

"I've seen one."

"What was it like?"

"Rather cheeky, to be honest."

He chuckled. "I can't imagine," he said, "what it's like actually to see those things most people only know from stories. If I were in your place, I think I'd dread every sunset."

"I used to be like that," I said. "That was why I first went to sea. You have a much better chance of avoiding

146

ghosts there than on land. That is, unless you happen to sign up aboard a haunted ship."

From the way he laughed, I suspected he thought I was joking.

"But now," I went on, "look where all that running away has got me. Besides, most ghosts aren't that frightening once you get to know them."

"That's another thing I envy about you," James said. "You were born in a country where boys like us can go to sea without a second thought. I always dreamed of sailing off and seeing the world. But these days, that's impossible."

"How did you become so interested in the world outside Japan?" I asked.

"Mainly from hearing my grandfather's stories from his voyage."

This astonished me, although on reflection, it shouldn't have. When Europeans were building ocean-going ships and sending explorers all over the world, there was no reason why Japan couldn't do likewise. "Where did he go?"

"He was one of four young men chosen to join an imperial delegation to Porutogaru and Itaria. He even got to attend the coronation of the divine emperor in Roma."

"Really?"

James nodded. "That was long ago, of course, before the Tokugawa clan came to power. Three of the delegates went on to become priests. Luckily for me, one didn't." He looked at me with sudden eagerness in his eyes. "Simon? What do you miss most about Igirisu? Besides your home and family, of course."

I answered with the first thing that came to mind. "Steak pie," I said.

"Steak...pie?"

I nodded. "My mother made it every Christmas. Sliced steak with pepper, herbs, and fruit juices, baked in a pie."

James' brow furrowed, and the corners of his mouth turned down. "Fruit juices…with steak?"

"Don't judge until you've tried it. Trust me, it's delicious." Even as I spoke, I could practically smell the buttery pastry as it emerged from the oven. My stomach growled audibly, and my mouth took on water as it hadn't done since our visit to Couckebacker's house. I found myself internally sending a thought heavenward: *Please, let me taste it again. Let me find my way home, and let my mother still be there to bake it for me.*

"If I went to Igirisu," James said, "would I be the first Japanese person ever to go there?"

I thought for a moment. "As far as I know."

"When all this is over, could you take me there?"

The question caught me by surprise. "Wouldn't your parents miss you?" Even as I asked it, the question tasted bitter on my tongue, because I had been asked the same one so many times even before our ill-fated visit to the palace of the Dragon God. People always asked it as if it were just an idle question, but I had to wonder: what kind of response were they expecting? *Do my parents miss me when I'm at sea? Why, yes, of course they do. Thank you for reminding me what a selfish, undutiful son I am.*

James was silent long enough for me to realize I had unwittingly touched a nerve.

"I'm an orphan," he finally said.

I could have kicked myself. Of course, he had come to Hara Castle alone and never said anything about his mother or father.

"I'm sorry," I replied. "Can I ask what happened?"

He looked out to sea. "A business rival of my father's told the magistrate my family was secretly Kirishitan."

"Were they?"

He shook his head. "It didn't matter. Just the accusation was enough." He was silent for a while. "Simon?" he finally said.

"James?"

"Why?"

148

"Why what?"

"Why does there have to be so much fighting over what to believe?"

I had no answer. I had been wondering the same thing.

"In my country," he went on, "we believe there are millions of gods. In yours, you believe there's only one. If we're right, there's more than enough for each country to have its own, right? And if you're right, then whenever anyone prays, anywhere in the world, the one and only god must hear them, right? Even if they use different names. I mean, even I have more than one name. You call me James. My other friends call me Jinzaemon. The musketeers call me 'Powder boy!' And what Komagine usually calls me, I'd rather not repeat."

We shared a chuckle, and he continued: "But I answer to them all. If even someone like me can manage that..." He looked up at the starry sky. "Surely the lord of heaven and earth can do the same. Right?"

I could find no fault in his logic.

I was apprehensive about taking this little craft across the rough waves of the Ariake Sea. But James knew a thing or two about navigation, and skillfully helped bring us across the water at its narrowest point, which was only about five miles. Once we were safely across, we rowed along the far coast by day, stopping by night on the most secluded beach we could find.

On the third day, we turned inland and rowed up the winding Chikugo River, passing lightly wooded hills varied occasionally by thatched-roof villages, with forested mountains in the distance. We rarely saw any other people, except for merchants carrying their wares between villages, or fishermen coming down to the riverbank to check the weirs.

It felt profoundly peaceful after the unremitting crowds, noise, and smells of Hara Castle. But as I continually reminded myself, I was in as much danger here as there, if not more. No matter where in Japan I went, I was an outlaw. The pastoral scene might have made a beautiful picture, but any attempt to paint myself into it could cost me my head.

"We're safest on waterways," James said, as the sun was setting and we began looking for a concealed place to camp. "We'll stay on the river until we can find a landing close enough to Mount Hiko and far enough from Hinokuma Castle."

"What's that?"

"The Shogun's outpost in this area."

I was about to reply, but before I could say anything, a loud shout off our port side nearly stopped my heart. By instinct, I dropped to the bottom of the boat, even though rational thought told me that if we had been discovered, it was a bit too late to hide.

James took a startled glance at the riverbank. Then, to my surprise, his look of alarm changed to one of relief.

I had been sure the shout had come from someone standing right on the riverbank. But as it echoed away, I realized it had come from some distance away, possibly as far as the mountains. If it sounded that loud even at that distance, I thought, then at the source, it could probably shatter a man's eardrums, or even his head.

"It's all right," said James. "No need to hide."

I sat up. "What on earth was that?"

"It sounded like a *yamajijii*."

It took me a moment to decipher the name. "Old man of the mountains?"

"That's right. They say it's a yokai like a one-eyed, one-legged old man, who wanders the mountains and gives out a shout that could wake a dead man or kill a live one. Usually harmless, unless you're foolish enough to accept its challenge to a shouting contest. Believe me, that's one contest no mortal can ever win."

"Have you ever seen one?"

"No. But I've heard them often enough."

Early next afternoon, we pulled the boat ashore, tried to find an inconspicuous place to leave it until James came back for it, and followed a path towards the mountains. Both of us were dressed in typical farmers' garb, with kerchiefs around our heads and wide-brimmed straw hats, carrying walking staves. If I kept my head down – which I had to do anyway to see my way on the rocky path – maybe no one would look twice at me.

The path led into the woods, where it suddenly grew steeper. We walked and walked, and the lower the sun sank, the more my anxiety grew. The sky overhead was still light, but under the forest canopy, the shadows were beginning to make our path even more treacherous than it already was.

"Are we going to make it by nightfall?" I asked James.

"We'll be fine," he said, in a voice that didn't sound entirely convinced. "But let's pick up the pace a little."

As I hastened to keep up with him, we heard voices up ahead. When we rounded a bend, we saw their source: two men, leaning on bamboo walking staves like ours. Just before I lowered my head to hide my face, I saw that they wore tortoiseshell-shaped helmets and coats bearing a crest. They each carried two swords, and had muskets slung across their backs.

"Just step aside and let them by," James said in an undertone. "If they question us, let me do the talking."

I was perfectly glad to let him. I could converse in Japanese well enough, but improvising answers to questions from officials was another matter entirely. As soon as I opened my mouth, I was sure to give myself away as a foreigner.

As they approached, we stood to one side of the path, with our heads lowered. Under the brim of my helmet, I saw their feet pass in front of us – and then, to my utter horror, stop and turn to face us.

"Hello," said one. "Where are you going?"

"To the shrine on Mount Hiko, sir," James replied smoothly.

"At this hour?" came the incredulous reply. "You'll never get there before dark. You should go home and start again in the morning."

"Thank you, sir. But I know the way well. No need to worry about me."

"What's your errand at the shrine that's so urgent?" asked the second one.

"To pray for the healing of my brother, sir. He's deaf and mute."

I had to admire James' cleverness. He had prepared a perfect excuse both for us to be going to Mount Hiko and for me to be silent.

"Why aren't your parents with you?" the second official pressed on.

James hesitated long enough to make me squirm internally before replying: "Our mother is ill, and our father is taking care of her. That's another reason we need to go to the shrine, to offer prayers for her and bring back a talisman."

"Do you have a travel permit?" the second official asked, the note of suspicion in his voice growing more pronounced.

"I wasn't aware we needed travel permits for a religious pilgrimage, sir."

"You don't," said the first official rather impatiently to his partner, before addressing James again in a kinder voice. "May the gods grant your prayer. If you can spare a moment, say one for me too."

James bowed. "I will, sir. Thank you, sir."

The first official continued on his way, but the second hung back.

"Mind how you go," he said. "These woods can be dangerous. There are venomous snakes about, like that one by your brother's foot."

Before I could think, I instinctively looked down and moved my feet closer together.

There was no snake. But by reacting to the false danger, I realized to my horror, I had exposed us to a real one. I was supposed to be deaf, but I had unwittingly given away that I could hear and understand.

"I thought so!" the official exclaimed in triumph. "Now, what kind of game are you really playing?"

Before I could react, he swung his staff and knocked my hat off. My hair was still swathed in cloth, but even in the fading light, there could be no mistaking my foreign features.

The official's eyes widened with shock and rage. "*Ijin!*" he shouted to his companion. "A foreigner!"

"Let's go!" James said.

I didn't need to be told twice. In a moment, he was off the path and into the woods, skirting the cedars on the steep slope with the agility of a deer. I scrambled to keep up with him as he wove deftly among the trees.

"Halt!" one of the officials shouted, as the two of them thrashed through the underbrush to give chase. James only ran faster, widening the gap between them and us.

From behind us, I heard the report of a musket. From somewhere near us, I heard a *thunk* as the musket ball embedded itself in a tree trunk.

"Halt!" came the voice again. "Stop in the name of the Shogun!"

We kept running. Another shot rang out behind us.

They only have two muskets between them, I thought. *That was the last shot they could take without stopping to reload, which should give us enough time to lose them.*

A sudden cry of pain came from James, and he stumbled and fell.

I rushed to his side. He lay on all fours, and I was horrified to see a dark red stain spreading across the back of his shirt.

He turned over and sprawled on the ground. The front of his shirt was also stained with blood.

Oh, no. No, no, no. This couldn't be happening.

"Don't move," I told him, as I wondered frantically what to do. I wadded up the cleaner parts of his shirt and pressed them hard against his wounds.

I heard a thrashing in the underbrush behind us as the officials struggled to catch up with us.

From the other direction, I saw a pale, flickering light moving among the trees. I would have thought it was a lantern, except it seemed to be moving up and down more than side to side.

"Help!" I shouted in the direction of the light. "Please! Help!" I was past caring whether it was friend or foe. Even the Shogun's enforcers, I thought, wouldn't leave a wounded boy to die.

"Simon?" James' voice emerged faintly through pale, parched lips, as he looked at me through dazed eyes. "When you get back…to Igirisu…"

"Don't talk," I said. "Save your strength."

He closed his eyes. "Have a…steak pie…for me…"

His voice trailed off. A moment later, the rasping noise of his breath stopped.

A thin wisp of blue, faintly luminous vapor curled out of his mouth.

The mysterious light in the trees drew closer, and I looked briefly away from James to see its source. It *was* a lantern, carried by someone about chest-height compared to me, and human-shaped, but clearly not human. It had only one leg, in the middle of its body, and hopped along with the aid of a bamboo staff. Its head looked bald at first, but its entire body – at least the parts not covered by the tattered traveling clothes it wore – was covered with fine grey hair. And it had only one eye, an enormous one in the middle of its forehead, with which it looked at me expectantly. This, I thought, must be the *yamajijii*.

I remembered what James had told me. "Are you hoping for a shouting contest?" I asked.

The creature grinned with its broad mouth and nodded eagerly.

"Well, I'm afraid I'm not up for it just now," I said. "But I'm sure those two men right behind me would love to accept your challenge."

As the creature hopped off in their direction, I looked back at James. The vapor rising from his mouth had coalesced into a glowing blue ball. The hitodama hovered above his head, casting an eerie light over his face.

From somewhere behind me, I heard a shout of alarm from the Shogun's officials. The yamajijii replied with a shout of its own that nearly blew out my eardrums.

I wondered whether I would ever be able to hear properly again after that, but the next sound was perfectly audible even over the ringing in my ears: the shot of a musket.

They asked for it, I thought vindictively, and clamped my hands over my ears as tightly as I could.

Even with that protection, the next shout from the yamajijii shook my bones. The tree branches overhead bent as if in a gale-force wind, and a shower of leaves fell from them.

When the echo of the shout faded away and I lowered my hands, the wood was silent except for the sound of the yamajijii's footfall as it hopped back to rejoin me.

I turned to face it as its single eye looked sadly at James. "I don't suppose you have anything like a shovel with you?" I asked.

By way of reply, the creature lowered itself to its knee, set down its lantern and staff, and began to dig in the ground with its hands. It worked so rapidly that in a few minutes, it had a hole big enough to make an adequate, if slightly shallow, grave. With the yamajijii's help, I carefully laid James' body in it and placed his staff vertically at his head. Together, we covered it with dirt and piled stones around the staff to mark the spot. The hitodama hung in the air above it, dancing to and fro. I hoped that meant James was satisfied with our handiwork.

I knelt before the grave to say a prayer, but then realized I had never learned exactly what James believed. I recited the twenty-third Psalm and the Our Father, since those were the only passages I knew by heart that seemed suitable.

The hitodama still hovered over the grave as though not quite sure whether it was dismissed. I could almost hear James asking, *Is that it?*

I turned my eyes heavenward.

"If there's only one of you," I said, "then you hear the prayers of everyone in the world. If there's more than one, then whichever one of you was watching over him: You probably already know this, but Jinzaemon, also known as James, was a good man whose life was cut short..." Tears began to flow down my cheek, and I wiped them away before continuing, "...before his dreams could come true. Please, welcome him. If he ever did anything wrong in his life, forgive him. And if you have any special reward for people who gave their lives in a righteous cause, then take my word, he's earned it." I paused a moment, then concluded: "I ask these things in the name of...well, in the name that you know better than I. Amen."

The hitodama flitted near me as if to say *thank you*. Then it rose and sailed off toward the twilit western sky. Wherever it was going, I hoped it could at least pass over England on the way.

I bowed my head until it touched the ground, and sobbed. The Grim Reaper had certainly been no stranger at Hara Castle, but this was the first time he had struck so close to home.

Once I had cried out all my tears, my grief turned to rage. Damn Matsukura Katsuie! Damn his castle! Damn Tokugawa Iemitsu and all his minions! If they had only been content to let their people go about their lives, eating whatever they grew, practicing whatever they believed, going wherever they liked, the rebellion need never have happened. James, and all the others who had perished in battle, would still be alive. And Oyuki and I would be free to find her father and sail back to England. But their greed, and their obsession with power and control, had brought about this catastrophe. No amount of gold brocade on their kimonos could hide the blood on their hands.

I stood up, with renewed determination. I had always felt that this was not my country or my battle, but now it was. To ensure James' death would not be in vain, I had to complete my mission. We had to win.

The yamajijii was still standing there, holding his lantern. I thought I saw tears in his eye.

"Do you, by any chance, know the way to Mount Hiko?" I asked.

He nodded, turned, and hopped off, leaning on his staff. I followed the light of his lantern.

Chapter 11:
Mount Hiko

I followed the path where the yamajijii led me until daybreak, when he abruptly turned and hopped into the woods, bound for wherever yokai go in the daytime.

If I had hoped that Mount Hiko would look like Mount Fuji, towering over the surrounding plains in unmistakable isolation, my hope was in vain. Everywhere I looked, I saw steep, cedar-covered slopes, and I could scarcely tell where one mountain ended and another began.

But once I had gone a little further down the path, I saw a stone *torii* gate, which I knew marked the entrance to a shrine – a clear sign that this mountain was regarded as sacred. Beyond it lay a flight of moss-encrusted stone stairs, hollowed as if by several centuries' worth of pilgrims' steps, extending upward as far as I could see.

I began to climb. The steps were so big that I wondered whether they were designed for humans or some type of giant yokai, and there were so many of them that by the time I reached the top, I was about ready to collapse from exhaustion. Then I passed under another torii gate, and into a courtyard in front of the red-lacquered building that formed the main shrine.

There, I saw a tengu.

Or, on second glance, at least a figure dressed like one.

158

He had the same tasseled coat and the same round, black box strapped to his forehead. But he had no wings, and his face was an ordinary human face.

"Hello?" I called tentatively.

He looked in my direction, and his eyes widened. He turned away from me and shouted towards the sanctuary: "*Sendatsu! Ijin! Ijin de gozaru!*"

I didn't know what *sendatsu* meant, but the next word was one I had heard often enough. It meant "foreigner," and when I heard it applied to me, it usually also meant trouble.

Another figure emerged from the sanctuary. This one looked much older, and although his costume was similar to the first, his coat was purple. Now that I had a closer look, I saw that, in addition to the tengu-like garments, they wore billowing white pantaloons, straw sandals, and hanging from the back of the red sashes around their waists, a broad strip of tawny fur. I wondered what animal it came from and what purpose it served.

"Hello," said the newcomer.

"Hello," I replied, then asked hesitantly: "Are you...are you a tengu?"

He seemed to find this highly amusing. "No," he said. "We are yamabushi."

It seemed I had come to the right place.

"My name is Shungen," he continued. "And you? Who might you be, and where did you come from?"

"Simon Grey," I said. "From England originally, but I came here from Shimabara."

Shungen raised an eyebrow. "The site of the rebellion?"

I supposed I shouldn't be surprised that the news had traveled even to this remote mountain shrine. "That's right," was all I said. I decided against telling him that I was part of it, since I couldn't be sure which side he would support.

The next comment from the younger of the two confirmed the wisdom of my decision. "Those Kirishitan!" he said with a contemptuous snort. "The last time we had a Kirishitan daimyo in this domain, he tried to burn down this shrine."

"Goto," Shungen admonished him gently, then turned back to me. "How did you come to be in Japan, Simon Grey? And what brings you to our mountain?"

"The first…well, it's a long story," I said. "As for the second, I came to find a tengu."

The one called Goto snorted again. "So you think it's that easy, do you? Just come looking for one, and it will appear? Some of us have been practicing for years, even decades, and have yet to see one of those divine messengers. What makes you think you'll be any exception?"

"Because I've seen one already."

Goto made a sound that needed no translation: *You're either lying or mad.* Shungen, however, looked at me with sudden, intense interest.

"You've seen a tengu? Where?"

"He came to me in Shimabara from time to time," I said. "I was told that this was the best place to meet tengu and learn the ways of the yamabushi."

Shungen and Goto exchanged a glance, and then Shungen turned back to me. "If you are willing to undergo the same ascetic practices that we do, to share the life of the yamabushi, then you may stay here and try to meet your tengu."

Goto's jaw dropped. "*Sendatsu*, are you serious? If word gets out that we harbored a foreigner, the Shogun will treat us no differently from the Kirishitan."

Shungen gave him a look of gentle reproof. "Even a hunter cannot refuse a bird who comes to him for help."

Goto glared at me. "Very well," he said. "We'll see how long he lasts."

* * *

I changed out of my traveling clothes into the simple white garment they provided for me, so thin that it offered practically no protection from the chill mountain air. When I was ready, Shungen handed me a scroll. "This is the Tengu Sutra," he said. "If you want to attract the attention of the tengu, this is the best incantation to use."

I unrolled the scroll. As I had feared, it availed me nothing at all. Thanks to the patient instruction I had received from Oyuki on our travels, I could speak and understand Japanese well enough, but reading was an entirely different matter. I only knew a bare handful of the thousands of complex characters that made up the Japanese written language, and even if I had known every symbol on the scroll before me, they were written with such highly stylized brushstrokes that I doubted I would recognize them. It looked as if someone had taken a rope used to teach newly recruited sailors all the various knots used aboard ship, dipped it in ink, and pressed it onto the paper.

Shungen must have noticed my hopeless look, for he went on: "Repeat after me. Keep repeating it until you know it by heart."

I did as instructed. It began with an invocation: *Namu daitengu, kotengu, ju-ni tengu, aromaya sumanki tengu.* "I take refuge in the greater tengu, the lesser tengu, the twelve tengu, the tens of thousands of magical tengu." Then it ran down a list of forty-eight names, and ended in a string of syllables that sounded like a magic spell: *On-aromaya-tengu-sumanki-sowaka, on-hira-hira-ken, hira-ken-no-sowaka.* Shungen patiently guided me through the sutra, name by name and line by line, until I could recite it from memory.

"Now, if by any chance you *do* encounter a tengu," Shungen continued, "be mindful: Tengu are very proud creatures. Flattery will get you a long way. But if you say anything a tengu perceives as an insult, it could be the last mistake you ever make. And it's best to try not to stare."

"At what?"

Before Shungen could answer, the door slid open to reveal Goto. "Is he ready?" he asked Shungen, without so much as a glance in my direction.

Shungen handed me over to Goto, who led me along a mountain path with steep precipices on either side. The path itself was a test of mindfulness – it was so covered with mud, mossy stones, and fallen pine needles that an unwary person could easily slip. The noise of rushing water grew louder as we went, until we walked into the chilling spray of a white waterfall.

Goto's next words confirmed my fears. "Sit there," he said, pointing at a rock directly under the waterfall, "and meditate until I come back to fetch you."

I waded into the pool at the bottom and approached the waterfall. To my mind, the roar of the water grew louder, and the spray colder and wetter, with every step I took. I hesitated a moment, then turned, planted my rear on the frigid stone, and leaned back into the cataract.

When Takeda's men put me in the water jail, I had thought there could be nothing worse. I was wrong. In that river, the cold water had been gently flowing around me. Here, it came thundering down from a great height, pounding on my head and shoulders before running down my body, soaking my clothes and chilling my skin. Within one minute, I was almost completely numb – "almost" because I still had just enough sensation left to feel the impact of the water as it struck me like a thousand hammers made of ice. Within ten minutes, I had forgotten how it felt to be warm and dry.

For a moment, I envied Oyuki. With the blood of her mother the snow woman flowing through her veins, this practice would be no hardship for her.

As the icy waters continued to beat on me, my thoughts flew to her. When I thought of holding her in my arms on the bridge at Hirado, the frigid cascade became marginally more bearable. But when I recalled how we had left things, and wondered whether a moment like that would ever come again, the cold hit me with renewed intensity.

By the time Goto came back, I was shivering from head to toe. I carefully unfolded my legs and stepped off the rock into the shallow water underneath, but my legs were so numb that I fell face-first into the pool. Goto made no effort to help me up. With an effort, I splashed to shore.

"Cold?" His voice suited the word.

I could only nod.

"Well, I know just the way to warm you up."

He led me along another trail, to a nook in the mountain side. There was a metal cauldron, large enough for a grown man to sit inside, with kindling piled underneath it and a stack of wood nearby.

I looked from him to the cauldron and back again. "You can't be serious. Are you planning to make me into soup?"

Goto's face was impassive. "You want to meet a tengu? You have to prove you're worthy of his time."

I climbed up the slope next to the cauldron and lowered myself in. The bottom was lined with stones, including one big enough to sit on. The water was icy cold, but I was used to that by now. At least it was standing still rather than falling on me.

"Go on, then," Goto said. "Recite the Tengu Sutra."

As I did, Goto struck a match and lit the kindling. It snapped and crackled as the fire spread, the smoke curling up around the edges of the cauldron.

My unscientific observation: For water in a large cauldron to heat from the temperature of an icy mountain stream to a nice comfortable bath takes forever. From there to the temperature of a stew pot takes only an instant. Twinges of pain shot through my skin as the water began to steam, and I shifted in a vain attempt to put myself a little farther from the heat source.

Goto noticed. "Have you had enough?" he asked. "Are you ready to quit?"

I was about to say yes, but realized just in time that he might be talking about my training in general. "No."

"No, what?"

I recalled the term of respect I had often heard used with teachers, doctors, and others in positions of superior knowledge. "No...*sensei*."

"Sensei?" Goto looked at me as if I had uttered a mortal insult. "'Sensei' means 'one who was born before you.' You think that's the only difference between you and me, do you? An accident of *timing*? You are to address those ahead of you on the path as *sendatsu*, 'one who has achieved before you.' Understand?"

"Yes, sendatsu."

"I can't hear you!"

"YES, SENDATSU!"

"Now, go on. Recite."

I recited one more time, as the steam from the water began to thicken. When I got to the end of the sutra, I felt that if I stayed in for one more repetition, I would turn red like a lobster. I stood up, jumped out of the cauldron, and sprawled on the rocks.

Goto drew a bucket of water from the stream and sluiced it over me. To go from hot to cold so quickly made me scream out loud.

"You'll be wanting something to dry you off," he said. "On your feet."

I struggled to my feet and followed him to a clearing in the woods. From a distance, I saw a billowing white cloud, which reminded me alarmingly of the hells of Unzen. But this time, I really could smell smoke and hear the crackling of burning wood. As we emerged into the clearing, I saw several yamabushi standing around the remains of a bonfire of cedar branches, now reduced to smoldering coals. One of them was beating a drum, and another was repeating a chant like the one at the end of the Tengu Sutra.

A pile of something white lay on the ground at the near end of the coal carpet. "Salt," Goto said, pointing to it. "To purify the body and protect it."

"Protect it from what?"

As soon as the words were out of my mouth, I knew the answer and I regretted asking the question. With a sweep of his arm, Goto indicated the coals.

Dear God, I thought. *If there really is a hell, and it's anything like what I've been through today, I'll be a better man for the rest of my life. I promise.*

"Don't hesitate," he told me. "If you do, you're sure to get burned."

I stepped in the pile of salt and looked apprehensively at the carpet of coals, which suddenly looked a mile long.

I imagined Oyuki waiting at the far end. Keeping the image firmly in my mind, I stepped out over the coals, not exactly running, but walking quickly and decisively. Before I knew it, I was on the other side, cooling my feet in another pile of salt.

Oyuki didn't know, and she might not have cared, that I had literally walked through fire for her. But I had.

* * *

Every morning, I was awakened by the sound of conch shells. Since the Shimabara rebels used the same instrument as a call to arms, the sound never failed to make me jump. Then, as soon as my heartbeat settled down, the day began.

I followed the same routine as the yamabushi: Long processions up steep mountain paths, chanting *Rokkon- shojo* – "purification of the six roots," meaning the two eyes, two ears, tongue, and heart. Meditation on rocks, and unlike the full-fledged yamabushi who had a lion skin always at the ready to cushion their backsides, I had nothing between me and the stone but a thin layer of cotton. Meals of rice, vegetables, and miso soup, admittedly better than the rations at Hara Castle, but still barely enough to sustain me. And after sunset, the fire ceremony where *goma* – wooden blocks with prayers written on them – were burned in a bonfire, in the belief that the smoke carried the prayers to heaven.

In addition to all of this, Goto had me recite the Tengu Sutra while enduring all kinds of torments, not just the waterfall and cauldron but anything else his imagination could devise. One particularly terrifying exercise involved hanging upside-down by ropes from a high cliff.

Naturally, during these endurance tests, my most frequent thought was, "How much longer?" But after a while, I noticed that whenever I asked myself that, my energy dissipated and a feeling of hopelessness overcame me. I soon realized that a better question would be, "Can I endure what's happening to me right at this moment?" When I put it that way, the answer was usually "yes." If nothing else, I reminded myself: *You need to save your energy. And it takes more energy to yell "Enough!" than to sit still and meditate.*

But I did wonder how long I would have to undergo this training until the tengu deigned to show himself. Remembering the stories I had heard of humans who had acquired superhuman powers after doing devotions at a shrine or in a river, like Takiyasha-hime and the Bridge Princess of Uji, the going rate seemed to be twenty-one days. If it took that long even to meet a tengu, let alone complete my training course with one, who knew what would happen at Hara in that time? My greatest fear loomed larger and larger in my mind: that after all this hardship and suffering, I would finally learn the secret arts to help us win the battle, only to return to Hara and find that we had already lost.

For me, however, the trial period was cut short. On the third day, in the midst of my austerities, I noticed some commotion at the entrance to the shrine. A few minutes later, Shungen came looking for me. I had never seen him rushed or worried before, but now, his pace and voice had an unaccustomed urgency.

"Simon," he said, "some men from Hinokuma Castle are here. They say two of their companions, who came here by the mountain road a few days ago, haven't returned. I don't suppose you know anything about that?"

I shook my head silently, fearful that my voice might give me away if I lied, and hoped that the yamabushis' supposed supernatural powers didn't extend to mind-reading.

"They're searching the shrine precincts," Shungen went on. "It wouldn't do for you to be discovered. Come with me."

At the top of it was a small wooden hut. Shungen slid the door open and ushered me inside. The hut contained a small altar, at the height of my knees, decorated with a miniature sword, a miniature bow and arrow, and a bamboo wand hung with a strip of white paper. Beside the altar was a brazier, with a pile of kindling already laid.

"Meditate here until I come back," Shungen instructed me. "They aren't likely to look for you here. And if they do...well, I doubt they'll be able to stay long enough to find you."

As I sat before the altar, Shungen struck a match and lit the kindling. When flames started licking the slender twigs, he took out a paper packet of some kind, laid it on top of the fire, and left, sliding the door shut behind him.

I hadn't understood Shungen's last remark, but once the packet started to smolder and smoke, his meaning became plain to see – or rather, smell. The mixture of herbs smelled as though someone had dried a fish when it was already rotten, tried to conceal the mistake by slathering it with hot peppers, and finally given up and burned the evidence. The smoke soon filled the tiny hut, stinging my eyes and making me cough and gag.

Meditate? How was I expected to meditate when I could scarcely breathe? I tried to recite the Tengu Sutra, even though I could barely get two syllables in between fits of coughing. I could hear the slurring in my own voice, and when I looked at the walls of the hut, I got the distinct impression they were spinning around me.

I heard voices outside the hut. Was I hearing things, or had the Shogun's men come to my door? I stopped reciting and desperately tried to hold my breath, even though a tremendous cough was hurling itself against the walls of my lungs, threatening to break through my rib cage unless I opened my mouth to let it out.

The spinning of the room intensified. The edges of my vision grew dark. I was vaguely aware of the door to the hut sliding open.

That was the last impression to register on my senses before I lost consciousness.

Chapter 12: Tengudo

When I opened my eyes, the hut was gone. I was looking up at a cloudless sky, a deeper shade of blue than I had ever seen before.

I sat up. I was lying on a flat slab of stone. Rocky crags rose up around me, before dropping off sharply into a vast expanse of white clouds. I had seen clouds from above once before, when a mystical flying horse-like creature called a *kirin* had given me a ride on its back from Kyo no Miyako to Edo Castle. But this time, the white cotton sea stretching from horizon to horizon was dotted with rocky islands like the one I was on, as if I were on one of many peaks in a vast mountain range permanently shrouded in clouds. From time to time, I saw a winged shape fly from one of the distant islands to another. Birds, I thought at first, but then I saw that they were human-shaped and wearing clothes. They were tengu.

"I was starting to wonder if I'd ever see you here," said a voice behind me.

I spun around. Perched on a nearby rock was the tengu who had come to visit me in Shimabara. Behind him rose a sheer cliff, so high I couldn't see over the top.

"Am I..." I looked around and tried to take in my surroundings. "Am I in Tengudo?"

"You are indeed. So I suppose it's time you learned my name: Hiko no Ajari. And now that you know where you are, the next question is why."

I turned to face him squarely. "I want to help our side win the battle."

"Sure that your side is the right one, are you?"

I opened my mouth, but no reply came out. Of course, if it came to a choice between our side and the Shogun's, there was no doubt which had the better claim to be right. But then I remembered the columns of smoke rising from the temples and shrines in Shimabara, and the common people who had been driven from their homes by the rebels' onslaught. You can always argue questions of right and wrong, I thought, but one thing was constant: To say that war made men into beasts was an insult to the animal kingdom.

"Is any side in war ever completely right?" I asked.

"Now that," Ajari said, "is the first sensible thing I've heard from you. All right, then, what is your true purpose?"

"I'm an exile in a hostile country. All I really want is for Oyuki and me to go home."

"Oh, I see," Ajari squawked. "You want to get the girl, and go home to mama and papa."

The undisguised mockery in his voice made my face flush. I made no reply.

"How did you come to be so far from home?" Ajari continued.

"I signed up as a cabin boy on a ship bound for Japan."

"What were you looking for?"

"I was trying to get away from the ghosts that always haunted me on land."

"So you got here by running away. And now that you're in danger here, you're trying to run back. Has there ever been a time in your life when you weren't running away from something?"

Another flare of anger and shame welled up in me. "I'd like to think I'm advancing. Toward victory for our cause, toward..." My voice trailed off before I spoke the other thought on my mind: *toward Oyuki.*

Ajari shook his head. "That's no better. Whether you're running away or running toward, something outside you is making you run. There is only one good reason to want to master the way of the warrior: Because you want to master the way of the warrior. That must be your only desire. And eventually, even that will fall away. The way of the warrior will be such a part of your nature that you'll progress along it just as naturally, and with just as little effort of will, as a tree grows. Are you prepared for that?"

I hesitated, then nodded. "I am."

Ajari, in his bird-like fashion, kept his head cocked and scrutinized me with an unblinking eye. "We'll see about that."

He hopped down from his perch, and indicated a trail. "This path will take you to meet Buzen-bo, the master of this mountain."

I looked. The path went directly to the sheer cliff face behind him, and up to a precipice. My heart caught in my mouth. Aboard ship, I had gotten used to climbing ropes and ladders in high seas, but this was another matter.

I walked to the foot of the cliff, examined the rock face, and began to climb. The protuberances that I could use as handholds or footholds were set widely apart, and it was a stretch to get from one to another. But after some careful climbing, and one or two heart-stopping moments when a foot slipped, I reached the precipice.

Not that it felt any safer than the rock face I had climbed. The ledge was scarcely wider than my feet. To make my way along the trail, I had to hug the cliff face, move one foot to the side, bring the other to meet it, and above all, never look down. I made my way, step by careful step, around a bend in the rock, to a place I couldn't see from where I started.

171

At the end of the trail, a chain hung from somewhere higher on the rock face. I looked up to see an outcropping of rock projecting over the trail. The chain was anchored to some spot above it.

"You must be joking," I groaned, even though neither Ajari nor any other living creature was close enough to hear me.

I took hold of the chain and began to climb, just as I would shimmy up a rope aboard ship: hold on with both hands and both feet, move one hand over the other, pull my feet up behind. I continued as the rock face curved back toward me, until I was practically hanging upside down.

My feet slipped. I was left holding onto the chain with just my hands, as my feet dangled above the clouds.

It was as if a hole opened at the point where my legs met, and my soul fell out, plunging into the depths just as my body would do if my hands lost their grip on the chain. If I were to fall into and through that expanse of clouds, who knew how much farther I would have to fall to whatever ground lay below them? One thing was certain: If I found out, I wouldn't be in any condition to share my discovery with anyone.

My feet flailed wildly as I pulled myself up, raised my legs, and locked my ankles around the chain again. Resolved, this time, that no force in the universe would pull them apart, I continued my climb until I was around the overhang. As soon as I rounded the bend and placed my foot on solid rock, I could breathe again.

The chain disappeared into a cave in the rock face. I followed it through the narrow opening. I soon passed the point where I could see anything by what little light came in through the cave mouth, but I continued to feel my way along the chain until it reached a fastening.

I felt around me. The passage curved, and probing with my feet, I found a step going down, and then another. I kept my hands on the walls of the passage, so narrow I could touch both of them easily, and felt my

172

way down carefully with my feet as the stairway spiraled down, descending into deeper and deeper darkness.

I have no idea how many steps I descended, but when I reached the last one and probed tentatively with my toes, I felt no floor. My foot met only empty space.

I drew my foot back, felt around with it for a loose stone on the step where I was standing, and when I found one, kicked it over the edge. There was silence for a few seconds, and then a faint echo of the crack of stone on stone. There was no knowing exactly how deep the pit was, but it was clear that if I fell into it, I had little to no chance of making it out again alive.

I stood still for a while, hoping my eyes would adjust to the dark. But without even the faintest moonlight or starlight to see by, it was a vain hope.

My hands felt up and down the walls, hoping there might be some other passage branching off from this one, some way around the pit. There was none.

I took a deep breath, and with all my strength, pushed against the walls with both hands and my left foot, while my right foot slid forward. Cautiously, I moved my left hand forward, then my right hand, then my left foot.

Don't forget to breathe, I reminded myself. *Breathe in, right foot, breathe out, left hand. Breathe in, right hand, breathe out, left foot.* Soon, my arms and legs were trembling, and the muscles of my midriff were aching with the unaccustomed exertion, but I kept moving forward, inch by inch.

Finally, after an eternity, I felt something solid underfoot. A tentative sweep of my foot revealed that it was the bottom step of another stairway, this one going up. With great relief, I placed both feet on the ledge and relaxed my arms, though still keeping my hands on the walls. Carefully, I made my way up, until the most welcome sight in the world met my eyes: a glimmer of light on the stone surface. I hurried up the last few steps and emerged, squinting and blinking, into the sunlight.

I was standing at the edge of the island, looking at a larger island some distance away, where Ajari stood waiting for me. Two flat rocks protruded from the white mist between the two, like stepping stones across a river of clouds. The first was a fairly easy jump from where I stood. The second was slightly farther away, and from there to the next island, the leap was too wide even to contemplate.

"Well?" Ajari called across the distance between us. "This is your path."

I looked apprehensively at the mist between the islands, and then back to Ajari. "Unlike you, I don't have wings."

"One who's worthy to be a yamabushi shouldn't need them."

I jumped to the first rock. From there, I took as much of a running start as the confined space would allow, and leaped to the second. But that distance was as far as I felt I could jump, and the second rock was no bigger than the first, offering me no chance to build up any more momentum.

I looked apprehensively at the island where Ajari stood. The distance between them looked as wide as the Ariake Sea, and the vertigo that I had felt while climbing the chain returned full force.

"If you're afraid," came Ajari's voice, "you can always turn back."

I stood frozen to the spot a while longer. Then, I retreated to the very edge of the stone where I stood. It only gave me space for three steps.

Here goes.

I ran. One step, two steps, three. I jumped.

To my horror, I felt myself falling well before I reached the edge of the far island. I pumped my legs frantically in mid-air, but even with that, even with my arms extended in front of me, I fell short. My feet disappeared into the mist.

And struck something solid with a force that nearly broke my ankles.

I stood, knee-deep in the mist, supported by some concealed surface underneath. Once the first shock of pain had passed, I laughed out loud with relief.

Once I felt ready to walk again, I took a step forward – cautiously, feeling with my toe to check whether the surface underfoot still continued – until I reached the far island where Ajari was waiting.

"Come," he said. "It's time for you to meet Buzen-bo, the master of this mountain."

He led me into a crater-like depression in the mountains. At the far end of it was a pool, recessed deeply enough that the surface was mirror-smooth, and something that looked like a stage. On it sat someone that, at first glance, looked like an old prophet with the wings of an angel.

He was dressed in a robe with a tasseled stole, like Shungen's, except that his was a color somewhere between brown and orange. The top of his head was bald, and the hair around it was long and white, as was his beard.

He looked like an ordinary man of advanced age, except for three appendages unlike any ever seen on any human being. Two were the feathered wings on his back. And the third was the nose that preceded the rest of his face by an arm's length. It was a good thing, I thought, that tengu lived outdoors. If he ever had to go through a door, then before his hand could reach the frame, his nose would already have poked a hole in the rice-paper screen.

Completely forgetting the warning Shungen had given me, I stared at this prodigious protuberance. Of course, Buzen-bo noticed.

"Feeling a little inadequate, are we?" he said. "Well, I suppose that's a natural reaction for a man to have when he sees one that's so much bigger than his."

I wasn't sure what to say to that. I decided just to proceed with the speech I had been rehearsing, as though that embarrassing moment hadn't happened.

"O mighty Buzen-bo," I said, "My name is Simon Grey. I have come to beseech you to teach me the mystical ways of the mountain warriors."

Buzen-bo held me for a moment in a penetrating gaze, his eyes partially concealed by the eyebrows that stuck out as far as the nose on an ordinary human.

"So you want to be a yamabushi?" he finally asked.

That was not exactly how I would have put it. But I said, "Yes, great one."

"You've heard of Minamoto no Yoshitsune?"

"Yes, great one."

"You know who taught him?"

I tried to recall what I had heard from Gensatsu. "Sojo-bo of Mount Kurama, great one."

Buzen-bo nodded. "The greatest of the tengu," he said, in a sarcastically exaggerated voice, with a bow and a dramatic flourish. "So, instead of him, what made you choose to come to Mount Hiko and ask the humble Buzen-bo, who's only ranked fourth among all the tengu? *Fourth!* Not even in the winners' circle. Sojo-bo of Mount Kurama, gold. Taro-bo of Mount Atago, silver. Sanshaku-bo of Mount Akiha, bronze. All of them look down their noses at me. So why not go learn from the best?"

The honest answer would have been, *Because you were closest.* But this time, I remembered Shungen's warning soon enough. In this case, honesty would probably not be the best policy.

"Because, great one, from what I've heard, you *are* the best. You trained Koba...Kobaya..."

I struggled to recall the name. Fortunately, Buzen-bo himself helped me out: "Kobayakawa Takakage."

"Yes, him. And may I say, great one, what a tragedy it was for Japan that his time came so soon. If he had lived long enough to fight in the Battle of Sekigahara, it might have gone the other way. The Toyotomi clan would now be ruling Japan, and the Tokugawas' persecutions would never have happened."

Buzen-bo was silent for a moment. With his eyes concealed by his eyebrows, and his mouth by his whiskers, I couldn't see his reaction.

"Where are you from?" he asked at last.

"England, great one."

In case Buzen-bo's grasp of European geography was on a par with the ordinary mortals down below, I prepared to explain, as tactfully as possible, the difference between England and Holland. But as soon as he heard the name, he clapped his hands with delight. "England!" he exclaimed. "Marvelous! In a mere century or two, you'll be the greatest imperial power the world has ever known! From Asia to Africa to the Americas, the sun will never set on your empire! Are you planning to help Great Britain conquer the world?"

"I…wasn't thinking that far ahead, sir," I replied with perfect honesty. "All I want is to help the Shimabara rebels win so I can go home."

But Buzen-bo's ears apparently weren't as extraordinary as his nose, because he went on as if he hadn't heard me. "And when you do, you'll let everyone know it was Buzen-bo of Mount Hiko who taught you. Won't you?"

I hesitated. "I give you my word, sir, everyone I…um…conquer will know your name."

"Brilliant!" Buzen-bo exclaimed, thrusting his fists skyward. "I'll be the first tengu whose name is known around the world! Let's see Sojo-bo make *that* claim! Yes, yes, he taught the greatest warrior in the history of Japan. And he never stops rubbing our noses in it. Yoshitsune this, Yoshitsune that. But hardly anyone in the outside world has ever heard of him. And it's likely no one will, for at least another two hundred years. Thanks to Tokugawa Iemitsu's seclusion edicts, none of his subjects will be able to put their noses outside Japan."

He tossed this out as an offhand comment, but as soon as I heard it, my blood froze. At least another two hundred years? Could Buzen-bo really see the future? And if he was right, what did that mean for our side's chances? It was already plain that the plan I had heard at first from Chijiwa, of an independent domain extending from Shimabara to Nagasaki, was doomed. But was it too much to hope that the rebels might wring even a few small concessions from the Shogun? And if not, what did that mean for my chances of surviving the battle and going home?

My mind was working so hard to fathom the implications that I scarcely heard Buzen-bo as he gleefully continued: "But now, *I'll* have someone who can make my name known throughout the world! Sojo-bo can take that and shove it right up his snotty snoot!" He turned his attention back to me. "Welcome, Simon Grey. Your apprenticeship begins today."

Chapter 13:
The Treacherous
Arrow

第十三章. 裏切の矢

There are many stories about journeys to enchanted realms, but do you know what none of them ever tells you? How hungry you get.

As far as I could tell, all Buzen-bo and Ajari ever ate was pine needles and bamboo leaves steeped in soy sauce, once every couple of days. It was hard to comprehend that so little food could nourish a body so big – and even harder, that it didn't seem to occur to them that a growing human male might possibly need just a little bit more. My diet consisted of grated mountain potato with dried gourd shavings and a bit of soy sauce, once a day. I hadn't thought anything could ever make me long for the meager portions of rice and soup we had at Hara Castle, or the salt pork and weevil-infested hardtack I had at sea, but here I was.

And this ration was supposed to sustain me through a training regimen that not only pushed the limit of human endurance, but kept pushing it until it fell on its bottom, then helped it back to its feet and pushed it some more. I punched a freezing waterfall until I could no longer feel my hands, then punched trees until my knuckles bled. I stood and endured sword-strokes while wrapped in a hundred layers of silk, then ninety-nine, then ninety-eight, with another peeled off every day, making it more and more urgent for me to learn how to harden my body against the blows.

After these warm-up exercises, the remainder of the day was mostly spent standing and holding things. Buzen-bo and Ajari spent hours teaching me the proper stance, the proper way to hold the bow, the proper way to hold the sword in the various guard positions. One day gave way to the next, without any sense that I was getting any closer to actually learning to shoot an arrow or fight a duel with the sword. Spending so much time on the fundamentals would be all very well, I thought, if my goal were to master the way of the warrior and ultimately train pupils of my own. But we had a battle to win, and every day I spent in Tengudo brought my companions one day closer to either victory or defeat, without me there to help tip the scales in favor of the first.

I wondered how long it would take. But whenever I asked Buzen-bo, his reply was always the same. "You humans! Always rushing. Always expecting things to happen instantly. Never willing to put your nose to the grindstone and give them the time they need."

After sunset, I would face the hardest test of all: staying awake through the long, rambling lectures Buzen-bo loved to give about military history, medicine, astronomy, or any other subject that happened to capture his interest. At night, I would retire to my cave, and dream that I was back at Couckebacker's house, seated at the table spread with a lavish Christmas feast, with Oyuki sitting beside me and Couckebacker urging us to help ourselves. But whenever I reached for any of the sumptuous dishes, Ajari would suddenly appear and give my knuckles a whack with his bamboo staff, squawking, "Oh, no, you don't!"

Finally, I had an archery lesson where I actually had the chance to release an arrow from a bow. Until now, I had never come any closer to a bow than reading stories about Robin Hood. Now that I actually tried to draw one, it was much heavier than I imagined. When I let fly, the string slapped my arm so hard that I cried out in pain. Of course, the arrow went wide of the target.

"You did two things wrong," said Buzen-bo. "First, you used strength to draw the bow. Second, you were preoccupied with hitting the target."

"Well...isn't that the whole point?" I asked. "How can I draw a bow this long without using strength?"

Buzen-bo made an impatient noise. "If you try to draw the bow with brute strength, you are acting against the character of the bow. You and the bow are in opposition. The goal is for you and the bow to become one. The bow is made of wood and bamboo. But when your spirit infuses it, its mystery will not be the same. When it seems as though your spirit fills heaven and earth, it will also fill the distance between the arrow and the target as water fills an empty shell. Clear your mind. When you release, the arrow should fly from the bow as naturally as a fruit falling from a tree."

I tried again, with no better result.

"Again, you're thinking too hard," he said. "Too much intention. When you force your will, you open a fissure in your mind for distractions and illusions to rush in."

I sighed. "I don't suppose you could show me some techniques to improve my chances of actually hitting the thing?"

He looked at me as though I had asked him to help me cheat on an examination. "The purpose of learning technique is to reach the point where you no longer think about technique. Strive to master it, yes, but let go of your preoccupation with it. Instead, let the bow be an expression of your mind. Let your mind be as still as the target. If your mind is clear, you can hit the target even with your eyes closed."

I tried again. Even with my eyes open, the arrow still missed.

We spent the morning on archery, and the result was a decisive victory for the target. Buzen-bo showed no sign of impatience, but when he saw my patience reaching its limits, he said simply, "Let's move on to swordsmanship."

I felt I was on somewhat surer ground here. I didn't have much more experience with the sword than the bow, but if I may say so myself, I had done reasonably well at fighting my way past the guards – both natural and supernatural – at Edo Castle.

Ajari brought a wooden sword for me and another for himself, and we squared off.

"Begin," said Buzen-bo.

Ajari let out a squawk that must have been audible as far away as the next island-peak in the cloudy sea. Involuntarily, I jumped. Before my feet even made it back to the ground, Ajari dealt me a jab with the point of his sword.

Ajari and Buzen-bo both laughed. When the levity had died down, Buzen-bo said, "Your opponent will do everything he can to create confusion and fear in you. But if your mind is clear, then whatever external sights and sounds assail your senses, you can simply observe them without reacting to them. Imagine a placid lake in the middle of the jungle. Around it, monkeys may be chattering, wild beasts may be fighting, trees may be burning. The lake reflects all those, but none of them makes the least ripple on its surface. You must become that lake. Try again."

Easier said than done, I thought as I faced off with Ajari again. At the signal from Buzen-bo, Ajari let out another squawk. My heart still skipped a beat, but when he lashed out, I was able to raise my blade to parry. His strike had been a feint, though, and he quickly changed direction and dealt me a stinging blow.

"Ya-ha-hah!" came Ajari's raucous cry. "Got you again!"

Flushed with embarrassment and anger, I took the initiative next time, and lashed out at Ajari as soon as Buzen-bo gave the word. He parried effortlessly and landed a decisive counter-stroke.

Ajari gave me another derisive squawk before turning to Buzen-bo. "Master, why are we wasting our time with someone so hopeless? Is this clumsy little boy really the best the Shimabara rebels had to offer? Even if the older veterans couldn't be spared, you'd think they'd send someone with real potential, like Amakusa Shiro – or that promising young warrior, Ashizuka Sanai."

The mention of that name ignited the blood in my veins like a match igniting a fuse. I lashed out again, without even waiting for Buzen-bo to give the starting signal. All I cared about was wiping the smirk off the beak of this mocking bird.

Again, he defeated me effortlessly.

Buzen-bo shook his head impatiently. "*Muga! Mushin!* No self! No mind! Don't you see? He's trying to get up your nose. He's attacking your pride, and you're falling for it. As long as you let your sense of self control you, he'll be able to lead you around by the nose. But if you let it go, your mind becomes like a mirror. When you've abandoned your own intentions, you can read your opponent's intentions so well that you know what he's going to do almost before he does." He added in an aside: "It's a good thing you came to me instead of Sojo-bo. You could never have learned this from him. His pride and vanity are higher than Mount Kurama. But I know more about overcoming the self than any other tengu. You'll never meet a tengu with less pride than I. Now, again."

We went around again. Ajari squawked and hurled insults, but I did my best to ignore them. I succeeded in fending off a few of his blows, but it wasn't long before he struck me from my undefended side.

"No," said Buzen-bo. "No, no, no! Let's take a break. Simon, bring me some water from that pool."

He pointed to the pool in a corner of the field. When I reached it, I saw that it was recessed from the ground level so that the wind barely disturbed it; its surface was as smooth as a mirror. I almost hated to make a ripple on it, but my master had ordered me. I cupped my hands, scooped up as much water as I could hold, and carefully carried it back to Buzen-bo. He received it in his own hands and took a grateful sip.

"Thank you," he said. "Now, bring me some more…in your fists."

I hesitated.

"Did you not hear me?" Buzen-bo inquired mildly.

"No, master. I mean, yes, master, I heard you, but…"

"But what?"

"But what you asked was impossible."

"Exactly!" Buzen-bo favored me with a half-smile. "What you try to grasp, you lose. Did you observe how smooth that pool was before you drew water from it? Like a mirror. Ten thousand forms and shapes may appear before it, and it reflects them all. But once they move on, no shadow or shape remains. That is how a warrior's mind must be. Everything that appears before it in the present moment, it reflects. To anything that is not before it in the present moment, it pays no attention."

By the end of the day, I might have become able to hold out against Ajari just a little longer than I could at the beginning, but I still had yet to land a blow on him.

That night, my body was exhausted, but my mind couldn't rest for fretting over how little progress I had made, how endless the road seemed, and what might be happening back at Hara Castle in the meantime. After fitful and fruitless attempts to sleep, I got up from my straw pallet and left the cave, hoping that a walk in the cool night air would help clear my mind.

To my surprise, I saw Buzen-bo sitting by the side of the reflecting pool, gazing into the water.

I remembered his earlier lecture. The pool only reflected what was in front of it at that moment. Was Buzen-bo so enamored of himself that he could spend so long simply gazing at his own reflection, like Narcissus from the Greek myth? From my experience of tengu so far, it wouldn't have surprised me.

Then I took a second look at the pool. Something seemed wrong, and it took me a moment to realize what it was: The sky over my head was black and starry, but the sky reflected in the pool was the bright blue of noonday.

Buzen-bo looked up and saw me. In an instant, the sky reflected in the pool changed to black, a mirror image of the sky overhead.

"What are you doing, master?" I asked.

"Nothing that need concern you."

I glanced at the pool. "This pool doesn't always reflect only what's above it, does it? You were looking into a different place or time."

"You need to get your rest," was his only reply. "You have a long day tomorrow."

I took a longing look at the pool. If it really could show other times or places, could I use it to see Hara Castle? Could I see as far away as England? Could I find out what was happening to my parents, or even to Oyuki's father?

"Could you teach me how to do that, master?" I asked.

"Do you know what I can teach you?" Buzen-bo replied. "How to keep your nose out of matters that have nothing to do with your training."

With that, he withdrew to his cave.

* * *

The next day, I fared little better. I was able to fend off a few blows from Ajari, but our contests were always painfully short – with the emphasis on "painful." And I was still unable to land a single blow on him.

Buzen-bo's disapproving scowl deepened as the day wore on. "You want to become a true warrior?" he finally asked. "Sharpen yourself to a razor edge, like the blade of a fine sword?"

"Yes, master." To my surprise, I found I meant it.

"There's only one problem," he said. "You're surrounded by magnets. Things you love, things you hate, things you desire, things you fear. Whenever one of these comes near you, it exerts a magnetic force on you. Victory. Defeat. Love. Loss. Home. Exile. Life. Death. As long as these forces are pulling you this way and that, you'll never be able to hold your blade straight. When your opponent attacks you, your mind must be completely at peace, without malice or fear. Forget about him, forget about yourself, forget about life, forget about death."

"I'm sorry, master," I said. "I just have trouble letting go of the idea that it's better to be alive than dead."

He either missed my irony or chose to ignore it. "The art of swordsmanship straddles the boundary between life and death. The essential first step is to cut through the root of confusion that causes you to regard life and death as two different things. Once you resolve that matter, you can move without moving, and stand still without standing still."

I was used to hearing Buzen-bo speak in riddles and paradoxes, but this was too much for me to wrap my mind around. "I'm sorry, master. Move without moving? Stand still without standing still? How is that even possible?"

"Have you ever seen a master horseman riding at a gallop?"

I nodded.

"Is he moving, or is he standing still?"

As I tried to work out an answer, I was silent long enough that Buzen-bo went on. "As the rider rides the horse, the mind rides *ki*."

"What's *ki?*"

"It's your life essence. It flows through all living things – humans, animals, plants, the earth itself."

"And yokai?"

"Of course. Some yokai have bodies animated by ki, like ours. Others are beings of pure ki, without a physical body. The point is, ki is present in all living things. To master the way of the warrior is to master your ki."

"And ever since I met you," Ajari chimed in, "your ki has been scattered. Part of it here. Part of it in Hara Castle, with her. Part of it in your home country with your family. Part of it, who knows where. This is no good. If you want to learn the way of the warrior, you need all of it here."

"Simon," Buzen-bo said, "remember the cave you passed through to get here? As you were crossing the chasm, where was your mind?"

I remembered the intense focus of mind and body I had exerted to cross the pit. "There," I said. "It was there."

"Of course," Buzen-bo said. "You needed all of it there, or you would meet with disaster. That level of concentration is what a warrior must maintain all the time. Come with me."

He stood up, spread his wings, and jumped. As I ran to follow him, he flew to the top of a tall cliff. Against the cliff leaned a ladder, with wooden supports and metal rungs.

"You must climb that ladder," Buzen-bo called down to me.

I approached the ladder, and as I got a closer look, drew back in horror. The rungs were not just metal bars, they were sharp swords, their blades facing up.

"You can't be serious," I muttered, half to myself.

"Turn your feet," he said, "so they meet the blade lengthwise rather than crosswise. Recite this mantra: *On-kiru-kiru-mata-uji-yaku-yasei-sowaka*. And send all your ki to your hands and feet. Every bit of it needs to be here. If any part of it is scattered..."

His voice trailed off, and Ajari, behind me, finished for him. "You'll know."

I walked up to the ladder.

Focus, he says, I told myself. *Send all your ki to your hands and feet.*

I took a deep breath, and felt something inside me drop, from just below my fast-beating heart to somewhere deep in my bowels.

"*On-kiru-kiru-mata-uji-yaku-yasei-sowaka,*" I recited.

With my hands, I took hold of one of the higher swords, gingerly, just enough to keep my balance without touching the blade.

"*On-kiru-kiru-mata-uji-yaku-yasei-sowaka.*"

I lifted my right foot, laid it carefully crosswise on the first blade, and tried to do as Buzen-bo had instructed: bring all my energy of body, mind, and spirit into the sole.

"*On-kiru-kiru-mata-uji-yaku-yasei-sowaka.*"

I lifted my left foot. My right felt no pain.

This is amazing! I thought. *I'm climbing barefoot up a ladder of swords! If only Oyuki and the others in Hara Castle could see me now!*

But the moment that thought arose, I felt a searing pain in my right foot. I quickly dropped my left to the ground, let go of the ladder, and with great trepidation, turned the sole of my right to examine it. A red line ran from toe to heel.

Buzen-bo flew down from his high perch to land at my side. He looked at my foot and waved his hand across my sole. When I looked again, the wound was healed, and I felt no pain.

"If you tell yourself to concentrate," he told me sternly, "that will break your concentration. Don't think.

Don't judge yourself, whether you're doing well or whether you're doing poorly. As you've just discovered, your body will tell you. Now, try it again. This time, keep all your ki here."

I turned back to the ladder. I laid my fingers on a blade, more tentatively than ever this time, now that I knew from firsthand experience how sharp they were. I laid my right foot crosswise on the bottom rung, and focused my energy on it. I tried to pick up my other foot, but fear kept it rooted to the ground.

"Whether you believe you can do it or you believe you can't," I heard Buzen-bo's voice, "you're right."

I closed my eyes, took a deep breath, and focused my ki. Reciting the chant, I lifted my left foot and laid it carefully on the next rung.

I felt no pain.

I climbed up another rung and recited the chant again. I did the same again, and again. The next thing I knew, I reached for a rung and my hand landed on rock. I stepped carefully up the last few rungs. When I opened my eyes, I was standing on top of the bluff.

"Maybe you're not completely hopeless after all," Buzen-bo said. That was the closest he had yet come to paying me a compliment.

* * *

For the next swordsmanship lesson, I squared off against Ajari.

"The defender has the advantage," Buzen-bo told me. "The attacker has to put his intention into the strike, and the defender can read his intention and react. And once your opponent is off balance, counterstrike at his vulnerable point."

I tried. But whatever I did, Ajari was ready for me.

"If your opponent becomes the mountain," Buzen-bo said, "you become the sea. If your opponent becomes the sea, you become the mountain."

He must have seen my blank look, for he went on: "Aren't you familiar with *The Book of Five Rings* by Miyamoto Musashi?"

I shook my head.

"How could you not be?" he demanded. "Musashi's book is holy writ for Japanese warriors."

A noise came from Ajari, which could have been a bird-like way of clearing his throat. "I don't believe it's been written yet, master."

Buzen-bo's expression suggested that he considered this a feeble excuse for not having read it. "Well, it will be soon. The idea is, stop doing what isn't working. If your opponent expects one tactic, use another. Keep him off guard. Learn to predict what he will do, but be unpredictable yourself."

No self, no mind, I told myself. *The mind, like a mirror, reflects with no intention. A clear mind can sense what the opponent intends to do before he does it.*

I waited for Ajari to attack. When he did, I parried and countered, but he was ready for me. He launched another attack, but I recognized it as the kind of feint he had used it before, and when his sword suddenly changed direction, I was ready. Clearly, Ajari was so taken aback that, for a split second, he wondered what to do next.

In that moment, I aimed a blow at his head. He raised his sword to block it, but I changed direction. My sword dealt him a tap on the shoulder.

I had done it! The first blow ever landed against Ajari!

Beaming, I turned to Buzen-bo. At that very moment, Ajari's wooden stick came down on my head.

"Hey!" I said, rubbing my head. "No fair!"

"When you go back to Hara Castle," Ajari said, "and rejoin the battle for real, what will your enemy's goal be? To play fair, or to kill you?"

The days wore on. I can't say I ever actually won a match against Ajari, but I became more and more able to hold my own against him.

"Well done," Buzen-bo said one day, after a duel that I was particularly proud of – which is to say, it took me significantly longer than usual to lose. "And I have something here for you."

He handed me a sword, in a sheath covered with tiger skin. When I drew the blade, I saw that it was a bit shorter and differently proportioned to the swords used by our ronin leaders. But even my untrained eye could tell that it was a masterpiece of the swordsmith's craft.

"This is a *tachi*," he explained, "slightly different from a samurai's *katana*. Yamabushi carry shorter weapons for use in confined spaces, and also because they might need to fight wild animals or cut their way through overgrown vegetation. Today, you'll have your first lesson with a real blade."

I saw that Ajari was armed, not with a sword, but with a bamboo stalk.

"Ready?" Buzen-bo asked.

I was about to answer his question with a question of my own: *Ready for what?* But before I could say anything, Ajari took the end of the bamboo stalk in his beak and blew. A small projectile flew out and hit me. On closer inspection, it proved to be a bean.

"The aim is to cut them," Buzen-bo said.

I swung, but couldn't hit. Ajari flitted this way and that, his wings flapping as he blew beans at me from all directions. I could barely keep turning to face him, let alone cut the beans in midair.

"Too fast!" I exclaimed in frustration.

"You're still attached to the idea of fast and slow," Buzen-bo said. "Nothing is fixed. Everything is always in flux. I shouldn't have to explain to you, of all people, that time doesn't flow at the same rate for everyone everywhere. You've been to Ryugujo."

I wondered how he knew. But before I could ask, he went on: "You know that a short time there was equivalent to a long time on the surface. And here in Tengudo, it's the reverse."

I felt a tremendous sense of relief. I hadn't, after all, walked into another time trap like the one in Ryugujo. I could take my time in Tengudo, and still return to Hara Castle in time for my training to be useful to our side.

"So you shouldn't have any trouble," Buzen-bo concluded, "wrapping your mind around the idea that *time is relative to your point of view.* Didn't some famous scientist from your part of the world say that once?"

When I failed to acknowledge, an expression of irritation crossed Buzen-bo's face, as it often did when he realized he had referred to something in the future. But he quickly put his slip to use: "There, you see? From your point of view, that hasn't happened yet. That only proves the point. Time is flexible. Use that flexibility to your advantage."

"How do I do that?"

"When do you feel time passes most quickly?"

Before I could answer, Ajari cut in: "I bet I know. When he's with that young lady who's always on his mind."

I blushed, I hoped not visibly.

"And when do you feel it passes most slowly?" Buzen-bo went on.

"I think I know the answer to that one too," said Ajari. "When he's listening to your lectures."

My blush deepened, but Buzen-bo laughed. "Very well, then." He took a seat, and began in the same droning voice he always used: "The history of Japan began approximately twenty-five hundred years ago, with the first Emperor, Jimmu."

I stood, sword at the ready, as he droned on and on. It really was as Ajari said: time felt as though it was going by at a slow crawl.

A movement from Ajari caught my attention. I looked in his direction to see a bean coming at me from his blowgun. But it seemed to be subject to the same dilatory effect as Buzen-bo's speech, because I could see it flying toward me in slow motion. I felt I had all the time in the world to raise my blade and cut it in half in mid-flight.

Ajari shot another, and then another. I cut them the same way. He began shooting two at a time, and then three at a time. As long as Buzen-bo was droning on, I never let one of them reach the ground whole.

"Well done," Buzen-bo said when the exercise was concluded. "Now, can you do it without my interminable voice slowing down time for you?"

I tried. But without his lecture, time seemed to revert to its ordinary speed.

The next lesson was archery. I reached for the bow as always, but Ajari grabbed it before I could.

"This is where you stand," said Buzen-bo, pointing to a patch of ground directly in front of the target.

I looked at him in sudden apprehension. Either I was expected to shoot the target from a ridiculously short distance – or I was expected to *be* the target.

Buzen-bo's next words confirmed my fears. "One of the secrets of the yamabushi is how to harden his body against arrows. Place your hand in front of the target."

I hesitated, then did as instructed. Since I was right-handed, I used my left hand.

"It needs to be your right," said Buzen-bo. "The left hand takes in, and the right hand gives out. For this exercise, you need to send out your ki."

I swapped hands. My palm prickled, as if my skin knew what was going to happen and was trying to ask my brain, *Are you serious?*

"Recite the chant of protection. As you do, send the ki flowing out of your hand as if it were a mighty waterfall."

I recited, "*On-kiru-kiru-mata-uji-yaku-yasei-sowaka.*" As I did, I tried to form the image Buzen-bo had described. A mighty waterfall was flowing from me, all right, but it wasn't made of ki from the palm of my hand – more like sweat from the rest of my body.

At a signal from Buzen-bo, Ajari drew back his bow and released the arrow.

Instinctively, I jerked my hand out of the way. The arrow embedded itself in the target.

Buzen-bo gave me an annoyed look. "Again."

I put my hand in place, and tried to focus on the meditation. I heard the twang of Ajari's bowstring.

If you don't know how it feels to have an arrow pierce the palm of your hand and pin it to a target…well, all I can say is, even if you don't feel you have anything else to be thankful for, you can be thankful for that.

I screamed in pain and looked in alarm at the shaft embedded in my hand and the blood dripping from it. The even more alarming part was that I could see no way to extract it without making the damage worse.

Buzen-bo pulled the arrow out. As I expected, the arrowhead hurt as much going out as it had going in. Perhaps more so, because I was anticipating it this time.

He held my hand in his for a moment. When he let go, it was completely whole and I felt no pain. There was still blood on my palm, but no wounds or scars or anything to show how it had gotten there.

"Again," said Buzen-bo unemotionally, as though nothing worse had happened to me than a tap from a wooden sword.

I put my trembling hand in place. I tried to focus on the meditation Buzen-bo had taught me, but more than half my mind was thinking of how much it would hurt if I failed.

Ajari let fly. It hurt exactly as much as I thought it would.

Again, Buzen-bo pulled the arrow out and healed my hand with a touch.

"You're anticipating," he said. "You're thinking of the worst outcome. You're imagining how much it will hurt if you fail."

I realized at that moment that I had never learned the Japanese for "No kidding."

"Those thoughts are blocking the flow of your ki," he went on. "If you dwell on the prospect of failure, you invite it. You need to be sending the full force of your ki out of your body. Concentrate on that and forget about the arrow."

Easy for you to say, I thought. I tried, but I couldn't stop myself from wincing as I heard the bow twang. Even knowing that Buzen-bo could heal me with a touch didn't make it any less painful when the arrow went home.

Buzen-bo heaved a disappointed sigh. "Let's take a break and do some meditation. Have a seat."

I gratefully sat down on a nearby rock.

"Close your eyes and put your hands together in the *gejishi* mudra."

I did as instructed, twisting my hands together in the complex gesture that involved crossing my forefingers unnaturally under my middle fingers.

"Picture this," he said. "At the lowest point of your trunk, where your legs meet, there's a doorway. Below it, there's a pipe running all the way down to the center of the earth. Open it, and the molten rock wells up into your body. At the top of your head, there's another doorway. Above it, there's a funnel that collects the fire from the sun and all the stars. Open it, and all the fire of the universe pours down into your body. The fire of the sun and the fire of the earth meet right at your heart and create an explosion. You become the molten rock. You become the fire of the stars. The fire radiates out from you, turning everything that comes near you to ashes. As you chant, imagine yourself becoming one with the fire."

I chanted and tried to envision the image he described.

And suddenly, I found I could.

I *did* feel something open at the top of my head. I *did* feel something open where my rear met the rock. I *did* feel fire flowing through me. I would have been surprised, except that fire can't feel surprise. All I could feel was a heat that would consume me if I were made of flesh, but I wasn't. I was made of molten rock from the center of the earth, and fire from the stars.

"Do you think you're ready to try again?" came Buzen-bo's voice.

"Yes," I said. And at that moment, I truly meant it.

"Open your eyes," he said. "Look down."

I did. An arrow was lying on the ground in front of me.

"The arrow hit you," Buzen-bo said with a smile, "and you didn't even notice."

I hadn't felt anything. Looking all over my body, I saw no wounds or other marks. I could only take Buzen-bo's word for it that the arrow had hit me at all.

"Now," said Buzen-bo, "it's only a matter of doing consciously what you've already done unconsciously. Let's do it again."

I put my hand in front of the target, closed my eyes, and chanted. I could still feel the fire coursing through me. I was so focused on the chant that I couldn't even hear the twang of the bowstring.

"Open your eyes," said Buzen-bo.

I did. My hand was whole, and an arrow was lying on the ground in front of the target.

Buzen-bo wore a broader grin than I had ever seen on him before. "Let's call that good for today."

* * *

That night, I was out and about again, and saw Buzen-bo peering into the reflecting pool. Again, the sky in it was a different color than the one overhead. But when Buzen-bo looked up and saw me coming, the image returned immediately to normal.

"Time is relative, you said," I said as I approached him. "You can see things that, from my point of view, haven't happened yet."

Buzen-bo nodded.

I dreaded asking the next question, but I couldn't let the opportunity pass me by.

"Can you see how the battle for Hara Castle is going to end?"

Buzen-bo gave me a stern look. "If you were to go into battle knowing your side was destined to win, you would be complacent. If you were to go into battle knowing your side was destined to lose, you would despair. In neither case would you fight to the best of your ability. A warrior must always fight as if everything depended on him."

I bowed. "Sorry, master."

Buzen-bo returned his attention to the scrying pool. "In any case, the outcome is cloudy. I can only tell you this: The battle for Hara Castle will be won when a million rocks have been hurled from its battlements."

"Can I see Hara Castle?" I pleaded. "Just once?"

His stern look returned. "We already talked about this. You've only just learned to keep all your ki in one place. If I were to help you yield to the temptation to send it off in multiple directions again, I would be cutting my nose off to spite my face."

"Fine," I said. "I understand. Not every tengu is proficient enough in the art of scrying to teach it to humans."

His eyes suddenly looked as though they were about to pop out to the tip of his nose. "What did you say?"

"There's no shame in admitting it," I went on. "Some tengu are more proficient in some of the mystical arts than others. Performing it takes one level of skill, but imparting it to others takes a whole different level. If it's beyond your ability, that's perfectly understandable. I can always go to Mount Kurama and ask Sojo-bo."

"Now you listen here!" Buzen-bo thundered. "Sojo-bo might be a great military tactician, but when it comes to the mystical arts, his nose isn't big enough to get into a sneezing contest with me! Come here and sit down!"

I sat by his side, suppressing a triumphant grin.

"Your ki is not confined to your body," he said. "You can project it outside your body, and use devices like this pool to amplify your senses. All it takes is for your spirit to be an integrated whole, and your mind observing it, still part of it but separate enough from it to master it." He stood. "There, I've told you everything you need to know. If you can't do it, that's on your nose, not mine."

I stayed there and meditated. I focused, with all my mind, on an image of Hara Castle, until I could practically see the warriors going about their training, the cooking fires burning, the chickens – by now as scrawny as their owners – strutting between the huts.

I opened my eyes. The reflection in the pool was unchanged.

I tried again. This time, I tried to project my spirit toward Hara Castle, not as I imagined it, but as it was.

When I opened my eyes, the reflection in the pool was still dark. I thought I had failed again. But when I looked more closely, I realized I was looking at Hara Castle by night.

I've done it! I thought. And of course, the moment this thought crossed my mind, the image began to fade.

Quickly, I closed my eyes, refocused my senses, and opened them again. The image came back.

If I had been hoping to catch a glimpse of Oyuki, I was disappointed. At this hour, scarcely anyone was stirring except for the warriors on night watch – and, unbeknownst to them, Don Protasio in the tenshu.

A movement in the courtyard caught my eye. Exerting the power of my ki, I tried to move in for a closer look.

The figure was carrying a bow and arrow. Its head was swathed in cloth, but even without that, distance and darkness would have made it impossible to see its features. Still, I distinctly saw it take a furtive look around, and when it saw that the coast was clear, raise the bow. When it drew back the arrow, I saw that there was something odd about the shape, and realized that it had a letter tied to it.

The figure released the arrow-letter towards the besiegers' camp, then hurriedly fled from the courtyard as though determined to avoid detection.

The image vanished. I sat back on my heels, scarcely believing what I had just seen. Someone – someone very anxious not to be seen by anyone on our side – had just sent a message to the enemy.

We had a traitor in our midst.

Chapter 14: The Orochi

The next morning, I told Buzen-bo what I had seen.

"I'm sorry, master," I said. "But I have to go back and warn them."

Buzen-bo gave me a look of utter disbelief. "What?" he demanded. "Now? You've come so far, but there's still so much farther to go. Other weapons besides the bow and sword. How to defeat an armed opponent when you're unarmed yourself. Mastery of fire. The secrets of crossing the boundary between human and beast."

"I'm sorry," I said again. "I wish I could. But if we really do have a traitor among us, passing inside information to the enemy, the castle could fall in a matter of days. I need to be there."

"Right now, you're at the most dangerous point in your training. You've mastered the fundamentals well enough to think you know all you need to know, but you have yet to learn how much you have yet to learn. If you drop everything and go back now, just because you thought something smelled fishy, you're more likely to be a liability to your side than an asset."

"If the castle falls without my having struck even a single blow for our side, everything you've taught me will have been for nothing."

"For nothing?" Buzen-bo echoed incredulously. "The outcome of this one little battle, whether Hara Castle stands or falls – is that the limit of your vision? Can you not see beyond the end of your nose? Do you not understand how little this matters in the grand sweep of history?"

"Forgive me, master, but I don't care about the grand sweep of history. I care about my companions in that castle."

But Buzen-bo was so worked up by now that I doubted he heard me. "My purpose is to shape you into a warrior for the world!" he ranted on. "For the ages! Such that when future generations of British schoolchildren open their history books, they'll see the name of Simon Grey right alongside those of Sir Francis Drake and Lord Nelson!"

Of course, I recognized the first of those, as the admiral who had led the British fleet to victory over the Spanish Armada. But as for the second, I could only guess that once again, Buzen-bo had absent-mindedly referred to someone who had yet to be born.

"Master," I said, "I'm sorry, but I honestly have no desire to see my name among theirs. I've seen enough of war to know that I don't want to see any more. All I want is to see the end of this battle, go back to England, and live out my days. I'd much rather read history books than have my name written in them."

Buzen-bo heaved a sigh through his cavernous nostrils that bent the grass at his feet.

"Fine," he muttered sullenly. "Go back and throw your life away in a desperate last stand with those rebels. No skin off my nose."

*   *   *

That night, I went to sleep in my cave. I had a vague dream of drifting gently through the air, looking down on Shimabara and the peak of Mount Unzen from a great height. The next morning, I woke up in my barracks in Hara Castle.

I might have thought the entire journey to Tengudo had all been a dream, if not for two things. First, I still had the sword Buzen-bo had given me. Second, the pallet beside mine that had once belonged to James was empty.

The first thing to do, I thought, was to find my commanding officer and report for duty. When I found Yamada, he looked surprised and delighted to see me.

"Simon!" he exclaimed. "When did you get back? And how? And did you actually meet the tengu?"

I answered this barrage of questions out of order. "Yes, sir, I did. I got back sometime last night, I'm not sure how." I paused. "How long have I been away, sir?"

"A couple of weeks."

I had lost track of the days in Tengudo, but it felt as though I had been there for several months. Buzen-bo had been right. Time really did pass differently in Tengudo than here below.

"What happened to Jinzaemon?" Yamada asked. The somber tone of his voice suggested he had already guessed the answer.

I looked down. "We ran into some of the Shogun's guards on the road between Hinokuma Castle and Mount Hiko. I managed to escape, but James...I mean, Jinzaemon didn't, sir."

Yamada bowed his head and crossed himself.

"I'll tell Shiro you're back safely," he said. "I'd love to hear more about your journey, but perhaps I should wait until we can call an assembly. Everyone will be eager to hear what you learned."

I paused a moment. "Sir? There's something else I should tell you. In confidence."

"Of course."

I looked around to make sure that no one could overhear.

"From Tengudo," I said, "I could see Hara Castle by magic."

He looked slightly taken aback, but went on listening.

"And I saw someone on our side, under cover of darkness, send an arrow-letter to the enemy."

Yamada thought a moment. "Did you see his face?"

I shook my head. "It was covered. Whoever it was, they were very anxious not to be seen."

"No distinguishing marks, or anything? Could you tell how tall he was?"

"From what I could see, neither taller nor shorter than most of the men in the castle. Nothing else to distinguish him."

Yamada was silent for a while.

"Do you have any idea who it might have been?" I asked.

He cast a glance at the tenshu. "I have my suspicions," he said darkly. "But it won't do to say anything without proof. I'll inquire into this, but it has to be handled with discretion." He turned his attention back to me. "Have you told anyone else?"

"Just you, sir."

"Until I find some hard evidence, I'll ask you to keep it that way."

* * *

Dark clouds roiled over Hara Castle. The air felt oppressively thick. Every movement seemed to take twice the usual amount of effort. It was like a muggy summer day, except that instead of being swelteringly hot, it was soul-chillingly cold. If a storm was about to break, I wished it would hurry up and get on with it.

Everyone's mood appeared to be as dark and heavy as the sky. At first, I put it down to the strange weather, but the more snippets of news I caught, the more I understood. Our provisions, never plentiful, had been stretched even more thinly. And as our side was wearing down, theirs was building up. Of the whispered rumors I heard, one was that Japan's most famous duelist, who had spent his life traveling throughout Japan leaving a trail strewn with the bodies of samurai rash enough to challenge him, had been persuaded to come out of retirement and lend his sword to the Shogun's side.

Yamada had arranged with Shiro for me to give a demonstration of what I had learned in Tengudo. As people began to gather in the archery range, I spotted Oyuki in conversation with the other women in the corps of archers. I stood near her, trying to catch her eye, and made my presence more obvious until the only way she could fail to notice me was if she was intentionally ignoring me. One of the others saw me and gave her a cue.

She glanced in my direction. "*Okaeri*," she said with a brief nod. "Welcome back." She said it as if I had simply nipped into the nearest town for a bag of rice, rather than having just returned from a perilous mission to an enchanted realm rarely seen by mortal eyes. Then, she turned back to the others and continued the conversation.

When everyone was assembled, Shiro called for order. "Brothers and sisters," he said, "Simon has just returned from his mission to Mount Hiko, where he learned the mystical arts of the yamabushi under the same great tengu who taught Kobayakawa Takakage. He's here to pass on these secrets to us. Please give him your undivided attention."

Shiro stepped aside and gave me the stage. I had never been in a position to teach anyone anything before, and facing a courtyard full of my comrades-in-arms, with everyone looking at me in rapt expectation except for the skeptical Sanai and the scowling Chijiwa, I felt more nervous and self-conscious than I ever had facing blades or arrows in Tengudo. I had no idea where to begin.

"Um…" was my eloquent introduction. I stalled for time by asking, "Well, first, does anyone have any questions?"

Komagine's voice, as usual, made itself heard above all others. "What did you learn about musketry and artillery?"

This was the most awkward possible question to start with. For all Buzen-bo's minute knowledge of present and future events, when it came to weapons, he seemed stuck in the past. Now that I thought of it, I couldn't recall him ever giving any sign that he knew there were such things as firearms.

"Well…actually, we concentrated on more traditional weapons, like the bow and sword."

"What about the bow, then?" asked the archery master.

I gratefully picked up a bow and arrow, and recalled Buzen-bo's archery lessons.

"The bow is made of wood and bamboo," I began. Somehow, when the words came out of my mouth in the courtyard of Hara Castle, they didn't sound like such a profound revelation as they did when Buzen-bo had said them in Tengudo.

"But when your spirit infuses it," I went on hurriedly, "its mystery will not be the same. When you use strength to draw the bow, you and the bow are in opposition. But when you become one with the bow, when you enter the state of no-self and no-mind, when it feels as though your spirit fills heaven and earth, the distance between arrow and target is filled like an empty shell."

Again, the words didn't sound anywhere near as impressive coming from me as from Buzen-bo. Deciding that actions would speak louder than words, I notched an arrow to the bow.

I let fly.

The arrow struck the target dead center. This evoked some gasps of awe and applause from the rebels, and I began to take heart.

"Impressive," said the archery master. "Did you learn anything that could help an archer hit a moving target?"

"Umm..." The boost in confidence I had just felt disappeared as soon as it had come. "I was trained on a stationary target."

"Brilliant," said a sarcastic voice. Without looking, I recognized it as Sanai's. "I'm sure all the Shogun's soldiers will be obliging enough to hold still while we let our spirits fill heaven and earth, or whatever it is they're supposed to do."

A moment of awkward silence ensued. Ashizuka broke it by asking, "How about swordsmanship?"

I felt more confident here. "Swordsmanship is nothing more nor less than the practical application of the mysterious function of the essence of mind," I said, again echoing Buzen-bo. "Coming, it has no form. Going, it leaves no trace. When your opponent faces you, be completely at peace, without malice and without fear. Forget about life, forget about death, forget about your opponent, forget about yourself."

Sanai made an exasperated noise. "Not this mystical drivel again! What *techniques* did you learn?"

I shot him an annoyed glance. "The whole purpose of learning technique is to reach the point where you no longer think about technique. To achieve this state is a matter of training the ki. It cannot simply be passed on. The instructor can point the way, but the swordsman must walk the path himself."

Sanai scoffed and rolled his eyes. "By the time we've mastered the ki or whatever, the enemy will have cut us to pieces!"

I knew how Buzen-bo would reply to that. *You are still regarding life and death as separate. The essential first step on the path is to cut through the root of confusion of life and death.* But that was an easy thing to say to a warrior who had already pledged to live and die in the service of his lord. These people were not looking to achieve a warrior's mind that transcended life and death. They were looking to survive. And who could blame them?

"Perhaps someone could assist me in a demonstration?" I picked up a second wooden sword and extended it to Sanai. "Ashizuka Sanai, would you care to do the honors?"

Sanai made no move to take the sword. He said nothing, but looked down his nose with an expression that said very clearly: *You are not worthy of me.*

"Go on," I goaded him. "This is your chance to get me back for beating you to Itakura."

As I expected, he took the bait and the sword. Before we could even square off properly, he charged and swung at my head.

I could see it coming a mile away. I hadn't quite got the knack of slowing down time the way I had while listening to Buzen-bo's lecture, but against Sanai, I didn't even have to. I pivoted effortlessly out of the way as his sword sliced through the air.

"Is that the best the son of a samurai can do?" I taunted him.

Further enraged, he turned and charged back toward me. I parried his stroke as he sailed past me.

"Stay at the center of the circle," I said. "Move without moving, stand still without standing still. Stoke the passions in your opponent that cloud his judgment, but be completely at peace yourself. Predict his movements, but be unpredictable yourself. When your opponent becomes the sea, you become the mountain. When your opponent becomes the mountain, you become the sea."

Sanai raised his sword for another stroke. I landed a blow across his forearms which, if I had been using a real sword, would have left him with no hands to strike with. It took a moment for the audience to notice, but when they did, they let me know with gasps and applause.

"Care for a rematch?" I asked Sanai.

"Pah!" he spat, throwing the wooden sword contemptuously to the ground. "If we have to resort to swordplay, it will mean the enemy has already overrun the castle and it will be too late. What else have you got?"

Sanai let the question hang in the air for an awkward moment. Then, just as I was opening my mouth for an answer, he provided his own. "I heard yamabushi can harden their bodies against arrows, sword blades, even musket balls. Is that one of the secrets you learned?"

It was the question I had been dreading. I had only accomplished that feat once, practically by accident, and I was far from confident that I could perform it on demand. But Sanai had issued the challenge, and something in me refused to back away from it.

"It is," I said.

"Now *that* would be a demonstration worth seeing."

I stood beside one of the archery targets and put my hand – my left this time, just in case – in front of the bull's-eye, as the master archer stood back and nocked an arrow to his bow.

I closed my eyes. While silently reciting the *On-kiru-kiru-mata-uji-yaku-yasei-sowaka* mantra, I practiced the meditation Buzen-bo had taught me. Energy from the stars pouring down through a funnel into the top of my head. Energy from the earth's core welling up from under my feet. The two forces meeting at my heart and sending a burst of energy radiating from my palms.

It didn't come.

I tried again. *Stars, head, fire, heart, hands.*

I felt a slight warmth in my hands, but nothing like the flames that seemed to engulf me when I tried this meditation in Tengudo.

I tried yet again. *Forget the audience, forget the archer, forget Sanai, forget everything.*

The harder I tried to forget them, the more keenly conscious of them I became. In particular, I was acutely aware of impatient murmurs beginning to spread through the audience. I couldn't catch everything they were saying, but the general meaning was clear: *Is he ever going to get on with it?*

I tried one last time. *Shut out all distractions. Concentrate only on focusing your ki.*

And finally, I felt some of the energy I had felt in Tengudo. Not as keenly, but enough for the purpose.

"Ready," I said before I could change my mind.

The master archer drew back and let fly.

And if his arrow had struck me square on the palm, who knows but that I might have succeeded in deflecting it. Unfortunately for me, his aim was not as good as Ajari's. The arrow struck me on the forearm, piercing through it and nearly transfixing it to the target.

I screamed in agony. As murmurs of concern and alarm spread through the audience, Gensatsu pushed his way through the crowd and ran to my side. I knew he would do his best, but I knew with equal certainty that he didn't have Buzen-bo's ability to heal with a single touch.

The demonstration came to an abrupt end as Gensatsu laid gentle hands on my shoulders and guided me to the infirmary. As we went, I heard Sanai's contemptuous voice behind me.

"That's all the secret knowledge you've got for us? I'd rather have Jinzaemon back."

His words pierced me more deeply than any arrow ever could. I was still heartbroken from James' death, and couldn't keep from blaming myself. To hear my internal voice turned external, and amplified in front of the entire assembly through the mouth of Sanai, helped matters not at all.

* * *

I'll spare details of how Gensatsu got the arrow out, except to say that, as I had confidently expected, it hurt as much coming out as going in.

"What were you thinking?" he demanded as he dressed my wound. Before I could answer, he went on, "You may not believe this, but you were extremely lucky. The arrow didn't break any bones or nick any major blood vessels. You won't be using that arm for a while, but in a few weeks, you should make a full recovery."

But how long, I wondered, would it take to recover from my humiliation?

It was frustrating to know I would be out of the action, but I didn't feel I would have had much to contribute in any case. I couldn't tell whether I was coming down with something or whether it was just in my mind after my disastrous demonstration, but I had no energy. I felt listless and sluggish, and every move I made took more than the usual effort, as though my body had become heavier, or as though I were moving through water instead of air. I had no appetite either, but perhaps this was just as well, since our provisions had dwindled to the point where one person's ration amounted to little more than a mouthful of rice and half a bowl of thin soup.

More than that, I felt hopeless. I wondered how I could have been so abysmally stupid as to believe that this rebellion could possibly succeed, or that I could possibly make a difference to the outcome, or that Oyuki could possibly see anything in me to make her return my feelings for her, or that I could ever possibly make it home to England. I tried to distract myself by focusing on happy memories from my past, but whenever I did, a mocking inner voice intruded. *Enjoy the memories,* it cackled, *because they're all that's left. You'll never experience happy moments like those ever again.*

I left the infirmary and headed back toward the barracks. A column of black, acrid smoke rose from the direction of the tsume-no-maru to join the dark clouds overhead, making me feel a wave of nausea every time the wind wafted it in my direction. I supposed they were burning some particularly noxious type of rubbish.

A figure carrying a bow walked across my path. It was Oyuki, presumably on her way back from archery training. Her gaze was focused on the ground ahead of her, and she gave no sign of noticing that I was there.

This hardly felt like the most auspicious day to talk to her, but there was no telling when I would get another chance.

"Oyuki?" I called.

She turned to look at me, and suddenly cringed, making a sound like "*Iyaaaugh!*" and a face that looked as if she had seen a giant spider.

Well, my gloomy inner voice told me. *Just as I thought.*

But a moment later, I realized my impression had been entirely correct. She *had* seen a giant spider, which I now saw too – a black and yellow striped one, as big as my hand, scuttling quickly across the ground between us as if on an urgent errand.

"Sorry," she said. "It startled me."

This was not the most encouraging start to this conversation, and even without it, I had been unsure as to what I would say. "Oyuki," I finally said, "before I went off to Mount Hiko, I didn't get the chance to see you…and apologize."

The corners of her mouth turned down, and her hand made a dismissive gesture. "Don't worry about it." The tone of her voice echoed the meaning of every word but the first.

"I should explain myself," I said. "Not excuse, just explain."

She turned her face away with a one-shouldered shrug. "Why bother?" she asked the wind. "What does it matter what you did or didn't do, and why? Or any of us? We're all going to die here. None of us is leaving this castle alive."

I had been prepared for anger. I was ready to take whatever she said, and apologize as many times as necessary until her anger was spent. But I had no idea what to say to this hopelessness. Especially since, in my current state of mind, I couldn't bring myself to gainsay her.

"You can't be sure of that," I finally said. But my voice sounded feeble even to my own ears.

"How else could it end?" she asked, still not looking at me. "The other side can just keep bringing in reinforcements until they overrun us or we starve to death. And even if, by a miracle, we *did* make it out alive, where would we go? My father's surely dead by now. We're alone on this island. It's death if we're found here, and there's no way off. One way or another, this island will be our grave."

I plumbed the depths of my mind to try to find some words to encourage her. But none came. *She's right,* said the voice inside me. *She's telling the truth you don't want to face.*

A sudden warning blast on a conch shell saved me from having to make a reply. Others around the castle took up the alarm.

By instinct, we rushed for our battle stations. But when we got close to the ramparts, we saw no more activity in the besiegers' camp than usual. No guns were firing, no arrows were flying, no soldiers were scaling the castle walls.

Oyuki glanced over her shoulder. "Behind us," she said.

The commotion seemed to be coming from the tsume-no-maru, near the source of the column of smoke. When we drew near, I saw something that would have made me think hunger was giving me waking nightmares, except that the multitudes of people screaming and running away clearly saw the same thing I did.

It looked like a cross between a giant snake and an equally giant scorpion. It was so big around that three tall men, holding hands in a circle, might have encompassed its girth – if it ever stopped thrashing long enough for them to try – and so long that its head could be in one of the courtyards and its tail in another. The front of its body had eight legs like a scorpion, and a pair of waving pincers that looked as though they could catch a man and cut him right in half. The rest of it was splotched in red, blue, and black, up to the angry red sting at the tip of its tail. It surveyed its prey through slitted pupils in eyes the size of barrels, and not just two of them – I saw several smaller pairs underneath the main pair. Its long red tongue flicked out, tasting the air, or perhaps licking its lips in anticipation at the feast before it.

As the noncombatants screamed and ran, the fighters rushed to the scene with their weapons. Ashizuka took command. "Swordsmen, spearmen, stand back and make ready!" he shouted. "Musketeers, archers, fire at will!"

Muskets cracked and strings twanged. The musket balls and some of the arrows seemed to strike their mark, but those that struck at an angle glanced harmlessly off its scales.

Oyuki drew back an arrow, took aim, and released. The arrow flew swift and true, and struck the creature in one of its enormous eyes.

It reared up on its two back sets of legs, as its front two clawed the air and its pincers waved wildly. Its mouth opened wide, revealing fangs as long and sharp as samurai swords. From its throat emerged a deep hiss, rising in pitch and intensity: *HoooAAAH!* It would clearly have been screaming in agony if it had vocal cords to scream with.

From the curved stinger in its tail, a jet of liquid sprayed out. Its tail swung this way and that so wildly that the drops of venom flying from it scattered over a wide area. I heard cries of pain from those within the sweep of the spray.

Oyuki was still standing firm, fitting another arrow to her bowstring.

I moved on instinct, without pausing to think. I stepped in front of her before she could draw her bow. I took another glance at the serpent-scorpion, to make sure any strike from it would hit me before her.

That proved to be a terrible mistake. A few drops of its venom hit me squarely in the face.

A burning pain seared my eyes. With a cry, I turned my face away and shut them, but the damage was already done. When I opened them again, I could see no more than I could with them closed.

"Simon!" I heard Oyuki's voice behind me. "Are you all right?"

"I can't see," I said, as the horrible realization took hold of me. "I'm blind!"

Chapter 15: Aragamigado

riendly hands took hold of me and guided me to the infirmary, where Gensatsu flushed my eyes with water several times. It eased the sting, and a salve he applied to my face eased it further, but I could still see nothing. He tied a bandage around my eyes and left me on a pallet to ponder my fate.

Alone, dark, and comfortless, my thoughts naturally turned to the worst. What if my eyesight never returned? In that case, any hope I had cherished of seeing England and my family again was gone forever. Even if, by a miracle, I made it home to them, I would never *see* their faces, or my house, or the white cliffs of Dover, or another sunrise, or another sunset, or another flower, or Oyuki's face, ever again.

"Simon," came Gensatsu's voice, mercifully breaking into my dark thoughts. "There's someone here to see you. On your right."

I turned, with a faint stirring of hope in my heart. But the voice I heard was not the one I had been wishing for.

"Hello, Simon." It was Shiro.

"Hello, sir," I said, still using the honorific by which even the most senior commanders addressed him.

"That was a very brave thing you did," he said.

I acknowledged his compliment with a nod. "Thank you."

"Can I say a prayer for you?"

215

I turned my head toward him. "Don't tell me you can restore my sight just by spitting in the dirt?"

Shiro gave a mild chuckle. "I'm sorry to say, that's a miracle I never learned how to perform."

"Go ahead, then," I said, although it wouldn't have been the best time to ask me how much faith I placed in the power of prayer.

He laid a gentle hand over my eyes and intoned an *orasho*. I had to admit, the touch of his hand felt warm and comforting, and the sound of his high, clear voice calmed my heart. Whether he really had a more direct line of communication to heaven than the rest of us was an open question, but he undoubtedly had the gift of making people believe he did.

"What happened to the monster?" I asked.

"It crawled back into its hole. We've sealed it off. Tomorrow morning, some of our warriors are going to go in and try to dispatch it." He paused a moment. "Simon, I don't see you often, so I want to take this chance to say thanks. You were swept up in this battle against your will, but even so, you've always gone above and beyond the call of duty. Our chances would be much worse without you."

"It's kind of you to say so," I said. "But I don't feel very valuable right now. What does a blind boy have to offer your cause?"

"You're talking as if a person's worth were based only on how much they can contribute. That's how Matsukura and his lot would think. They see things only through the lens of this world, not through the eyes of Deus. To him, each of us is equally beloved."

I scoffed. "Ask anyone in this castle, and they'd probably say some are more beloved by Deus than others. And they'd look in your direction when they said it."

"They flatter me," Shiro said, with a smile in his voice. "Perhaps Deus has assigned me a task that's a bit out of the ordinary. But at the end of the day, I'm a child of

Deus like any other, no more and no less precious in his sight than you or anyone else."

I suddenly felt closer to him than I had since our walk together on the road to Fukae, which felt like a lifetime ago. For a moment, I could forget that he was the supreme general, or the savior of Shimabara, or whatever other titles people called him. We were just two young men, only a year or two apart in age, having a conversation.

"Shiro?" I asked.

"Yes, Simon?" If he was at all surprised by my casual use of his name, his voice gave no sign.

"What are you going to do when this is over?"

He was silent long enough to make me wonder if he had given the question much thought.

"We have to win first," he finally answered. "After that...well, I'll go wherever Deus leads me."

"Do you ever think of settling down someday?" I asked. "Getting married, raising a family?" I circled obliquely around the question that had been burning in my mind but I could never ask out loud: *Are you in love with Oyuki?*

"To tell the truth, I don't think much about the future," he said. "I suppose, if I had been born in another age, I might have gone into the priesthood. But that's not exactly what you would call a viable career option these days. Unless I could find some way to go to Roma, which I would love...but then I could never come back to Japan. For now, I just live each day doing what Deus requires of me. Sufficient unto the day is the work thereof." He patted my arm. "You're the one with something to go back to when this is over."

I devoutly hoped that was still true.

"And by the grace of Deus, we'll see that you get there," he went on. "You and Oyuki."

It was the first time I had heard him put our names together like that. Hearing them from the mouth of the

Chosen One made me feel for a moment as though her destiny and mine really were entwined.

Before I could reply, I heard the door slide open and felt a rush of chill air from outside. When Shiro spoke again, his voice sounded slightly more distant, as if he had turned his head to face the newcomer. "Speaking of which."

"Hello, Simon," came a voice on my left.

My heart leapt. This time, it *was* the one I most wanted to hear.

"Well, I'll leave you to it," said Shiro after a pause. "Again, Simon, my deepest thanks."

I heard the door open and close again as Shiro left, and the rustle of Oyuki's kimono as she knelt by my pallet.

"How are your eyes?" she asked. "Has Gensatsu said anything?"

"Not yet. Would you believe, he doesn't seem to have much experience treating people blinded by the venom of a giant serpent-scorpion."

There was a moment of what would have been silence, if it hadn't been for my heart pounding so hard that I felt sure Oyuki could hear.

"Thank you," she finally said, "for putting yourself in danger to protect me."

"You've done the same for me. Many times."

There was another pause, which Oyuki again broke. "Oh, by the way. Obotan passed on your message, and this. I suppose I should give it back to you."

I couldn't see what she meant by *this*, but when she pressed an object into my hand, I knew by the feeling that it was the tamatebako. My fingers started to curl around it, but then I opened my hand again.

"Perhaps you'd best hold on to it for the time being," I said.

"Otohime gave it to you."

"She gave it to *us*. And I don't exactly feel I can be trusted with it."

"Why do you say that?"

I took a deep breath. I didn't see anything for it but to tell her the truth.

"That day, before I left for Mount Hiko – it wasn't the first time I thought about opening it. If it contains the time we spent in Ryugujo, I thought, it could make me instantly into a grown man. And we've been caught up in such huge events, and I felt so powerless to do anything. I felt like…well, exactly what I am: a boy who somehow blundered into a place where men were making history. The temptation was almost too great to resist. I didn't give any thought to the consequences for you. Or even for myself, now that I think about it. What would I gain by walking around in a thirty-year-old body if I was still only fourteen at heart, and hadn't had the ordinary chance to grow into it? I put myself at a terrible risk, and what's far worse, you too. It was a foolish, foolish thing even to think of, and I'm sorry."

Her response to my confession was a long silence. More than anything, I wished I could see her face.

"Well," she finally said, "I have some idea how you feel. You were very kind and never blamed me for what happened, but I've been constantly feeling that I got us into this. And there's been precious little I've been able to do to get us out. You're the one who's been on the front lines with the warriors, or training with the tengu. I've been in the rear guard. So, if you were feeling desperate to do anything that might give you a little more power over our destiny…well, I can certainly understand."

"Is there such a thing as 'our destiny' anymore?" I couldn't help asking. "Even if we survive this battle, if my eyesight is completely gone, I'm just a burden to you. What am I going to do, smell my way to England? You're better off without me."

"Don't talk like that," she admonished me sternly. "Whatever we face, we face it together. We've gone through too much together already for that to change now."

"Thank you," I said, from the heart. "I just feel so small. So helpless. So alone."

I felt the touch of her hand on my arm. A warmth quickly spread from there to envelop my whole body.

"Small, maybe," she said. "But 'helpless' has never been a word I would use for you. And as long as I'm alive, you'll never be alone."

Her hand lingered on my arm a moment longer before she took it away. I wanted to say something, but my heart was so full I couldn't find any words.

"Rest well," she said. "I'll see you tomorrow."

I heard her receding footsteps, and the sliding of the door. A blast of chill air came in as she left, but strangely, I didn't mind the cold at all.

I had no idea how long I lay there in darkness, or when I fell asleep. I only knew that I dreamed of England and my family. And when I was on the cusp of waking, and knew the dream for what it was, the thought pierced my brain like a barbed arrow: *From now on, the only sights you ever see will be in dreams.*

I tried to hold on to the dream for just a few moments longer, but of course, the image faded as consciousness returned. But when I opened my eyes behind the bandages, I saw a solid field not of black, but of dark red.

"*Sensei!*" I called.

Gensatsu was at my side in a moment. "What is it, Simon?"

"Take off my bandage! I think my sight might be coming back!"

He laid a cautious hand on my arm. "Simon, let's not rush. Rest is the most important..."

"Take it off! Or I'll take it off myself!"

After a moment's hesitation, Gensatsu helped me to sit up, untied the bandage, and began to unwind it. With each layer he unwound, my heart leapt higher as the red light grew brighter. Finally, as he peeled off the last layer and I opened my eyes, I could see his silhouette in the faint light before dawn.

I sat up. Gensatsu laid a restraining hand on me. "Simon, you need to…"

I shook off his hand, stood up, and made my way out of the infirmary. To the west, towering above the enemy camp, I saw the hulking form of Mount Unzen. To the east, I saw the outlines of the huts, and the towering form of the tenshu. None of them had ever looked so beautiful.

Maybe, I thought, Amakusa Shiro really could perform miracles. Or maybe Oyuki was herself a miracle. But, the more rational part of my brain reminded me, the most likely explanation was that the effects of the monster's venom were temporary.

Hardly anyone was stirring. If I hurried, I thought, I might be able to see Don Protasio before sunrise.

I made my way to the tenshu and found his chamber. "Don Protasio," I said, "there's something important I need to ask you. Have you ever had to deal with monsters under the castle?"

"I beg your pardon?"

I told him about the serpent-scorpion. His eyes widened in alarm as he listened.

"Under the castle, there's a cave," he finally said. "We called it Aragamigado, the Cave of the Fierce God."

I stared at him wide-eyed. "You mean this creature has been living under the castle the whole time we've been here? And you never thought this was worth telling us?"

Don Protasio swiveled his shoulders from side to side – the nearest, I gathered, that he could come to shaking his head without the risk of dislodging it. "The cave was named after a spider spirit believed to live there. But this is the first I've ever heard of such an *orochi*."

I made note of the name. "Where did it come from, then?"

"My fear is that it was summoned."

221

"By whom?"

"I believe that when the latest round of reinforcements arrived in the Shogunate camp, they had among them a *gunshi* from the Bureau of Onmyodo."

I had never heard the word *gunshi*, but I knew about *onmyodo*, the Way of Light and Shadow, the Japanese magical arts. I had previously crossed paths with the onmyoji who served as a personal advisor to the former Shogun, and I had barely escaped from that encounter alive. "What's a gunshi?"

"An onmyoji who specializes in military matters."

"I don't suppose you can tell us anything about how to defeat this...orochi?"

"I've never had to deal with such a creature," he said. "But you say it's a cross between a snake and a scorpion? Neither of those care much for fire, smoke, or the smell of cedar."

"Thank you," I said. "That's useful to know."

"And they say if arrows are moistened with human spittle, they will be especially effective against monsters. Oh, one other important thing. I've heard that some varieties of scorpion, possibly including the giant ones, can..."

Outside, a rooster crowed.

Distracted, I momentarily turned toward the window. When I turned back, Don Protasio was gone.

* * *

As I headed back out into the courtyard, the sun was rising over the mountains across the Ariake Sea. By its light, I saw a group of armed and armored ronin heading for the Tsume-no-maru. It included Ashizuka, Chijiwa, Mori, Yamada, and Gensatsu, along with four others whose names I hadn't learned.

I ran up to Ashizuka. He turned as I approached, looking surprised to see me. "Simon!" he said. "It's good to see you up and about so soon."

"Sir," I said, "are you heading for the lair of the orochi?"

He seemed surprised that I knew its name. "Yes."

"Let me go with you," I said, forgetting my manners until a moment later when I hastily added, "If you please, sir."

He gave me a look of astonishment, then shook his head. "Simon, you've just barely recovered. You need to rest."

"I can see just fine," I said. "And this is personal now. I want to get that thing back."

"I appreciate your eagerness," Ashizuka said, "but this is a job for samurai."

"You don't think a yamabushi is up to it?" I countered. "Besides, even samurai could benefit from some extra information. For example, have you brought any cedar branches?"

"Cedar?"

"The smoke is repellent to snakes and scorpions. Take me with you and I can give you more help."

Ashizuka gave me a look of resignation. "Very well," he said. "Go arm yourself." He turned to the others. "The rest of you, gather as many cedar branches as you can carry. Meet back here in half an hour."

I reported back to the meeting point as the ronin were reconvening. They carried straw baskets on their backs, of the kind people used to carry firewood, filled with green branches.

The entrance to the orochi's lair, I now saw, was the bare patch of ground I had first noticed in the tsume-no-maru. It had been covered with boards, with heavy stones piled on top of them. Grunting, we cleared away the stones. When we removed the boards underneath, a few wisps of the noxious black smoke curled out. I felt a sudden wave of nausea and hopelessness. I hastily moved upwind and took a deep breath of clean air.

When the vapor had dissipated, Ashizuka lowered himself into the hole. Chijiwa, Mori, and the rest followed. I was second from the last, with Yamada bringing up the rear.

We inched our way down the long shaft, until we finally reached a cave chamber large enough to move freely. Ashizuka lit a torch with a match, and the other ronin lit theirs from his. The torchlight only extended to part of the cavern, but perhaps because I had spent a night in near total darkness, I found my eyes adjusting to the dim light more quickly than usual, and I had a nearly complete view of our surroundings.

We were in a long gallery, with a high, vaulted ceiling covered with stalactites. To my anxious mind, they looked like serpent's teeth ready to clamp down on us any moment. We made our cautious way to the end of the gallery, where we found smaller tunnels branching off in two directions.

Ashizuka turned to face us. "Any idea which way?" he asked.

"Perhaps we should split up?" Mori suggested. "Five one way and five another? Whichever party encounters anything can withdraw back here, and..."

"Just a moment," I interrupted, pointing at the cave floor. A large, black-and-yellow spider – the kind that had startled Oyuki – was scuttling out of the left-hand tunnel and towards the right-hand one. It was soon followed by another, and then another.

"What are you suggesting?" asked Yamada. "Follow the spiders?"

"No," I said. "I saw a spider like this on the castle grounds yesterday. If they live in this cave, it's a good bet the orochi preys on them and they're running away from it. If we go in the opposite direction, we're likely to find it."

Ashizuka nodded agreement, and led us down the left-hand passage. The narrow passage continued for a while, until it emerged into another large gallery.

And there, among the stalagmites, lay the orochi. In the darkness of the cave, its body appeared to glow with a faint greenish-blue light. It might have been sleeping, but it might equally well have been lying in wait for its prey to come within reach of its pincers.

The acrid smell was at its strongest here, and the inner voice of hopelessness surged back louder than ever. *You think the ten of you have any chance against the orochi? This cave will be your tomb!*

We advanced until the gallery widened enough to accommodate all of us, and then, as quietly as we could, spread our cedar branches from one side of the gallery to the other. Once the barrier was in place, we touched our torches to the branches to ignite them, and used our hats to fan the flames. The wood was still green and the fire was slow to spread, but it yielded plenty of smoke.

In whispers, Ashizuka gave us our orders. Two groups of three muskets each. Archers on their flanks, their arrows moistened with spittle, to provide cover for the musketeers during the vulnerable moments when they were reloading. As for me, my orders were to stay in back and try to keep out of harm's way.

We took our positions behind the pile of burning branches. The front rank of musketeers lowered themselves to one knee.

"Ready," Ashizuka commanded in a low voice. "Aim. Fire!"

The report of the muskets echoed deafeningly in the subterranean space.

The orochi came to life at once, rearing up on its hind legs and wildly waving its pincers. Its one remaining eye glared balefully at us. But it came no closer. The barrier of smoke and fire seemed to be working.

The archers released a volley of arrows, each one following hard on the tail feathers of the one before, as the first rank of musketeers drew back to reload and the second moved into firing position. Their muskets cracked, and the orochi opened its mouth to let loose its chilling hiss – of rage, or agony, or both.

A jet of venom sprayed from the sting in its tail.

"Cover your eyes!" Gensatsu shouted. I quickly backed out of range of the spray as the ronin stopped their attack long enough to lower their heads, shielding their eyes with their armored sleeves and the brims of their helmets. I heard a faint hissing sound and saw wisps of white vapor rise where the drops of venom struck the rock.

"Fire!" Ashizuka ordered.

The muskets let loose a third volley. The unearthly noise from the creature's throat intensified, but it showed no sign of weakening. The smoke from the pile of branches was gradually filling the cavern and having the same effect on us that we meant for it to have on the monster. My eyes stung and I coughed, and the sound echoed from the samurai around me.

The orochi put all eight legs on the ground, curled its tail, and crouched. Then, without warning, it sprang. It leapt almost as high as the ceiling of the gallery, sailed over the wall of fire, landed behind us, and scuttled around quickly to face us. We were now trapped between it and our own fiery blockade.

This must have been what Don Protasio had tried to tell me before cockcrow cut him short. *Some varieties of scorpion, possibly including giant ones, can jump.*

"Swords!" commanded Ashizuka.

The ronin quickly lay aside their bows and firearms, and drew their swords. Chijiwa drew both his short and long sword. He stepped directly in front of the creature and held his long sword straight up and his short sword across it, to form the sign of the cross.

"*Exorcizo te, spiritus immundissime!*" he shouted. "Most unclean spirit, I cast you out in the name of almighty Deus and his..."

The orochi's tail shot forward over its head, and then drew back. It happened so fast that I could barely see, but it stinger had clearly struck Chijiwa. He collapsed to the cave floor.

Ashizuka and Gensatsu rushed to his side, took an arm each, and dragged him toward a place of relative safety. His body twitched and convulsed, his mouth foamed, and his eyes rolled.

The remaining ronin ran to outflank the monster, stabbing and slashing at its sides. Yamada succeeded in cutting off the end of its tail. When it struck the floor, it continued to writhe as if it were alive and looking to reattach itself.

One of the creature's pincers reached out toward Ashizuka. He let go of Chijiwa's arm and raised the sword that he had been carrying one-handed, but the pincer clamped around his waist with a force that, if not for his armor, would likely have cut him in two. It lifted him, armor and all, off the floor.

I had my sword, but with the creature standing at the full stretch of its legs, I could barely reach its body with it, let alone inflict any serious damage. I cast around desperately for something else to use as a weapon. Several muskets lay scattered about, but I couldn't tell if any were loaded.

I ran to Chijiwa, and from his twitching, unresisting body, took his powder flask. With my sword, I cut a length of matchcord from one of the muskets. I unstoppered the flask and pushed in the matchcord as far as it would go.

The orochi drew Ashizuka closer to its head, and opened its red, serpentine mouth wide enough to swallow him whole.

I lit the matchcord off the fiery barrier behind me, and hurled the flask at the monster's mouth. It sailed right into its throat.

The orochi appeared not to notice. Its pincers held Ashizuka in its mouth, as its jaws prepared to bite him in two. The long fangs looked sharp enough to pierce right through his armor.

Ashizuka thrust his sword upwards. This was no easy feat, since the monster was holding him facing down. The stroke went over his head and behind his back, carrying only a fraction of his full strength. Still, it struck true, piercing the creature right in the roof of its mouth.

Then came a sound like the muffled shot of a cannon.

It would be dramatic to say that the orochi blew apart into a million pieces that splattered all over the cave walls. It would be nearly as dramatic, and rather less unsettling to the stomach, to say that it tottered unsteadily on its eight legs before collapsing with a crash that shook the cave and made the rebels in the castle above brace themselves for an earthquake. But neither would be true. The only change to be observed was that its pincers fell limply to the cave floor. Ashizuka, with his gauntleted hands, pried the chelae far enough apart to extract himself from its grip.

We all gazed warily at the orochi's body. It couldn't even be called motionless, since its serpentine tail continued to thrash as though it hadn't yet gotten the message that it was dead. The light from the wall of fire flickered in its giant, unblinking eye.

"Have we done it?" asked Yamada cautiously.

"I believe so," said Ashizuka. He turned to me and nodded. "Thank you, Simon."

I returned his bow. It would have been nice to take the credit for singlehandedly dealing the monster its mortal blow, but Ashizuka's sword-stroke might well have been just as decisive as my improvised grenade. As long as it was done, I thought, what did it matter who did it?

The others looked in the direction of Chijiwa and Gensatsu, and my gaze followed theirs. Chijiwa was breathing heavily, but his convulsions had eased to only an occasional twitch. His eyes, though dazed and confused, had stopped their wild rolling.

"He'll live," said Gensatsu. "I gave him something to slow the effects of the venom. Once we get him to the infirmary, I can treat him more properly."

Yamada looked back at the body of the beast. "There must be a ton of meat on this carcass," he said. "Anyone know any good recipes for cedar-smoked orochi?"

There was scattered laughter. "A good thought," said Mori, "but even the mountain tribes that eat giant snakes have to pickle them in miso for at least three years to get all the poisons out. Imagine how long it would take for this one. We should burn it, or dispose of it in the sea."

He clapped a hand on my shoulder. "Thank you again, Simon," he said. "Never let it be said that you're anything less than a true warrior."

Chapter 16:
The Raid

第十六章・襲撃

A document had been circulating among us called the "Rule of Shiro," supposedly written by him, although some suspected it was written by someone like Chijiwa over his signature. Among other things, it urged us to be diligent about fasting during Lent.

As if we had a choice. Our rations had grown so short that a grim pun was going the rounds: *Hara-jo*, Hara Castle, became *Hara-hetta-jo*, the Castle of the Empty Stomach.

My parents had lived through a time of severe famine before I was born, and my mother had acquired a book that had mercifully sat untouched on the shelf since: Hugh Plat's *Sundrie new and Artificiall remedies against Famine, written uppon thoccasion of this present Dearth*. I wished I had it with me now. If I ever got back to England, I thought, I might publish a companion volume: *Receipts learnt by Simoune Grey at Hara Castle in Japan, for various Plantes, Sea-Weedes, and other stuffe never heretofore imagin'd as Fitte for human Consumption*. It might be short, but it would include some advice I was sure even Plat had never thought of:

1. Anything at all from the sea can be considered edible. This includes barnacles, all kinds of seaweed, any type of fish that's not poisonous and – if you cut very carefully – a few that are.

2. To make clam soup for one person, put one clam into a bowl of hot water with a pinch of miso. To make clam soup for a hundred people, follow the recipe as above, but with a hundred bowls of water instead of one. And remember, even after the meat inside has been eaten, clam shells will *always* add flavor and nutrition to the broth, no matter how many times they have been made to serve this purpose already.

3. When the very last grain of rice in the bag has been consumed, don't let the bag go to waste: boil and eat that too. It's made of rice husks, after all, so it must have *some* nutritional value.

4. Grass and tree leaves are essential ingredients in soup. If they can nourish an animal the size of a cow, horse, or deer, then surely they can nourish an animal the size of a human being.

5. If you have to go to bed hungry, place a hot stone on your stomach. This technique can be used until all your firewood has vanished along with all your food.

6. If your name is Amakusa Shiro and everyone thinks you're the Japanese reincarnation of Jesus Christ, do please understand that the thirty thousand ordinary mortals who entrusted their lives to you don't all have your skill at fasting. If you ever learned how to perform the miracle of turning stones to bread, now would be an excellent time to demonstrate. Of course, "man doth not live by bread alone," but man hath a very hard time living without it.

It was, perhaps fittingly, the morning of Good Friday when Ashizuka found me and called me aside.

"Simon," he said. "Shiro has asked me to convey this message to you personally. You have been chosen to be part of a very special mission."

"What is it?" I asked cautiously.

"A contingent is going to conduct a raid on the enemy camp. To bring back whatever they can in the way of food and ammunition. It's a very dangerous mission, and only our strongest and fastest warriors have been chosen for it. You've proven yourself worthy to be included in their number. Are you willing?"

My heart gave a leap, and then caught in my throat on the way back down. Now that I had been recognized as a true warrior, I wasn't sure whether this was the kind of recognition I wanted. But it was a mission that could shift the outcome of the battle. I couldn't refuse.

"I'm in," I said.

Ashizuka nodded in satisfaction. "We meet at Oe Gate, at the Hour of the Rat. Until then, tell no one."

When we parted ways, I noticed that there was some commotion in the courtyard. I hurried to see what was happening.

"There's been an arrow-letter from their side," I heard someone say. "They've asked for a parley."

I could sense the feeling in the air: excitement mingled with apprehension. On one hand, with the tide of battle so clearly turning in Izu's favor, I wondered what purpose a parley would serve other than to offer terms of surrender. On the other hand, it was a sign of how far we had come. At first, the Shogunate saw us as criminals to be rounded up and executed. Then they saw us as rebels to be crushed, then as a military foe to be outmaneuvered, and now as a worthy adversary to be negotiated with. Come what may, at least we had made the Shogun and his forces take us seriously.

A great crowd gathered on the ramparts overlooking Oe Beach. Those who had arrived later stood on tiptoe and craned their heads to see, as the two delegates went to meet on the beach below. Izu had sent one of his most trusted lieutenants, someone by the name of Arima Naozumi. Yamada, with Shiro's approval, had volunteered to represent us.

"When thou fastest, anoint thine head and wash thy face, that thou appear not unto men to fast." Yamada had clearly taken this verse to heart. He presented himself at Oe Beach freshly shaven, with every hair in place, wearing a gold-threaded brocade garment that I had never seen on him before; either he had borrowed it from someone, or else he had been saving it for an occasion like this one. It hung rather loosely on him, but that was the only clue anyone would have that he was starving. As for the envoy from their side, he was dressed in basic black, relieved only by a gold crest on the breast and sleeves: a five-petaled flower in a circle.

The two were too far away for us to hear their conversation. But when they went their separate ways and Yamada came back through Oe Gate, the crowd parted before him as if he were Moses and they were the waters of the Red Sea. He walked up to the steps of the tenshu, where Shiro was waiting with Ashizuka, Mori, and Chijiwa.

Shiro stood and made as if to escort him back into the tenshu, but Yamada stopped and stayed where he was.

"Sir," he said, "I have a specific request to convey Izu's message to you in front of the assembly."

Shiro turned back to face him. "Very well, then."

Yamada unrolled a sheet of paper. "Amakusa Shiro," he read aloud, "you must be aware by now that this battle can have only one outcome. If you truly regard yourself as the chosen messenger of Deus, now is the time to prove it. You have the chance to follow in the footsteps of the Lord you claim to serve, and sacrifice your life as a ransom for those who put their faith in you."

A collective gasp went up around the courtyard at these words. Oyuki's hands flew to her mouth.

"You are to surrender yourself to the Shogun's justice," Yamada went on. "If you do, any of your followers who confess their crimes against the Shogun will be granted amnesty. If you refuse, then when Hara Castle falls, no quarter will be given to you or anyone who follows you."

This recitation was greeted with a silence as profound as Hara Castle had known since before we arrived. Shiro stood, unmoving, for what seemed like an eternity before he turned and made as if to head back into the tenshu.

"I must pray," he said.

"Sir!" Ashizuka seized him by the arm. "You can't seriously be thinking of taking him up on it."

"There is no greater love than to lay down your life for those you love," Shiro said. "What is one life compared with thirty thousand?"

"And what is one earthly life compared with one immortal soul?" Chijiwa shot back. "You know that if anyone applies to the Shogun's forces for amnesty, they'll be made to step on the fumi-e and renounce their faith. What will it profit any of them if you buy them a few more years of mortal existence, if their souls are doomed to eternal perdition?"

"Sir?" came a tentative voice from the crowd.

All eyes turned to look as a man shouldered his way to the front. It had been a while since we had seen him, and he had grown much thinner than last time, but there was no mistaking the scars he bore courtesy of Matsukura and his minions. It was Totoemon, the fisherman who had first rescued us.

"I'm just a simple fisherman," he said. "I don't pretend to know about gods or heaven or hell or anything like that. All I know is, if there is a hell, it can't be much worse than life under Matsukura."

Heads all around nodded in fervent agreement as he continued: "Do you know how it feels to wake up every morning knowing that everything you produce that day will be taken from you? And then to be told you'll have to produce twice as much the next day, or you and your loved ones will face torture, maybe even death? That was our life, before you appeared. It's true, this rebellion didn't go quite as planned. And it's true that we've endured plenty of hardship here too. But this time, it was for no one's sake but ours. We were our own masters. Whatever we faced, we faced it all together. We had hope. And even if it turns out our hope was in vain…still, I would rather die here, on my own terms, than go back to the life I left to follow you." He looked around him. "Does anyone else feel the same?"

A voice answered, "Aye!" Another echoed it, and another, and another, until the chorus had swelled to fill the entire courtyard.

Shiro looked around, and a faint smile crossed his lips.

"So be it," he said. "Yamada, you may return to Naozumi with this reply: You are welcome to come to Hara Castle. For those who follow the Way, it is the gateway to heaven. For those who persecute them, it is the gateway to hell."

Yamada stood still, looking as if he were either expecting Shiro to say more or he had something to say himself.

"You may go and convey the message now," Shiro said. His gentle tone conveyed an unmistakable command.

"Yes, sir." Yamada bowed and departed.

As expected, Shiro's reply put an end to the negotiations. Everyone spent the rest of that day however they spent it, but as for me, I mainly spent it fretting over the upcoming mission. I knew I should try to get some rest, but I was too anxious.

The Hour of the Dog, soon after dark, found me pacing in the courtyard, looking up at the full moon that illuminated the entire castle with a pale light except when clouds veiled it. If I had been looking to the sky for guidance about our upcoming mission, all I saw was a mocking mystery. Would our way be clear? Or would something unexpected happen to hide our goal from sight?

In one of the moments when the moon shone its brightest, I noticed a movement around the powder shed. My gaze automatically followed it, and I saw a figure leaving the building. My first thought was that it was Komagine, checking to see how much – or, more accurately, how little – powder we had left. But if he was simply conducting a regular inspection of our supplies, why would he do it in the dark of night? And as the figure left the building, it skulked furtively around to the other side, as if anxious to keep out of sight.

Could this, I wondered, be the same person I saw from the scrying pool in Tengudo?

I hesitated, then moved in for a closer look, keeping to the shadows myself and trying to avoid being seen. The figure had gone around to the back side of the shed, and I stood there for a moment debating with myself whether to follow it and risk discovery, or wait for it to move.

"Simon?" said a voice near me. It was the voice that, ordinarily, I would be happier to hear call my name than any other in the world. But this time, I jumped about a foot and put a hand over my heart.

"Simon?" Oyuki repeated. "What are you doing out here?"

"I couldn't sleep," I said truthfully.

I took a surreptitious glance in the direction of the powder shed. I saw no sign of movement. My mind was torn between continuing my pursuit, or taking advantage of this precious opportunity which might be my last.

"Me either," she said. "It feels…it feels as though things are about to come to a head."

She was more right than she knew. I remembered how Ashizuka had urged me to secrecy about our upcoming mission. But seeing Oyuki there in the moonlight, and knowing that this might be the last night I could ever talk to her, made that concern seem suddenly distant.

"Oyuki," I said, "I've been chosen for a special mission. We're going to raid the enemy camp tonight."

Her eyes widened, and she drew in a sharp breath.

"Of course, it's extremely dangerous," I said. "None of us has any assurance of coming back. And if I don't…"

I swallowed, in a vain attempt to relieve the dryness in my mouth. "I couldn't bear to leave this world with questions left unanswered between me and the girl I…"

Oyuki held up a hand. "Simon, stop. Don't talk like that. You *will* come back. But once you do, we'll still have to win this battle. And after that, you and I will still have to make it to Nagasaki, find my father, and find a way to England. What I need from you is your help. And you'll need my help. I can't think of anything beyond that right now. First things first."

I sighed. "Very well."

There was a moment of silence. Seeing that she wasn't likely to break it, I awkwardly took it upon myself. "Well…good night."

I turned to go. I took a glance toward the powder shed, but I saw no more sign of the mysterious figure.

"Simon?" Oyuki called.

I turned back. A tiny wellspring of hope broke through the parched ground inside me.

She took a step toward me. "Having said all that…" she began, then paused. "I have so few chances to talk to you alone…there's one thing I'd like to say to you. Something I've been meaning to say for quite a long time."

My heart pounded. "What is it?"

She looked up, as if hoping the stars would spell out her next words for her. Finally, she took a deep breath.

"*Ho-ro.*"

The sound was like the croaking of a bullfrog. But it was so loud and deep that any frog who could produce it, I thought, must be as big as a horse.

Oyuki's head turned sharply to look at me. "What?" we both said in unison.

"*Ho-ro,*" came the voice again, from somewhere behind me.

Oyuki looked over my shoulder, and her eyes widened. I turned and looked behind me, and gasped.

My intuition had been almost exactly right. It was a bullfrog, or toad, but big enough that a grown man could ride astride it like a pony. And it was a ghost. I could see through it, and wisps of green vapor rose from its back.

"*Ho-ro,*" it croaked again. It hopped up, turned around in mid-air, and landed facing away from us. It took a leap, and then performed another mid-air turn to face us again.

"*Ho-ro!*" I didn't speak Bullfrog, but to my ear, the croak sounded higher and more insistent.

"Do you suppose it's trying to talk to us?" Oyuki asked. "Is it trying to say 'follow'?"

We followed the giant toad as it hopped down the slope toward the Lotus Pond Gate. When it reached the bottom, it gave one final leap and passed straight through the gate, leaving no trace but a few wisps of green vapor rising from the wooden planks.

I hesitated. Could it be leading us into an ambush? But the lotus pond lay nestled between steep embankments on two sides, and on the third, only a thin strip of earth separated it from the sea. If any enemy troops wanted to position themselves for an ambush there, they would have to walk on water. And if no one on our side could do that, I strongly doubted anyone on theirs could.

I drew aside the bar and opened the gate.

The light of the full moon illuminated an expanse of floating green leaves, growing so thickly you almost felt you *could* walk across them, varied with pink and white blossoms, extending to the point where the narrow earthen barrier separated them from the calm sea. Frogs – presumably the ordinary rather than the giant ghostly kind – croaked happily, as comfortably at home among these flowers as the frogs back home were in lily pads.

In the middle of the pond, standing on the lotus leaves without bending the petals, was the translucent figure of a woman. Her mortal life had been

238

comparatively short, judging by both her youthful face and the long, flowing sleeves of her kimono (which, I knew by now, meant she had died unmarried). Her hair hung down past her waist, and her feet were invisible; her kimono faded from translucent to transparent before it reached the green carpet of lotus leaves. Her face was beautiful, but her eyes held both a sadness that suggested someone had hurt her deeply, and a steely resolution that suggested anyone who did the same again would be making a grave mistake.

"Oyuki," she said. "And Simon. It's wonderful to meet you at last. I suppose there's no need for me to introduce myself?"

Oyuki's puzzled expression suggested otherwise.

Noticing, the apparition gave a further hint. "You put on a lovely play about me. Although I beg to correct you on one point. It was the frog-wizard Nikushisen who taught me my craft, not the god of the Kifune Shrine. Kyo no Miyako was far from me, after all, and hostile territory after that episode with my father. But I don't blame you for getting confused, since so many conflicting stories have been told about me."

Oyuki's eyes bulged. "Takiyasha-hime?"

"In the flesh. Well, in the spirit."

Oyuki's eyes still threatened to fall out of their sockets.

"You look as if you'd seen a ghost," said Takiyasha-hime. "And I wouldn't have thought that was anything new to you."

"Well…I'm surprised to see you all the way down here," said Oyuki. "I thought you were from somewhere on the far side of Edo."

"I am. But unlike some spirits, I'm not bound to the place where my physical body was buried. I can travel anywhere. And I do – anywhere where the downtrodden common people are rising up against the rich and powerful." She glided across the lotus flowers to speak to Oyuki more closely. "In you, I see someone like myself. A young woman, dwelling between the natural world and the spirit world, at home in both and in neither, with formidable supernatural powers ready to be tempered and forged into a weapon to fight for justice."

"And you've only made yourself visible now?" I asked.

Takiyasha-hime turned to me. "The charming gentleman who built this castle – Don Protasio, is that his name? – and the dashing young man in command of your forces, are both something called Kirishitan, correct?"

"Very true," I said.

"I admit, I'm not entirely sure what that is. It's so hard to keep track of all these new crazes, here today, gone tomorrow."

I opened my mouth to protest that a religion that had been spreading throughout the world for sixteen centuries could hardly be called a passing fad. Then I remembered that it had only been in Japan for one of those centuries, as opposed to six for her. If she chose to regard Jesus of Nazareth as a Johnny Newcome, I didn't see a way to convince her otherwise.

"But my guess was," Takiyasha-hime went on, "they wouldn't take too kindly to the sudden appearance of a notorious witch in their castle."

"That's probably a safe bet," I agreed.

"So, you're probably wondering why I chose to appear to you now," she said. "Since you put my story on the stage, I assume you know what powers I had. How I learned the secrets of frog magic from Nikushisen. How I raised an army of yokai to avenge my father. How I summoned a *gashadokuro* to defend against Mitsukuni. It's true…" She took a rueful look down at her spectral body. "…they did defeat me in the end. But you have to admit, I gave them the fight of their lives. I struck such a blow against the corrupt Heian court that Japan is still talking about it six hundred years later."

"When I heard your story," I interjected, "I was hoping you would win."

"Thank you." She favored me with a brief smile before turning her attention back to Oyuki. "Those spells were written on a scroll. After Mitsukuni killed me, he took it back to the capital. It's been kept under lock and key at the Bureau of Onmyodo ever since. But apparently, they've made some copies. And one, I believe, is close at hand."

"How close?" Oyuki asked.

"You may have heard that the new commander of the Shogun's forces brought a *gunshi* with him. Domon Yasunari."

The name didn't mean anything to me, but I remembered what Don Protasio had said about the military magician. I nodded.

"I strongly suspect," Takiyasha-hime went on, "that among the spell-scrolls he brought with him, he has a copy of mine."

"Does that mean he can use your magic?" Oyuki asked in alarm.

"Possibly. The scroll can tell him the *words* of the incantations, but it can't tell him the intonation and gestures I learned from Nikushisen himself. Whether he can use it is a question. As for me, of course, in my present state, I can't." She gave Oyuki a significant look. "But *someone* could, with the proper instruction."

Oyuki drew in a stunned breath.

"I've been watching your struggle, from a distance," Takiyasha-hime went on. "I know about the raid you're planning on the enemy camp. I can help you. I can scout ahead invisibly and tell you exactly where to find what you need. And if you can get the scroll from Domon's tent, I can show Oyuki how to use its magic."

Oyuki was looking at Takiyasha-hime with a half-hopeful, half-doubting expression, as though thinking what I was: this offer sounded almost too good to be true. "So you'll help procure supplies for our army and magical power for me," she said. "What about you? What do you stand to gain?"

Takiyasha-hime sighed, exhaling a bluish-white cloud of spectral vapor into the night air. "I've been walking this earth for six hundred years," she said. "And in that time, I've seen the same story repeated over and over. Those at the top spend their lives in pursuit of wealth and power, and then use it to keep those at the bottom from rising any higher. But every so often, someone comes along with the courage to lead the downtrodden to rise up and shake off the yoke of tyranny. Your Amakusa Shiro – well, I don't know what he'd say if he met me, but I do know that if my father were alive today, he would be fighting alongside him. So if there's any power that can still be drawn from my scroll, I'd much rather see it in the hands of the oppressed than the oppressor. Does that satisfy you?"

Oyuki and I exchanged a glance and nodded. "It does," she said.

Once we were back inside the castle, I ran and asked Yamada for a piece of paper, which he provided even though his supply had dwindled to almost nothing, along with a brush and ink stone. The next challenge was to find light enough to draw by, since the few lamps in the castle and the precious store of oil were reserved for the use of Shiro and the most senior commanders. I eventually found the smoldering remains of a cooking fire, and blew on the embers until I had a flame just barely bright enough to distinguish between ink and paper.

Once all my materials were ready, I proceeded to draw a map of the enemy camp, following Takiyasha-hime's descriptions. She could penetrate deep into the enemy's camp invisibly, then be back at my side in an instant to tell me exactly where to find the stores of food and ammunition. Every army, I thought, should have a ghost on reconnaissance duty.

"Here," she said, as I filled in the southwest corner of the map, "is the Matsudaira camp. This is where Izu's command post is, and also Domon's quarters. Once the rest of your raiding party has secured its objective, I'll show you where you need to go."

"All right."

"And on the way, be sure to pick up a bone."

For a moment, I wondered whether I had heard her correctly. "A bone? What kind do you mean?"

"Any kind will do, but something big, like a thigh or shin bone, will work best. On a battlefield, you shouldn't have much trouble finding one."

By the time we finally finished, it was the fourth quarter of the Hour of the Boar, just a few minutes before rendezvous at the Hour of the Rat. I furled the scroll and took a deep breath.

"Well," I said to Oyuki, "here I go. Wish me luck."

Oyuki stood silently for a moment, looking down. Then, so suddenly I could scarcely believe it was happening, she threw her arms around me.

"Good luck, Simon," she whispered. This wish was followed by a sound, so slight I wasn't even sure I had heard it, that might have meant she had kissed the air next to my ear. "Come back safe."

She let go of me, turned, and walked quickly towards her barracks without a backward glance. Takiyasha-hime watched her go for a moment, then turned back to me with an encouraging lift of her spectral eyebrows.

I made my way to the Oe Gate, my heart hammering inside my chest – from nerves, or for another reason, I couldn't tell. But one thing I knew was that, despite the chill of the night, I felt warm all over.

Some of the raiding party had already begun to assemble. The leader, I noticed with some trepidation, was Chijiwa.

I walked up to him. "Sir," I said, "I have some information that I think will prove useful."

I handed him the map. By the light of the small lantern he held, he gave it a glance. Then, his eyes widening, he held it closer to the light and leaned in to examine it closely.

"Where did this come from?" he demanded. "How did you learn all this?"

I hesitated long enough that he answered his own question. "By the arts you learned from the tengu?"

His voice contained a note of disapproval, but something told me he would approve even less if he knew the truth. I didn't deny his words.

He turned the map this way and that, holding it closer to the lantern. It looked as though he were debating with himself whether to make use of it or burn it as the product of black magic.

"I can vouch for its accuracy," I said. "Use it as you see fit."

Chijiwa apparently decided that any information about the enemy would be helpful, wherever it came from. "Thank you," he said, dismissing me.

I bowed and took my place. I noted with apprehension that Sanai had also been selected.

Chijiwa called the troops to order. "You know our mission," he said, without preamble. "We will divide into three raiding parties, each striking one of the three camps nearest the castle. Ashizuka will lead the assault against the Terazawa camp, Mori against Kuroda, and myself against Nabeshima."

My heart sank. Of course, striking the closest targets made perfect strategic sense. But it put the Matsudaira camp, where my own target lay, beyond the bounds of our mission.

Chijiwa read out our assignments. I was in the Kuroda party, under Mori's command. To my dismay, Sanai was in the same group.

"The first stage," Chijiwa went on, "is to take as much as you can without alerting the enemy to your presence, especially food, weapons, and ammunition. Our watchwords are speed and stealth. As soon as anyone raises an alarm, the second stage begins: retreat while inflicting as much damage on the enemy camp as possible. Those of you with firearms and fire arrows, that will be the time to use them. Understood?"

Murmurs of assent came from the assembled rebels.

"One more thing," said Chijiwa, his ordinarily grave voice turning even graver. "If you see any of our number captured and it proves impossible to rescue them...then save them from whatever horrible torture Izu has in store for them. Deus will welcome them directly into paradise and crown them with a martyr's crown."

My mouth went dry as soon as I heard these words. I scarcely dared glance around at my comrades in arms. If I had to carry out Chijiwa's order on one of them, could I do it? I strongly doubted it. And I doubted even more strongly that, if one of them were to carry it out on me and keep me from seeing Oyuki or my family ever again, I would find paradise and the martyr's crown any consolation at all.

"Let us pray," Chijiwa concluded.

All of us sank to our knees. Chijiwa intoned an *orasho* that I couldn't follow. As he chanted, I prayed silently in my own language. *God, if you really are on our side, if we really are your chosen ones...now would be the perfect time to show us. Guide and protect us, and bring our mission to a successful end.* And in one corner of my mind, I added, almost involuntarily: *And please, bring me back safely to Oyuki. Amen.*

We cautiously opened the gate and started down towards the tidal flats. Everyone kept a close eye on the steep slope underfoot, and for my own part, it was for more than one reason. The embankment between the tidal flats and the castle wall, difficult to reach from the enemy's side at low tide and all but impossible at high tide, was a place where many of the besiegers had perished and their bodies lay unrecovered. It seemed the most likely hunting ground for bones.

Sure enough, I soon discovered what might have been a thigh bone. With a silent apology to its former owner, I picked it up and concealed it under my shirt.

The tide had gone out far enough that the ground underfoot was as solid as it ever was, meaning it was only thick, sticky mud, as opposed to thick, sticky mud under seawater. We stepped carefully across it, our only light coming from the moon overhead. And of course, if I glanced behind, I could see points of light from the smoldering matchcords of muskets, like fireflies turned red with anger about having to make an appearance so far ahead of their usual season.

Takiyasha-hime went ahead, invisible to all but me. I envied the way she could glide effortlessly over the mud without even having to worry about getting a stain on her transparent kimono. When she glanced over her shoulder at me, she must have noticed my difficulty, for she raised a hand and said, "*Kitsunebi!*"

A ball of pale blue light appeared in the air over her shoulder. It was a comforting sight. A foxfire like this one had lit the way for Oyuki and me as we traveled by night from Edo toward Hirado. It wasn't much brighter than the moonlight, but by its light, I could see my way even in the shadows, or when passing clouds obscured the moon. Since it was a spectral light, visible only to those with my gift of seeing yokai, it was unfortunately of no help to my companions, but more importantly, it wouldn't give away our presence to the enemy.

When we reached the solid ground on the far side of the flats, I took my assigned position in the vanguard. Mori took his direction from me, and I, unbeknownst to him, took it from Takiyasha-hime. She led us through the labyrinth of bamboo fences that separated one lord's forces from the others, until we arrived at what appeared to be the most solid structure in the camp: four walls, of odd-sized stones held together with mortar, and a tiled roof. This had to be the powder shed.

Two strong raiders used an iron crow to pry open the lock. Our guards, armed with bows or muskets, stood guard at intervals, forming a corridor where the raiders could run back and forth, passing powder kegs one to the other.

When everyone was occupied with their tasks, I took a sidelong glance at Takiyasha-hime, and saw her beckoning me. I tried to slip away inconspicuously, but Mori just happened to glance in my direction.

"Simon!" he said in a sharp whisper. "Simon! Where are you going?"

"I'll be right back, sir."

I ran between the bamboo palisades and the sea, following the swiftly gliding figure of Takiyasha-hime. With every step I took, my anxiety grew. Every step took me farther away from the protection of my companions, and farther away from what was meant to be my mission. Even if I survived the raid, my commanding officers might call for my head for deserting my post.

Takiyasha-hime abruptly turned and glided through the palisade, leaving me alone on the other side.

Panic overtook me. I debated risking detection by calling out to her. But before I could say anything, she reappeared.

"Sorry," she said sheepishly. "I forgot you can't do that."

She led me around the fence and into an enclosure where several tents stood. Judging from their size and splendor, they had to be the quarters of the senior officers. The unbidden thought flitted through my mind that it would be a simple matter for someone to slip in, and then slip out again after putting a musket ball through Izu's head or a blade between his ribs. But quite apart from the knavery of killing a man as he slept, I couldn't see that it would change anything. When

Matsukura fell into disgrace, Itakura replaced him. When Itakura was killed, Izu replaced him. If Izu were to die, undoubtedly the Shogun had someone waiting in the wings to replace him too. Our fight against the Shogun's forces was like Hercules' battle with the Hydra: if we cut one head off, another would grow to take its place. I wasn't sure what our side would need for victory, but I knew that simply to separate the enemy commander's soul from his body wasn't it.

Takiyasha-hime veered toward a smaller tent just next to the command tent. By the entrance, a huge mastiff stood watch. It looked too solid to be a ghost, but it seemed to be outlined in a pale bluish light that didn't come from the kitsunebi. It sat up as we approached, and an ominous growl came from its throat.

"The bone," said Takiyasha-hime. "Quickly!"

I took out the bone and threw it to the dog. It eagerly took the bone in its paws and began gnawing it.

Takiyasha-hime bent down and gave the spectral dog's head a pat. "*Yoshi, yoshi,*" she crooned. Apparently, ghostly dogs liked a bone and a little affection just as much as their living counterparts.

While the dog was occupied, we slipped into the tent.

I had seen an onmyoji's laboratory once before, in Edo Castle when I had the misfortune to cross paths with the court magician to the former Shogun, and this looked like a makeshift version of the same. On a long table, celestial globes and astrolabes shared space with astrological charts covered with incomprehensible symbols. In one corner, Domon lay snoring on his pallet.

"It must be one of those," Takiyasha-hime said, pointing.

I followed her point, and my heart sank into my bowels.

I wasn't sure what I had been expecting. I suppose I had some vague image of books lined up on shelves, their titles clearly embossed on their spines in letters I could read: THE BOOK OF MAGICAL SECRETS STOLEN

FROM TAKIYASHA-HIME, TO WHOM PLEASE RETURN.
What I saw instead was a free-standing wooden case
divided into niches like a honeycomb, in which boxes
and cases, each of a size to contain only one scroll, lay
piled in no apparent order. I thought about taking the
whole thing and sorting them out later, but the case
looked so heavy and unwieldy that it would take at least
two strong men to carry it.

There was nothing for it but to go through them one
by one. I took out each box in turn and showed it to
Takiyasha-hime. The boxes usually had labels, written
in a flowing script that I couldn't read but she clearly
could, because she would glance at them and shake her
head. But some of the scrolls were in leather or
lacquerware cases, which their owner could apparently
tell apart just by differences in shape and material. In
such cases, the only way to determine the contents was
to unfasten whatever strap or cord was holding the case
closed, take out the scroll, untie the ribbon that
invariably bound it, and unfurl enough of it to get a
sample of the writing.

I heard a stirring from Domon's pallet. And then, I
heard a voice utter something that sounded like a
magical incantation.

I froze in terror, steeling myself for the spell to strike
me.

But I felt nothing. After a second or two when
nothing seemed to happen, I risked a glance in Domon's
direction. He was facing a different way than he had
been when we first came in, but his eyes were still closed.
He hadn't been casting a spell, just talking in his sleep.

It was a small relief, but not enough to stem the rising
tide of panic I felt. There were still a great many more
scrolls ahead of us than behind us. At this rate, I thought
frantically, we could be here all night. And with each
passing moment, the chances increased that some
disaster would befall us: Domon would wake up for real,
or the ghostly dog would bark, or one of the enemy

soldiers would see our raiding party and raise the alarm, or someone from my own side would come looking for me.

I opened another case, slid out a scroll, unbound it, and unrolled it enough to show Takiyasha-hime the text.

She suddenly leaned in more closely. "Let me see more."

I unrolled it further, and Takiyasha-hime nodded in delight. "Yes! That's the one. Let's go!"

I quickly rolled the scroll, slipping it back into its case as I hastened out of the tent. But just as I passed under the flap, I heard a howl that chilled me even more than the night air.

The sound had startled me so greatly that it took a moment for me to see what had alerted the ghostly dog. Someone was standing across the enclosure, holding a musket pointed in my direction.

My first panicked thought was that the enemy had discovered me. Then I realized that the figure wore neither helmet nor armor, and looked too small and thin to be one of the Shogun's soldiers.

It was Sanai.

As soon as I registered his presence, four guards burst out of the command tent and converged on me.

At the same time, something slammed into me from behind. I had only a split second to fling the scroll in Sanai's direction before I fell face down on the ground. The dog might have appeared translucent, but it weighed just as much as any mortal mastiff.

"Take that to Oyuki!" I could barely raise my face far enough to shout the instruction to Sanai.

For the next few seconds, everything seemed to be moving so slowly that I suddenly understood what Buzen-bo had said about the relativity of time. Unfortunately, I had no way to use that to my advantage.

Shouts and alarms broke out all over the camp.

Arcs of fire streaked across the night sky, as our archers, following Chijiwa's orders, released their fire arrows. Flames and smoke began to rise as the arrows struck their mark.

The four soldiers seized my arms and pulled me to my feet. I looked desperately around for Takiyasha-hime, but she was nowhere to be seen.

Sanai, after a moment's hesitation, raised his musket and pointed it in my direction. With horror, I realized what he had in mind. There were four soldiers holding me, and he had only one shot.

If you see any of our number captured and it proves impossible to rescue them...then save them from whatever horrible torture Izu has in store for them.

"Take it!" I shouted again.

Suddenly, night turned into day. In the distance, a ball of fire billowed up from the ground, casting a red glow over the entire camp. A fraction of a second later, an enormous explosion shook the ground, not to mention my bones, and nearly burst my eardrums. Another followed it, and another, and another.

I realized what had happened: one of the retreating raiders had shot a fire-arrow into the powder shed. Sanai, almost involuntarily, ducked as bits of stone and tile showered down on us.

That was the last thing I saw before the soldiers dragged me out of the enclosure.

* * *

They took me to a rectangular palisade, where a space along one of the walls had been fenced off with a bamboo lattice. Behind it knelt at least a dozen people, their wrists bound with straw rope, their bowed heads covered with rice sacks. Two burly, scowling guards, armed with spears, patrolled the near side of the fence.

The soldiers bound my wrists in the same way and put a rice sack over my head. Rough hands pushed me behind the fence, then shoved down on my shoulders to bring me to my knees.

Once the guards had gone their way, I tried to speak to the prisoner next to me. "*Abé,*" I began in an undertone.

Before he could reply, the butt end of a spear struck me hard in the ribs. "Silence!" barked an unseen voice.

I couldn't see, but over the next few hours, I could hear a great deal more than I would have wished. From what I supposed was the nearest tent, bone-chilling screams rent my ears.

"Aaugh!" came a cry of agony. "Aaugh! Deus!"

"There is no Deus," came a sharp, high-pitched, nasal voice that carried even over the prisoner's anguished cries. "You've thrown your life away following a false god. Do you see the heavens opening? Do you see an army of celestial beings swooping down with flaming swords? Do you even see any of your own companions coming to your rescue? No. No one is coming to save you. You can only save yourself. Repent of this madness. Turn away from the demon Yaso and the traitor Amakusa Shiro. Then, your crimes against the Shogun might possibly be forgiven."

The silence that followed was broken only by low moans from the prisoner. Then, I heard a startlingly loud noise that sounded like two boulders colliding.

"Aaugh!" came another cry, this one, if possible, even louder and more agonized. "I repent! I repent!"

"Excellent," said the other voice. "You made a wise decision."

That was the last sound I heard from that direction for a while.

Then, I felt a commotion near me as guards entered the enclosure. Their hands gripped my arms and pulled me roughly to my feet.

"Your turn," said a voice.

Chapter 17:
Izu the Wise

第十七章・知恵の伊豆

My captors took me out of the enclosure and marched me somewhere far enough away that when we stopped, I was uncomfortably wet from the light drizzle that was starting to fall. A kick to the back of the knees made my legs buckle. I fell hard on my knees, and it was only the guards' iron grip on my arms that prevented me from falling on my face. As I winced and stifled a cry of pain, an unseen hand pulled the rice sack roughly off my head.

My surroundings were quite different from what I was expecting. I was afraid they were going to take me to whatever they used as the mobile equivalent of a torture chamber. Instead, I was in a wooden building, one that looked fairly sturdy for a structure only meant to last for a matter of months. By the light of two braziers, I saw a white curtain covering the whole opposite wall, with a crest emblazoned on it in black: a circle enclosing three broad leaves whose points met in the center. All around the room stood banners bearing the same crest. In front of me, flanked by armored spear-carriers, sat a man of about forty, with a fleshy face that suggested he enjoyed his food and drink.

I didn't have to guess. I knew I was facing Matsudaira Nobutsuna, otherwise known as Izu the Wise, supreme leader of the Shogunate forces.

Surprisingly for such a high-ranking military commander, I saw none of the haggard lines that battle-weariness had etched into the faces of the veteran samurai on our side. The first word that came to mind when I saw him was "fatherly" – the sort of father who could be kind and indulgent toward his children who pleased him, brutal to those who displeased him.

Two others sat alongside him. I knew one of them from his black dress and five-petaled flower crest: Arima Naozumi. I had only seen him from a distance, and now that I saw his scowling, pinched face up close, I wished I could have kept it that way. The other wore a purple robe with voluminous sleeves, and a tall, black hat that looked like a bishop's miter worn sideways. I had seen a costume like it before, at the Seimei Shrine in Kyo no Miyako. And I had seen this person's face, at least in its sleeping form: Domon Yasunari.

The guards untied the ropes that bound my wrists. I kept my hands behind my back and flexed my fingers a few times, waiting for sensation to return.

Izu looked me over silently for a few moments. Then, he gestured to one of his attendants. To my utter astonishment, the attendant came bearing a low-lying lacquerware table, and set it on the ground in front of me. On it was a bowl of soup, a bowl of rice, and a small fish still sizzling from the fire. Under ordinary circumstances, I might have called it a modest meal, but by the standards we had grown used to at Hara Castle, it was an unimaginable feast.

"Please, help yourself," Izu said, with a gesture of welcome. "You can't fight on an empty stomach."

Not long ago, I would have found this enticement impossible to resist. But now, I was so far beyond hunger that I felt myself reverting to the state I had been in during my long fast in Tengudo. I had a vague recollection that there was such a thing in the world as food, that most people were very preoccupied with it and spent a great deal of time either producing or consuming it, and that at some point, I had been one of them. But all of that now seemed like a dim and distant memory. And this meal, I realized, was part of his strategy. If I ate the food he offered me, I would be placing myself in his debt.

"No, thank you," I said.

The attendant started to take the tray away, but Izu stopped him with a gesture. He bowed and backed away, leaving it in front of me, possibly to test my resolve.

"Simon Grey," said Izu. "That's your name, right?"

I nodded.

"They say you've been to Ryugujo."

This caught me off balance. "Yes, sir," I replied warily, remembering how everyone else who heard that story had laughed at me or called me mad.

Izu leaned forward with sudden eagerness. "What was it like?"

I looked up at him. His face showed no sign of skepticism. On the contrary, all I saw in it was childlike wonder.

"Well..." I hesitated, then gave the best description of Ryugujo I could. The more I spoke, the more delighted he appeared. He drank in every word I said, and when I paused, he filled the silence with questions. Had I met Otohime? Was she really as beautiful as the legends said? How long had I spent in her palace, and meanwhile, how much time had passed on the surface?

"Ever since I was a boy," he said when I had finished, "I've been fascinated by stories like Urashima Taro. Every time I looked out to sea, I dreamed about the city under the waves. It was only a story, but part of me always wanted to believe it was real. And now I know it is." He gave me a wistful smile. "I can't help envying you a little."

Naozumi cleared his throat. "Begging your pardon, sir," he said, "you realize there are other rebels to be questioned."

The voice was respectful, but it sent a chill of fear through me. I had heard it before – through the fabric of the tent and the rice sack over my head, as it interrogated one of my companions.

The sound of his voice reminded me I had to be on my guard, which I had come perilously close to letting down. This could all be part of Izu's grand strategy: fill me with fear first, and just as I was expecting the worst, turn the tables by offering me food and a sympathetic ear. He could simply be playing with my mind. And if he was, I had to admit, it was working.

"And which country did you say you were from?" Izu went on.

"England, sir."

"I'm sorry you got caught up in this," he said. "After all, it isn't your country and it isn't your battle. I'd imagine what you want more than anything is just to go home."

I did my best not to show him how right he was. "I wouldn't mind that," I said cautiously.

"You and I both know," Izu said, "that time is running out for the rebels. I know your provisions have run so low that you've been reduced to eating grass. As for our side, we have fresh supplies coming in constantly. Perhaps you were hoping to hold us off until ships from abroad came to your rescue? Surely you've realized by now that none will be coming. No one outside Japan knows or cares about your cause."

The wind went out of my sails. At my most honest, I had known the chances of any other nation coming to our aid were near zero. But still, a part of me had continued to cherish that secret hope. To hear Izu say aloud that he knew about it, and knew it was in vain, made me feel even smaller and more helpless.

"Or were you simply hoping to call the Shogun's attention to the plight of the people of Shimabara?" Izu continued. "In that case, you've already achieved your goal." He gestured to one of the guards. "Bring him."

The guard and his companion bowed and left the tent. A minute later, they reappeared, holding between them a prisoner with his wrists bound behind him. From the look of him, he had been a high-ranking samurai or member of the nobility. He was dressed in a fine kimono and wore his hair in samurai style. But his clothes were dirty and disheveled, as if he hadn't changed them for days or even weeks. His hair was starting to grow back on the scalp around his topknot, where samurai usually shaved. He cast a baleful look around him as the guards brought him in.

Izu looked at me as if expecting to see some sign of recognition on my face. "You don't know him?" he asked when none was forthcoming. "Well, I suppose that's to be expected. Perhaps his face isn't as familiar to you as it would be to the rebels." He turned back to the prisoner. "Well, go on, then. Tell the young gentleman your name."

The prisoner glared fiercely and kept silent.

"Tell him your name," Izu repeated, in a calm but firmer tone.

In a sullen voice, the prisoner replied, "Matsukura Katsuie."

My mind reeled. This was the man who had started it all – the architect, not only of the monstrous castle that insatiably gobbled the common people's livelihood, but of the persecutions that had ignited our rebellion. He had loomed large in our imagination as a master villain, untouchable, unaccountable, unassailable, raining slings and arrows down on his hapless vassals from the high keep of his castle, with the Shogun giving full support to every new scheme he plotted. And now, the mighty one had been cast down from his throne.

"As I said before," Izu continued, "the Shogun's only desire is to preserve the peace and order of the nation. It was Matsukura's duty to uphold it in his domain. He failed. Instead, he poured more and more of his scarce resources into fulfilling his father's foolish dream, while his domain edged closer and closer to revolt. For this, his lands and titles are forfeit, and he himself will be subject to the Shogun's justice."

He made a dismissive gesture. As the guards took Matsukura away, Izu turned back to me. "Did you want to write yourselves into the history books?" he asked. "You've done that. The only question is, how do you, Simon Grey, want your own part in the story to end?"

A moment of silence followed this question. Izu broke it with another one. "What would you say if I told you I could see you safely escorted to Nagasaki and put aboard the next ship bound for Europe?"

Despite everything, my heart gave a leap. I had to exert all my effort to keep it from showing in my face.

"I would wonder what you wanted in exchange," I said.

"What I want is the same thing you and your leaders want: an end to this siege. And by now, as you surely know, there's only one way that can happen. All I would ask of you is to spare your people any further suffering by hastening the inevitable." He paused, then continued in an abstract tone: "Hunger weakens people's minds and makes them forgetful. It would be completely understandable if someone, some night, were to commit a small oversight like neglecting to bar one of the gates."

It took a moment for the import of his words to sink in. When it did, I felt a chill that had nothing to do with the rain. He was asking me to be a Trojan horse.

I shook my head.

"Your loyalty is commendable," Izu said. "Tell me this: Does your side return it? What have they done for you, that you should put your life at risk for their sake?"

The image of the stealthy archer I had seen from Tengudo came vividly back to mind.

"Simon," Izu continued, "I'll make you this offer one time and one time only. One way or another, this siege will end, and end soon. Help make it happen, and I'll help you on your way. If you refuse, then when Hara Castle finally falls, you will share the fate of the other rebels."

"I've been sharing their fate all along," I said. "I see no reason to do any differently now."

Izu stared at me for several moments. "It grieves me to do this," he finally said with a sigh, and gestured to the guards. "Prepare him for interrogation."

* * *

The guards took me out of the command post. The rain was falling harder, and I felt a twinge of disappointment that it would help extinguish the fires we had started.

They took me back, not to the place where I had been confined, but to a nearby tent. They leaned me against the central pole, bound my wrists behind it, kicked my legs out from under me so I fell to my knees, and bound my ankles in the same way as before. However, they didn't cover my head this time, so I could see my surroundings. Particularly, in the corner, I could see a stack of smooth, rectangular stones, about the size and shape of tombstones in an English cemetery, each one with straw ropes tied around it.

I was left there for several minutes to speculate on what use they might be planning to make of the stones. The rain hammered on the roof of the tent. Some wayward drops found their way around the ventilation flap, slid down the pole, and trickled down my back, sending additional chills down my spine as if I didn't already have enough of those from fear.

The tent flap rustled. Two guards came in, carrying between them what looked like a large, clearly heavy box, draped with a cloth. When they had set it down beside the entrance, they held the tent flap open for one more arrival. I was expecting Naozumi, but instead, I saw the man in the purple robe and black hat.

"You know who I am," he said.

"Domon Yasunari," I said. "From the Bureau of Onmyodo."

He nodded. "My father advised Tokugawa Ieyasu at the Battle of Sekigahara. He always said that he would be the last of the gunshi. Now that the Tokugawa clan had unified the nation and brought peace and order, our profession would no longer be needed. It's been my great honor to prove him wrong. *I* will be the last of the gunshi." He took a step toward me. "But it would seem I have some competition for that title. You got past my inugami. You got into my tent. And from my collection of scrolls, you carefully chose the one containing the spells of Takiyasha-hime. Why that one, and only that one?"

"Its rightful owner wanted it back," I said.

Domon scoffed. "Don't play games with me. She's been dead for centuries."

"That doesn't seem to have slowed her down much."

"You mean, her ghost? I doubt she'll be able to make much use of that scroll. But clearly, there's someone on your side who can. Who is it?"

I kept silent.

"I see," said Domon. "You're not going to talk. I expected as much." He gestured toward the stone slabs stacked in a corner. "Do you know what those are used for? An interrogation technique called *ishi-daki*, 'embracing the stone.' They're stacked on the subject's lap until he talks. Most people become very talkative with only one. The strong ones take two. I've never seen anyone hold out for more than three."

I mentally prepared myself. The incantation I had learned from the tengu was supposed to protect from blades and projectiles. Would it have any effect, I

260

wondered, against the weight of stones crushing the bones in my legs?

"However," Domon went on, "I see no need to resort to such primitive measures. Not just yet. Not when I have my assistant here."

With a flourish, he drew away the cloth covering what I had first thought to be a box. What it revealed instead was a bamboo cage. The creature inside looked like a monkey about my size. Its face, however, was eerily human-like, except for its eyes, which looked even more eerily like those of an owl: perfectly round, with enormous pupils that stared unblinkingly at me. They looked at me as if their gaze could pierce through my skull.

Its mouth moved, and words emerged in a human-like voice. "He thinks I'm eerie."

I realized with alarm that my impression had been right: its gaze *could* pierce through my skull.

I had dealt before with a *hihi*, a yokai that could read human thoughts. I couldn't help wondering what type of yokai this new one was, and how Domon had managed to capture it.

"He's seen yokai like me before," the creature reported, "but he's wondering what I am and how you captured me."

"Ah, yes." Domon allowed himself a self-satisfied smirk. "Capturing a *satori* – that's a very difficult undertaking indeed. But he's proven to be an invaluable resource for intelligence-gathering." Domon stared at me with eyes almost as intense as the satori's. "Now, let me ask you again: Who is the onmyoji on your side?"

Don't think of… I stopped myself just in time. If I told myself not to think of…*that person,* it would be the same as thinking of that person.

"He's trying hard not to think of that person," the satori reported.

Domon nodded. "Excellent. Don't think of him. Don't form a picture of him in your mind. Don't think of his name. Right now. Don't think of him."

I conjured a mental picture of a clear blue sky, grateful for Domon's assumption that an onmyoji could only be male.

"He's relieved that you think it's a man," the satori reported.

My next thought was unrepeatable. That, however, didn't prevent the satori from repeating it. I hoped Domon couldn't understand English.

Domon smiled, with the look of one who had just set a Flying Dragon on the board to threaten my King. "Her, then. Don't think of her. And by all means, don't think of her name."

Before Oyuki's name could spell itself out in my mind, I concentrated as hard as I could on one of the bawdy sea-shanties I had heard sailors sing on numerous voyages. The satori sang along with me, although it mangled the words and the melody almost beyond recognition.

My lady and her handmaid, upon a merry pin,
A contest had at farting, who would the wager win?
The girl first took three candles, and stood them all upright,
Wi'th'first fart she blew them out, wi'th'next set them alight.

"Who is she?" Domon shouted over the cacophony.

"He thinks you look like the front end of a pig," the satori informed him on my behalf, "and smell like the back end."

"I'm sorry," I said. "Did I think that out loud?"

"Enough!" Domon's eyes shot fire at me. "Congratulations, Simon Grey. You're the first prisoner I've seen who could hold out so long against a satori. And you'll be the first subject for an experiment I've always wanted to try: the combination of the satori with more...*traditional* interrogation techniques."

Domon gestured to the guards. With practiced motions as though they had done this many times before, they crossed over to the stack of stones and took hold of the top one. Seeing the exertion it took them to lift it, the thought of how it would feel to bear the full weight on my lap practically made my kneecaps break themselves.

Then, two more armored figures pushed their way through the tent flap. At first, I thought they were more guards. But the look on the faces of the guards as they dropped the stone showed me that they were as startled by the new arrivals as I was. At second glance, not only were the newcomers not part of the Shogun's forces, they weren't even part of the human race.

They looked like gigantic frogs, with splotchy skin ranging in color from dark brown to light brown to greenish-white. They walked upright and carried spears, and they wore cuirasses that seemed to be made of turtle shell.

The guards drew their swords. In almost perfect synchronicity, the frog-creatures opened their mouths. With a motion so fast I could scarcely be sure I saw it correctly, their long, pink tongues shot out and adhered to the sword blades. When they drew back, they took the swords with them, for the frog-creatures to take in their webbed hands just before their tongues rolled back into their mouths.

A third figure entered the tent, armed and armored similarly to the others, but much bigger; it would tower over even the tallest man I knew. I had always felt that even ordinary toads – at least the ones in my garden – had a naturally dour appearance, but to see that scowl magnified onto a face a yard across was downright terrifying.

Domon assumed a defensive stance and drew a slender rod from somewhere in his robe, which I could only assume was a magic wand. The giant toad gave him a baleful look through its orange-and-black eyes, and opened its mouth.

Instead of the long tongue I had been expecting, an iridescent mist, refracting all the colors of the rainbow, billowed out and swirled through the tent. As soon as it touched the guards, they froze as though rooted to the spot. Domon took a step back, but as soon as the tendrils of the mist touched him, he froze as well.

The giant toad spoke, in a deep, rolling voice that sounded like – well, the croaking of a giant toad.

"You think you can defe-eh-end yourselves against us?" it demanded. "You're no more thre-eh-eat than the flies I had for break-ek-ek-ek-ekfast! Ge-eh-et in our way, and *you'll* be the ones who croak!"

He turned his bulging eyes on his troops. "Frogmen! He-eh-elp him! Hop to it or I'll have your legs saute-eh-ed for my dinner!"

"Ribbit!" the others responded in unison. They set about untying the ropes that bound me, but their webbed hands were awkwardly suited for the job, and they eventually gave up and cut through the ropes with the swords they had taken from the guards.

I couldn't help wondering whether this was really happening, or whether hunger, sleeplessness, and fear were playing tricks on my senses.

"He's wondering whether this is really happening," said the satori, "or whether hunger…"

The giant toad-man dealt a blow to the bars of the cage. The satori fell silent.

"Who are you?" was all I could say.

He raised a webbed hand in salute. "Captain Bufo, sir. Amphibious Operations Squadron O-Gamma. We're here to re-eh-escue you, on the orders of Ge-eh-eneral Oyuki."

The frogmen took hold of my arms, helped me to my feet, and guided me out of the tent.

A deafening chorus of croaks greeted us as soon as we were outside. Thousands, even millions, of frogs covered every surface in the camp – except our path, which they apparently knew to jump clear of. My amphibian escorts, still keeping a firm grip on my arms, frog-marched me back the way I had come, along the path between the bamboo palisades and the sea.

The enemy was apparently too preoccupied with the sudden deluge of frogs to put much of an effort into stopping us. A few arrows sailed in our direction, but no musket balls – firearms were useless in this rain.

My escorts, on their webbed feet, made it across the tidal flats without even breaking stride, and hopped up the slope to the Oe Gate, which was open as other members of Captain Bufo's squadron were guiding the rescued captives home.

Oyuki rushed to greet me just as the frogmen let me go. Some sensation had returned to my limbs, but I was still a little unsteady on my feet, and I staggered without their support. Oyuki quickly grabbed my arms to steady me. Once I had regained my balance, she held on to me for a blessed moment longer than necessary before releasing her grip.

"Welcome back, Simon," she said, with a huge smile of relief.

"Thank you." It was all I could manage.

She gestured around at Captain Bufo and his warty warriors. "Not bad for a first try, wouldn't you say?"

The transparent figure of Takiyasha-hime, standing beside her, nodded warm approval.

Captain Bufo stood to attention – or as close as he could manage on his bowlegs – and saluted. "Mission accomplished, ma'am," he said. "Are there eh-eh-any further orders?"

"Not at the moment," Oyuki replied. "Thank you, Captain. Excellent work."

Captain Bufo gave another salute, then turned to his team and raised his voice. "We-eh-ell done, frogmen! Dis-*missed!*"

"Ribbit!" they replied in chorus, and hopped away.

Chapter 18:
The Trial

第十八章. 裁判

From what I heard people saying about the raid the next day, the results had been mixed. It had accomplished its purpose of wreaking havoc on the enemy camp, leaving over three hundred of the besiegers dead or wounded, and depriving their side, in quite a spectacular way, of a shed full of gunpowder. But it had brought back little in the way of ammunition for our side, and even less in the way of food. Worse, about two hundred on our side had been killed or wounded, and despite Chijiwa's orders, a dozen or so had been taken alive. Captain Bufo's team had managed to bring them back, but in several cases, not before Naozumi had taken a turn with them.

When I next saw Yamada, his face looked grave. "Simon, Shiro wants to see you in the tenshu."

A sudden jolt of anxiety went through me. I had rarely spoken to Shiro, but when I did, it had usually taken the form of a casual conversation. This was the first time he had sent a formal summons down the chain of command.

I reviewed last night's events in my mind, and wondered how much trouble I was in for. A hostile eyewitness could make a compelling case that I, by disobeying orders and breaking away from my team, had been solely responsible for the failure of the mission. And the only eyewitness I knew of was Sanai.

What was going to happen to me? Aboard an English ship, sailors who had committed offenses were flogged in front of the entire crew. I hoped nothing worse would await me, but knowing the Japanese penchant for fiendishly inventive punishments and interrogation techniques, I couldn't be too sure.

Silently, partly because my mouth was so dry I probably couldn't have spoken even if I had anything to say, I followed Yamada back to the tenshu, to the upper room that I had only seen once before. Shiro sat in front of Yamada's banner, with Ashizuka and Mori on one side as Yamada joined Chijiwa on the other.

The room certainly looked set up for a trial. In fact, it was eerily reminiscent of Izu's command post. But the spot that I had occupied there – kneeling on the floor facing the general – was already taken, by Oyuki.

"Simon, thank you for coming," said Shiro. He gestured to the floor. "Please, have a seat." His words were polite as always, but his face was as grave as the others.

I knelt beside Oyuki and stole a sideways glance at her. She made no acknowledgment of my presence. Her face was like a kabuki mask, revealing nothing of the thoughts of the person underneath.

"Simon," Shiro began once I was settled, "just before the raid, you presented Chijiwa with a highly detailed and accurate map of the enemy camp. He asked if you had made it using the gifts you learned from the tengu, and you neither confirmed nor denied it. Is this true so far?"

"Yes."

"Can you tell us exactly how you got the information for that map?" When I hesitated, Shiro prompted further: "Specifically, did you have any supernatural aid?"

"Yes."

"Who was it that helped you?"

I couldn't see anything else for it but to tell the truth. "The ghost of Takiyasha-hime."

I thought I heard a sharp exhalation from Chijiwa, but he, like the others, sat still. Shiro continued: "How did you make her acquaintance?"

I told him the story of our encounter with Takiyasha-hime and her assistance on the raid. When Shiro had finished questioning me, he turned his attention back to Oyuki, who confirmed that Sanai had given her the scroll as I asked, and Takiyasha-hime had taught her how to use it.

When Oyuki finished, Chijiwa turned to Shiro. "You've heard it from her own lips," he said. "She's admitted to practicing witchcraft."

"What?" I said aloud before I could stop myself.

"Simon, your turn to speak is over," Chijiwa said sharply. "Once we've finished with her, we'll settle with you."

"Witchcraft?" Mori echoed, in a disbelieving tone. "She saved the captives' lives by conjuring a plague of frogs. That was not only effective but an elegant Biblical touch. Reminiscent of what Mouze did to the king of Egiputo."

As usual, it took me a moment to decipher the Japanese pronunciation of Biblical names, but I soon figured out that he was talking about Moses and Pharaoh.

Chijiwa glared at Mori. "If you're going to play that game, Soiken, I'll remind you that every time Deus performed a miracle through Mouze, the sorcerers of Egiputo managed to duplicate it by black magic."

"What are you proposing?" Shiro asked.

Chijiwa glared at both of us. "Turn them out. They never wanted to be among us in the first place. Let them hop to Nagasaki on the back of a giant toad."

My heart started hammering even harder. "This is no joking matter," I said. "To be turned out of the castle would be a death sentence."

Chijiwa said nothing, but his face conveyed one word very clearly: *And?*

"Oyuki saved my life, and the lives of the other prisoners," I said. "What does it matter whether she had supernatural help? When I used the fighting arts I learned from the tengu to fight the orochi, everyone hailed me as a hero. Why is her case any different?"

"I never approved of enlisting the aid of tengu, or ghosts, or any other occult creatures," Chijiwa said. "As far as I was concerned, we would have been much better off trusting solely in the power of Deus. On those occasions, I was overruled. But this time, let these others say what they will, witchcraft is a bridge too far."

"I see," said Oyuki. "You're afraid of a woman with power beyond your reach."

"Silence!" Chijiwa thundered at her.

"Can you prove her wrong?" I asked. "This is how you thank her for saving us? With a witch trial? What are you planning to do next? Make her drink holy water? Duck her in the lotus pond? Shave her head and lead her into the tenshu backwards?"

Oyuki gave me a look of alarm, and I realized too late that my audience had no way of understanding these ironic references to the Pendle witch trials, which had been notorious in England before I left. In fact, Chijiwa was looking at me with a sudden expression of avid interest. I had the horrible feeling that, if he had paper and a brush ready to hand, he would be taking notes.

"You know," I went on hurriedly, "I can think of an easier way. Yamada-sama is a talented artist. I'm sure he could draw a good picture of Takiyasha-hime from our description. Why not just have him do that, and then have Oyuki step on it?"

The heavy silence that followed told me my words had hit their mark. Chijiwa's jowls were quivering with barely suppressed rage.

"Have we become the very thing we're fighting against?" I pressed on. "What difference is there anymore between you and Matsukura?"

"Do I really have to explain the difference to you?" Chijiwa demanded. "Matsukura, Izu, the Shogun…the lot of them are *persecuting* the one true faith. We are *defending* it. And *you* are consorting with the enemies of Deus, the enemies of humankind, the agents of the Adversary himself."

"Enough." Shiro's high, calm voice pierced through the argument, as he raised a pacifying hand. "We already have our hands full fighting our enemies. Do we have to fight among ourselves as well?"

Chijiwa gaped at him. "You too, Shiro? If someone like Soiken defends her," he went on with an accusing glance at Mori, "that's no surprise. He's always taken a keener interest in the occult than befits a Kirishitan. But *you*, I always thought, were a true man of Deus." He exhaled sharply again before continuing, "It seems even a man of Deus is still a man, and a young man is still vulnerable to the charms of a young woman. She's bewitched even you."

With an indignant expression, Shiro opened his mouth to reply. But before he could say anything, Chijiwa pressed on: "Well, if you won't settle the matter, I will." He turned to confront Oyuki. "You're either with us or with the devil. So tell us, once and for all: which is it to be? Are you on the side of heaven, or hell?"

Oyuki looked him straight in the eye. "If being on the side of heaven means being on the side of people like you, I don't see much to choose between them."

Fire flashed from Chijiwa's eyes. He looked as though, if he had been closer, he would have struck her.

Things had come to such a pitch, I thought, that there was nothing to do but turn the tables. I took a deep breath and said a silent prayer.

"Izu thanks you for doing his job for him," I said to Chijiwa. "Are you going to report your success in your next arrow-letter to him?"

Chijiwa glared at me, wide-eyed. "What?"

"Someone on our side has been sending arrow-letters to the enemy. Perhaps you know who?"

The reaction on his face was not what I expected. The rage was still there, now mingled with astonishment, but I didn't see the slightest sign of guilt.

"What are you talking about?" he demanded. And, I realized, it was a genuine question. He hadn't known.

I felt as though the floor of the tenshu had dropped out from under me, but I did my best to bluster my way through. "Well, if it wasn't you, who was it? That's what I thought this meeting was going to be about. Wouldn't our time and effort be better spent finding the traitor in our midst than conducting witch trials?"

Everyone looked at me with bewildered expressions. Everyone except Yamada, who was looking at no one at all, his gaze fixed firmly on the floor.

"Simon," said Shiro, "what are you saying? What do you know that we don't?"

I told him what I had seen in the scrying pool in Tengudo. He looked at me, wide-eyed. "And you didn't tell anyone about this until now?"

"Of course I did," I said. "I told my commanding officer."

"Indeed?" Shiro turned to face Yamada. "How strange that this is the first I'm hearing of it."

Yamada cleared his throat. "Naturally, this is a very serious matter. I took it upon myself to investigate, but I didn't wish to cast undue suspicion on anyone until I had proof."

"And on whom did your suspicion fall?" Shiro asked.

Yamada continued to look down, and made no reply.

"On whom did it fall?" Shiro repeated more sharply.

Yamada was silent for a few seconds that felt like hours.

"You heard what Chijiwa proposed," he finally said. "To spread our remaining powder around the walls of the castle, and when the Shogun's forces finally forced their way in, ignite it and blow us all to eternity."

So *that* was the mysterious figure I had seen skulking around the powder shed.

"Is this true?" asked an incredulous Mori.

Not only did Chijiwa not deny it, he proudly returned Mori's gaze.

"It would have been so simple," he said. "One flash of fire. Then, everyone on our side would be on the way to Paradise to claim their martyr's reward, and everyone on their side would be on the way to hell. Much better than running the risk of any of us being taken alive. You know what tortures the Shogun's forces are capable of. But at this stage, they would scarcely even need them. How many of us do you suppose would gladly step on the fumi-e and trade their last hope of heaven for a bowl of soup and rice?"

Ashizuka gaped at him. "I can't believe what I'm hearing."

I wholeheartedly shared his sentiment. Chijiwa's plan would have been a horrific revelation under ordinary circumstances, but at the moment, I barely had enough shock left to spare for it after the confession of Yamada. He had been more than a commanding officer to me. He had practically been a substitute father – a dependable, reassuring presence in these perilous times. To hear that *he* was the traitor sucked the breath right out of my body.

"Do you, of all people," Ashizuka continued, "need to be told that Deus forbids suicide?"

"How could it be called suicide if it wasn't of their own volition?" Chijiwa replied, still looking completely convinced of the righteousness of his idea. "That charge could only stand against the one who lit the fuse, and that would have been me. I would willingly accept whatever judgment Deus passed on my soul, knowing that I had saved thousands of others from perdition."

Shiro kept his scrutiny on Yamada. "Did you really think I would take his suggestion?"

"You didn't dismiss it," Yamada said. "How was I to know? You're a young man, and your mind has always been on matters of the spirit, of the next world. You haven't lived in this world long enough to have anything invested in it. Going out in a blaze of glory is all very well when your own life is the only one at stake. You haven't learned what it means for the lives of others to be bound together with yours."

"Have I not?" A fiercer anger blazed from Shiro than I had ever seen before. "Do you think I don't see the lives of all these thousands as bound together with mine? Do you think I don't feel the constant weight on my shoulders of all the hope they place in me?"

"And do you really think their hopes can be fulfilled?" Yamada asked. "How do you imagine we can win? What does victory even mean anymore?"

"What does victory mean?" Shiro shot back. "I'll tell you what it means. It doesn't mean achieving the goal we had in mind at first. It doesn't even mean survival. Even if we make it out of this castle, in the long run none of us will ever leave this globe alive. Victory means not losing your soul. It means writing your chapter of the Great Story so that, no matter how it ends, men and angels will read it and say, 'This was a true and good man.' Do you think they'll be able to say that of you, Yamada Emosaku?"

Yamada hung his head.

Shiro, his eyes still on Yamada, gestured to the others. "Keep him confined until we decide what to do with him."

"What about them?" Chijiwa asked, pointing to Oyuki and me.

Shiro fixed him in a baleful gaze. "One who proposed to take the lives of my people has no standing to bring a charge against two who did their best to save them, even by sorcery." He turned his attention back to Yamada. "Take him away."

Chapter 19:
Easter Sunday

第
十
九
章
・
復
活
祭

T he twenty-eighth day of the second lunar month in the fifteenth year of the Kan'ei era, the Year of the Tiger. Or, by the calendar I was more used to, Easter Sunday of the Year of our Lord 1638.

Since we had no priest among us, we celebrated the same way we did every Sunday, with Shiro leading us in a "dry Mass." He intoned the words of the Mass in the Japanized Latin that I had become somewhat able to follow by this point, but without administering the sacraments. Not that he could have in any case, since there was no bread or wine to be had in the camp.

"When the sun rose on the first Easter morning," he said during his homily, "it followed the darkest night the disciples had ever known. The one in whom they had put all their trust was dead, and for all they knew, there was nothing they could do but give him a proper burial. Perhaps they had forgotten the promise he made to them before he went to his death: 'Your grief will turn to joy, and that joy no one can take from you.' And it turned out exactly as he said. Have faith in this, brothers and sisters: Miracles happen when you least expect them."

After Mass, Oyuki shouldered her way through the crowd and rushed up to me. "Simon!" she cried excitedly. "Look!"

I looked where she was pointing. Over the top of the outer wall, I saw the masts and sails of a tall ship – not one of the Shogun's vessels, but a European merchantman. Atop the crow's nest flew the Dutch colors.

I never imagined I could be so happy to see them.

We ran to the ramparts for a closer look. It was a three-masted cargo fluyt, bearing the name *De Rijp*.

Oyuki and I turned to look at each other.

"Could this mean..." she asked hesitantly, "Couckebacker has had a change of heart?"

"If so," I said, "Shiro was right. Miracles do happen when you least expect them."

And I dared to believe it. I held out a glimmer of hope, on this Easter morning, that there really was a God in heaven and he had not abandoned his followers in this besieged castle.

A sound like a thunderclap echoed through the cloudless sky, accompanied by a flash of fire and a puff of smoke from one of the cannon ports of the *Rijp*. A ball sailed over the ramparts of the castle. As we watched in disbelief, it fell to the dry ground of the courtyard, raising a cloud of dust as it embedded itself in the earth.

Oyuki and I exchanged another glance, our joy suddenly turned to shock and horror, as another cannon fired. This one struck one of the huts, breaking a hole in the thatched roof. We heard a scream from within.

The Dutch *had* joined the battle...but not on our side.

"Couckebacker!" I shouted at the top of my lungs, not caring that there was no way he could hear me from this distance. "You vermin! You traitor! You...*Judas!*"

My rant was cut short by another explosion, much louder and closer than the cannon blasts. It came from somewhere behind us.

I turned. From around the northern part of the outer wall, smoke rose as if pouring out of the ground itself. It took me a moment to realize what had happened: The enemy had undermined the castle wall. They had dug a tunnel and packed it with explosives.

Before the smoke even cleared, cannons thundered from the enemy camp. We hastily took cover as the bombardment began in earnest, from both land and sea.

Amid the fusillade of the cannons, I heard the shouts of thousands of soldiers as they charged. The cannons were artillery preparation for one final, all-out assault.

It reminded me of our first battle, just before the New Year. But since that time, the enemy's ranks had swelled: more men, more weapons, more capable leaders. As for our side, many of the rebels were so weakened with hunger they could barely stand. There was no use in the musketeers manning their battle stations, since we had no more powder or shot left. Oyuki and her fellow archers were our only hope of striking the foe from a distance.

The besiegers leaned their bamboo ladders against the walls. As before, our side struggled to push them away with poles, and hurriedly heated oil and sand in cooking pots, preparing to rain them down on the heads of the soldiers scaling the walls. There were rocks standing by the ramparts, but scarcely anyone with enough strength to lift them alone. Two or more people had to lift them into position and let gravity do the rest.

Fire-arrows sailed over the walls. The huts along the outer wall had had just enough time to dry out after Friday's rain, and now they burst into flames. Some of the defenders seized on the idea of using the burning timbers as weapons. They wrapped their hands in their sleeves, pried burning timbers away, carried them to the battlements, and hurled them down onto the heads of the attackers. It was an ingenious tactic that also bespoke a dreadful finality: *This is it. This is the end. One way or another, after today, Hara Castle will be no more.*

The northern gate caved under the force of a battering ram, and the Shogun's forces poured into the outer courtyard. As they surged forward, our side retreated – except for one figure in red amidst all the others in garments so dirty and dusty that you could scarcely tell they had once been white. Obotan ran towards one of the leading samurai with outstretched arms and a look of desperation on her face.

"Sir!" she cried. "Please! These madmen have abducted me! Save me and take me back to Edo!"

The samurai hesitated as she ran up to him and threw one arm around him. With the other, she deftly drew her pipe out of her sash. I didn't see what must have happened next – Obotan using her considerable strength to drive the sharpened mouthpiece of the pipe through a chink in the samurai's armor – but I heard his cry of pain.

"That's something like it," she said as he fell to the ground, then turned and caught my eye. "Remember, boy," she called. "The pipe kills!"

Her satisfied smile was etched onto her face for eternity, as a thrust from the sword of another samurai stained her kimono a darker shade of red.

Those on our side who still had some strength left tried desperately to hold the line, while the women, children, and men too weak to fight, herded through the second gate into the inner courtyard. Once they were all through, the warriors retreated after them and hurriedly swung the gate shut.

As soon as the gate was closed, we did our best to barricade it. Some people leaned wooden beams against it, while others used what little remained of their strength to pile rocks, cooking pots, anything that could possibly impede our attackers, in front of it. Take-taba were brought into place to provide cover for the archers, Oyuki among them. And the warriors stood in front of the gate, waiting. It was my dubious honor to be among them.

With a noise that made us all jump, the gate shook as the battering ram struck it.

I turned to Ashizuka. "I don't suppose we're up to a million rocks yet?"

The battering ram landed another blow, causing the bar across the gate to crack and splinter.

Chijiwa's head snapped about to face me. "What did you say?"

"I...uh..." The ram struck the gate again. "It was something I heard from the tengu. The battle for Hara Castle will be won when a million rocks have been hurled from its ramparts."

Chijiwa turned his gaze back to the gate. "Superstitious nonsense," he said, but with less conviction than usual. For some reason, the words appeared to have shaken him.

At the next blow from the battering ram, the bar split almost in two. One final blow forced the gates wide enough apart that the soldiers began pouring in. Our archers loosed a volley of arrows the moment they came in sight, and many of them fell, but they continued to come through the gate, in numbers too great to pick off one at a time.

Just behind the vanguard came a samurai, whose unhurried stride set him apart from the inrushing hordes. He appeared to be as old as Ashizuka and the other senior officers on our side, but his armor looked new, without the dents and notches you would expect on a seasoned warrior. The skin on his face was pockmarked, and he regarded us with an expression both disdainful and wary, as though he deemed us unworthy of him but was still not going to let any of us surprise him.

I stepped into his path.

He took one look at me, then made as if to move on, as though I were beneath his notice. He said nothing, but his attitude spoke as loudly as any words could: *Stand aside, boy, so I can go seek out the real warriors.*

I started to draw my sword.

In a flash, the hilt of his sword pressed down on my hand. He had closed the distance with me so quickly that he only had to unsheathe a few inches of the blade to send the unmistakable message: *Don't even think about it.*

I took a step back and drew my sword all the way.

The point had barely cleared the sheath before his blade came flashing at me. I raised my own sword to parry, but his blade quickly changed direction and slashed at my unprotected wrists. The stroke would have cut my hands clean off, but I took a desperate jump backwards and it narrowly missed.

He gave a shout like a lion's roar. It startled me, and in that moment of disorientation, he swung. I barely managed to parry the blow.

Buzen-bo's voice echoed in my mind. *Your opponent will do everything he can to cause confusion and fear in you. But if your mind is clear, then whatever external sights and sounds assail your senses, you can simply observe them without reacting to them.*

I recovered my balance, and we squared off again. I tried to move to the east so that the rising sun would be behind me, but he had the same idea. All I could do was to keep it to my right.

Predict what your opponent will do, but be unpredictable yourself. This warrior seemed to embody this principle. He would lash out, and I would move to parry, only to realize that his strike had been a feint. If I felt a moment of relief afterwards, he would sense my lapse of mindfulness and attack. If I attempted a counterstrike, his blade would always be there a fraction of a second before mine. If I feigned fatigue to lull him into overconfidence, he saw right through the deception.

It was like fighting Ajari again. And I had never won against him.

The defender has the advantage, I reminded myself. *His goal is to kill me. My goal is to stay alive. If the fight ends with neither of us landing a blow, it will mean my victory and his defeat.*

The unknown warrior finally spoke. "I've never fought anyone like you," he said. "Where did you learn your swordsmanship?" From the conversational tone of his question, you would think we were in the garden having a cup of tea rather than in a besieged castle fighting a duel to the death.

"From the tengu," I replied.

Before I could finish the last word, he slashed. I was ready for him, though, and my blade parried his.

I noticed an unusual movement on top of the gate, behind my opponent. I tried to look more closely using only my peripheral vision, without moving my eyes and alerting my opponent. There was an armored figure standing on top of the gate, and it looked like Chijiwa.

My opponent took advantage of my momentary distraction to launch a blindingly fast strike. I barely had time to raise my sword to parry. The tip of his blade bore down on the hilt of mine, and before I knew what was happening, my sword was on the ground.

The armored figure on the gate took a flying leap.

It was so unexpected that I couldn't stop my eyes from giving me away. Now that I had been disarmed, my opponent risked a glance above and behind him, to see the bulk of Chijiwa, like a cannonball, hurtling down towards him, his sword ready for a downward thrust.

The unknown warrior tried to step aside and raise his sword simultaneously. But there was little space and less time to do the first. All he could manage was the second.

The two bodies collided, fell to the ground, and rolled apart.

Both of them lay there, grunting and groaning in pain. Neither rose. The unknown warrior clutched his leg.

I picked up my sword and held it on guard, wary of another trick.

"Simon," said Mori's awed voice behind me, "do you know who that is? Miyamoto Musashi."

It took me a moment to recall where I had heard the name before. When I did, my mind reeled. I had just fought the greatest swordsman of the age, the one who had never lost a duel. I wondered fleetingly whether history would record this one as the one that broke his streak, or whether it would be regarded as a draw.

Musashi looked up at me, still grimacing and clutching his leg. "Go on, then," he said through clenched teeth. "Finish what you started."

I remembered Buzen-bo's words: *Musashi's book is holy writ for Japanese warriors. Well, it will be soon.*

Buzen-bo could see the future. If I were to strike the final blow against Musashi, would that change the predestined course of history? It was too complicated a question for me to wrap my mind around, but one thing I knew for sure: I had no desire to drive my sword into the body of a helpless man, especially one who had such a gift yet to be given.

"Man wounded!" I shouted in the direction of the attackers.

Several of the Shogun's warriors surrounded Musashi, picked him up, and carried him toward the gate. One of them glanced in my direction and, without meeting my gaze, gave a slight nod that I took for an expression of thanks.

Mori and I looked at Chijiwa. He looked back at us through glazed eyes.

"Deus," he murmured, "into your hands I commend my spirit."

His rasping breath ceased.

Mori's gaze stayed on Chijiwa's lifeless form a moment longer. "Your tengu's prophecy is fulfilled," he told me sadly.

"How?"

"*Chi-ji-iwa.* A thousand thousand rocks – a million rocks. That was what his name meant." He turned back to me. "When your tengu said the battle would be won, I don't suppose he happened to mention by which side?"

I looked into his eyes, full of determination.

"It can be ours," I said. "All we have to do is hold out until sundown. After that, we'll be able to summon the yokai to fight on our side."

And I wish I could say that was what happened.

I wish I could say that as soon as the sun set on the battle, General Seto ordered all the plates in the castle to throw themselves at the Shogun's troops. I wish I could say that Captain Bufo and his amphibian army saw to it that they dropped like flies. I wish I could say that Takiyasha-hime rode to our rescue with an army of yokai marshalled behind her.

But on that Easter Sunday, the Shimabara Rebellion failed to outlast the daylight.

* * *

Let the chronicle show that the rebels fought to the very end. We gave it everything we had. But everything we had still wasn't enough to make us a match for an army of well-trained, well-armed, well-nourished warriors who outnumbered us five to one.

Once again, I understood keenly what Buzen-bo meant about the relativity of time. The battle unfolded with the speed of lightning, but to my eyes, everything seemed to be moving slowly. I could see every step, but I was powerless to stop any of it.

I saw a young warrior, in red armor bearing the same crest as Itakura Shigemasa, striding through the courtyard escorted by four guards. Sanai put up a brave fight against them, but it was one against five. The guards used the butt ends of their spears to pummel him within an inch of his life, then stood aside and let their young master strike the final blow.

I saw Ashizuka crossing blades with Naozumi. I saw his face as his son fell, and heard his scream of anguish.

I saw Naozumi take advantage of his moment of distraction to run him through.

I saw Mori fall, right beside me. I rushed to his side and cradled his head in my arms. Keeping his flair for the dramatic even to the very end, he spent his last breath reciting a poem he had clearly prepared for the occasion:

Last year and this year,
Gone like dreams upon waking.
Great horse, great rider,
Their souls all take flight like birds.
Plum blossoms, scent of heaven.

And the next thing I realized, all was still. The only sound in the castle was Naozumi's voice, shouting in triumph: "Behold your savior! Behold your Chosen One! Behold the almighty power of your Deus!"

I hurried to the main courtyard. A crowd had already gathered there. Oyuki was among them, tears streaming down her face.

In the center of the courtyard, the light from the setting sun shone on a bamboo cross. Standing beside it was the wretched figure of Yamada, one samurai holding each of his arms. And hanging from the cross, still alive, but just barely, was Amakusa Shiro. His face was streaked with dirt and blood, but still, heavenly light seemed to engulf him.

"Behold your savior!" the jubilant Naozumi repeated. "Behold your Chosen One! Behold the almighty power of your Deus!"

As we looked on helplessly, Shiro summoned the last of his strength to raise his head and address his final words to the heavens.

"Forgive them, Father," he murmured. "They know not what they've done."

With these words, he gave up his spirit.

Chapter 20:
The Fall of Hara Castle

第二十章・落城

This is the end of your rebellion," the triumphant Naozumi declared. "You trusted in your god to save you, but now you see that your *Deus* is nothing more than a *dai-uso,* a great lie."

He grinned smugly at his own pun before continuing: "And your Chosen One, Amakusa Shiro, was nothing more than a false prophet. You should have accepted the Shogun's offer of clemency when you had the chance." He turned to the samurai nearest him. "Leave none alive," he ordered. "And leave no stone of Hara Castle standing."

"Sir!" Yamada called as he strained against the grip of the samurai who held him. "You said we would be shown mercy!"

The smirking Naozumi turned to him. "And perhaps you shall," he said. "In the next world...if there really is a Deus to grant it." He turned back to his lieutenant. "You have your orders. Kill them all."

"Just a moment, please."

The new voice was quiet and polite, but it resonated across the courtyard, drawing more attention than Naozumi's bluster. All heads turned to look for its source. When people saw it, they gasped. Some clapped hands over their mouths. Some on our side made the sign of the cross.

It was Don Protasio. His spectral figure, outlined in blue light, calmly made its way from the tenshu to the courtyard where we stood.

"I might have something to say about that," he continued, "since this is, after all, my house."

Of all the expressions on all the faces looking at him, none looked more terrified than Naozumi's. If he looked as if he had seen a ghost, that would be entirely understandable. But he looked more as if he were face to face with the Devil himself than this mild-mannered apparition. Sweat poured down his face, and he shook in every limb. He backed away, but tripped over an uneven patch of ground and fell hard on his backside.

Don Protasio continued to approach him. "Miguel," he said gently, "why do you feel you need to fear me?"

Miguel?

"I must admit," Don Protasio went on, "this was not exactly how I imagined the return of my prodigal son."

Son?

Now that I thought of it, Don Protasio had only ever told us his son's baptismal name, never his Japanese name. And I was so used to calling Don Protasio by his Christian name that I had never noticed the coincidence until this moment: Arima Harunobu, Arima Naozumi.

"When the Shogun's men came to take my head," Don Protasio continued, "I thought that, as a martyr, I would go straight to heaven. For the longest time, I couldn't guess why I had to stay here below. When Amakusa Shiro and his followers took refuge in my castle, I thought I had finally found the answer: I had to stay here long enough to give them what help I could. But now I know the real reason."

He extended a spectral hand. It penetrated through the face shield of Naozumi's helmet to caress his cheek.

"I couldn't go to heaven because it wouldn't be heaven without you."

Naozumi blinked several times. I couldn't be sure, but it looked as if his eyes were beginning to well up with tears.

"When I ascend, I want to be sure that you'll ascend too," Don Protasio went on. "My son, what does it profit you if you win the battle? What does it profit you if you win honor, titles, wealth, lands, castles, but lose your soul? When you lie alone at night, do you ever have dreams of facing a shadowy foe from which no sword, no gun, no vassals can protect you? Heed them. They are warnings of the fate that awaits you in the life to come, unless you mend your ways."

Naozumi's breath came in ragged gasps. "If what you say is true," he said, "it's too late for me. My soul is already lost."

"As long as there's breath in your body, it's not too late," Don Protasio replied. "You can still repent. You can still have your name written among those who chose the right path."

Naozumi swallowed hard. "I have my orders."

"Are you going to obey them and save your life?" Don Protasio asked. "Or obey your conscience and save your soul? It's one or the other."

Naozumi was silent a moment longer. Then, he laid a trembling hand on the hilt of his short sword.

"No, Miguel!" Don Protasio's voice was sharper than I had ever heard it before. "Deus forbids it. There's no easy escape for you that way."

"I would have to anyway," Naozumi said miserably, "if I disobeyed my master."

"You could refuse, as I did. You could insist that those who pass sentence on you carry it out themselves."

Suddenly, a ball of blue light flitted before my face. It was a hitodama, as I had seen when James died.

It hovered before me for a moment, flitted away, then came back. It seemed to be beckoning me to follow it.

I took a glance at Oyuki. She clearly saw it too.

Slowly and cautiously, we made our way to the edge of the crowd, following where it led. Everyone's attention was so focused on Don Protasio and Naozumi that we managed to slip away, strategically threading our way among the taller rebels, undetected by the enemy.

The hitodama led us to the tsume-no-maru, to the entrance to Arigamigado. The boards and rocks were still there, having been put back in place as a precaution even after the orochi had been defeated. The hitodama hovered over it.

"The cave!" I whispered to Oyuki. "Where we fought the serpent-scorpion. Maybe it has an opening outside the castle."

As quickly as we could, we started to move aside the stones.

Then, one of the Shogun's soldiers came into view. As soon as I saw him, he saw me. He called to his companions: "Someone's trying to escape!"

Oyuki and I redoubled our efforts. Two more soldiers came running to catch up with the first. They aimed their muskets at us and fired.

Time is relative to your point of view.

And suddenly I understood, at the most basic level, what Buzen-bo meant. I could see the musket balls making their leisurely way toward me. I could trace their trajectory. I saw that one was going to miss, but the other was headed straight for Oyuki.

I chanted under my breath, "*On-kiru-kiru-mata-uji-yaku-yasei-sowaka.*"

The floodgates opened. Ki from heaven, and from the center of the earth, flowed through me. I had all the time in the world.

I put my hand in the path of the musket ball.

As if my hand were made of stone or iron, the musket ball struck it and fell harmlessly to the ground.

The soldiers exchanged an incredulous glance, as if wondering whether I was the second ghost they had seen today.

One of them drew his sword and charged.

I drew my own sword. Still in the time-dilated state, I executed the technique Musashi had used on me, and sent the sword falling to the earth.

Oyuki had cleared away enough of the barrier to make an opening that we could just squeeze through. The hitodama dived in. I motioned to Oyuki to go ahead. While she was lowering herself into the passage, I dealt a blow to the soldier's breastplate that sent him staggering backwards, and followed it with a kick that sent him sprawling.

Once Oyuki was through, I squeezed in after her.

We slid down the rough shaft, and emerged into the main gallery. The faint light from the hitodama illuminated our way. When we got to the place where the gallery divided, the hitodama led us to the right – not the passage that led to the orochi's former lair, but the other one we hadn't taken.

That passage took us into another gallery almost as big as the one we had left. The high, vaulted ceiling reminded me of a church. In fact, the grooves time had carved into some of the larger stalagmites made them look like clusters of organ pipes.

The hitodama stopped. It grew larger, and its light grew brighter. A moment later, the radiant figure of Amakusa Shiro stood before us: translucent, in that we could still see the cave wall through it, but glowing with a light as white as its kimono.

"Shiro," said Oyuki with a smile. "Thank you for saving us."

Shiro inclined his radiant head. "I wish I could have saved you all," he said. "But you two, at least, can see me in this state, so I was able to give you a little help." He pointed down the gallery. "Go a bit farther this way, and you'll find the tunnel the other side dug. That will lead you into their camp. All their warriors are in the castle now, so you'll find it practically empty."

"Thank you," I said.

"Once you've gotten away," said Shiro, "there are two things I ask of you. First: Izu and the Shogun will want to make us disappear. It won't be enough for them to see our cause go down in history as a failure. They'll want to erase it altogether, to make it as if the Shimabara Rebellion never happened. Don't let them. Tell our story. Tell the world how we, the common people, dared to stand up to the Shogun of Japan. And all his forces, even though they could destroy our bodies, failed to break our spirits."

I nodded fervently. "We will. And the second?"

He extended a hand to Oyuki. After a moment's hesitation, she raised hers, and he took it. His new body must have had some substance, because her hand rested in his as naturally as if he were still flesh and blood.

He held out the other hand to me. I took it. It felt warm, as if it were made of solid light.

Shiro brought our hands together, joined Oyuki's to mine, and put both of his around ours.

"Take good care of each other."

He released our hands, spread his arms with palms upraised, and turned his face toward heaven. For a moment, he was standing in a column of brilliant light. Then it, and he, were gone.

Without his hitodama, we were standing in total darkness. I felt a moment of panic, but then I heard Oyuki's voice say, "*Kitsunebi!*"

Another ball of blue light appeared. With it illuminating our path, we proceeded further down the gallery. As Shiro had said, we soon encountered a place where rocks lay strewn about as though the cave wall had been blown apart. Beyond it was a narrow tunnel, clearly dug by human hands, and with the walls scorched black where it met the gallery.

We emerged from the tunnel into the fast-darkening evening. Standing at the exit, waiting patiently for us, was Domon, flanked by two soldiers.

He took one look at Oyuki, and his eyes widened in disbelief. "It was *you*?"

A slight expression of puzzlement crossed her face, but she promptly fired back, "Who were you expecting?"

"A proper sorceress. Someone who would be a worthy successor to Takiyasha-hime." Before she could retort, he went on: "No matter. Your army of frogs put a bit of a damper on our battle plans, I'll say that for you. But still, history will show that the Shogun's forces crushed the Shimabara Rebellion. And the last of the gunshi helped secure their victory."

He took a step back, put his hands together with his fingers twisted into an arcane gesture, and with eyes half-closed, began to recite a long, monotonous chant.

"*Shi-kotsu-ren-ketsu-soku-kotsu, soku-kotsu-ren-ketsu-sho-kotsu, sho-kotsu-ren-ketsu-kyo-kotsu...*"

I felt vibrations in the ground underfoot, like the beginning of an earthquake. Mounds began to appear in the earth, as if a whole colony of moles had simultaneously decided to dig their way to the surface. Then the mounds burst, and from them emerged not moles, or any other burrowing animals, but human bones.

As I watched in horrified fascination, the bones flew across the battlefield to a spot near us. As they converged, they connected. The smaller bones fused into larger ones, and they joined together to form skeletal feet, legs, hips, spine, ribs, shoulders, arms, and hands. Finally, all the skulls, both whole and fragmented, flew to the top, to fuse into one skull so big it looked as though a second moon had appeared in the sky. The creature had the proportions of a human skeleton, but it stood as tall as the keep of Hara Castle. Inside its cavernous eye sockets, a blue fire blazed.

As Domon continued his chant, the eyes turned their horrific gaze on us. The massive skeleton bent at the waist and extended its arms toward us, its bony fingers outspread to grab us.

Suddenly, a figure appeared beside Oyuki: the ghostly form of Takiyasha-hime.

"Oyuki," she said urgently, "that's a *gashadokuro*. A yokai made from the bones of those who died in battle, animated by their anger and thirst for revenge."

Oyuki turned to her in desperation. "How do we fight it?"

"You can control it. Just as I did, when I fought Oyataro no Mitsukuni."

"How?" Oyuki's voice was practically a scream. "How can I compete with such a powerful onmyoji?"

"It's *my* magic he's using," said Takiyasha-hime. "And my power aligns itself naturally with the oppressed against the oppressor."

I suddenly heard James' voice in my head, echoing the words he had said to me across the shogi board. I gave it voice for Oyuki. "She's right. The greatest strategy is to get your opponent to do your fighting for you."

"Chant along with me," Takiyasha-hime instructed, "and trust in the righteousness of your cause."

Oyuki took a deep breath, twisted her fingers into the same gesture Domon was using, and began to chant, following Takiyasha-hime's lead.

"*Kyo-kotsu-ren-ketsu-kei-kotsu, kei-kotsu-ren-ketsu-shitsu-gai-kotsu, shitsu-gai-kotsu-ren-ketsu-dai-tai-kotsu...*"

Imagine a marionette so large and complex that it requires two puppeteers. Now imagine those two in a fight, each viciously pummeling the other with one fist while the other hand strained to keep his own controller out of reach. Now imagine that the marionette is as tall as twelve grown men. Then, you will have some image of how the gashadokuro looked as its skeletal arms and legs flailed about at impossible angles, its skull swinging madly from side to side, as Oyuki and Domon fought their battle of wills.

The guards charged at me. I drew my sword and stood in front of Oyuki, with only one thought in mind: *Protect her.*

I heard Buzen-bo's voice in my mind. *If multiple enemies attack you, position yourself so they get in each other's way. Keep the weaker of your opponents between you and the stronger. If you can master this technique, you can fight five, ten, or twenty enemies as easily as one.*

The first of the soldiers swung his long sword at me. As I parried the blow, I stepped in close and drew his short sword from its sheath.

"*Okari shimasu,*" I said. Japanese formalities are wonderfully compact. It took less than a second to say, "I will humbly accept the favor of being graciously allowed to borrow this."

I now had two swords. When one of the guards attacked me, I could parry his blow with the short, and counterattack with the long.

I did my best to follow Buzen-bo's principle. But as sensible as it was when I had only myself to defend, I knew that in this case, I was not the primary target. Oyuki was, and everything depended on my keeping them away from her. If either of them were to outflank me while I was engaged with the other, he would have a clear pathway to her.

In the background, I could still hear the chant going on, slowly as if I were hearing it under water: "*Dai-tai-kotsu-ren-ketsu-kan-kotsu, kan-kotsu-ren-ketsu-seki-chu, seki-chu-ren-ketsu-to-gai-kotsu...*"

James' voice echoed in my head again. *If your King is in check,* it reminded me, *you have to see to his safety before you launch a counterattack.*

Praying that these guards would follow the same principle, I charged at Domon.

The guards turned and ran after me, as though competing to see which would be the first to strike me down. Out the corner of my eye, I saw one of them rapidly close the distance between us and raise his sword.

I turned, stepped aside, and let his momentum carry him past me. As soon as his back was to me, I dealt him a kick in the backside to help him on his way.

He tumbled forward, collided with Domon, and both came down. Behind me, Oyuki's voice went on chanting.

The gashadokuro ceased its macabre dance. It turned in our direction, bent down, and stretched out an arm.

The soldier hurriedly scrambled to his feet. Domon tried to do the same, but before he could, the skeletal fingers closed around him. The gashadokuro rose, lifting him high into the air. As he squirmed and struggled frantically, the huge jawbone swung open, and the bony arm conveyed him towards it.

I averted my eyes. I heard a horrible crunching noise from above, and saw a soft, black shape fall to the ground in front of me. On closer inspection, it proved to be Domon's hat.

The guards gaped for a moment, then ran away in terror.

"Well done, Oyuki," I heard Takiyasha-hime's voice say. "I knew you could do it."

Oyuki let out a sigh of relief and exhaustion. "Thank you," she said.

"Thank *you*," I said, sheathing my sword. "You saved us."

I looked up at the gashadokuro, who seemed to be awaiting further orders. Behind it – or through the gaps between its bones – I saw the masts and sails of the *Rijp*, passing by us as it sailed away from the castle, its treacherous mission accomplished.

A red veil of rage came down over my eyes.

"Oyuki," I said, "could this…this gashadokuro possibly take us to the quarterdeck of that ship?"

She must have caught the dark undertone in my voice. "What do you have in mind?" she asked warily.

"Could it?"

"I suppose."

"Ask it."

Oyuki uttered another incantation. The gashadokuro turned toward us, lowered itself to one kneecap, and reached out its skeletal arms. The phalanges and metacarpals of one hand curled gently around me, and another around Oyuki.

I held on tight as the gigantic skeleton stood up, taking us high into the air. It crossed the battlefield with twenty-yard strides and waded into the sea. The water was more than deep enough for the keel of a tall ship, but it only came up to the gashadokuro's pelvic bone. It walked through the sea with surprising swiftness, its bony legs offering only minimal resistance to the water, until it caught up with the ship. A cannon fired, followed by some muskets from the deck, but the balls flew harmlessly between the enormous bones. If any of them struck, the gashadokuro gave no sign that it felt them.

It set us down gently on the quarterdeck, next to a terrified Nicolaes Couckebacker. Its mission fulfilled, it turned and waded back to land, heading toward the castle, presumably in search of some samurai to snack on.

Couckebacker looked from one of us to the other, pale and trembling, as well he might. His fear filled me with vindictive satisfaction.

"Simon! Oyuki!" he stammered. "What...how...?"

I drew my sword. "Thought you could attack us and just sail away, did you?"

"Simon!" Oyuki said in alarm, but I was too enraged to pay her any heed. I kept my focus on Couckebacker.

"So what changed your mind?" I demanded.

Couckebacker continued to stare wide-eyed at the point of my sword. "I didn't want to fight you! Believe me, I didn't! But the Shogun insisted. If I had refused, he would have driven all the Dutch out of Japan."

295

"Oh, how tragic. The struggle of poor farmers against cruelty and oppression couldn't move you. A plea for help from fellow Christians couldn't move you. Only a threat to your nice little monopoly on trade with Japan could move you. Now draw your sword and fight!"

He looked at me in a mixture of fear and bewilderment. "What?"

"Fight! You came here to fight us, didn't you? You had no hesitation when all it meant for you was standing on your quarterdeck, firing cannons from a safe distance. Let's see how you do in a real fight, with a real sword, against a real warrior!"

He raised his hands as if hoping they could ward off a sword. "Simon, please..."

"*Fight!*" I bellowed. "Are you a real man? Or just a lubberly Dutchman?"

"Simon!" Oyuki said in shock.

Just the way she said my name suddenly made my face burn. What was I hoping to accomplish? If I defeated Couckebacker in a duel, what then? Was I acting out some swashbuckling fantasy of defeating the captain and taking the ship? As much as I hated to admit it, Couckebacker was now our best – perhaps our only – chance of finding a way home.

I slowly lowered my sword.

"Forgive me," I said, in a small voice. The red veil in front of my eyes was lifting, but the redness moved to my cheeks as I recalled the words I had said under its influence.

"Heer Couckebacker," Oyuki said calmly, "I think Simon might be willing to withdraw his challenge to a duel...if you'll do us one small favor."

Couckebacker nodded.

Oyuki continued: "Take us to Nagasaki."

* * *

As Hara Castle receded from view, conflicting feelings swirled within me. My heart was buoyed with relief that Oyuki and I had survived, but weighed down with sadness and an odd sense of guilt. What had I done to deserve to live, when so many others much braver than me had perished? I thought sadly of Shiro, Ashizuka, Mori, even Chijiwa, and all the others who had given their lives for their faith. I prayed that the Deus they trusted in would welcome them into the paradise they had always longed for.

As for those who had joined Shiro's cause wishing for nothing more than the basic right to eat the fruits of their own labor, I hoped they would get their wish. I hoped, in the confusion caused by the gashadokuro, at least some of them would escape with their lives. I hoped, with Matsukura gone, the next lord of Shimabara would treat them like human beings. I hoped.

The next day, the *Rijp* sailed up the inlet toward Nagasaki. As we drew closer, I saw that it was the largest city I had seen in Japan except for Edo. A few other tall ships, rigged unlike any European ships I had seen – perhaps they were Chinese – sailed to and from the harbor. Just beside the harbor was a projection that I thought at first was a promontory, but as we drew closer, I saw that it was an island connected to the mainland by a long, narrow bridge. Furthermore, it had a man-made look: fan-shaped, too perfectly to be natural, and surrounded by walls and watchtowers. If I were to guess at its purpose, I had to admit, my first thought would be a fortress or a prison. But then a gust of wind billowed the Dutch flag out from a flagpole in the center, and I realized I was looking at Dejima. In the Tokugawas' Japan, prisoners and foreigners seemed to be regarded the same way: they couldn't simply be done away with, but they needed to be kept at a comfortable arm's length from ordinary society.

"Heer Couckebacker," Oyuki asked, hesitantly as if she feared the answer to her question: "Are there...do you know of any Englishmen on Dejima?"

"Some sailors from Britain or other countries come and go aboard the Dutch ships landing there," he replied. "But the only Englishman I know who lives on Dejima year-round is the one who runs the brewery."

"The brewery?"

Couckebacker nodded. "He came here aboard a Dutch ship some years ago, and somewhere along the line, he got the idea that someday, everyone in Japan would be drinking beer. From his success so far...well, let's just say the sake brewers of Japan don't have much to fear from him. But I'll admit, his ale isn't bad, even if it *is* English. And he is, after all, the only brewer on Dejima, so many of us Dutch are regular customers of his."

The ship dropped anchor near the artificial island. Couckebacker, Oyuki, and I were lowered to sea level in a boat, along with two sailors. They rowed the boat up to a set of stone steps, leading from the sea to a landing in front of a wooden gate where a samurai stood guard. One of the sailors offered a hand to Couckebacker as he stepped ashore. No one offered us similar assistance, so we made our own way out of the boat and followed him.

"Greetings, Heer Couckebacker," the samurai said with a bow, in surprisingly fluent Dutch. "What brings you to Dejima?"

"Just a regular meeting with Chief Caron," Couckebacker replied.

The samurai's gaze shifted to us. "And these children?"

Who is he calling children? I thought indignantly. *We were probably born before him. And we've certainly seen more in our lives than he has.*

Couckebacker indicated me. "That one's my ship's boy," he said.

"And the girl?"

"My daughter."

The samurai looked surprised. Oyuki and I tried very hard not to do the same. I had to admit, I was impressed with how casually and convincingly the lie flowed from his mouth.

"I never knew you had a family, mijnheer," said the samurai.

"Yes, I have a wife in Hirado. My family has never come out this way, so you haven't seen them before."

The corners of the samurai's mouth turned down. "Mijnheer, you must have heard the Shogun's edict. Wives and children of Dutch merchants are no longer allowed to remain in Japan. They must move to Jagatara at their earliest convenience."

I wondered for a moment where Jagatara was. Then I realized it was probably the Japanese pronunciation of Jakarta, the closest Dutch colony to Japan.

"I know," Couckebacker replied with well-feigned sadness. "And my wife is packing up and preparing to go. But my daughter has never been to Dejima. I'd like for her to see it, just once, before she leaves Japan for good."

The samurai looked from Couckebacker to us and back. "I'll have to get permission from the magistrate."

"Just a brief visit. On and off. I really don't think it's worth troubling the magistrate for such a trivial matter, do you?"

The samurai stood with his arms folded, and made no reply.

"I'm sure you'd be within your rights to make that call yourself," Couckebacker went on. "You do your job with such sound judgment, you're worth much more than the pittance they pay you."

Couckebacker's hand reached toward the samurai's folded arms, and deposited something in his voluminous sleeve. I heard a slight clink as it hit the bottom.

The samurai was silent a moment longer. "As you say," he finally said. "A brief visit, on and off, without attracting the magistrate's attention."

Couckebacker bowed. "Many thanks. I knew you were a reasonable man."

The samurai shouted an order to someone within. We heard a bolt being drawn aside, and the gate creaked open. As soon as we were through, and well past the guards, I said in an undertone: "Thank you."

Couckebacker gave us a stern look. "You can thank me by leaving Dejima as soon as you can, and not causing any further trouble."

I looked at our surroundings. It was as though the gate we had just passed through were a magical portal out of Japan and into Holland. Dutch merchants in their hats, coats, and ruffled collars walked up and down a cobblestone street, among wood-and-plaster buildings with gabled roofs that would have looked completely at home in Amsterdam. The occasional samurai, dressed in kimono and carrying swords, also appeared among them, but in these surroundings, *they* were the ones who looked like visitors from a distant land.

Farther down the street, I saw the spire of a wooden church. A cross stood placidly atop it, in full view of heaven and earth, as though it had every right to be there. As though it neither knew nor cared that if it dared to show itself anywhere else in Japan, it would bring suffering and death in its wake.

Couckebacker turned into a door under a wooden sign showing a terrestrial sphere with the words *De Globe*. We followed him into a small, cozy pub, where a few merchants sat at the counter and tables, conversing in animated Dutch over frothing mugs made from the ubiquitous blue-and-white delft porcelain. The man behind the counter stood with his back to us and his face to a barrel, busily filling a tankard, and could only spare a glance over his shoulder as we entered.

"Welcome, mijnheer!" he said, speaking in Couckebacker's general direction while keeping his eyes on his work. "Indeed, it's been a while. You must be parched. What can I offer you?"

My jaw dropped. He had significantly less hair than I remembered, and of what remained, the proportion of reddish-brown to grey had shifted in favor of the latter. What loss he had suffered on top of his head, he had more than made up for down below; his waistline bespoke many years of sampling his own product. But there could be no mistaking his voice or the cadence of his speech.

It was Captain Shakespeare.

"Actually," Couckebacker said, "I'm here on business. I have two young compatriots of yours with me."

Oyuki and I stepped around Couckebacker. When Captain Shakespeare's gaze shifted to us, he froze in place. His eyes and mouth opened wider than I could have imagined possible. The beer from the barrel flowed unheeded into the tankard in his hand, over the rim, and onto the floor, before he noticed and hurriedly shut the tap.

"Dear God," he said in a soft voice when he could speak again. "What apparitions see I here? Does some disease or madness fool my eyes? Do I see ghosts? A vision? Or a dream?"

"None of those, sir," I said. "We're real."

"Truly? Oyuki Winter? Simon Grey?" He set down the tankard, came slowly to our side of the counter, and reached out a tentative hand to touch my sleeve, as if to confirm that I was solid. "And neither aged a day? How can this be?" He looked from one of us to the other, his amazed expression unchanging. "Art truly Simon? Art thou Oyuki? Or are you both some sort of changelings?"

"It's really us," said Oyuki. "I promise you."

Captain Shakespeare's expression went from wonder to exultation. "Praise the good Lord!" he cried, throwing an arm around each of us and pulling us into a rib-cracking embrace. "I prayed this day would come!"

Couckebacker cleared his throat. "I'll be about my business, then, and leave you to catch up."

Captain Shakespeare eased his grip on us long enough to look up at him through eyes still filled with joyful tears. "A thousand thanks, mijnheer. A million thanks!"

As Couckebacker went his way, Captain Shakespeare returned his beaming gaze to us. "So tell me, what adventures have you had? That morning, when you vanished 'neath the waves, we hoped and prayed that you would reappear. We waited all day, all night, all next day. When you never came back, we thought the worst."

"We can tell you everything," said Oyuki, "but first, one question. What happened to my father?"

Captain Shakespeare drew a deep breath and exhaled. "In truth, my dear, that tale is long to tell."

"Please, sir, just tell me this." The words came from a mouth so dry, they sounded as if they were written on parchment. "Is he alive?"

Captain Shakespeare looked down.

"I cannot say that he is in this world."

I had only a momentary glimpse of Oyuki's grief-stricken face before she covered it with her hands and sank to her knees.

Captain Shakespeare took hold of her arms and went on hurriedly, "But neither can I say that he is dead."

I lost my patience. "Captain!" I shouted at him. "Just once, could you give us a straight answer? No riddles, no poetry, no flowery phrases, just a simple yes or no?"

He turned to me. His eyes were full of such pain that I immediately regretted my outburst.

"Simon, dear lad," he said gently, "I spoke the truth to you. His story is not soon nor simply told." He gestured to the counter. "Perhaps you'll join me in a cup of tea?"

Oyuki lowered her hands from her now tear-streaked face, turned her anguished gaze up to meet Captain Shakespeare's, and silently nodded. The captain took one arm, I the other, and we helped her to her feet.

She and I took stools at the counter. Captain Shakespeare set a kettle on the hob, then turned back to us and began his tale.

Glossary of
Japanese Terms

BYAKUJUTSU: The Japanese name for an herb known in Chinese as *bai zhu* (white atractylodes rhizome), often used in traditional medicine.

CHON-MAGE: The hairstyle of a SAMURAI, with the hair on top bound into a knot, and the area around it shaved.

DAIMYO: A great lord.

DEJIMA: An artificial island off Nagasaki. During the EDO Period, when foreigners were banned from entering the Japanese mainland, Europeans (mainly Dutch) were confined here.

DEUS: The word for "God" in both Latin and Portuguese, used in EDO-period Japan to refer to the Christian God.

EDO (now known as Tokyo): The administrative capital of Japan from 1603 to the present. It was the seat of the Tokugawa Shoguns from 1603 to 1868, a time known as the "Edo Period" or "Tokugawa Period."

FUMI-E: A painting or carving of a cross, the Virgin Mary, or other symbol from Christian iconography. During the Edo period, when Christianity was banned, suspected Christians were required to step on them as a symbolic way of renouncing their faith.

GASHADOKURO: A YOKAI in the shape of a giant skeleton. Often appears on battlefields or other places where many have died in agony without proper burial.

GUNSHI: An ONMYOJI (practitioner of traditional Japanese magic) in service to the military. A war wizard.

HAIMUSHI: One of many types of tiny YOKAI believed to dwell in the body and cause disease.

IGIRISU: The Japanese name for England. From a mispronunciation of the word "English."

KAMON: The symbol of a noble family. The equivalent of a European coat of arms.

KAPPA: A YOKAI that dwells in rivers. It looks like a frog the size of a human child, walking upright, with the shell and beak of a snapping turtle.

KATANA: A long, slightly curved sword used by SAMURAI.

KI: The energy that flows through, and animates, all living beings.

KITSUNEBI: Foxfire. A type of YOKAI that appears as a ball of pale blue light.

KYO NO MIYAKO (now known as Kyoto): The symbolic capital of Japan and home of the Emperor.

MUDRA: A hand position used while reciting a SUTRA.

NASU: An eggplant. Considered lucky to see in the first dream of the new year, since the word "nasu" can also mean "to achieve your goals."

ONIGIRI: A ball of pressed rice, often with a pickled plum or small piece of fish in the center.

ONMYODO (literally "the Way of Light and Shadow"): Traditional Japanese magic.

ONMYOJI: A practitioner of ONMYODO. A magician or sorcerer.

OROCHI: A type of YOKAI, appearing as a cross between a giant snake and an equally giant scorpion.

ORANDA: The Japanese name for Holland (the Netherlands).

ORASHO: A prayer, originally in Latin but with Japanese pronunciation, chanted by secret Christians during the EDO period. From the Latin word *oratio* meaning "prayer."

OTOHIME: The princess of an undersea realm off the coast of Japan.

OZUTSU: A light, shoulder-mounted cannon.

RONIN: A samurai with no allegiance to any lord, often because his former master was killed or disgraced.

RYUGUJO: The Palace of the Dragon God. An undersea palace, home to Ryujin (the Dragon God) and Otohime.

SAMURAI: A warrior, usually in service to a DAIMYO (great lord).

SHOGI: Japanese chess. Unlike Western chess, captured pieces can be used by the player who captures them.

SHOGUN: The military dictator of Japan during the EDO period. While the Emperor was the symbolic ruler, the Shogun was the actual head of government.

SUIKO: A "water tiger." A river-dwelling yokai, related to the kappa but more aggressive.

SUTRA: A Buddhist chant, sometimes also used as a magical incantation.

TACHI: A sword with a blade slightly shorter and wider than a KATANA, used by YAMABUSHI.

TAKE-TABA: Bundles of bamboo stalks tied to a frame and used as a shield against cannon fire.

TAMATEBAKO: A jeweled treasure box.

TENGU: A type of YOKAI that lives mainly in TENGUDO, but occasionally descends to the ordinary mortal world. The kotengu (lesser tengu) appear as humans with the wings and heads of birds, while the daitengu (greater tengu) have human-like features except for their remarkably large noses. They are exceptionally skilled at martial arts, and many of the greatest warriors of Japanese history and legend were said to have been trained by them.

TENGUDO: The realm of the tengu, located among the clouds and high mountaintops.

TENSHU: The central building in a Japanese castle.

TSUME-NO-MARU: A courtyard near the center of a Japanese castle. The place where residents of the castle would retreat if the outer walls had been breached.

URASHIMA TARO: In Japanese folklore, a young fisherman who visited Ryugujo, and returned to find that many decades had passed on the surface.

YABUMI: An arrow-letter; a letter tied to an arrow and shot from a bow. Often used in wartime to send messages to the other side, such as challenges or terms of surrender.

YAMABUSHI: A mountain warrior. A practitioner of the religion of Shugendo, which involves performing ascetic rituals deep in the mountains in the hope of meeting TENGU. These practices are believed to grant them supernatural powers.

YAMAJIJII ("Old Man of the Mountains"): A one-eyed, one-legged YOKAI that lives in the mountains, famous for its ability to shout loud enough to wake the dead or kill the living.

YOKAI: A term encompassing various monsters, ghosts, and other supernatural creatures in Japan.

Acknowledgements

When *Simon Grey and the March of a Hundred Ghosts* was released in 2019, I confidently expected to have the sequel ready the following year. However, like Simon, I felt that I suddenly slipped into a realm where time worked differently. The global pandemic brought all travel to a halt, preventing me from going either to Shimabara to research the story or to the States to take it to potential readers. Before I knew it, five years had passed. But now, the next chapter in Simon and Oyuki's story is finally ready to share...and it couldn't have happened without the help and support of their friends around the world.

For this second Simon Grey adventure, as for the first, I am greatly indebted to Daisuke Kamiya of the Department of Japanese History at Tokai University. His profound knowledge and patient guidance were a treasure beyond any tamatebako. Any errors or historical liberties that remain are mine alone.

I am also indebted to others who gave generously of their time and expertise. Toyohiro Hirata of the Amakusa Christian Museum shared his minute knowledge of everything to do with the Shimabara Rebellion, and gave me the rare and unforgettable opportunity to see Amakusa Shiro's actual battle flag. The staff at Shimabara Castle graciously arranged for Shiro himself to descend from heaven and give me a personal guided tour (with the aid of virtual reality). Thanks also to Yohei Ideguchi of the Hirado Dutch Trading Post, Shiori Hirata of the Asakura Akitsuki Museum, and the staff members at the Arima Christian Heritage Museum, the Mt. Hiko shrine, and the Dejima historic site in Nagasaki. And special thanks to the *sendatsu* on Mt. Takao who initiated me into the ways of Shugendo, and treated me much more kindly than their analogues in the book treated Simon!

I'm also grateful to John Paul Catton of Excalibur Books for his guidance and encouragement, and to Edith Hope Bishop for her comments on the manuscript.

Among the many authors whose writings I drew on to write this book: As always, Matthew Meyer, Matt Alt and Hiroko Yoda for yokai lore. Jonathan Clements, Go Idekubo, Chisato Kanda, Seiichi Konishi, M. Paske-Smith, Kurazo Tsuruta, and the anonymous author of the Edo-period novel *Amakusa Sodo* for the history, legends, and colorful characters of the Shimabara Rebellion. Issai Chozanji, Roald Knutsen, Atsutane Hirata and his translator Carmen Blacker for inside information about tengu. Antony Cummins and Tetsuo Owada for details of Japanese military magic. Shodo Koshikidake for the history and practices of Shugendo. Jennifer Mitchelhill for Japanese castle architecture.

Finally, many thanks to everyone who believed in Simon and pledged their support to help me share his story with the world: John Bigelow, Matthew Boroson, Christina Curlett, Emilie Fevrier, James-Henry Holland, Rachel Koldewyn, Chris LeCluyse, Stacee Mandeville, Cindy Matthews, Matthew Meyer, Wayne Miller, Eric Ostby, Janna Bernstein Rhodes, Kim Ekey Roth, Sharina, Emily Winslow Stark, and Loren Waller. May Deus richly bless you!

And of course, thanks to Kento for providing the first inspiration for Simon Grey, and to Yuki and Kay for being patient with me and helping me bring his story to life.

Charles Kowalski
Kanagawa, Japan
September 2024

www.ingramcontent.com/pod-product-compliance
Lightning Source LLC
Chambersburg PA
CBHW021204250626
47155CB00008B/2664